BLOOD
JADE

Tor Books by Julia Vee and Ken Bebelle

THE PHOENIX HOARD

Ebony Gate

Blood Jade

BLOOD JADE

The Phoenix Hoard, Book 2

JULIA VEE
and
KEN BEBELLE

TOR PUBLISHING GROUP
NEW YORK

BLOOD JADE

A Tor Book
Published by Tom Doherty Associates / Tor Publishing Group
120 Broadway
New York, NY 10271

www.torpublishinggroup.com

The Library of Congress Cataloging-in-Publication Data
is available upon request.

ISBN 978-1-250-83792-9 (hardcover)
ISBN 978-1-250-83793-6 (ebook)

Our books may be purchased in bulk for promotional, educational, or business use. Please contact your local bookseller or the Macmillan Corporate and Premium Sales Department at 1-800-221-7945, extension 5442, or by email at MacmillanSpecialMarkets@macmillan.com.

First Edition: 2024

Printed in the United States of America

0 9 8 7 6 5 4 3 2 1

This is dedicated to the booksellers.
Thank you for putting magic into the hands of readers.

~Julia and Ken

CAST OF CHARACTERS

SOONG CLAN

Soong Zhènmíng—Head of Soong Clan, father to Emiko and Tatsuya, member of Bā Tóu

Sara Hiroto—mother to Emiko and Tatsuya, member of Bā Shǒu, also known as the Walker of the Void

Emiko Soong ("Emi-chan")—elder daughter of Soong Clan, former Blade of Soong, also known as the Butcher of Beijing, current Sentinel of San Francisco

Tatsuya Soong ("Tacchan")—younger son of Soong Clan, currently finishing his schooling at Lóng Kǒu

Bāo—Emiko's foo lion companion, jade pendant that she can activate to bring him to life, enjoys napping under sunny windows

Sugi—Zhènmíng's constant companion, an animated Hokkaido wolf constructed out of Japanese cedar tiles, eats acorns

Fujita-san—Soong Zhènmíng's majordomo

Uncle Lau—leads the Iron Fists

Kubota-san—leads the Pearl Guard

Uncle Jake—breakfast cook

Lulu Ayi—groundskeeper

Yoko-obaachan—healer

Huang si-fu—dinner chef

Nami—member of Iron Fists, Disciple of Raijin

TRAN CLAN

Fiona Tran—head of house in San Francisco, gāo wind talent

Freddy Tran—Fiona's twin brother, gāo wind talent, currently not involved in clan affairs
Franklin—aegis, Fiona's personal bodyguard
Willy—Fiona's majordomo
Linh—Fiona and Freddy's cousin, head of Tran security

LOUIE CLAN

Raymond "Dai Lou" Louie—elder patriarch of the Louie Clan, not involved in clan operations due to age
Raymond "Ray Ray" Louie—heir to Dai Lou, lost a hand in reparation to San Francisco for his part in the taking of the Ebony Gate
"Uncle" Jimmy Louie—Dai Lou's younger brother, uncle to Ray Ray and acting Head of the Louie Clan
Leanna Louie—Ray Ray's elder daughter, Emiko's only martial arts student
Lucy Louie—Ray Ray's younger daughter

MOK CLAN

Stella Mok
Stanley Mok

KOH CLAN

Koh Lǐ Qiáng "Old Li"
Sabine Koh
Awang Koh
Nayla Koh
Nura Koh

TANAKA CLAN

Tanaka Kenichi
Tanaka "Junior" Hideo
Watanabe Haruto

SOMAC SALVAGE

Tessa MacNeil—Emiko's business partner, curator at the Tien Pacific Museum

Andira "Andie" MacNeil-Wijaya—Tessa's wife, IT security for SOMAC and Emiko's home

JŌKŌRYŪKAI (THE ASSOCIATION)

Ogata-sensei—Emiko's sensei during her time at Jōkōryūkai

Saburo—a fire talent from Jōkōryūkai who was temporarily contracted with the Louies

OTHERS

Big Ricky Sun, Mama Sun, Baby Ricky, Sally—family that owns the Sun Emporium on Lotus Lane, purveyors of Emiko's supplies and her favorite steamed pork buns

Grandma Chen ("Popo")—gāo-level Herbalist/purifier, owns Vitality Health Services day spa in Inner Sunset

SYNOPSIS OF *EBONY GATE*

Magical dud EMIKO SOONG always compensated for her lack of magical talent with more sword swinging. She dutifully served the Soong Clan for years as its Blade until the stains on her soul drove her out of Tokyo to seek a life free from bloodshed.

She likes San Francisco. She grows her salvage business, SO-MAC, with her business partner, TESSA MACNEIL. She transacts with the working-class magic dealers on Lotus Lane and she stays out of the way of the two elite Jiārén families up on Nob Hill. The thing is, folks keep calling on her to pick up her sword and deal with their small problems. Like rampaging Japanese yetis in Golden Gate Park. But Emiko's day job now requires her to work with ADAM JØRGENSEN, the wealthy patron backing Tessa's museum. Adam has somehow inherited a rare Jiārén sword, Crimson Cloud Splitter, which Emiko now must requisition from him to honor the First Law—protect the Hoard.

Cleaning up magical mishaps has garnered the attention of the city's burgeoning magic sentience, and the city wants to make it official. In fact, everyone seems to be urging her to become San Francisco's Sentinel, but Emiko's not eager to replace one benevolent master with another.

When a shinigami demands Emiko honor a Talon, an old blood debt, she finds herself in danger of losing her soul to eternal servitude. To keep her hard-earned freedom she must recover the Ebony Gate, an ancient artifact sealing a portal to the underworld, and its blood jade anchor, the Lost Heart of Yázì, to prevent the ghosts and demons of the Yomi underworld from destroying San Francisco.

Emiko allies with FIONA TRAN and FREDDY TRAN, scions of a powerful clan of magic users. Emiko's relationship with Fiona

Tran is further complicated by the fact that Fiona has started dating Emiko's ex, KAMON APICHAI, one of the Thai Tigers.

With Freddy's help, Emiko follows the Ebony Gate across San Francisco and ties the Louie Clan to the Gate's disappearance. They confront the thieves in a bloody battle that leaves them two dead bodies as the thieves make off with the Gate. In a strange stroke of luck, Adam buys a lead on the Lost Heart of Yázì, leading Emiko and Adam to a mysterious auction.

Emiko and Adam fight their way through multiple Jiārén families, a horde of undead kappa, and ice mages (why is it always ice mages?!), and lose the Lost Heart of Yázì. An old enemy of Emiko's shows up and unleashes a torrent of lightning, striking Adam in the process. Emiko swears an oath to invoke the protection of the Soong Clan to save Adam from further harm.

Emiko and Freddy catch up to the Gate at the Port of Oakland. They manage to prevent the Gate from leaving, but the Gate is shattered to pieces in the fight.

Emiko's only hope now is to repair the Gate and find out why it was stolen. She confronts RAYMOND LOUIE, who traps her and her friends in an underground vault. Her deadline approaching, Emiko faces the destruction of her soul and failing her new friends and those who count on her.

Emiko takes the mantle of the Sentinel of San Francisco and uses her newly granted power to free herself and her friends from captivity. As they escape, Emiko reveals Raymond to be a disciple of the cult of the Ninth Dragon, a fanatic devoted to resurrecting a long-dead evil. Raymond flees.

Emiko, Fiona, Freddy, and Kamon rush back to repair the Gate and stem the tide of ghosts pouring forth from Yomi. Emiko relinquishes Sword of Truth to anchor the Ebony Gate, the souls of generations of Soong Blades before her now serving in her place to seal Yomi.

She endures a truth seeking for Freddy, and reveals to Kamon that her mother was the one who traded the Talon to the shinigami.

Emiko finally finds the peace she's been searching for and accepts the friendly overtures of her business partner and her wife to socialize. Adam has amnesia from the lightning strike, leaving Emiko on borrowed time to address his custodianship of the legendary Jiārén sword.

The Ebony Gate is repaired, San Francisco is saved, and Emiko doesn't get turned into garden statuary. She has made a powerful ally in the Tran family and a powerful enemy in the Louie family, and she is the new Sentinel of San Francisco.

BLOOD JADE

SURF'S UP

I was supposed to be stopping a turf war but instead I'd been commandeered into a wet suit and was now holding on for dear life to a kiteboard. Worst of all, my weapons were in a backpack tied up high on an electric pole. I blamed the air talent in front of me for all of this.

A spray of water kicked up from my board and a thousand droplets scattered in the air, catching the spring sunshine like a waterfall of diamonds. I had a fraction of a second to marvel at the beauty of it before the kite lines jerked me forward and the freezing salt water smacked me in the face. I blinked furiously and tensed my arms, trying to wrest control of the kite before the wind dragged me into the south tower of the Golden Gate.

So far, I was bad at this and I despised being bad at anything.

This was entirely Freddy's fault.

Freddy Tran slalomed past me in a graceful arc with one hand on his kite handle and the other carelessly dragging through the bay. He leaned into his turn with an ease that I would have admired if I wasn't resenting the fact that he had roped me into this misbegotten adventure.

I had gone to his sister, Fiona, when the Ebony Gate had been stolen, sealing the request for aid with a Talon. I'd really been bargaining for Fiona's help, since she was the rising head of the clan, but she'd stuck me with her pot-smoking surfer twin brother, Freddy, who had turned out to be somewhat less of a slacker than his reputation spoke of.

Now he showed up on my doorstep at random times and tried to make me have fun.

Against the backdrop of the bay, his royal-blue aura fanned out in a soft blur, and with his deep tan and white rashguard, he was a poster child for water sports. Jerk. He kicked up a rooster tail of green-gray bay water as his board dug deep into the surf. The kite at the end of his lines was identical to mine, a great billowing swath of sparkling silver nylon. It was a picture-perfect moment, made complete by his slicked-back dark hair and laughing eyes.

Above our kites, the Golden Gate Bridge rose out of the water like a titan, massive supports of orange-red girders growing out of hulking concrete pilings. Road traffic rumbled over the bridge and seagulls wheeled against blue skies.

Freddy tacked and raised his hand out of the water, waggling a shaka sign at me. "Looking good, Emiko! Sick moves!"

The wake from his board moved past me, forcing me to bob to stay on top of my board. I yelled back at him over the wind. "This is crazy!"

He whooped like a maniac.

I was only out here because Freddy had kidnapped me. There was still plenty of work to do. The Trans and the Louies, the two strongest Lóng Jiārén clans in San Francisco, were on a collision course. Jiārén were descended from dragons and wore their civility like a neatly pressed jacket. It could come off at any time, and it looked like the time was here. War was brewing, and when it hit, San Francisco would be ground zero. The very city I had just bound myself to.

Fiona, the responsible Tran, had given me assurances that she wouldn't break the peace just yet. As the Sentinel of San Francisco, I was attuned to the heartbeat of my city and, for now, things were quiet. I trusted her word, but it didn't resolve the sensation that my city was a simmering pot of soup, on the cusp of boiling over.

After I ignored Freddy's texts for several days, he'd used his air talent to funnel himself right onto my porch, setting off all my alarms.

When I'd run to the front of the house, ready to take down whoever had been stupid enough to try my security, Freddy had opened another funnel and sucked us both away to Crissy Field.

I'd gotten even with him though. Right after we landed, I threw up on his shirt.

A sea salt aroma flared around us, cleaner and more vibrant than the seawater currently crusting in my hair. The scent had nothing to do with the water, just the unique smell of Freddy's talent as he created a miniature vortex of air just behind his kite. He whooped as his kite took off and launched him into the air. His back arched and he executed a neat flip as he was carried into the shadow of the bridge.

I risked unclenching one hand to quickly swipe my hair from my eyes. Around us, other surfers sped along the tops of the waves, carving neat turns and making little jumps. I was the Sentinel of San Francisco. I'd spent six years being trained as a world-class assassin by the Jōkōryūkai. This was just kitesurfing in some of the most challenging waters in the world.

I could do this.

I closed my eyes and shut out the world around me, concentrating on the sensations in my body, narrowing my focus down to each individual moment as it occurred.

My father had taught this to me when I'd been struggling with even basic mastery of my qì. Rather than dwelling on past failures, or the anticipation of any future success, he trained me to instead learn what I could from each instant in time.

The control rod in my hands twitched and jumped as my kite snapped in the wind, pulling me across the water. My legs flexed as the board bumped and bobbed under my feet, rising and falling with the swells in the water. The breath of my city whispered through the cables of the bridge, over the tops of the whitecaps, and tickled the hairs at the back of my neck.

I hadn't considered that my connection to San Francisco would extend out into the bay, but it made a kind of sense that the city would claim the waters around it as well. The city's power ran under me as a cool current of energy. When I reached for it I felt an answering pulse from the . . . thing that the city had left inside my chest. I still didn't know what it was, and my research into it had yielded little. Add in the impending clan war and a fledgling antiques business that I was still trying to run, and some things had been put on the back burner.

Fresh energy from the city surged up my legs and I spread my toes. The choppy action of the waves calmed, and now staying balanced atop the board was as easy as standing on a sidewalk. A briny wind picked up behind me and I shot forward. I tightened my arms and pulled in, leaning to my right. My board carved through the water. I sailed through a spray of fine mist, the acceleration sending a thrill down my spine like a shot of electricity.

Freddy whooped again, his voice sounding closer now. "Yeah, that's how the Sentinel does it!"

I wasn't sure if it comported with Sentinel etiquette, but tapping into the power of the city certainly made kitesurfing more enjoyable. And, credit to Freddy, it *was* good being outside in the elements. With the sun on my face and the salt-tinged breeze at my back, I felt freer than I could remember.

Taking the mantle of the Sentinel had been a scary choice, but at least it had been my choice. Well, the choice had been forced on me by my mother's blood debt to a shinigami. But with the welfare of my adopted home at stake, I'd chosen to become the embodiment of the city's power, and with that power I had earned back my mother's Talon. In addition to the return of the Hiroto Talon, I retained my soul instead of anchoring the Ebony Gate for eternity as a ward against the restless demons and ghosts of Yomi. I thought it was a fair trade.

The city and I had gotten off to a rough start. The fledgling magic sentience had tried to run roughshod over my will, but years of being someone else's attack dog had inured me to brute-force tactics. Our relationship felt more like a partnership now, if one could be partners with a city.

I opened my eyes and found Freddy cruising next to me as our kites towed us through the noontime shadow under the bridge. We angled slightly to the north, heading out of the bay and toward the far end of the bridge. Freddy's discreet funnels kept our wind steady and we slewed back and forth, crisscrossing and spraying each other with our wakes. I spluttered and laughed as Freddy hit me with a spectacularly large wave that almost bowled me over.

Freddy pointed back toward the bay and yelled, "Race you to the north side!"

I gave him a thumbs-up.

"Loser has to show me their new temple, okay?"

He sure knew how to motivate me. The Merchants' Association of Lotus Lane had donated a Sentinel's Hall to honor me, with offices and staff intended to *manage my calendar*. It was just too much.

"It's not a temple, Tran!"

Freddy's air talent swirled around him and he gave me a lazy wink as he shot forward on the burst of air. Of course, like any respectable Jiārén, Freddy was going to cheat. As descendants of the Eight Sons of the Dragon, nearly all Jiārén "inherited" Dragon talents, like wildflowers grown near a nuclear test site. Those talents came with us when Jiārén came to this world from the Realm, fleeing the Cataclysm and the death of our Dragon gods. Our talents made us powerful and dangerous. Most of us, anyway. Some of us became powerful and dangerous through sheer training and sacrifice.

My meridians were so blocked and twisted that I could barely do the basic things that all other Jiārén took for granted. I grew up as the Broken Tooth of Soong Clan, and I'd spent my life learning ways to overcome my failings the hard way, through work and attention to detail.

But now, with the mantle of the Sentinel, I'd tapped into a wellspring of power bigger than I ever could have imagined. It was like going from riding a bike to suddenly piloting a rocket ship.

I centered my energy and allowed myself a satisfied smile. This rocket ship was going to leave Freddy drenched in my wake. The thing in my chest thudded like an extra heart as I reached again for the city's power. My stomach dropped out as I lurched forward. I tightened my grip and dug in. In an eyeblink I crested over the surf and flew past Freddy. The wake from my board pushed him to the side and I waggled my hand at him as I blew by.

Freddy crowed as I sailed past him. I leaned my head back and let the wind and spray wash over me like a cleansing shower. As much as I hated to admit it, Freddy had been right. I needed this. Not just the sunshine and the exercise, but being with, in, a part of my city. I needed it like I needed air and water. I wasn't going to solve the coming crisis from inside my home. Fiona had cried feud on the Louies, but that didn't guarantee a clan war, did it? As Sentinel, I would make my intentions known to all clans and all Jiārén. Chaotic times were coming, but I needed to find a resolution and deescalate it.

I cruised north, the beautiful town of Sausalito entering my view.

A wave of nausea rolled through me and sent a barb of agony through my gut. My fingers went slack and the kite ripped away from me. The once-steady double thump in my chest skipped a beat and all the strength drained from my legs. My knees buckled and the world slewed sideways. The comforting weight of San Francisco's power vanished from my body like kindling in a bonfire.

The sensation folded me in half and then light and sound disappeared as I plunged headfirst into the bay.

The biting cold of the water shocked my system back to functioning and I had the good sense not to open my mouth. The pain in my gut was already fading, but I couldn't trace the sensation. My mind blanked, and my hands clenched instinctively, searching for my weapons. But I had none.

Dim sunlight filtered in from above as I floated for a moment, trying to figure out what had happened.

I reached for the city's power again, trying to trace the same paths, only to find that not only was the city not there, but even the paths were gone. It was like I'd been transported to the other side of the planet. A spark of panic ignited as I called out to the heart of San Francisco, and was again answered with cold, absolute silence.

Why was the city ignoring me?

I bit back on the panicky sensation trying to crawl out of my throat. As far as I had researched, the only way to stop being the Sentinel was to die, and I definitely wasn't dead yet, judging by the burning sensation in my lungs. Something had happened. I would just have to figure it out, after I dragged my butt out of the bay. I kicked for the surface.

The ache in my lungs became a sharp ball of spikes behind my ribs, and my muscles burned as my exertions used up the remaining oxygen in my system. And still the surface looked no closer. The sour taste of panic crept into the back of my mouth even as I kept my lips glued together against the water trying to worm its way in. The chill of the water faded as my limbs went numb from the cold.

My mind must have started to slip a gear as well, because I heard, clear as day, low throaty laughter coming from beneath me.

"Lost little dragon. So far from home."

Even though I was underwater, the words rang inside my skull. It was a woman's voice—melodious, refined, and menacing.

I flailed my arms and legs even as I felt them weakening. Below me, from the dark depths, a single flickering point of white light grew closer, pulsing as mocking words floated past me.

"You call yourself dragons. You are barely a fish."

The light stretched and spun until it was a swirl of arms reaching for me. As my movements slowed, the tug of the current dragged me down. I was going to drown, or fall victim to whatever menace was below me.

I reached out for the city and again got nothing. My heart pounded in my chest and every instinct ripped at my jaw, clawing my mouth open.

"This will teach you to leave your seat of power."

The light became a vortex, sucking me deeper into the frigid depths. The cold was a living thing now, massive teeth of ice biting through my limbs, marching toward my torso, turning me bite by bite into a frozen block of numbness. My vision darkened into a long tunnel that ended at a mouth of very white, very sharp teeth.

THE OLD ONE

Rough hands grabbed at me, pawing at my neck and shoulders, fingers digging cruelly, grasping for purchase. I twisted, trying to get away, but they found the straps of my harness and wormed underneath, pulling me like a marionette. Sudden, sickening movement sucked away what little sense of self-preservation I had left as my mind slipped away. Greedy fingers of water slipped past my lips and barreled down my throat. I sucked in a breath and got nothing but cold, salt, and pain.

Light exploded around me just as sound returned in a rush of cries and screams. I coughed and would have jackknifed back into the water but for the strong arms wrapped around my chest. Those arms kept my head above the water as I vomited up what felt like half the bay.

"Emiko, you scared me to death!"

It was Freddy who'd pulled me back from the black. I sucked in lungfuls of beautiful, crisp air and hacked around the burning ruin of my throat. My skin flushed hot and cold with sensation and relief at being alive.

Freddy's legs kicked beneath, his sheer athleticism holding us afloat.

My voice was a hoarse whisper.

"What happened?"

I felt him shrug behind me. "Don't know. One second we were cruising, the next . . . this."

All around us, the surfers struggled with twisting winds, trying to make their way back to the beach. The once blue skies had darkened to an ominous gray and storm clouds advanced into the bay, whipped by onshore winds. My hair lashed across my face as the waves pounded us. The wind sang through the cables of the Golden Gate, the mournful song dangerously loud. Figures ran along the edge of the bridge, pedestrians seeking safety.

And in the midst of all this, my chest still felt strangely hollow, my limbs bereft of the city's power.

I had gone past the city's boundary and now I was paying the price.

I kicked my legs until I could pull away from Freddy and tread water on my own. He kept a hand on my harness until I waved him off.

"Freddy, I heard something. Someone. Down there. We have to get out of the water."

"What are you—"

Whitecaps frothed around us in a vortex that expanded before our eyes. I turned in place, my gaze tracking movement, my old skills coming back like bad habits. More white slewed around us and the surface of the bay undulated and sparkled.

"Freddy . . ."

The incoming storm reached the bridge and sheets of rain slammed into us, blotting out the daylight and filling the air with the sound of angry water. The vortex strengthened, and it was taking all I had just to keep from getting sucked down. The whitecaps broke and an elongated shape slipped through the waves, blinding white and covered in glistening, chitinous scales.

Dread sank into me, threatening to sap me further.

"Emiko!"

I kicked through the water. "Freddy! Get us out of here!"

Freddy grabbed my harness a split second before the salty scent of his talent surrounded us. I held my breath as the water beneath us drained into his funnel. Nausea gripped me as gravity disappeared then reappeared in quick succession. The deck of the bridge jumped up and slammed into my feet, buckling my knees. I tucked into a roll that didn't quite work because Freddy's hand was still attached to my harness. We landed in a tangle of limbs and tumbled to a stop next to a minivan.

An inch of water flooded the deck of the bridge. Rain hammered down like the great dragons themselves had returned with a vengeance. Traffic was wrecked, with cars crushed together at severe angles and jammed against the center divider. Doors hung open wherever I looked, cars abandoned in the sudden torrential onslaught. In the distance, dim shadows ran for either end of the bridge.

Good. At least the Wàirén were gone. Because someone was throwing around some serious Dragon power, and the last thing I needed was a bridge full of outsiders as witnesses.

I got up and put my back to the minivan, trying to see through the raging storm. Freddy groaned and I pulled him up and set his back to the van. If he lay on his back he would drown in this rising deluge.

"Maybe not the best day for kitesurfing, then? And the day started out so nice," he mumbled.

I made out the blurred outline of the north tower about a hundred yards south of us. Whatever was going on, we had to get off the bridge. Better yet, I needed to get across the center of the bridge, and back inside my city.

"This isn't an ordinary storm, Tran. We need to move."

His head rolled back and bonked on the side of the van. "I'm wiped . . ."

Skies. His aura was a bare sliver of pale blue. He'd used his talent to search for me under the surf. Between that and fighting the twisting currents, I was lucky he was even conscious.

Muffled, panicked cries pulled my attention from Freddy. I edged up until I could see into the minivan and my heart went cold. The front of the van was crumpled in half against the tailgate of a delivery box truck. The driver, a woman in a sensible navy cardigan, lay slumped against a deflated airbag, a spreading bruise across the bridge of her nose.

In the backseat, two small children, red-eyed and snot-nosed, safely strapped into their car seats, wailed at the tops of their lungs. I yanked at the door and just about ripped my fingernails off as my hand slipped off the wet handle. It was jammed shut. I banged on the window but that just made the kids scream even more. The mom didn't move a hair.

I reached down and shook Freddy. "Tran, wake up! I need your help!"

Thunder and lightning cracked the world apart like a nut, leaving me flash blind, my senses overloaded with the smell of ozone and my singed hair.

The dark clouds parted. A brilliant white, serpentine body tipped with a triangular head undulated through the opening. Another jagged fork of lightning split the sky, casting the serpent in a silver glow. Light danced and glittered off luminous rippling scales and feathery wings.

The serpent plunged from the clouds and landed south of us, on the center of the bridge. When its forelegs hit the concrete, it dissolved into a billowing cascade of pristine white silks. Golden light radiated from the center of the silks as the fabric writhed into a whirling ball. A majestic woman emerged, clad in a voluminous white dress, her inky black hair pulled high in a tall bun.

Although rain crashed all around us, the woman stood tall and unperturbed in a tidy ring of sunlight. Even the bridge looked dry under her feet, the flooding waters stopping short of her in a perfect circle.

Freddy audibly swallowed. My own mouth was agape. There were few beings I knew of with this kind of control over their physical shape as well as weather and water, and I thought Jiārén had left all the dragons behind in the Realm when we fled the Cataclysm.

The dragon, if that's what she was, sauntered toward us, hips swaying dangerously under her dress. Her voice was the same deadly one I'd heard while drowning in the bay.

"Come, little fish. Show me that this world hasn't robbed you of your spine. Hold your head high as I end you."

This was my would-be killer and I was undeniably outmatched. But I had people counting on me. I wrenched Freddy to his feet. The appearance of a possible dragon had awakened him considerably. My heart beat in my ears and all I could hear were the cries of the kids in the minivan.

"Freddy, you need to get the kids off the bridge."

His eyes darted to the woman who continued to advance on us, seemingly in no hurry at all. "Emiko, I'm not leaving you here with her. She's . . . *Old*."

I heard the emphasis. With the level of power needed to control the weather with this exacting precision, she had to be centuries old. Maybe she'd even crossed over from the Realm herself, one of the lesser dragons fleeing the world-rending conflicts of our Dragon gods.

In terms of talent, Freddy was far above me, but this woman was exponentially stronger than Freddy. We were outclassed. Freddy staying at my side wasn't going to change the odds.

"I'm telling you as your Sentinel, Tran. Get the kids out of here. I'll deal with this."

Freddy looked from the Old One to the kids in the van, and then back to me. The carefree surfer dude was gone for a moment, replaced by the man he might have been molded into had he not ceded clan leadership to his sister. The expression was there for just a fraction of a second, and then it was gone, like a shadow across the sky.

He gave me a tight nod. "I'll get help."

Until then, I was on my own.

I pivoted and strode to face my ancient opponent. A bloom of clean salt air washed over me from behind and I knew Freddy had cleared out.

With any luck, he'd get ahold of his sister. Fiona could task her fleet of drones to assess the situation. Maybe send a small battalion of wind talents to create a distraction for me.

As I walked, I stretched out with my senses, trying to reestablish my connection to the city. Nothing. I was still too far from the boundary.

This was extraordinarily bad timing for me, or maybe it was exactly what this Old One had been waiting for: me to step outside of the city.

The Old One tilted her head and studied me, her eyes contemptuous. I stopped just outside of her little circle of sunshine.

Her face had the strangely ageless quality I attributed to beings who did not spend much time in human form. Like a certain shinigami I'd dealt with recently.

A few loose locks of jet-black hair fell to her shoulders, framing her pale face. Her gown was so white it glowed, with long, wide sleeves that hid her hands. She didn't appear to carry any weapons, but I knew from experience to be wary of the unseen.

As the rain coursed down my face and neck I clasped my hands before my chest and gave the woman a deep formal bow. "Honored guest, the Sentinel welcomes you to San Francisco."

It never hurt to be polite, especially when you were at a disadvantage.

Large, gray eyes examined me as if I was a bug pinned to a board and her lips quirked into a snide smile. One arm came up and a delicate hand with slender fingers covered her mouth as she laughed.

Her eyes sparkled. "I'll give you points for decorum, little fish, but that won't save you. Once you stepped beyond the boundaries of your city, you placed yourself at the mercy of those stronger than you."

Her gaze traveled up and down my body, lingering above my head, where my Sentinel aura would be if I was only another fifty meters south, at the center of the bridge. She was right, I had foolishly left the boundaries of my city and now I was merely a weak mortal compared to this being. She mocked me for the barest edge of the muddy aura I kept furled tight.

She tsked. "Not that it seems to be much of a loss." She waved a negligent hand in my direction. "Your talent is so broken . . . I doubt I'll even gain a decade of longevity from your Pearl. What a waste."

Old anger flushed up my neck. The words spilled from my mouth without any input from my brain. "I'm not broken."

The Old One and I were twenty feet apart. When I said the word *broken* she moved, and before I finished, she slammed me against a parked car, one pale hand clamped like iron around my neck.

I went up on my tiptoes, my hands scrambling for purchase on the rain-slicked car to take the pressure off. The woman leaned in close enough that I could feel the heat baking off her smooth skin. When she whispered in my ear her voice held the weight of centuries.

"I am Iron Serpent, and if I say you are broken, then you are broken."

Shock coursed through me. She wasn't just an Old One, she was *the Old One.* She who had defied all the others. The Old One we'd whispered about at Lóng Kǒu. She'd stolen immortality for herself and her younger sister, the Green Serpent. If there was anything Jiārén feared, it was a thief of this caliber.

I didn't stand a chance. At least not on speed, brute-force, or talent. But I was more than just the Broken Tooth of the Soong Clan. I'd been underestimated my whole life. The anger I'd felt a moment ago hardened into resolve. I didn't want to die here.

Iron Serpent pulled back a little and blew out a breath through her nose. She'd brought the sunlight with her, and the rain was finally out of my eyes. With her other hand she trailed a finger lightly across the top of my chest. Her gaze seemed to go through me.

"The blockage is extensive. How have you survived even this long?"

She was right, I was a survivor. My mind raced furiously. She was ancient and overconfident. I would use that.

She placed two fingers over the knot on the right side of my chest, below my collarbone. "And yet you were chosen. Curious."

For two years, I'd denied the city's call. But in the end it had been me choosing the city. I gave Iron Serpent a cool smile.

Iron Serpent made a face. "You don't even know what the Pearl is, do you? You Sentinels die so young."

That got my attention. What did she know about Sentinels? She was distracted enough that her hold on my neck had loosened. Also, she clearly liked to talk. I needed more time. I didn't need to beat Iron Serpent—I just needed to buy Freddy enough time to get to Fiona and provide me with some distraction. With that, I could sprint the fifty meters to cross into San Francisco's magical boundary.

A dicey plan, but it was a plan.

I licked my lips. "Perhaps you would indulge me with a lesson?"

A lazy smile stretched her lips, making her look only more dangerous. "Be careful what you ask for, little fish."

With her free hand Iron Serpent grabbed my wrist. The flowing white sleeve rippled and snapped, tightening around her slender arm. As the fabric contracted, her arm morphed: glittering white scales sheathed her forearm and razor-sharp talons tipped her fingers.

"Your Pearl is a rare delicacy, prized by those of us who long for a taste of the Realm. You Jiārén are poor imitations of the True Dragons, but a Sentinel's Pearl is . . ."

Her eyes went wide and distant, as if remembering a particularly good meal.

"No. Words will not suffice. Let me show you."

Iron Serpent dug between my tendons and a fat drop of blood welled at the wound, stark against the white claw. She applied pressure and—

A shock jolted through me. Iron Serpent's power poured liquid fire into my meridians. Her qì surged through my system like high-voltage electrocution.

Moving my qì had always been a difficult task. Rather than following sensible, flowing patterns, I was forced to find awkward paths to move my energy, routing around the blockage. Iron Serpent disregarded all of that, spreading through the blockages.

Heat flashed across my entire body. A cloud of steam rose as the water on my skin and wet suit vaporized. I opened my mouth in a wordless scream of agony. Iron Serpent was cooking me from the inside out. Power flowed into the thing she'd called the Pearl. I closed my eyes and reached for the city again, hoping against hope that I could tap into its power, but those fifty meters might as well have been a mile.

But as I searched for the city, something else in me awakened, stirred out of its slumber by Iron Serpent's qì. Something dark and empty, like desolation.

Iron Serpent leaned in. "Do you feel that, little fish?"

My whole life, I'd been forced to fight against those blessed with Dragon talents, more powerful than me by the luck of their birth. As powerful as they had been, I'd learned that I could stand toe-to-toe with them. As the Blade of Soong, I'd bested many of them. I'd learned to use whatever I had to do it.

I didn't know what this thing inside me was, but it felt big. Hungry. Maybe it was big enough to handle Iron Serpent.

The darkness, the emptiness in my belly pulsed like a living thing. It shook my core like a caged animal, furious at its imprisonment. The hunger roared and demanded to be set free.

I opened my eyes and reached for Iron Serpent's qì. It was like trying to gather water in my hands, but I managed to redirect enough of it and I funneled it into my core and unlocked the cage.

The yawning, aching emptiness inside me swelled up from within and reached out through my meridians, spreading like eager flames over a river of oil. An alien power coursed through me and surged against Iron Serpent's qì. When our powers clashed, Iron Serpent's spine went rigid and her eyes widened. Her grip on my neck slackened and I used the opportunity to grab her by the wrist and peel her hand off my neck. I dug the tips of my fingers into her meridians.

The look of disgust on her face was worth it. "Impertinent child!"

I pushed off the car and took a step into her, bringing my dirty, grimy self closer to her pristine gown. I wasn't sure what my power was doing just yet, but it was giving me leverage, and I would take whatever I could get. New strength bloomed in my legs and back and I leaned forward, staring the Old One down.

"Don't wrestle with pigs and then complain when you get dirty."

My fingers found Iron Serpent's meridian and the hunger in my chest bellowed anew. My heart felt like it would burst. I had nothing left to lose. I threw the new power into Iron Serpent.

The qì flow didn't reverse. The strange power didn't push Iron Serpent out of me. Iron Serpent's qì just . . . disappeared. Swallowed whole like a school of krill vanishing into a whale's maw. Strange images flashed across my eyes, purple and pink skies at twilight, strange constellations of stars, an ornate arched bridge over a placid lake. She tried to twist out of my grip, but my fingers were steel around her wrist. Where her claws pierced my wrist, my blood stopped flowing and my skin turned pale white.

Iron Serpent tried to jerk away. Her nostrils flared in alarm. "What are you?"

Delicate white scales formed on my skin, growing outward. As the scales spread, my muscles bulged. My fingers lengthened, the nails extending into deadly points. I swayed as a vision rushed through me, a white serpent with delicate wings, soaring through clouds of pale violet.

Iron Serpent screamed and the sound was an exquisite stab of pain to my ears. "Enough!"

I jerked forward as the rest of Iron Serpent's gown whipped around her in a storm of thrashing silk. The deck of the bridge rushed up to me and I barely got my hands up in time to protect my face. My arm with the white scales landed first, and the impact carved a gouge into the concrete. I rolled over and found myself directly under Iron's Serpent's gaping muzzle.

She loomed over me in her true form, her enormous, sinuous body crushing several cars behind her. Her mouth was large enough to swallow me whole and lined with rows of small, sharp teeth. Luminous eyes like pools of quicksilver pinned me to the concrete. Along her torso, a small patch of skin lacked the protective layer of scales.

I watched in wonder as the scales faded from my arm, to reappear on Iron Serpent. My wrist was smooth and unmarked where her claws had pierced me only moments before. The deep, dark emptiness inside me was also gone. Without the addition of Iron Serpent's qì, my body sagged against the deck.

Even in her serpent form, her voice carried the same tone—a casual threat of death. "So, not a fish after all. That old fox was right. Interesting."

Her body flexed, tossing cars like toys. I stayed very, very still and held her gaze. I refused to show any sign of weakness. After another moment of studying me, she seemed to come to a decision and the rain slacked off. Blue skies crept through the storm clouds.

Iron Serpent tossed her head toward San Francisco. "Return to your city. Today's lesson is done."

I got to my feet, never taking my eyes from the Old One. I gave her a short bow. "Thank you for the lesson."

She nodded again. "Cultivate your strength. A storm is coming, and you will need to be strong."

Her pale gray eyes drilled into me. "I look forward to our next meeting, little phoenix."

Phoenix?

I backed away slowly and gave her another short, respectful bow. Iron Serpent huffed, something between a laugh, a cough, and exasperation. The way Popo often did when scolding me. Her body coiled and she sprang into the air, feathery wings flapping. As she spiraled up, the storm clouds parted. Her brilliant white form melded into the bright light of the sun, and then she was gone.

I ran back to my city. When I crossed the center of the bridge my body drank up the city's charge like a battery. Between one step and the next, my connection to the city returned and it was like sound and color flooded my world in that instant.

From here on, I would have to be more careful about when I left the bounds of San Francisco. I sensed that the bridge was thankfully empty of residents, just a mass of stalled and wrecked cars. A murder of crows perched along the bridge railings as if welcoming me back.

New energy refreshed my legs and soothed my battered neck. The city greeted me with relief and I felt the same. As I hoofed it back to the heart of my city, the crows took wing and circled above me like a dark honor guard.

Emergency services had set up in the parking lot of the welcome center at the south end of the bridge, triaging injured tourists and bikers. Fortunately a freak spring storm that flooded the bridge wasn't too far from the realm of possibility. Most locals would forget about the storm shortly, and by the weekend the story would be folded neatly into the city's ever-growing lore.

In all the confusion, no one noticed me walking off the bridge. Or maybe it was the crows obscuring me. Before the crows departed, a few of them teamed up and dropped my bag of weapons at my feet. How thoughtful.

I found Freddy sprawled across a concrete bench, talking to a drone.

Must be Fiona.

"Hi."

He hopped up in surprise. "You won?"

"Call it a draw."

He raised his eyebrows.

"What happened to the kids?"

Freddy pointed to the array of emergency vehicles with flashing lights. I zeroed in on an ambulance where an EMT tended to a woman wrapped in a blanket. Two young children clung to her legs like needy koala bears.

I clapped him on the shoulder. "Good job, Tran."

The drone buzzed off.

"I didn't do anything! I was coming back for you with Linh's team."

I shrugged. "It worked out."

"You faced down an Old One! Spill!"

He wasn't wrong. It wasn't every day that a legend tried to kill you. Our kind liked to stay hidden. Our monsters, even more so. After the Cataclysm and our escape from the Realm, Jiārén were the only ones who lived openly. Iron Serpent's presence alone was worrying enough, but her parting words seemed to portend even worse. At a conservative estimate, she was at least a thousand years old. No one got that old by being stupid.

But I was still reeling from my confrontation with her. I didn't even know where to begin explaining to Freddy what had gone down. Especially the dark . . . thing . . . that had awoken in me. What had Iron Serpent done to cause that? Was it still in there, waiting for another chance to break free? The power had felt wild, like an untamed animal.

A ravenous beast.

My world seemed a little darker now, the shadows heavy with sharp blades, the air thick with the scent of Dragon talents. Father would be right at home.

My brother's Lóng Yá Tourney was right around the corner, a cross between prom and a gladiator fight. What better way for Jiārén to show off the next generation of powerful children? It was the highlight event of the year, sure to be stacked with all of the most powerful, scheming Jiārén. Two of them were right here in my city, threatening clan warfare. And now I knew I couldn't leave the city without leaving an essential part of my power behind.

I chose my words carefully. "Things got weird."

Freddy sobered. "Bad weird?"

"Yeah."

"She let you walk?"

I nodded. "And she gave me a warning."

He waited a beat but I didn't elaborate. He slung an arm around my shoulders and squeezed. Somehow, Freddy had become my friend. I leaned against him and we sat in silence. I watched the EMTs take care of their patients, my people. The woman with the two kids was bundled into the back of an ambulance and another woman arrived to corral the kids and take them home. My city had taken a hit today, but it was resilient. It would bounce back.

A pearlescent Escalade with mirrored windows pulled up, navigating smoothly through all the emergency vehicles to stop right in front of us. The driver's door opened and the Trans' chief enforcer as well as Fiona's personal aegis, Franklin, stepped out, six and a half feet of brawny boxer stuffed into a shiny sharkskin suit. Hoard silver winked in the sunlight along his fingers and wrists, and at the understated tiepin on his chest. From behind his dark sunglasses he gave the parking lot a quick once-over before opening the rear passenger door for us. His jaw could have been carved from granite and he didn't so much as smile when Freddy beamed and waved at him.

Freddy popped up. "Come on, we'll give you a lift back home."

After the day I'd had, a lift from Freddy that didn't involve vomiting was a welcome change of pace.

THE ARCHIVE

Franklin took me back to my house. I hadn't managed to lock the door when Freddy had stolen me away, but the murder of crows clustered on my front porch seemed to be more than enough deterrent. More perks of the new job.

The sight of my home calmed me as always, its modest exterior a reminder of the life I was building for myself in this city. I'd used my salvage earnings to buy this double lot in Dogpatch, which was not in one of the fancy parts of the city. It was slowly getting gentrified but had none of the charm of Potrero Hill and bordered on an industrial area. I didn't worry so much about Wàirén crime from the industrial fringes. My security measures were top-notch, and magically enhanced.

Anyone looking from the sidewalk saw just a small house with a cheerful blue door. I slept better at night because I knew the reinforced door could stop a tank or hold out against a fire talent to buy me precious time to retreat to either my panic room or my back lot where my cottage sat. The windows on the front house were bulletproof, which also helped against the many kinetic talents in the Jiārén community.

A soothing water fountain sat on the porch, next to the bamboo planter and the shoe rack. The fountain was new, and a change in color in the water let me know if Dragon talents had been used on the porch. Not as good as the protection on the back cottage, but still helpful. It had been a gift from the Sun family after my assumption of the Sentinel mantle.

Freddy got out as the car stopped and stood with his arms wide, expectant. I hesitated a beat and held up my fist. He scowled but managed to smile at the same time. We bumped knuckles. Freddy climbed back into the Escalade and hung his head out the window. The afternoon sunlight glinted off his mirrored shades.

"You withstood a truth seeking for me, Emiko. I'll get my hug out of you yet."

I rapped my knuckles on his forehead. "If you ever kidnap me again, I will smash your surfboard into tiny pieces."

I was kidding. Sort of.

He shuddered. "That's just mean, Emiko." He waggled another shaka at me as the car drove off.

The crows flapped away from my porch as I approached, until only one remained as I crossed my threshold. I tried to ignore it. I'd already lost every staring contest with them. Was it always the same crow? Or did they take turns? Was I meriting closer observation after leaving the city boundary?

My phone pinged and my mood lifted when I saw the text notification.

sifu uncle asked if we could move our lesson to the afternoon this week

Only one person in the world called me si-fu. Leanna Louie, eleven-year-old princess of the Louie household, and my first and only private martial arts student.

No problem, see you at 3:00 then?

yay! ive been working on some new tricks

I smiled.

And practicing the routines I gave you?

That got me a string of crying emojis.

can you get on Yíchǎn? texting is sooo boring

More crying emojis.

The next message was a link to download an app, followed by machine-gun, rapid-fire messages.

it's the newest thing!!
everyone's on it
omg you're going to love it
aaaaaaaa

A cascade of plump red hearts drifted across my screen. Texting with a tween was painful. I swiped them away and clicked the app link. In a moment the app had loaded and presented me with a list of possible contacts to add as friends.

I quickly tapped on Leanna's and Freddy's smiling faces, but hovered over Fiona's imperious not-smile. It still felt odd to call Freddy a friend, but I enjoyed his company. Perhaps it was his own bad experience with clan politics that drew me to him.

Fiona, on the other hand . . .

If Freddy reminded me of me, then Fiona reminded me of my father, which made me wary. People like my father didn't have friends. But I couldn't live like that. Not anymore. I tapped Fiona's face.

They were a matched set, and I would make an effort to make allies, if not friends. Popo would be proud of me.

The Yíchǎn app pinged with a new message.

aaaaaa so happy your here

More puffy heart and smile emojis blanketed my screen, this time accompanied by a shower of glitter and sound effects.

Ok, you can show me the rest of the app later.

k bye!

The app was populated with glamor shots and highly curated images of Jiārén elites. I had zero interest in their doings beyond professional curiosity. I shook my head in amazement. It used to be so much work to keep tabs on them. Now they told me where they were, what they were doing, and who they were doing it with. If only I'd had access to this back in my Jōkōryūkai days.

I peeled out of my gear as I walked to the back of the house and the hottest shower I could stand. Going beyond the city limits had cut me off from the city's power, and the effect had wiped me out. The limitation was obvious in hindsight and I berated myself for missing it. From now on I would have to be careful anytime I left the city.

But this was just a symptom of what had been bothering me ever since I'd taken the mantle of Sentinel. There wasn't any lore for me to learn from. And the less I knew about my powers, the more vulnerable I was. Especially if I was attracting the attention of beings like Iron Serpent. Becoming Sentinel had moved me into a much deeper pool, with bigger predators.

In my years as the Blade, I'd taken a page from my father's book, noting my enemies' strengths and weaknesses. I never went into a fight without a sure edge and the appropriate weapons. Today I had been caught unprepared and without my weapons. I wasn't going to let that happen again.

I closed my eyes and as the hot water sluiced over me, I replayed my fight with the Old One. I flexed my arm—the one that had been covered in scales. That feeling of absolute strength that had surged through it, and the way I'd been so overcome with hunger before. Like something inside me was ravenous. Was that me? Or the city?

Something tickled the edges of my mind, buried in the murky shadows of the past. Like forgotten dreams, only fragments of hungry sensation washed over me. I wanted to remember. Or did I?

My eyes snapped open. I knew that feeling, which meant it wasn't something the city had imposed on me. But something about the battle with the Old One had unleashed it.

I placed my palm over that area on my chest where Iron Serpent had attempted to carve me open. This scar was visible and new, but the ones in my mind were old. And they often showed up as nightmares, the kind that left me waking and gasping but unable to remember. Not for the first time, bitterness rose up in me at the awareness that the nightmares were the memories that my waking mind hid from me.

I couldn't do anything to recover those, but maybe I could do something about the new threats to my life. So I fell back on my training. What I needed was information and preparation.

Being the Sentinel made me stronger, but it had painted a target on my back. There was one place in the city that might have even a shred of information that could help me.

It was time to go to the Library.

Of course, not the Wàirén library. Nearly every city with a substantial population of Jiārén had a Library, a repository of our lore and history. Like everything else we had, it was hidden in plain sight and well guarded.

The San Francisco Public Library hummed with activity, a popular place for my city's residents. Teens skateboarded up and down the broad expanse of sidewalk. Well-dressed urbanites dodged the skaters while balancing steaming cups of coffee. Along Larkin Street bikers wove in and out of the afternoon crush of cars. I stood on the sidewalk for a moment, savoring the feel of the life of my city pulsing around me like coursing river water.

In this crush of humanity, I could wear my weapons and people wouldn't give me a second glance. I had carried Truth and Hachi together for years in public. Wàirén didn't see them at all or thought I was carrying an umbrella or flashlight or some other mundane item. Occasionally I had to draw my sword in front of a Wàirén—then all bets were off.

But I was just going to the Library. Hopefully I wouldn't need to draw my weapons today.

I turned toward the massive concrete building and mentally readied myself. My last visit to the Library had been like so many incidents in my life. It hadn't ended well. I'd been attacked by a ghost and kicked out by the Librarian. The Librarian was a powerful entity in the seat of her power. Even as the Sentinel I did not look forward to seeing her again.

Inside the Library the massive interior skylight acted as a filter, keeping out the bustling noise of the city while letting in calming gray San Francisco sunlight. A group of kids carrying skateboards crossed the main lobby, whispering among themselves as they headed for the teen center. A clutch of young children sat in a wide circle, at rapt attention around an aged Asian woman. The old woman unrolled a scroll painted with fantastic creatures, adjusted her horn-rimmed glasses, and began speaking in soft Cantonese, telling an ancient tale of dragons and phoenixes. The pulse of the city quieted, relaxing a knot of tension I'd been holding between my shoulder blades.

I headed to the third floor on the east side, where the Wàirén Chinese collection was housed. The wrought-iron gates enclosing the collection looked innocuous, fashioned into climbing wisteria and jasmine flowers, but the flowers obscured intricate figures of the Eight Sons of the Dragon. Hidden in plain sight.

Even from a distance I felt the power of the jeweled eyes of those dragons. The no-look spells that concealed the Library hadn't been obvious to me before, but the city's magic gave me a new lens. It was shocking, honestly, how unaware I'd been before, my magical ignorance shielding me from how much truly separated Lóng Jiārén from Júwàirén.

For two years I'd immersed myself in this city, making Wàirén friends and growing my business. I'd started to feel like I was making progress. Though I'd always have my history as the Blade, my nightmares had become less frequent and I'd felt like I'd gained some needed distance from Jiārén society. I should have known the other shoe was about to drop. Then the pendulum swung so far the other way and knocked me ass over teakettle back into Jiārén intrigues.

I passed through the gates and entered the Chinese collection, a small rotunda bordered by walnut bookshelves that stretched to the ceiling. Dark paneled cabinets broke up the shelving with ceramic antiques set under museum lighting. The Librarian sat inside a circular desk in the center of the room. She stood as I approached, stretching out to her full height, her jet-black eyes flashing. I remembered the way she'd shut down my hecklers last time. They'd left bleeding. She was terrifying. Maybe she wouldn't remember me though. I was just one face among many, right?

Her brow creased and her dark eyes drilled into me before looking above my head. After seeing my golden aura that marked me as Sentinel, a war of emotions passed over her thin face. She seemed to come to some sort of decision and placed her hands in front of her, sketching a shallow bow.

"Honored Sentinel, I apologize, but I do not have time to escort you through the Library today."

Escort? "That's fine. If I could mark the guest register, I can find my own way. Do you know where—"

The Librarian interrupted me. "My sincerest apologies, Sentinel, but it would not be proper for an honored guest such as yourself to not have a guide through our Library."

My nose twitched. Somehow her apology didn't seem sincere at all. She remembered how my last visit ended. Did she think I needed supervision? It's not like I had asked to be attacked. "A guide isn't necessary, I just—"

The Librarian's power flared, the sclera of her eyes darkening and whorls of inky smoke curling around her hands. "Unfortunately there is no—"

A quiet, raspy voice, no louder than a whisper, spoke behind me. Although barely audible, the voice silenced the Librarian and stilled the room. "She doesn't want you here, Sentinel."

An ancient, stoop-backed woman entered the rotunda behind

me, pushing a walker in front of her. Her gray hair was permed and sprayed into a stiff nimbus around her head. Battered yellow tennis balls capped the front legs of her walker. Leaning heavily, the old woman shuffled her walker into the room and I recognized her from the reading circle on the first floor. She coughed, the sound wet and rattling in her lungs. An age-spotted hand searched through the pockets of her threadbare pink housecoat and came out with a wrinkled pack of unfiltered cigarettes.

That was enough to break the Librarian out of her shock. "Gu Ma, no! There is no smoking inside the Library!"

I looked between the Librarian and the interloper, the Librarian's elder auntie. I didn't see much of a familial resemblance between them. Gu Ma lifted her head, spearing the Librarian with a look. Her eyes, initially watery, sharpened and her pupils grew large and dark. Oh, there it was.

Gu Ma clucked softly in disapproval. "Siu jie."

My hackles went up until I realized Gu Ma was talking to the Librarian.

As if hearing my thoughts, Gu Ma turned to me, her penetrating stare skewering me for a moment before returning to the pack in her hands. With slow movements she shook a crooked cigarette out of the pack and carefully plucked it out with her lips.

She spoke around the cigarette as she stowed the pack. "Fine. I won't light it. Nothing in your rules says anything about that."

The Librarian's hands clutched into tight fists, more black tendrils snaking out of them and spilling over the top of her desk. "This. Is. A. Library!"

Gu Ma grabbed my hand and began pulling me around the Librarian's desk. For an old woman, her grip was exceptionally strong. She muttered as she dragged me along. "Silly girl. Who ever heard of a dragon afraid of a little smoke?"

She raised her voice as we approached the elevator hidden behind the far shelves and yelled in Cantonese, telling her niece not to be afraid. "I'll make sure she stays out of trouble."

I wasn't so sure about that.

With a word, the bookshelf split open, revealing a gleaming metal door that slid open to accept us. We stepped inside and turned around, giving me one last look at the apoplectic Librarian, still stunned and standing at her desk. I gave an awkward wave. This incident hadn't won me any favors.

Gu Ma smiled around her cigarette and waved as well before slapping her hand on the panel of buttons. Power, old power, flowed from the small woman and nine buttons lit up on the panel. My eyebrows threatened to crawl up into my hair. This woman's talent felt even older than Iron Serpent's. But maybe it didn't belong to her. Maybe it was like the Librarian's, whose power came from the institution itself? My eyes were drawn to the bottom button, which had not lit up for me during my last visit. Gu Ma grinned even wider when she caught me looking and pressed the number nine with one nicotine-stained finger.

The elevator slid quietly into motion, taking us down into the bowels of the Library. The Library mirrored the structure of the San Francisco main library above us, with each floor ringed around a circular open space. Delicate walkways like spokes on a wheel radiated out from the elevator at each level.

We dropped beyond the fifth level where I had visited last time. As we dropped lower I marveled at the breadth of the artifacts on display. One level looked to be entirely covered in huge maps drawn on a variety of surfaces. Massive animal skins adorned the walls, alongside slabs of stone and sheets of parchment as big as flags.

Gu Ma lifted her head and looked up, seeming to peer through the ceiling now several floors above us. With a satisfied grunt she snapped her fingers and the end of her cigarette ignited. She inhaled deeply and blew out a plume of fragrant blue-gray smoke. "You don't mind, do you?"

I stifled a cough in the cramped confines and shook my head. "Of course not."

Gu Ma took another drag on her cigarette as the elevator continued to descend, her eyes tracking up and down my body and then lingering just a bit above my head. "Well, it seems you have at least some sense."

I bowed deeply. "To whom do I have the pleasure of speaking with?"

Gu Ma snorted, amused by my question. Her eyes bored into mine and the silence stretched until I started to fidget under her stare. I broke first, turning away from her and then nearly throwing myself through the glass as the elevator plunged through the bottom of the Library and into darkness. Heart hammering, I looked up to find a small circle of light shrinking above us.

The embers of Gu Ma's cigarette glowed red, now the only light inside the elevator car. In the near darkness Gu Ma was an oppressive presence, turning the air into syrup. I struggled to breathe and stay upright as she spoke. "The Library above us, and all the other Libraries around the world are branches of a tree. This tree contains the collected knowledge of all Jiārén since before the Cataclysm."

I had the sudden intuition that in the darkness, Gu Ma no longer looked like a stooped old woman. I strained to see her in the dim light, trying to convince myself that I wasn't seeing a massive, hulking shape next to me.

She crushed out the cigarette on the floor of the elevator, plunging us into total darkness. "I am taking you to the root of the tree, the place from which all our knowledge springs. And we will see if you are truly worthy to be called a Sentinel. Only after you prove yourself, will we bother with names."

A chill ran down my spine. Iron Serpent had hinted that Sentinels died young. Perhaps they'd all been killed by an Old One masquerading as an octogenarian bingo jockey. The elevator would stop at the bottom of the shaft and Gu Ma would toss my body upon a pile of corpses, the rotting remains of other failed Sentinels.

A spot of red-orange light flared before me and Gu Ma's wrinkled face swam out of the black as she drew on her second cigarette. "Aiya. You worry too much."

The elevator slid to a stop and Gu Ma turned, dragging her walker around with her. The doors hissed open and she hobbled out into the darkness, the glowing ember showing her movement. As she walked, a soft glowing light appeared, revealing a rough passage hewn out of bedrock. The walls of the corridor looked like they'd only recently been cut and the passage disappeared into the darkness.

The walker scraped over the rough surface of the floor as Gu Ma walked. "I suppose I should thank you, girl. I've always wanted to visit San Francisco, and a city's Library doesn't join with the Archive until a Sentinel rises. Even if you die today, at least you have done me this one thing."

I had already almost died this morning. I was not eager for a repeat.

The glowing light seemed to be coming from the walls of the corridor itself, and the light followed us as we made our way down the path. "This Archive, it will help me understand the Sentinel powers?"

"All that, and more. If you are worthy, and only when you are ready."

My hand drifted up to my collarbone, where the Pearl pulsed under my skin. "What about the . . ."

Gu Ma caught the movement of my hand and gave me a grim smile. "Yes, had a bit of an adventure this morning, didn't you? Not to worry, I don't think the white snake would have eaten you."

She blew out a plume of blue-gray smoke and laughed. "At least, not yet. Not when she could save you for later and make eating your Pearl worth her effort."

My head swam at the implication of Gu Ma's words. If she was telling the truth, both of these beings were thousands of years old. I was descended from those in the Realm. Gu Ma and Iron Serpent were from the Realm. I was dangerously out of my depth. My hand tightened on Hachi's grip, the wakizashi I wore on my hip. I still felt unbalanced without the weight of Sword of Truth on my back, but the familiar silk knots on Hachi were some comfort.

Gu Ma waved a dismissive hand at my sword. "That will not help you here. It is a crude instrument, the weapons of those who are unable to comprehend the greater path of the world."

The passage widened and the light around us grew brighter until we stood in a round antechamber. A circular labyrinth had been carved into the floor, and the opposite wall of the chamber was a massive face of polished rock at least twenty feet high. A circular mosaic covered the majority of the rock face, a sea of gray and blue stones set in what looked like a random pattern.

Gu Ma came to a stop before the mosaic. "You must learn, or you will die. And the only true weapon is knowledge."

I couldn't tell if she was giving me advice, or threatening me.

She raised her hand toward the wall of polished rock. "Behind this door lies the Archive, more that has been forgotten than remembered, a vast trove of knowledge that I have been charged with protecting for a millennium. The most powerful weapon in all of Jiārén history. Entry to the vault is restricted to me and those who can truly claim the title of Sentinel."

She took a long drag from her cigarette. "To open the door, you must be the Sentinel. To be the Sentinel, you must open the door."

Gu Ma turned, and in that instant, she no longer looked like she needed the walker to stand. Power flowed from her like heat from a bonfire. Light blazed from the rock around us, throwing crazed shadows on the wall behind her. None of the shadows looked like a frail old woman. Several looked like they had wings. Her eyes shone, crystal bright, and seemed to pierce through me.

"Only a true Sentinel may open this door. You will open the door, or you will die."

No pressure. I clenched my fists to quell the shaking in my hands. "How do—"

"A true Sentinel knows how to open the door."

Frustration rumbled in my belly. "I took the mantle. I traded my freedom to protect my city. I am the Sentinel."

Gu Ma narrowed her eyes. "So the little dragon closes a door to the underworld and now she knows everything, does she?"

The old woman scooted her walker forward a step. My hindbrain betrayed me, and I took a half step back.

Gu Ma's voice was the low grating of crushed gravel. "You. Are not. A dragon. You are an insect that has tasted but a hint of the true power of dragons. Your lives are here and gone in less than the blink of an eye. You Jiārén make plans and scheme, never comprehending that your power was never more than the least of your master's leavings."

As she spoke, she took slow steps forward until she pinned me against the rock wall. The power Gu Ma gave off rivaled what I'd felt from Iron Serpent, power with the quiet, crushing depths of the ocean. She leaned over me until her face hovered over mine and the heat from the tip of her cigarette warmed my cheek.

"You are not the Sentinel simply because you took the mantle. The power of the Sentinel is not something you take."

Gu Ma straightened. "It is what you become."

She turned and gestured to the mosaic. "Now show me what you can become. Show me you can become more than a foot soldier."

She didn't quite spit out the last word, but she said it with enough disdain to rankle me. I wasn't proud of my past, but I had done my duty. I edged around her and sat down inside the carving of the labyrinth, hoping the pattern would provide some kind of clue for me. I crossed my legs and placed my hands lightly on my knees, closing my eyes and stretching out with my senses.

I had done it once, on Lotus Lane. Some kind of melding of my mind and the city, allowing me to perceive far more than humanly possible. If I could tap into that, it might give me a clue to opening the Archive. Naturally, I'd already tried this several times in the last week, and come up empty-handed each time. Trying to find it here under the crushing metaphysical weight of the bones of the city wasn't much easier.

The labyrinth had to be the key. Instead of reaching for the door, I projected my senses into the floor. I traced the pattern of the maze in my mind and timed my breaths to the ebb and flow of the carved lines. I pictured my qì flowing through my body and then along the lines of the maze.

Iron Serpent had nearly cooked me, but her brute-force had managed to move a lot of qì through my meridians. Now the flow was back to its former weak state. It was like trying to dance with two different shoes. Every other step threw me off the rhythm, forcing me to back up and start over. Sweat beaded on my neck. I pushed until my mind was blank and I visualized myself sinking into the labyrinth under my legs.

On my next breath my lungs filled with salty sea air. As I exhaled, cool fog passed through my lips. The sounds of the city, birds calling, car horns, ringing cable car bells, echoed off the rough stone walls and filled my ears. I took another breath and set my hands on the stone. I pushed a meager flow of my qì through the maze and the life of the city leapt up in my chest like a caged animal straining against its bonds.

My eyes flew open. The door to the vault shone with brilliant blue light. The mosaic flashed once, the sudden light blinding and searing through my mind. Images leapt out of the chaos of the mosaic now, the curve of a cheek, a crow in flight, a bridge wreathed in fog. I inhaled again, gasping as the power of the city pushed back through me.

It was similar to the sensation with Iron Serpent. My meridians were preventing the city from merging its power with me. Whatever had happened in the vault of the Louie bank, I wasn't replicating it today.

But this was it. It had to be. I grabbed the city's power, bending it to my will, like I was trying to divert a river with my bare hands. I stood and stumbled to the wall. I just needed to put my hands on the mosaic. The city's power hammered on my meridians, trying to beat through a closed door.

I fell forward and my hand landed on the wall, the sharp edges of the stone cutting into my palm. Blood welled from the cuts and smeared across the mosaic as I fell to my knees. The power inside me twisted like a fish out of water and wrenched itself out of my grasp. I cried out but it was too late. The city vanished from my mind like a snuffed candle and I collapsed. The light in the chamber died down to just the original soft glow from the walls.

I had failed.

I lay there for a moment, my shoulder to the door, before I remembered that Gu Ma had been watching me the whole time. I raised my eyes to her slowly, the way a deer watches a wolf.

Gu Ma twisted one hand into the front of my shirt and hauled me off the floor. She did it as easily as picking up a scrap of garbage, which was probably how much she thought of me. I clutched at her wrist but she was even stronger than Iron Serpent, her grip unrelenting.

With shuffling steps she dragged me toward the door and pinned me to the stone wall. I reached frantically for San Francisco, but Gu Ma's presence swelled and filled the entire chamber, displacing all the air, space, and power.

Gu Ma sucked on her cigarette and the tip glowed red, yellow, then white hot, a shining star I had to squint against. On the far wall, a massive shadow loomed to the ceiling and gave the impression of curving fangs and sharp claws. Gu Ma raised her other hand and a shadow as thick as a tree matched her movement.

I closed my eyes and said a prayer to the Great Dragon Father. Not for me, but for my brother, who would go into Lóng Yá wondering why I'd failed to show up for him.

One heartbeat.

Another.

I opened my eyes and found Gu Ma looking just to my left. She dropped me unceremoniously and I landed in a heap, my clothes soaked in cold sweat. Gu Ma leaned over me, her eyes right next to the wall. I followed her gaze to where a tiny seam, just a few millimeters, had opened at the edge of the mosaic.

Gu Ma turned and her gaze pierced through me. It was as if she could see the twisted wreckage of my meridians. Old shame rose up my neck.

Gu Ma clucked and lit another cigarette. "Not bad."

She bent down until she was eye to eye with me. "You have the key. You need to learn to turn it."

I sucked in a breath. "I will."

"Next time, do better." She thumped me on the forehead with one stubby finger.

I heard the unspoken "or else . . ."

Gu Ma blew a plume of smoke in my face. I flinched, shutting my eyes against the smoke.

I opened my eyes and blinked against the sudden brightness. I'd returned to the main rotunda of the Chinese collection, surrounded by a dissipating cloud of Gu Ma's tobacco smoke. I coughed and waved the smoke out of my face, only to find the Librarian looming beside me, her eyes glittering with anger.

I batted more of the smoke away and backed up. "It's not mine! I wasn't smoking, I swear!"

The Librarian closed the distance with me, getting right in my face. She hovered close for an extra beat, as if debating internally. Finally she raised an arm toward the door. Her words came out stilted, forced past the smile she'd pasted on.

"We hope you enjoyed your visit today, honored Sentinel. Let me know if you would like an escort to the exit."

I shook my head and made for the door. At least she let me leave under my own power this time.

I wasn't sure she would let me back in next time.

SAN FRANCISCO CALLING

A good morning always starts with a fight. Which was why I started two mornings a week at Big G's, my local BJJ gym, grappling with my fellow students and learning new ways to express my emotions without injuring anyone.

Call it exercise and therapy rolled into one neat package. I needed plenty of it given the beatings I had taken the day before from Iron Serpent and Gu Ma. I'd recovered physically but my confidence had definitely taken a hit. Old wounds never really healed, you just forgot about the pain for a while.

Two years hadn't been long enough.

The city's power hadn't been enough, either.

I'd left a lot behind when I came to San Francisco. My failure from Lóng Kǒu, my failure from Jōkōryūkai, my failure as the Blade of Soong. All my efforts to make something useful out of my life culminated in the bloody ruin of Beijing's Pearl Market, and a name that I would never get away from: the Butcher.

But Iron Serpent had called me broken. *Broken.* It was an older wound, but the pain was still as fresh. I needed to remind myself what I was good at, and that was getting close and getting dirty.

At Jōkōryūkai I had learned innumerable ways to take my enemies apart with a dazzling variety of weapons. When engaging Jiārén with Dragon talents, there was no such thing as an easy fight. Like our lives, our conflicts were quick and brutal. Studying Brazilian jiujitsu gave me an opportunity to keep my reflexes fresh without hurting anyone. It also taught me something I hadn't had as the Blade: restraint.

For the last rolling session this morning I paired up with Marshall. Our size difference was comical, but for all of his greater reach and barrel chest we both knew who was the better fighter. Not that I let that hold me back. Our instructor, Charlie, would never let me go easy and it was ingrained in me anyway.

Marshall made a valiant attempt, coming in fast and trying to lock me down with speed and brute strength. An admirable effort, but I slipped away easily. When your enemies weren't coming after you with spears of fire or blades of ice, anything else was less intimidating. I rolled Marshall onto his back and wrapped him up in an arm bar. He tapped out graciously and got up with a rueful smile on his face.

"I'll be fast enough for you one of these days, Emiko."

I nodded. He was getting faster, but anything less than life or death wouldn't motivate him to improve fast enough to take me.

As we all gathered and packed up our gear Marshall said, "You're going to get bored if Adam doesn't get back in the gym soon."

That comment got me a knowing look from Ellie, who thankfully said nothing. It was still enough to drive a flush of heat up the back of my neck. Hopefully I was still sweaty enough to hide my reaction. I tried to downplay it, but Ellie had spotted a change in me at the mention of Adam.

We had been seeing a lot of each other of late.

Our meetings were all business. Usually Tessa was there, too. It wasn't like Adam and I were alone. Much. Or dating. Or anything like that.

"The doctor told him to lay off anything strenuous for at least another few weeks," I replied.

Marshall and Ellie made sympathetic noises.

Truly, lightning strikes were no joke.

But the resulting short-term amnesia from the lightning strike had been a blessing and a curse. It meant I could dodge the most pointed of Adam's questions of why he had been struck with lightning, under the auspices of the doctor's advice not to rush things. But the longer I avoided telling him that the Tanaka Clan had unleashed a death strike on both of us and that I'd taken a blood oath so that the Trans would heal him, the harder it got to tell him the truth.

Though I didn't like to think of myself as a liar, lies of omission were still lies. But I obeyed the First Law because it was the primary pillar of Jiārén life.

Protect the Hoard.

It was literal and figurative. Protect our power base, the artifacts and treasure we collected, soaked in Dragon power. And protect our way of life, keeping our ways secret from outsiders.

It was so ingrained that I couldn't wrest free of its stranglehold.

Adam had somehow inherited Crimson Cloud Splitter, a sword so epic, most Jiārén families would make a play for it, and they would take out Adam and everyone in Adam's orbit to be on the safe side. He thought it was a lost work of legendary swordsmith Kunimitsu. To be sure, if it was a fifteenth-century sword from that genius, it would be a spectacular find in its own right. Which was why he and Tessa wanted to display it in their big upcoming exhibit at the museum.

I couldn't let that happen and so far I had been spinning my wheels trying to stop it.

Ore from Lóng Jiā was so hard that it could only be melted by dragon flame. Of the Nine Sons of the Dragon, only one had the fiery breath. This swordsmith had then imbued the blade with lightning power. Crimson Cloud Splitter had been lost with the Jiārén diaspora in the eleventh century and somehow resurfaced briefly in Tokyo, the engraving on it inspiring the great Kunimitsu.

Those very similarities were what had Adam convinced that this was a lost work of the Kunimitsu school. Now he was dead set on displaying the sword with the rest of his collection at Tessa's museum. As the museum's consultant, I had to find a credible reason to pull the sword from the exhibit while keeping Jiārén secrets from Tessa.

If I didn't protect the Hoard, someone else would, and I wouldn't like how they did it. My relationship with Adam had changed since our first contentious meeting at the museum. He had started out as a thorn in my side, but he'd taken a hit for me that had almost killed him. And when I'd brought him to Tessa and Andie's house, I'd done so under the theory that I was supposed to keep an eye on him for the sake of the new clan ties I'd invoked. But I hadn't expected to have a good time. It was like there was magic in Andie's kitchen, and I was different with them. Which only made things worse whenever I realized that everything would change once he knew about our Jiārén ways.

Adam wasn't just under my protection, he was under the Soong Clan's protection. Which meant my father was involved. At the time, I hadn't seen any way around it, desperate to have Fiona's healer save Adam, but unwilling to tinker with his mind. A *cleaning.*

That was considered a gentle way to protect the Hoard. To wipe out Wàirén memories of things they shouldn't have seen or heard. Everything inside me rebelled against it. Yes, I had been the Butcher, and my ways had never been gentle. But I never took anyone's memories. That was the cruelest excision.

I had a jagged tear in my own memories and I would never wish it on anyone.

So I had to bring Adam into the fold. I just needed to figure out how. And we were supposed to have coffee in a few minutes. With a low curse, I yanked out my change of clothes.

I swapped the baggy gi pants for black leggings and pulled on low-top Onitsuka sneakers, black with gold accents. With my black cowl-neck tank, black cropped cardigan, tight black pants, and black sneakers, I probably looked like a cat burglar.

Adam waited for me by the entrance. A heathered blue sweater stretched across his broad chest. The man had a penchant for cashmere. Worn-in gray jeans completed his outfit. He'd dressed casually, the way a billionaire executive did casual. Not the usual uniform of tech drones that populated the city.

No matter how many times I'd seen him, it always startled me the way he smiled at me. Like he was really pleased to see me. Like I wasn't the reason he had a concussion and amnesia now.

"Hey. Ready?"

I smiled in return, unable to resist the easy warmth in his voice, and the welcome in his piercing blue eyes. "I just need to drop my bag in the car."

He held the gym door open for me but didn't step aside. I accepted his unspoken invitation to move in close. He was so tall that my head didn't quite reach his shoulder. I brushed against his extended upper arm and I caught the faint smell of soap and lavender. I wondered if the lavender was from his skin or his sweater.

I stopped myself from leaning in to sniff him and walked through the doors to the parking lot.

The city was just starting to wake, sunlight dispersing the morning fog. The hum of the city's power reached up through the ground, almost vibrating up my legs. Despite the morning workout, I felt refreshed. I looked up at the big man standing in front of me.

Sunlight limned his frame and haloed his blond hair, treating him like a favored son. The battering he'd taken from the lightning strike had faded, and his skin looked golden and warm.

Adam cleared his throat. "I heard back from Professor Ōtsuka last night."

I closed my eyes and pictured the morning light washing me away into blissful nothingness or maybe teleporting me away from my problems—namely Adam. If he had his way and put the katana on display at the museum, all hell would break loose.

When I opened my eyes, I was still in the parking lot, and Adam's expectant expression hadn't changed. Too bad. "Is that so?"

His eyes lit up with excitement. "Yes, she has an opening in her schedule next week."

I grunted.

Adam tilted his head. "I've already chartered a flight. You should come with me."

I thought about spending hours alone with Adam in a cozy private jet for a trans-Pacific flight.

Absolutely not.

I took a deliberate step away from Adam and his inordinately good scent. "Endure jet lag and airplane food just to prove you wrong? Thanks, but I'll pass."

Adam matched my step away with one closer. "I have a five-star chef aboard the jet."

His lips quirked into a lazy half smile. "We could watch a movie."

Was it getting warmer? My cheeks flushed. "And none of that will convince me that the sword is a Kunimitsu. Neither will Professor Ōtsuka. You're wasting your time."

Professor Ōtsuka was the premier authority on medieval Japanese sword metallurgy. She'd seen photos, but now Adam wanted to take the sword to Japan for her to examine up close. She would likely confirm that the sword was missing some key elements to authenticate it as a Kunimitsu. Unfortunately she would also be unable to identify the alloy used to craft the sword. And word of a mysterious ancient sword in the professor's keeping would raise far too many eyebrows and gather far too much notice from Jiārén.

Adam's sword could not go to Japan.

He shrugged his big shoulders. "If that's what it takes to convince you and the museum, it's worth it to me. I made a promise to the Yamamotos. My word means everything to me. I'll see it through to the end, wherever it takes me."

The Yamamotos were his host family during his extended stay in Japan. The sword had come to Adam through the Yamamotos. I had a hunch that they were descendants of Jiārén who became Outclan, those with marginal talents, or blood so thin they could pass as Wàirén. Over a few generations, the one artifact that they managed to keep with them turned into a family myth that Adam now fervently believed in. The Yamamotos were like family to him and I didn't doubt he meant to keep his word to their deceased patriarch.

My word meant a lot where I came from, too. Especially after it had been sealed with blood. Unlike Adam's, my word often meant life and death, and this time it was his life in the balance. The stick clearly wasn't working here. Perhaps Adam needed the carrot.

And maybe this was also how I could get his oath to the Hoard.

"I can make the case that it's not a lost Kunimitsu. We don't even need Professor Ōtsuka."

Adam's gaze sharpened. "And how will you do that?"

I could just tell him. Come clean. The thought of the weight off my shoulders made me nearly giddy and lightheaded. I'd lay bare everything that he'd forgotten about the auction at the Palace of Fine Arts, make him remember the caliber of people we were dealing with, and how everything could blow back on his host family.

Picturing the look on his face, when he finally understood who I was, and how I had lied to him . . .

Gods, why was it so hard to talk to this man?

A wave of darkness swarmed down from the roof of the building across the street, a murder of crows all beating their wings in thunderous rhythm. My emotions whipsawed. I clutched at the distraction like I was drowning, while also dreading the reason for the crows' visitation. The flowing wall of jet-black bodies swooped down to street level and settled on and around my Jeep. In a blink, rows of bright-eyed crows sat on the hood and roof of my car, nearly all of them looking at me. Dozens more crowded the space on the asphalt around my car, making the approach to my vehicle nearly impossible.

Adam's eyebrows drew together in confusion. "Well, there's something you don't see every day."

I turned so Adam wouldn't see me throwing stink eye at the birds. I tried for lighthearted and hoped it didn't come out as desperate. "Ha, well, once you've lived in the city a while, you'll get used to it."

Nudging my way forward I inched through the birds until I reached my Jeep. They parted enough for me to open the door and throw in my bag, at least. Whatever they were here for, maybe it wasn't urgent. My hand brushed against one of the crows as I closed the car door and an image flashed across my mind, so vivid I had to grab the door to stay upright.

Checkered tiled floors, blue and white. A darkened room with broken furniture. A body dressed in a suit, lying in a pool of fresh blood, the scent thick and cloying.

The vision faded and a burst of salt water hit my nose and I knew that the rest of my day was not going to go as planned. Adam jumped back a step as Freddy Tran appeared out of nowhere on the other side of my Jeep.

"Emiko! You need to—"

Freddy broke off when he saw Adam.

I blinked at this version of Freddy I'd never seen before. Today he wore a fitted dove-gray suit that accented his swimmer's physique, offset with a silver tie, his normally unruly hair combed back. I blinked, gobsmacked. He was wearing pants. I'd never seen him in anything other than board shorts. He looked like an Armani gangster.

Ever agile, Freddy pivoted to address a visibly confused Adam. "Oh, hey man, you must be Adam."

Freddy came around the Jeep, his hand extended. "Nice to finally meet you."

Adam shook off his surprise and shook Freddy's hand. "You, too. Does Emiko talk about me much . . . ?"

Freddy laughed and ran a hand through his hair. "Yeah, sorry, I'm Freddy. I'm Emiko's . . . assistant."

Now Adam turned to me, eyebrows raised. "Assistant?"

I stared daggers at Freddy. "Yes, we're still just on a trial basis, aren't we? What are you doing here, Freddy?"

Now I saw the tension around his eyes, and the tight set of his shoulders and neck. Skies, something was wrong. "Oh, I forgot, didn't I?"

Freddy relaxed when I caught on. "Yeah, sorry to bug you on your day off. My car's around the corner. I have the . . . paperwork there for you."

Adam watched our awkward interplay, visibly confused. "If you need to go, Emiko, we can catch up later. You can show me your proof about the sword at our meeting."

The hits just kept coming from every direction, but I had to table my concerns about Adam. I'd let him have this round. "Sure, see you then."

When Adam turned to go, Freddy led me away from my Jeep and around the corner. Once we were out of sight his poker face dropped and I saw hints of real panic around his eyes. My stomach lurched and I connected the dots. I beat Freddy to the punch.

"Who died?"

Freddy's voice cracked. "Franklin."

Skies. Had the Louies made the first move already? Franklin was as close to family as you could be without sharing blood. Fiona would be devastated.

And furious.

I had to keep this from blowing up. "Where's your car?"

Freddy made a face. "We don't have time. Please don't break all my surfboards."

The crisp tang of salt water appeared and Freddy's talent blossomed around us. He wrapped his arms around me and pulled me into the swirling vortex.

DUTY

I vomited on the sidewalk, my gut roiling as my body protested Freddy's violent mode of travel. Some people just weren't meant to be hurled across the city through a twisting tunnel of air.

Freddy pulled me to my feet and kept his hands on my arms until he saw that I wasn't going to fall over. Between the transportation and the news, it was a close thing. I'd been away from Jiārén life too long. I'd grown soft. Franklin was dead. He'd been stoically alive just a day ago. And for some reason, Freddy had tunneled us to just across the street from the Hotel Bellavista.

"Emiko? You okay?"

I waited a moment for my guts to settle down and nodded. "How'd you find me?"

Freddy rolled his eyes. "Drones. Remember? When you didn't answer your phone, I searched for your Jeep."

The Trans controlled all magical imports and exports out of San Francisco. They had planes, trains, ships, and drones at their disposal. Even I couldn't hide from them.

Freddy looked around us quickly, but no one was looking in our direction. He opened his suit jacket and reached inside. "It's not the same, but I have some gummy bear edibles if you need to level out the nerves."

Okay, there was the Freddy I was used to. I didn't drink, smoke, or gamble. I wasn't about to start chewing CBD gummies. I swiped at my mouth with the back of my hand and pushed him away. "Thanks, but no. I could use some water though."

As usual, he shrugged it off. His eyes, normally bright with laughter, were dull and somber today. He nodded and led me across the street to where a Tran security team waited, two men and two women, all dressed impeccably in varying tones of gray and silver, and all radiating a quiet menace.

Freddy handed me a bottle of water. While I chugged with undignified thirst, he pulled a couple of the gummy bears out and popped them into his mouth before rebuttoning his jacket. "We better get in there. Come on."

Fiona's gray-suited security detail had formed a perimeter around the building. More of her team stretched around both sides of the massive hotel. It looked like she'd had her people cordon off the entire hotel.

As we approached the massive white facade of the hotel entrance, the white rosebushes that flanked the entrance began blooming with speedy profusion. A shower of petals blew down and coated my hair and face like kisses. Crows flying in V-formation arrowed down over the building and began circling above me and cawing.

Freddy turned to look at me, covered in rose petals and being serenaded by crows. He shook his head. His expression plainly said, *Is it always going to be like this with you?*

I wiped the petals off my face and shrugged. This Sentinel gig remained mysterious to me. After what had happened with the crows yesterday morning, I had a pit of anxiety in my stomach. Was the city just helping me make an entrance, or laying some kind of claim over me? I still didn't know.

Freddy exchanged nods with the guards we passed and they waved us through. I tried not to notice the stares I was getting as we moved through the arched entrance to the hotel. I didn't know if it was the gold aura, the crows above me, or the flower petals. I would've been dropped from the assassin's roster at Jōkōryūkai for standing out so much. I guess the city didn't want her Sentinel to blend in. My new aura was like a beacon and I had mixed feelings about that.

I ignored the Tran security detail and their stares and just followed Freddy.

The Bellavista was one of the iconic properties perched on top of Nob Hill. The property dated back to the times of the robber barons. The interior had the quiet hush of lavish wealth. Gleaming floors of white marble set the stage, and walnut panels and mature plants provided discreet nooks for quiet conversation. A small fountain burbled in the atrium, surrounded by a dazzling array of greenery.

Normally the lobby would have guests and staff, and the usual hum of well-heeled guests checking in and being assisted by the concierge.

Not today.

Silence pressed down in the deserted lobby. Not a single staff member manned the front desk. No bellhops were to be found.

My eyes widened as I took in the scene. "Where is everyone?"

His lips thinned. "After what happened to Franklin, we called my father. He contacted the owner of the hotel. We booked out the rest of the hotel suites and conference rooms. The staff are currently offering replacement accommodations to the present guests."

The Trans were a power here in the city. Though more recent to town than the Louies, they had a lot of pull and enough money to buy this hotel from the loose change in their Louis Quatorze sofa if they wanted.

I followed Freddy through the silent lobby and then down the plushly appointed hotel hallway. The thick scent of rotting ginger assaulted my nose. The smell brought me to a stop in the middle of the hallway. It was similar to the scent of my mother's talent. She traveled far afield for Bā Shǒu but this didn't feel quite right. There was something about the scent of this talent that felt off. I stopped for a moment and closed my eyes, trying to use the city's filter to see the hallway.

Freddy's footsteps stopped. "Emiko?"

"Shh. Sentinel stuff."

I concentrated and saw the dark walnut paneling and an afterimage of footsteps that vanished in the shadow of the alcove. In the next room I felt, rather than saw, the oppressive weight of death.

Dread trickled down my back like ice water. The vision the crows had given me was unfolding before me. I was the Sentinel. This was my city, and it wanted me here. I opened my eyes and moved forward.

As we turned into the waiting area in front of the conference rooms, the flooring changed to brilliant blue-and-white Spanish tile.

I knew what I would see next.

Fiona and her security detail stood silent watch around Franklin's fallen body. Fiona shone like a beacon amidst all the soft-gray tailored suits, resplendent in a white Gucci dress with a fitted silver logo belt snug at her tiny waist. That cobalt blue of her aura was tightly coiled but a pretty foil for her outfit. Her long silver-tipped curls were tied in a loose bun under a perfect white hat and Swiss-dotted fascinator. Fiona looked perfect, as usual, even in her abject grief.

Goatee Guy held out a package of facial tissue and Fiona dabbed at her eyes. Fiona and Freddy's cousin, Linh, stood off to the side. She was small like Fiona, but stood ramrod straight in her tailored gray suit. Linh's pageboy cut was so razor straight it looked like it had been ironed.

Fiona spotted me and bowed deeply. "Sentinel."

She bowed two more times with her staff and Freddy in unison. No hugs or air kisses this time. Even with the body in the room, I hadn't expected Fiona to be so formal. But Fiona was cunning, like my father, and her actions were carefully planned to send a message to the last two people in the room.

These two people were a middle-aged couple a few feet behind Fiona. The couple clearly avoided my eyes as they watched Fiona and her crew pay their respects to me.

The gentleman was slightly younger than my father, late forties, balding, and a bit taller than Fiona. His wife had her hair in an elaborate updo, expertly tinted to blend her grays. Her deep red blazer and skirt had the forgiving stretch and gold hardware to mark it a St. John exclusive. Her tiny feet were in red flats with gold buckles. Both of them had the skin that spoke of decades spent in sunny humid climes—deeply tan with large pores.

Stanley and Stella Mok, heads of the Mok Clan on the Malayan peninsula.

The last time I'd seen them had been as the Blade of Soong. I'd wiped their cousin's blood off Truth on Stella's dupioni silk drapes. Their cousin's hand was the only one I took that day, a message my father deemed sufficient to convince the Moks to maintain their household in better order. My father's message was more subtle than I had anticipated, but I doubted that Stella felt the same.

Stanley Mok sneered at me and turned to Fiona. "You're bowing to the Butcher?"

Outrage and contempt dripped from his words.

Fiona's gaze didn't waver. "She is our Sentinel. And you stand within her city."

That statement seemed to give Stanley pause, but Stella lifted a delicate shoulder and looked down her nose at me. "I'm not bowing to someone who won't last the year."

Apparently the Moks shared the same opinion that Iron Serpent did. I was tired of everyone telling me I was going to die soon.

I studied Mrs. Mok. Between her and her rooster of a husband, she was the true threat. Her aura slowly loosened, revealing a burnt umber hue that promised a world of hurt if I didn't get to her first. Her earth talent was extremely lucrative for their mining operations, and unfortunately for me, very problematic if she opened a crevasse the size of the Grand Canyon underneath me. After she sealed up the canyon and pulverized my bones to sand, her husband could then helpfully filter and sort my valuables from the rubble. Their talents had made them good partners for the Soong family's jewelry empire. At least, until I showed up.

But I wasn't the Blade anymore, I could think for myself, and

I wasn't about to start carving up a Bā Tóu member here. I might have bad blood with the Moks, but it was Fiona who had called on me today. Alone, I could still take Stella but with her husband here, they'd give me a run for my money. And that wasn't even factoring in the Moks' security detail. Though much smaller in number than the Tran cohort, their five-man security team exuded self-assured confidence. Unlike Fiona's detail, they weren't quite as stylishly attired, but the gleaming rubies they all wore on their fingers and wrists sent a clear statement. Their watchful eyes and active stances made it even more obvious why they were present.

Stella Mok was very powerful and could cause a lot of damage in my city. The idea of diplomacy, when the Moks were clearly in the wrong, grated on me like chewing tinfoil. I decided it was probably best to ignore them. For now. Whatever had brought the Moks here, it likely had something to do with Fiona. The least I could do for her was not step on her toes.

Very deliberately I turned toward Fiona, returning her bow. I angled my body just enough to be insulting to the Moks, but not so far as to move them out of my periphery. "What service can the Sentinel render for the Trans?"

Stella blew out a breath but did not move.

Fiona ignored them and stepped lightly over to Franklin. Unshed tears glittered in her eyes and her voice was thick with tightly leashed fury. "Find his killer. Find who did this and bring them to me."

I knelt next to Franklin's body and studied the wound. A neat puncture wound marred the immaculate front of Franklin's shirt and jacket. I hovered as close as I could without stepping in the spreading blood, taking in the rest of the scene. Other than the killing wound there was nothing else to indicate a fight. No bruises on his knuckles, no torn fingernails, his bloody shirt was still neatly tucked under his belt and his hair wasn't even mussed.

At least he'd died doing his job. It was safe to assume that Franklin was not the type of person to attract assassins. Fiona had been the target. "What happened?"

Fiona took a deep breath then spoke. "We were here to meet the Moks to discuss an alliance. Franklin's team arrived early to set up security. When I arrived he escorted me into the building, but the lights in the entryway had gone out. We'd barely stepped into the room when he pushed me back into the hallway."

She stopped and took another breath, taking the moment to compose herself. It must have been hard, to lose someone who was with her day and night, and still maintain the appearance of strength before me, the Moks, and all her other subordinates. Fiona steeled herself and met my eyes, her own gaze hardening. "Before you ask, I didn't see anything. I heard him cry out when the killer struck, but that's it. I ran in and swept the room with wind blades."

I looked around and noted the precise line cut into the walnut paneling. Her wind blade had cleared the entire room at waist level. All the consoles and cabinets along the walls had been neatly cut apart. Anyone caught by that would have been sheared open like a Pez dispenser. Fiona was nobody's easy target.

When Fiona spoke again, a ragged edge of anger seeped into her voice. "By the time we got the lights on, this is all there was. Whoever did this was gone."

I shot a questioning look at Linh. Fiona's head of security glanced to her boss, then back to me, clearly annoyed. "The hotel is clear. The killer escaped by magical means."

Outrage burned low in my belly. Some upstart assassin had come to San Francisco, to my city, to kill my people. I'd only been the Sentinel for two weeks, but that was more than enough time for the Jiārén grapevine. Whoever had done this knew they were spitting in my face as they did it. The fire in my gut inched higher, burning hotter. The need to fight, to protect what was *mine,* thundered through my veins, the sensation making me a little lightheaded.

And here in the room with me were two newcomers to my city. Two people who had disrespected my clan in the past. Two people I had cleaned up after before. Emiko Soong, Jiārén janitor.

I stood and turned to the Moks. I made a fist and reached out for the city. It was surprisingly easy with my hackles up. I reached down and pulled the city up to me and draped its power over my shoulders like a cloak. Power thrummed through my fingers and danced across my skin like needles.

A heavy shadow appeared in the back of my mind. San Francisco, its magic-born sentience, hovered behind my eyes like a voyeur, looking out through me. I pushed it back, until it was no more than a quiet presence, staring intently at the Moks.

I had much the same idea.

"Where were you two when this was happening?"

Stella's eyes widened and her nostrils flared. "If you—"

I cut her off with a hand. An ocean of power rocked beneath my feet and the hotel rumbled as a minor earthquake shook Nob Hill. A chorus of distant car alarms blared and everyone in the room cried out. Stella and Stanley both tumbled to their knees.

Power flushed my skin and when I spoke, the very earth seemed to reverberate with my voice. The presence in my mind moved up and the words that flowed out didn't feel like I was speaking them. "I am the Sentinel. This is my city. I will protect what is mine."

Stanley pulled his wife to her feet and she shook herself out of his grasp, her eyes blazing. Her aura flooded with color now, no longer restrained. "How dare you! We are guests, invited here by the Trans! We—"

My patience snapped. Power geysered out of me and soaked into the ground under the hotel. The city and I both felt it at the same time, the Moks' filthy talents seeping into the earth at my feet, like an uninvited guest snooping through my house.

The anger made it easy. I took hold of the earth under the hotel and held it in the iron grip of my power. I brushed away the Moks' talent like an errant bug. I claimed the very dirt beneath their feet. As earth talents, the Moks must have felt like their air had been choked off. They were angry but now a hint of fear tinged the edges of their eyes. *Good.* Fear was sometimes as good as respect.

Fiona cleared her throat. She had her fingers pinched over the bridge of her nose. "It's not them, Emiko. I got here early to get things settled before the Moks arrived. I didn't even give them the location until just before I left my house."

The shadow in my mind loomed forward and my vision darkened. The city was not satisfied. But I believed Fiona. The city might have basic instincts, but it was up to me to temper them with conscious thought.

It was harder, so much harder, to let go. Like a muscle cramped in place, I fought to release my hold on the earth. Slowly, the power drained away and it was as if the entire room finally exhaled. The mantle of my city slid off my shoulders, leaving me feeling cold and exposed. Without the city in my head, I felt small and alone in a room full of people staring at me like I was crazy.

That part was unfortunately something I was used to.

So much for easy answers. I wasn't inclined to play the diplomacy game—I left that to experts like my father and Fiona. I nodded to Fiona, trusting her to salvage the situation. Stella watched me closely but the umber of her aura quieted.

I knelt to examine Franklin's body again. The smell of ginger was fading, but still sickly sweet enough to nearly make me gag. I sniffed again, discreetly, hunting for clues, but hiding what I was doing. Not many people could smell talents, and I wanted no one in this room to know what I could do.

Still offended and embarrassed, Stella Mok voiced her displeasure. Broken Claw, but she was shrill now. From the floor I gave Fiona a pointed look, asking for her help. She gave me an exasperated puff through her nose and dragged the Moks to the far end of the room to give me some space. Fiona made the kind of soothing sounds you used to maintain relations with someone you didn't like very much.

Even if the killer had struck before Franklin could activate his talent, he shouldn't have died from the wound. He was Fiona's first line of defense, and she wouldn't have hired him if he could be taken out so easily. After he'd been cut his stone limb talent should have started sealing up the wound instantly. Against anyone with an edged weapon, Franklin should have been able to get at least a few licks in.

I drew in the mixture of scents through my nose. The heavy scent of the killer's talent nearly masked it but there was something else here near Franklin's body. My brain tried to identify the smell and finally landed on squid ink. Weird.

Freddy had wandered close. "What's that look on your face mean?"

I stood up. "It means I need to see Grandma Chen. Or rather, she needs to see Franklin. There's more to this wound."

If anyone could determine what was contaminating Franklin's wound, it would be the finest Herbalist in the States.

I waved Fiona back. Thankfully the Moks stayed in their corner shooting daggers at me through their eyes. Fiona's eyes were glassy. Her adrenaline was running out and the numbness was setting in. I put a hand on her shoulder and squeezed. That seemed to get a little life back in her eyes. "I need you to get Franklin's body to Grandma Chen. That wound shouldn't have killed him. There's something else going on here and the sooner we get her involved, the more answers we'll get."

She nodded once, clawing herself back together, pulling on the mask she wore as the head of the Tran Clan. "Consider it done. What about you?"

I had to prepare for my meeting tonight with Tessa and make my last attempt to convince her to keep Adam's sword out of the museum's exhibit. Because I was going to Lóng Yá soon after and I wouldn't get another chance. I just hadn't expected to have a murder to deal with. At least the details here seemed to point away from the Louies.

"Uncle" Jimmy Louie, the ostensible head of the Louie Clan, was an old-school Lóng Jiārén. When he came for you, he did it out in the open, because he wanted you to see it coming, knowing you had no way of avoiding it. Much like my father, at times.

This murder was a puzzle. Whoever was responsible clearly had skills and talent. But little details struck me as amateurish. Why kill

Franklin and then run from Fiona? Had the killer lost their nerve? I doubted that Uncle Jimmy would expend his resources on such a sloppy attempt on Fiona's life. No, someone else was at work here.

Freddy stood beside me, a look of concern on his face. "Emi? You look like you're going to barf."

I grunted. "No, I'm fine."

There were just a million things to take care of at once. No problem.

I tilted my head at their cousin, Linh, gesturing for her to join us. She walked over and nodded to Fiona and Freddy before acknowledging me. I needed to get in one last set of instructions before I could leave.

"I want two sets of eyes on her at all times."

Linh nodded, her lips thin with annoyance. I got it. No one wanted to be told how to do their job. I leaned in close to breathe in her ear. "No staff that hasn't been with you at least a year. Clear everyone else out of the rotation."

Linh blinked and then nodded. I looked at Goatee Guy, Fiona's majordomo. He owned Fiona's calendar, but by necessity, a lot of people had to know about Fiona's itinerary today. I didn't see a way to plug that hole.

The idea of a killer loose in my city was a cold weight in the pit of my stomach. I needed Fiona to be a little less Fiona until I could get a handle on this. "Can you lay low for the next day or two?"

Linh's eyes widened and snapped to Fiona. "I don't—"

Fiona interrupted, her voice a whip crack. "Impossible. Lóng Yá is next week. There are affairs to settle before we leave. Preparations must be made. I'm simply too busy."

Freddy and Linh just shrugged their shoulders, unable to contradict Fiona. I tried again. "Someone who could go through Franklin so easily is a trained killer, Fiona. We have no idea who we're dealing with. You're taking unnecessary risks."

At the mention of her bodyguard, Fiona's eyes went cold. "We are

Jiārén. Life is risk. I would have thought you would understand that better than most."

I did, but that didn't mean I would stick my neck out for something as trivial as the Lóng Yá Tourney. With that, Fiona turned her back on me, neglecting to bow as she returned to the Moks on the far side of the room.

Linh stared at me for a long moment, her sharp eyes a little sad now. "We will mourn Franklin, but we won't hide. You're not wrong, Sentinel, but we are Trans. This clan does not bow to threats. I'll do what I can to lower her profile until we get out of San Francisco. No guarantees, though."

It wasn't much, but it would have to do.

I grimaced. "Hey Freddy, can you give me a lift back to my car?"

CORPORATE RESOLUTION

All I wanted was to draw a nice hot bath, dunk my head under the bubbles, and pretend today had never happened. But that wasn't in the cards. On the one hand, I had a smoldering clan war that could blow up my city. On the other hand, I had a dangerous artifact on the verge of blowing up my life. My limited menu of bad options spoke either to my historically bad decision-making, or to my epically rotten luck. I wasn't sure which.

My schedule dictated that Adam's sword was my highest priority. Tessa and I needed to have it out over that cursed sword. She had humored me before when I'd objected to Crimson Cloud Splitter but tonight was my last shot.

I owed Tessa answers but couldn't reveal Jiārén secrets. Giving her too much information would put her in danger. Threading this needle was going to be as much fun as untangling my Adam problem.

Tessa was the person I'd known the longest during my time in San Francisco. She was also the second closest to knowing the truth about my double life. Tessa's wife, Andie, was a hard-core data wonk. Andie had teased out some of the unwritten details of my past life, but had been gracious enough to let me slide on the trust that I had Tessa's best interests at heart.

Knowing that I was abusing that trust to some degree hurt me in ways I never expected. Tessa had helped me get SOMAC Salvage up and running, and to the point where I was actually making a living for myself. She deserved honesty from me. I just didn't know how to do that.

As I approached my house, I reflected that in a lot of ways, my home was a mirror of my life, with one face I showed the public, and another that I kept hidden. Behind my front house, tucked behind more wards and defensive systems, was the rear house, where I slept and kept my true valuables. Two stone foo lions flanked the small porch on the rear house. On the right, the male lion stood with a woven ball under one paw. One the left, the female stood with a pup under her paw. The statues were both adornment and security.

I passed my hand over the head of the female lion and a slight tingle of power crawled across my palm. I pushed back with my qì and the front door popped open.

Once inside, I sealed the front door then entered my bedroom and secured that door as well.

I slid aside a bookshelf and palmed open a biometric scanner. A small drawer clicked open and dull red light crept out around the seams. I pulled out the tray and took a moment to look at my own, small Hoard.

Hoard families all guarded a collection of treasures that had been carried to this world when we fled the Cataclysm. The Soong Hoard sat safely in my family home, which was secreted away in a Realm Fragment, a piece of our old world, anchored to this one with Old Magic. It was the only way to truly protect anything from hostile Jiārén.

It said volumes about me that I'd come to San Francisco to escape Jiārén intrigues, and then immediately started my own Hoard.

The major pieces were two Talons, a triple-stranded pearl necklace, a gold dragon cuff, and a pair of jadeite bracelets, each with their telltale red gleam. The Talons were from my father and mother. The rest were items that I'd been reluctant to sell from my share of SOMAC's finds. Now the Lost Heart of Yázì had been added, nestled on a folded white linen napkin, its dull red light filling the small cubby. The shinigami had claimed it was too corrupted to anchor the Ebony Gate but that didn't mean it was powerless. The opposite was true—so much power poured out of it that I felt the city pulse in response.

I might not have the meridians or talent to use them, but I knew powerful Hoard gems when I saw them.

With the Lost Heart, I would have to move my Hoard, and soon. My wards would not be enough to shield this much power. I needed a Realm Fragment, but those weren't exactly lying around on the street. But that was a problem for future me.

For now, I needed to appease Tessa.

I would start by making tea.

Two hours later, and I was ready. I'd brewed Tessa's favorite tea and packed it in travel mugs. I'd picked up her favorite takeout. I wished her wife, Andie, could join us to help dilute the tension of the discussion, but no such luck because Tessa was working late at the museum so I was going to her.

Which I dreaded.

These meetings had become a marathon of trying not to lie to Tessa about that thrice-damned sword, but also not tell her why it wasn't a Kunimitsu and why it could not be put on display.

But a lie of omission was still a lie.

I hated lying to her. Crimson Cloud Splitter was a constant reminder to me that Tessa knew nothing about me and my past, and it was safest for her if I kept things that way. This was exactly why I shied away from spending time in her home and with Andie. My visit to their home with Adam had only confirmed my worst fears. I liked spending time with them.

The drive eastbound across the bridge was thankfully reverse traffic as everyone was trying to get into the city on a Saturday night. But traffic was the least of my worries.

I held my breath as I passed through Treasure Island in the center of the bridge. Crossing beyond the city boundary once again hit me with the subtlety of a hammer blow. I went lightheaded for a moment as my Sentinel powers faded away, leaving the world a quieter, less vibrant place. In the light traffic I doubted anyone noticed as my Jeep nearly wobbled out of my lane. Leaving the Sentinel mantle behind was a risk, but my life had been nothing but managing risk, and I wasn't going to let it make me a prisoner in my own home.

The Tien Pacific Museum rose above the city landscape, lights bouncing around a juxtaposition of angled glass and concrete. It was a small but prestigious institution, and also one of my best clients. I thanked the parking gods when I found a spot right in front of the museum and walked to the back entrance, my stomach in knots.

I pressed the call button on the intercom.

"It's me."

"Come on back!"

The door unlocked with a buzz and my business partner appeared at the end of the hallway. As always, Tessa packed a punch with her presence despite her tiny trim frame. Her frizzy blond hair was back in a loose knot with a pen sticking out of it. She looked chic and comfortable in navy joggers and a cropped cream sweater. She waved an overloaded clipboard at me. "Emiko! Thank goodness you brought food!"

When Tessa spoke, exclamation points followed. A wave of affection rushed over me. She had battered down all my careful barriers, relentless in her warmth and friendship. I couldn't let the violence of Jiārén life spill over to this relationship. Somehow, I needed to convince her that Crimson Cloud Splitter couldn't go in the exhibit, and I had to do it tonight.

I followed her bouncy strides down the dim hallways, past gray cement walls stacked high with metal shelves. Tessa was relentlessly Californian, her steamroller extroversion paired with radiant health. It was unnerving but made her a perfect business partner. She worked long hours, but unless her boss moved, retired, or died, Tessa had no hope of getting the top spot. And assistant directors of small academic museums didn't make much money. That's where I came into the picture.

Tessa had all the aboveboard relationships. She knew everyone in the academic community and she was happy to talk to them—leaving me free to hunt for the good stuff. While Tessa shone in the light, I stayed in the dark where I did my best work.

I was subject to the First Law, which meant I always protected the Hoard. So my methods and means were a little more shadowy when I came across a Hoard artifact. I shopped those items around to Jiārén families. I knew which families had affinities to certain metals or gems. My family had dibs on pearls. Fiona's father paid a premium for any silver I got my hands on.

It was a good system. Tessa earned extra money, and I brought Hoard artifacts back to their rightful owners. We made good partners, and, against my best intentions, good friends. Now my involvement in her life had brought her perilously close to the world of Jiārén. I prayed to the Great Dragon that I could keep Tessa safe.

When we reached her offices, Tessa turned and took a tea out of my hands.

"Your timing is perfect, Adam just got here."

A small part of me died on the inside. "Oh. I hope I brought enough food for all of us."

I had come early because I did not need to the two of them tag-teaming me. My lips flattened in annoyance at Adam's uncanny ability to insert himself into my life.

Tessa pushed open the shabby blue door to her office. While the display areas for the patrons were meticulously maintained, these rear offices showed their age.

As the door swung wide, Adam stood, filling the cramped confines of Tessa's messy office. Adam had changed out of his casual clothing from this morning, and he now wore the kind of pin-sharp, executive attire I rarely saw in the city. His gray wool suit jacket was unbuttoned, the collared shirt underneath a pale blue. Heavy square cuff links flashed as he moved. His only concession tonight was the lack of a tie. It should have looked cold and imposing but somehow the effect was the opposite against his sun-warmed skin. He gave me a crooked smile and rushed forward to take the bags out of my hands.

"Emiko, thanks for picking up something to eat. I'm starving."

I smiled in return, unable to resist the genuine welcome in his clear blue eyes. This was the whole problem—I *liked* seeing him. But it was a mistake to pretend we could be anything other than what Jiārén rules dictated.

My mouth responded on autopilot. "Sure, my pleasure."

Adam busied himself by clearing a mountain of papers off Tessa's desk. For all his sharp attire, he looked at ease even assembling our impromptu dinner. Despite my mental picture of him as an idle member of a yacht club, I really had no idea what he did all day. He always came to these meetings dressed like he was ready for a board meeting and maybe for him, that's what these were.

That was a sobering thought. I'd been so focused on Crimson Cloud Splitter I'd lost the context of why we were all here in the first place.

For Tessa's exhibit. Adam's exhibit.

And by extension, this was my exhibit, too, in a way. The issue wasn't them—it was my Jiārén rules threatening this part of my world. I needed to focus on what was important, and how to help them have the best exhibit they could put on.

I set aside my annoyance and helped pull out plastic chairs and clear enough space for us to eat. Adam and Tessa fussed a bit, gathering napkins and pulling out cartons of food. The easy familiarity of their company soothed my restlessness. It felt the same as when Adam and I had met Tessa and Andie for dinner. The feeling was nice.

And dangerous.

Lóng Kǒu and Jōkōryūkai were not institutions known for instilling camaraderie. Eating with friends was a new experience, and one I had never expected to have.

Tessa ripped into the bags and let out a soft sigh of pleasure. "My favorite."

I'd spent much of my life taking every advantage I could, so I was not above softening my business partner up with good food. Tessa was a vegetarian and I ordered her favorites from the Shanghainese restaurant I liked. Dishes my father loved and that I had been eating since I was very little. Minced dandelion greens with bean curd, giant rolls of vegetarian goose stuffed with diced sweetened shiitake mushrooms, and chewy braised gluten for Tessa. Giant lion's head meatballs on a bed of bok choy and bamboo shoots, as well as braised pork belly for me since I was most decidedly not a vegetarian.

We dug into our food and after a blessed reprieve where I shoved protein into my face, Tessa put her chopsticks down and fired her opening salvo. "So, why haven't you worked out the sword issue with Adam?"

The easy mood of our meal disappeared like fog in the sun.

I swallowed my rice and gave Adam the side-eye. He smiled blandly. "We've been talking about it."

Which was true. I sipped my tea and chose my next words carefully. "I stand by my assessment. I do not believe this is a lost work of Kunimitsu and feel it would be misleading to display it."

Also true. Tessa leaned in closer.

Tessa's eyebrows drew down in a sharp V. "I don't have to display it as a lost work. I can simply say it has a number of similarities that mean some could conclude it is a lost work."

Adam picked up his drink and leaned back in his chair, thankfully quiet for once.

"I still think it's a mistake for the museum."

The tension in the room thickened. Tessa's expressive mouth turned down. "Do you think I would risk my professional reputation and jeopardize the museum?"

My throat tightened at the look in her eyes. "No, of course not. But you asked me to vet the weapons and this sword is a problem. Rumors it is a Kunimitsu will bring a lot of dangerous elements out of the woodwork."

Namely Jiārén I would rather keep away from you, I didn't say.

In the heavy silence that followed, Adam stood up, his chair scraping the floor. He made a show of fiddling with his phone. "I'm sorry, I need to step out for a call."

I didn't blame him. I wanted to step out, too.

Tessa set her tea down with a thunk. "So it's not a sword problem, it's a security problem."

I swept my hand around her dilapidated office. "The museum does not have sufficient security."

Adam's strides echoed down the hallway as he beat a hasty retreat.

She narrowed her eyes. "Do you understand how important this exhibit is to the museum? To me?"

I had some idea, but I shook my head.

"We struggle to get pieces of this caliber. Adam has single-handedly opened new doors for us, where private collections are agreeing to loan pieces for this exhibit."

I nodded, my eyes going to the stacks of photos and files on the side of her battered desk.

Tessa pointed to the photos. "If Adam wants this sword in, I need to make this happen and I can display it ethically. If we need more security, Adam has offered to help. If you want us to make infrastructure upgrades, Adam endowed the museum with abundant funds to do so."

His generosity was impressive, and also a problem.

"There isn't enough time to do the type of upgrades you need to safeguard this sword."

Frankly, if a Jiārén of any gāo-level talent wanted to get the sword, no conventional security that Tessa and Adam devised would offer even a modicum of resistance.

"This clearly isn't about the security. What aren't you telling me?"

I stalled by tidying my plate and chopsticks, my thoughts cascading as I tried to determine what I could or couldn't tell her. Finally I settled on a half-truth.

"You know I don't tell you everything that happens on my side of SOMAC."

Tessa nodded, her eyes wary.

I barreled on. "I've come across certain sword collectors before and they are dangerous. They will do anything, including hurt people, to get this sword. The only thing that's kept Adam safe so far is that the very existence of the sword is a secret."

Her eyes widened in alarm. "Is he in danger? Am I?"

"If you display the sword? Yes. Both of you."

She took it a lot better than I expected. "You have to tell him."

I had been trying to. "I will."

Tessa's face turned mulish. "Am I your partner or not?"

"Of course you are." I didn't know how to get out of this hole I had dug for myself.

"Am I your junior partner?" Her voice rose a bit at the end. Tessa was livid.

"What? No. Of course not." How had I ended up on the defensive?

Her jaw jutted out in a way that said she wasn't taking no for an answer and her eyes speared through me. "We work well together because we trust each other. So you're going to *trust* me with the curation of this exhibit. And I'm going to trust you to ensure we have the security we need for it."

Tessa held out her hand. "Shake on it, partner."

I looked at her hand hanging in front of me, a sword dangling over our fragile relationship. She was my closest friend and I needed her to be safe. How was I going to do that when the next attack came?

Of course, keeping a Wàirén safe was exactly how I'd ended up bringing Adam under my clan's protection. I'd told Freddy that Jiārén needed to change how we dealt with Wàirén. How could I not give Tessa the same respect? She'd more than earned it, as my partner, and as my friend.

I reached for Tessa's hand and gave a firm shake. "Deal."

Tessa tidied up the rest of the take-out boxes and turned to face me, her eyes clear and bright. "I know you're good at your job, and I trust you to secure this thing."

My insides roiled. This whole exchange made me queasy. I also couldn't steamroll over her, no matter how much I wished I could. That was what made friendship so precious, so dangerous—the fact that you had something to risk.

My only remaining option was to convince Adam to withdraw the sword from the exhibit.

I found Adam outside, leaning against a cherry tree, half in the glow of the lamppost, half in shadow. The tree had blossomed, leaving its branches bare, but there were still scattered piles of petals on the ground. He slid his phone into his pocket and in two long strides he reached me. In the lamplight and shadow, the chiseled planes of his face looked hard. Severe. But when he addressed me, his smooth baritone invited confidence.

"Hey, everything okay in there?" he asked.

I resented his relaxed posture and warm tone. His actions had forced my hand with Tessa. "You're the one that instigated this. You can go in there and find out yourself."

He straightened, all six and a half feet of him looming over me. "What's that supposed to mean?"

"It means I don't appreciate you going over me and complaining to Tessa."

"That's rich."

I bristled. "I'm doing my job, Adam."

"Is that all? Because it feels like a lot more than just the fact you don't think it's a Kunimitsu. You're hiding something from us, and Tessa and I are entitled to know what it is—that's your job."

I hated that he saw through me. That he was right. His reasonable words made me want to lash out, to treat him like a foe I could cut down. The way First Law dictated. But that was the old way, the easy way, and I wouldn't do that. My words were the next sharpest thing.

"You can't have everything you want, Adam. That sword is not a Kunimitsu, and it will draw unwanted attention to the exhibit, the museum, and by extension—Tessa. I will not let that happen."

His jaw tightened. He was getting angry. Good. Now we were on the same plane. "Emiko, you're a liar. Even now when I'm calling you on it, you're lying to my face. I've tried to work with you, but you won't tell me the truth."

His eyes narrowed. "You're also not telling me what really happened at the auction. I've been waiting for my memories to come back, but we both know you were there."

We weren't talking about the exhibit anymore. My anger dissipated, flimsy in the face of my debt. I owed him, and my clan did, too.

I deflated. "I will."

His eyes widened, his surprise at my easy capitulation clear. "When?"

"When I figure out how."

"Emiko . . ." His voice lost its earlier harshness.

I very much wanted to respond. But I wasn't ready. And I wasn't about to air Jiārén secrets here on the street. I turned away, eager to end this confrontation before I made an even bigger mistake.

"Good night, Adam."

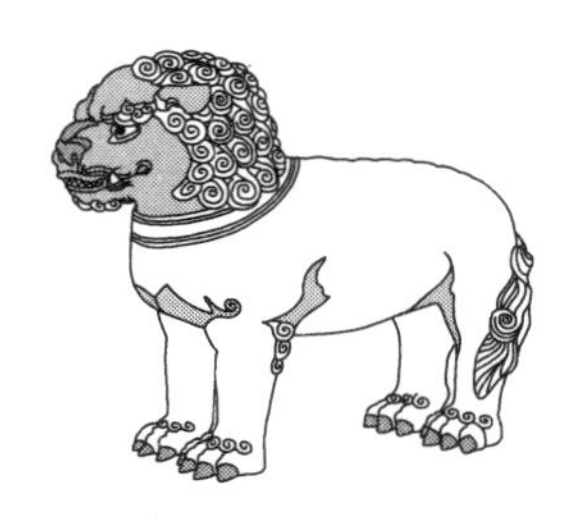

NIGHT WATCH

After tonight's miserable performance I figured I might as well take my chances and check in on Fiona. She still had a killer after her. Somehow that seemed simpler to deal with than trying to navigate the complexities of friendship and loyalty with Tessa. Or Adam.

I hadn't heard anything from Linh, but if Fiona had been my target, I'd try again—and soon. The assassin had already tipped their hand. There was no reason to wait any longer. Always best to take out the target before they could bolster their defenses.

My phone dinged, a new tone that I hadn't heard before. I fished my phone out, and nearly swerved out of my lane when I saw it. The Legacy app had alerted me to a new photo from my good friend, Fiona Tran. She sat in an antique wingback, resplendent in a Burberry trench, surrounded by open suitcases overflowing with party dresses and formal wear. Silver bangles covered one arm to her elbow and she held a glittering silver gown aloft in front of her with a column of air.

This was her idea of keeping a low profile? She was practically begging the assassin to strike again. I jerked the steering wheel and slalomed across four lanes of traffic. Horns blared in protest as I took the turnoff to the Tran château. Maybe tonight would give me a chance to deal with this killer once and for all. The sooner the better.

Fiona lived in Pacific Heights, along a strip of stately homes that comprised San Francisco's version of the Gold Coast. The neighborhood was thick with large Edwardians and charmingly painted Victorians, each house shielded behind tall black wrought-iron gates.

The Trans had acquired a coveted double lot with a long driveway. I parked a few blocks away and pulled a dark gray beanie out of my glove compartment. The beanie covered my ridiculous skunk stripe, one of the ways the city chose to mark me when I accepted the Sentinel power. At least the tattoos that had appeared on my arm were usually out of sight.

I rummaged through my trusty duffel bag, but my bag of tricks was getting low. My last Dragon Breath crystal and a few throwing knives would have to do. Hachi on my hip, I made my way over on foot, noting who had cameras and which way they pointed.

It was getting dark and there were plenty of shadows for me to work with. Old skills born of long years of training came back as naturally as breathing. I hugged the dark corners underneath ivy-covered walls, my soft-soled boots quiet on immaculate landscaping.

Lampposts were scarce in Pacific Heights, and they cast dim pools of illumination in small pockets on the sidewalk. An occasional resident strolled by, sometimes with a dog. This was not a Saturday night hot spot. I crouched in a dark recess and scanned up and down the street. It would be easy for the assassin to do exactly what I was doing.

A part of me really wanted them to.

The fact that the assassin had made their move in the daytime at a public venue meant a couple of things. It was possible they'd cased the Tran estate already and found it too well fortified. Fiona had a veritable army of staff and security personnel on-site. That didn't make the job impossible, but it was always better to hit a target where they were softer. Alternatively, maybe the kill needed to take place at the Bellavista because of the Moks. I didn't have a clue why that would be. I would need Fiona and Linh to walk me through the possible suspects and motives.

The last explanation was timing. The killer wanted to hit Fiona now, and the time deadline drove them to make a high-risk attempt in public.

If that was the case, they were sure to try again very soon.

The neighbor to the south had dogs who barked as I passed. I paused at the château gates and waited. The Tran home was three stories tall and set back a considerable distance from the sidewalk. Pruned hedges and ornate wrought-iron gates maintained their privacy. Security cameras and the Trans' well-trained clan members and staff handled the rest.

I suspected it wouldn't be enough tonight.

When I drew on my Sentinel power the guards stood out in my vision as blurry spots of light in the early evening. A handful of guards circled the property, inside and outside of the main building. Judging by how they deformed San Francisco's magic, they were strong talents. Experience with Fiona told me her guards sported a variety of weapons, traditional and modern. But too few. They had blind spots all over the property as the pattern shifted. When the gap appeared I strolled past the gates and to the neighbor to the north. No dogs.

What Fiona needed was a multilayer of magical booby traps, security patrols, dogs, and lights. I turned my phone brightness down to almost nothing and texted Freddy.

Are you in the city?

Fi is home. I'm at a buddy's place in Santa Cruz.

Why don't you guys have more patrols at the house?

Don't need them. We have drones.

Drones were noisy. There would be plenty of time for someone to avoid those.

I sighed. I couldn't let this go. The Trans' northern neighbor had no wrought-iron fencing, just ivy-covered stone walls. I slowed at the border. Fiona's cameras didn't point toward the neighbor's property, probably a nod to privacy. Inconvenient. The neighbor's charming Victorian only had a doorbell camera facing the walkway. Between the fog and the poor lighting, it was too easy.

I took hold of the ivy and hoisted myself into the neighbor's yard. The shared fence along the side yard was also stone. This time I paused on top of the fence instead of leaping down into the Trans' side. I closed my eyes to tune in to the city, seeing with that other sense. The magical plains of the city undulated softly, a welcoming wave of color and texture.

What kind of booby traps would air elemental talents like?

I hummed softly and felt a soft ping above me. Without opening my eyes, I turned my gaze slowly up, watching the waves of Jiārén energy ripple along the house. It was beautiful when viewed with the city's sight. The city's magic washed over the château and the resulting crash revealed the outlines of the Tran defenses like surf against the coastline.

There.

I opened my eyes and blinked to adjust. Lanterns and wind chimes hung from the balconies and from the tall trees in the yard. A moment ago with the city's magical sight, it looked almost like a chain of Christmas lights twinkling in the night between the chimes and lanterns. Now they looked ordinary, nearly invisible in the heavy fog.

But what did they do?

I picked up a twig and tested its heft. With a gentle toss, I lobbed it at the nearest lantern. The round lantern bobbled, the faint light it emitted sputtering as the lantern moved. I waited.

Nothing.

I climbed down off the wall. Scooping up a handful of pebbles, I flung them just under the lantern. It brightened, going from faint to like a hundred watts instantly. I liked that. Trust Fiona to have yard lanterns that were pretty and useful. Problem was, there weren't enough of them to deter the most persistent of intruders. It certainly wasn't enough to keep out a killer like me. Even worse, the patrols from the front didn't even notice the brighter patch. No one came to investigate.

Keeping my eyes up, I wove my way between the lanterns, avoiding their path. I found a spot behind a coastal redwood that let me watch one of the side doors, which I suspected led to the kitchen. The rear of the house had two French doors that pushed out to a beautiful deck. Too open. I would never go in that way unless I knew the house was empty.

I wrapped my hands around the narrow trunk of the young redwood and shimmied myself into the cover of its thick branches. From here I had a clear view of the property's northern border. My position was also shielded from that approach, where I was sure the assassin would come in from. I settled in, letting myself go to that place where I became merely a weapon waiting for a target. It was a pose that I had cultivated well after years with Jōkōryūkai, and one that I had honed as the Blade of Soong. My breathing slowed and I became still enough that nighttime insects buzzed around me as if I was just another part of the greenery. My vision expanded, drinking in the field before me, eyes ready to spot any change.

Behind me, life continued to hum in the Tran château. Light spilled out of the windows and guards and house staff moved back and forth. The evening gray faded to full dark, and the shadows in the corners grew, reaching out to swallow more and more of the property.

After an hour of waiting, I expected to endure agony in my ankles from maintaining my balance on the narrow branch. By the second hour I expected my back to spasm. None of that happened. Soothing energy flowed into my hands through the tree, calmed my muscles, and even sharpened my senses. I marveled at the seemingly limitless potential at my fingertips. The night air grew heavy with moisture and my clothes grew damp and cold, along with all of my exposed skin.

This ease was the city's gift, and I was grateful.

But it didn't make the waiting any less dull. By the third hour I was beginning to question the assassin's work ethic. What kind of killer made only one attempt on their target?

A clammy chill crept up my spine and set the left side of my head buzzing. I turned slowly in that direction, my eyes drinking in the faint light. Someone with power had arrived, and their talent had deformed the city's magic like weight on a vast sheet of fabric. In the far corner of the property, the night's darkness . . . flexed.

The scent of rotting ginger filled my sinuses, rocking me back with surprise. I hadn't been mistaken at the Bellavista. The last time I'd smelled an active dark walker had been when my mother walked out of my life. An iridescent sheen appeared in the depths of the shadow and reality tore itself open. The assassin, Franklin's killer, stepped out of the inky darkness and set foot in my city.

The hole in space sealed behind the assassin with a pop. Clad in dark clothing from head to toe, the intruder stayed well inside the shadows and approached the house, their power pressing in on me like a splinter in my mind. As I'd suspected, the killer hadn't needed any doors at the Hotel Bellavista. They'd simply entered through the deep shadows in the meeting room.

The assassin dashed out of the shadows and across the lawn, coming to a stop beneath my redwood tree, a lithe figure, taller than me, with the unmistakable outline of a sword off the left hip.

I was not letting that assassin enter the house. I dropped like a stone, silent, hand on Hachi's grip, ready to draw and strike in one smooth movement.

The assassin's head jerked up. Rotting ginger flared again, making my eyes water, as the assassin fell sideways, into the lee of the tree. Reality tore open again and my target stepped into the void. I spun, twisting my hips and pulling Hachi free in the same motion.

Steel crashed against my sword from above, where the assassin had fallen out of the dappled shadows of the tree branches. I braced my arms as my back hit the grass and the impact drove the air from my lungs. I turned my sword, forcing my attacker's momentum over my head and sending them rolling across the grass.

I jumped to my feet and advanced, keeping the assassin hemmed into the light spilling from the Tran château. Without the shadows my opponent was stuck without their escape hatch. I twitched my left arm and a kunai dropped into my palm.

The assassin came smoothly to their feet and turned to face me, free hand coming up and tearing off a black hood. A young woman's face emerged from the black cloth, straight black hair tied back, eyes blazing like fallen stars under slashing brows. She wore half a Noh mask covering her nose and mouth, porcelain pale with the eerie, dead smile of bloodred lips. She threw the hood at her feet and came at me, katana coming up to high guard as a bloodcurdling scream ripped out of her.

Fiona's security measures exploded as the assassin's qì burst from her like a ruptured dam. I got Hachi up and blocked a vicious flurry of attacks, steel ringing high and clear in the night. The buzz of security drones filled the air as I gave ground to the young woman. Stinging pain lanced through my palms when our blades crossed. She was strong, and my arms burned as I blocked strike after strike.

A loud voice came from the house along with pounding steps. I was going to have to have a talk with Fiona about her tardy security response. A lone Tran enforcer ran into the light from the back of the house, a barrel of a man barely squeezed into his sharkskin Armani suit, with hands the size and shape of cinder blocks.

The assassin pushed back from me and broke off, her eyes snapping back and forth between me and the new heavy. The air crackled with energy and the hairs on my arm stood up. A nimbus of blue sparks glowed around the enforcer's fists as he approached. He flexed his hands, knuckles cracking audibly, and slammed his fists together, sparking a jagged ribbon of blue-white electricity from his hands to the ground. The grass exploded at his feet, digging a three-foot crater in the sod.

A Disciple of Raijin. On Fiona's payroll. The Trans were just full of surprises. The assassin hesitated only a split second before leaping away and running toward the Tran enforcer.

Well. That was more than a little insulting.

I ran after her and immediately dodged a hammer blow of electricity that thundered past me and cracked the redwood. The assassin rolled out of the way as well and came up running, sword held low. I yelled at the enforcer to get back but he ignored me, sending out blast after blast of blue-white energy. I veered off, getting away from the friendly fire.

The assassin crossed the grass in an eyeblink, avoiding the Disciple's lightning with sublime grace. He dropped to one knee and slammed his fists into the blasted grass at his feet. I jumped back as lightning burst forth from his hands and expanded in a circular wave around him, crawling over Fiona's ruined lawn like a swarm of crackling snakes.

My jaw dropped as the assassin dropped at the last moment, falling through the darkness of her own shadow. That was not an easy trick, and deadly if done wrong. And she'd pulled it off while evading a wave of lightning. The young woman popped out of the Disciple's shadow, behind him now, and leapt. I shouted a useless warning. She twisted in the air, spine bowed, and her katana flashed out, striking the Disciple across his back and opening him from shoulder to hip in a spray of gore. The Disciple screamed, the wave of electricity dying like a snuffed candle, and collapsed to the ground. The assassin landed neatly on her feet and flicked the blood from her sword as she turned to face me.

A thrill of real fear crawled up the backs of my legs. She was an exceptional swordswoman. Maybe as good as . . . the best I'd ever seen. I'd been out of regular practice for two years now. If we had met then, it would have been an interesting challenge. But her attack was . . . odd. I didn't have another word for it. At first she had seemed like a professional. But this felt strangely personal.

The assassin ran at me and lunged, slashing at my belly. I sidestepped and whipped out my left arm as she passed. I goosed my qì, pouring energy into the ruby crystal in the palm of my glove. My success rate with these crystals used to be awful. Now, augmented with the power of the city, the effect was better, if sloppy. A wide spray of sparks and flame burst from my hand and crawled up the assassin's arm.

It was more than enough to catch her eye and cause her to miss the kunai that popped out between my knuckles. The woman wrenched herself out of the way at the last moment, the point of my blade drawing a thin line of blood across her exposed neck.

Stomping feet and slamming doors sounded behind me as the assassin tumbled past me. She came to her feet and her dark eyes glittered with rage, flashing between me and the rest of Fiona's approaching enforcers. Her eyes drilled into me, as if she recognized me, and dread landed like a frozen ball of lead in my belly.

The woman's voice was a hoarse whisper like crushed glass. "You win again, Emiko."

My world fractured as she fell backward into the shadow of the redwood and disappeared.

I closed my eyes and called on the city's sight. Layers of magic bled into one another and I made out the faint blue of the killer's steps behind the redwoods for a few yards.

Then nothing.

Fiona's guards ran past me, but I knew it was too late.

The French doors pushed open and Linh stepped out into the night's chaos. Her sharply tailored suit of earlier was gone, replaced by a sleek pair of gray trousers that nipped in at the waist and tapered at the ankles, topped with a gray cashmere sweater and a puffy gray vest. Despite the unreasonable hour, her hair looked smooth and even, the pageboy framing her pointed jawline.

Chewing out Linh might feel good, but she was merely a stand-in for my true target. Fiona ruled her home as surely as my father ruled mine. If she hadn't authorized greater security measures, Linh couldn't implement them.

"Does she value her own life so little?"

Linh met my eyes steadily. "She's dealing with it the only way she knows. We all are."

"There will be more bodies to bury and grieve over if she doesn't take this seriously."

I gestured around the property and ticked off each weakness in the perimeter, spelling out to Linh in full detail just how I'd gotten in, how many hours I'd spent, and just how close the killer had gotten.

Linh's eyes tracked behind me.

Fiona emerged from the rear double doors and surveyed the scene.

Her aura unfurled, the royal blue muted in the night. At her side was a familiar sight, but out of context for me.

Kamon.

Here. In Fiona's house.

His dark hair was glossy and tousled under the lanterns. While Fiona was in her trademark spike heels, Kamon's feet were bare. The top buttons of his white shirt were undone, and his sleeves rolled up. It was stupid, but I couldn't help the flutter of response within me, followed by a pang of regret when I saw him.

Fiona rushed to her fallen enforcer, her movements accelerated by a gust of air. She knelt next to the healers who worked frantically to save him. Fiona laid a hand on his good shoulder and squeezed gently. The big man groaned and lifted his head to look at her. His eyes were wet with pain, but blazed bright with defiance. Fiona smiled grimly and tipped her head to him. I stalked over to them, anger boiling up from my belly. Linh hurried to catch up with me.

Before I could say anything, Fiona spoke up, addressing Linh. She kept her eyes on her enforcer as she spoke. "Denji was part of the Tokyo detail. He will need to be replaced."

"I'll call up Hyeon." Linh hesitated a moment. "It won't be the same, Fi."

Fiona's voice was low and quiet. "No, of course not. But we do what we must."

Linh turned on her heel and left. Fiona passed a few more low words with the healers before standing and facing me.

This was asinine. Fiona was going to keep losing good enforcers if she insisted on playing it this way. "Are you going to reconsider attending Lóng Yá?"

"What did you learn about the assassin?"

I blew out a breath and forced myself to count to ten. "I know she's trying to kill you. Isn't that enough?"

Fiona glared at me. "There is more going on here. I need to know who hired her."

I despised clan politics, lies stacked on top of deception, wrapped up in innuendo. I'd lived in it long enough to see knives hidden in every word and poison behind every smile. Long enough to nearly lose myself to it. I hadn't missed this part of clan life at all.

"No, you need to not die," I gritted out.

"That's not the same as living, is it?"

"Fine. The assassin is a gāo-level dark walker. And well trained."

I watched Fiona carefully as I spoke but she didn't flinch. Maybe I'd gotten lucky and she wasn't familiar with dark walkers. "If you want my opinion, you're better off taking care of her quickly."

Fiona took a deep breath and held it a moment. "It must be nice, to always deal with problems so directly."

"Direct solutions are the most efficient."

"No. The assassin may be trying to kill me, but whoever hired that assassin is trying to destroy my clan. The worst thing we can do before Lóng Yá is show weakness. Or did you think the assassin's timing was a coincidence?"

I hadn't considered the timing as related to the upcoming Lóng Yá. If Tatsuya and Father hadn't summoned me home, I would not have been thinking of Lóng Yá at all.

Kamon prowled over and wrapped an arm around Fiona. She leaned into his big body briefly before standing straight. He gave me a nod and I returned it with an uplift of my chin.

Fiona waved her hands and a gentle gust of wind pushed some torn-up sod back into place. "If we do not show ourselves at Lóng Yá, other clans will see us as weak, and seek to take our territory and overtake our businesses. Whoever sent the assassin is trying to take down my clan. I will not cower in a Realm pocket as someone else dismantles what I have built."

It was always about territory with Jiārén.

"You can't protect your clan if you're dead, Fiona."

Kamon's face went dark and his fingers give her shoulder a squeeze, as if to assure himself she was fine and that she would stay safe. A small ache thudded in my chest at seeing it. He didn't seem to be having much luck finding women who stayed out of harm's way.

Fiona turned to me, eyes bright with anger and unshed tears. "I'm as good as dead if I'm hiding away in fear. I will have my retribution, for Franklin, and Denji, and anyone else who gets hurt. We are going to Lóng Yá."

"This isn't going to end well."

"For them. It isn't going to end well for them."

My lips tightened with annoyance. "But at what cost?"

Fiona slashed her hand down. "Whatever it takes." She pivoted on her heel. "I'll see you at the Herbalist's tomorrow."

Kamon and I watched her stalk away, agitation in the sharp strike of her heels against the pavers.

Kamon shook his head. "I didn't hear anything, or scent anything."

"You wouldn't with a dark walker."

Our eyes met, memory and loss tangling in that gaze. Finally I said, "Good night, Kamon. Please talk to her about Lóng Yá."

Kamon's lips quirked in a sad smile. "I know better than to tell her what to do."

He turned away and I stood in the dark long after he'd disappeared into the house. I wrapped my hand around my lion pendant, my hand craving contact of some kind. It was only cool jade but the weight of it was still a comfort. Bāo had been with me through everything, even my darkest times. The animation energy that powered my foo lion was gone, spent on that fateful battle with the ghosts of Yomi, but I knew Bāo and I would be reunited once I returned to Tokyo.

In the meantime, Fiona was readying for war and I was on the front lines with my city. Denji was a Tran, but he was mine as well.

All of it left a sour taste in my mouth.

I had a killer to catch before I lost any more of my citizens.

FIRST LAW

There was simply too much on my plate. I was at my best when focused on clear, defined objectives. Like wrists. Or necks.

When my attention split into too many directions, I needed to ruthlessly pare down my distractions. Adam was one such distraction. I'd run from him earlier and that wasn't like me. Send me to do a job and I wouldn't stop until it was executed. Send me to communicate and I was an abject failure.

It was time to put this problem to rest.

My Adam problem concerned the First Law, and that superceded all other issues for Jiārén. The First Law defined our lives. The other laws were derived from it, and of course the First Law was always the exception to the others.

Adam's memory loss had given me the luxury of pretending that the problem had gone away, but that wouldn't last forever. I had brought Adam under the protection of my clan on the strength of my word. It was time to make good on that word and tell him the truth.

It was child's play to bypass the building's security. I also had the advantage that I'd lived there before.

When I slid the door open to Adam's penthouse, the lights were off. I listened for sounds of movement or the shower.

Nothing.

I stepped lightly to his bedroom. The bed was massive, accommodating his gigantic frame. He slept in a careless twist of white sheets, his broad shoulders exposed. With some effort, I looked away to scan the room for Crimson Cloud Splitter.

He'd taken it out at some point, and it lay gleaming in the open black case. Even in the dark, the sword glowed with a deep inner fire that hinted at Realm ore. It was truly breathtaking and I could understand Adam's obsession with it.

I could take it from him now.

But I wouldn't do that to him, either. It would torment him and I didn't want him to think he had been a bad custodian. He was just the wrong custodian.

I stood over Adam, reluctant to wake him.

Finally I placed a hand on his shoulder. His skin radiated heat. "Adam."

He stirred but didn't wake.

I shook him. "Adam!"

With a start, he blinked and his dark-honey lashes fanned out across those slashing cheekbones. Finally his eyes opened, slow and then startled at the sight of me looming over him.

To his credit, he didn't freak out. One big palm dug into his eyes as he forced himself to wake with a groan. He sat up, the duvet falling to his waist and baring his chest. I kept my gaze fixedly on his face. His eyes looked soft with sleep despite the earlier jolt I'd given him. He blinked and then his eyebrows drew down into a sharp V.

"I don't recall giving you a key." His voice was rough, and decidedly chilly.

"I needed to talk to you."

"Can I get dressed first?"

He wasn't flirting with me. Hearing annoyance in his voice almost made me feel better. It was worse when he was being nice to me.

I pivoted and stalked out while he rolled out of bed.

The hallway had one framed photo, a single black frame in a stark expanse of white walls. Curious to know what could get on Adam's sentimental list given how sparse the place was, I studied the photo. Adam looked more than ten years younger. Maybe this was taken just before college. He towered over a family of three, beaming as the four of them posed near Mount Fuji.

I looked at Adam and this smiling family. The Yamamotos, I presumed. Their son looked very young here, maybe eight or nine years old. He had round cheeks and fluffy flyaway hair that stood straight up. The bespectacled Mr. Yamamoto had that same hairstyle, though thinning.

Adam was carrying on this Kunimitsu crusade for this family. I needed to show him why it had to end.

I drew Hachi and set it down on his kitchen island.

Adam padded out in his bare feet, clad in faded jeans and a snug gray T-shirt. His eyes weren't sleepy and low-lidded anymore. His golden cheeks still had creases from his pillow. He stared at me, unsmiling. It was the way he had assessed me that first time we met on the jiujitsu mats.

Like we were opponents.

"Shall I make tea for us, or would you prefer coffee instead?" His tone was neutral, and I couldn't tell if he was being sarcastic with me.

"No thank you, I'm fine."

"Something stronger, then."

He reached up to a glass shelf and pulled down a snifter and a premium bottle of Japanese whiskey.

I waited as he poured, the rich scent of the liquor permeating the air. "I needed to show you something. Please bring out the katana."

He took a sip and nodded. "Give me a minute."

Moments later he returned with the sword and turned it with the handle toward me. I placed it above Hachi.

"Adam, this sword is not a lost Kunimitsu. I'm going to show you why."

"We've been over this, Emiko." He sounded tired.

"Not this part, we haven't."

I picked up Hachi and gave her a boost from my qì. The petals of blood jade glowed deep red, the light eerie in the quiet of the kitchen. The more qì I fed her, the more the red fire sparked with gold streaks.

After Hachi's light show, I put her back down and picked up Crimson Cloud Splitter. The weight of the katana was perfect and I resisted the urge to take a few practice strokes. Adam watched me closely but didn't say anything.

With a careful turn, I placed my fingers under the tsuba of the katana. It was beautifully carved, the round guard a strangely delicate ornament to this deadly blade. The artisan's skill of the carving and inlay were obvious, delicate gold tracings with the barest circles of mutton-fat jade serving as the eyes of the dragon curved around the guard.

I skimmed my fingers over the mutton-fat jade, feeding it the smallest trace of qì. It brightened slowly and then shone a radiant white, as if lit from an inner sun.

Adam's eyebrows lifted high and with a quick movement, he hit the light switch in the kitchen.

The eyes of the dragon still glowed bright under the kitchen's recessed lighting.

Adam picked up the katana and turned it slowly. He ran his own fingers over it, feeling each minute groove. The carving dimmed and a moment later, it was dull again. He tapped it, then ran his fingers over the carvings once more. It remained dim. After a moment he set it down.

His lips turned down. "I don't know what that was about, but I'm not sure what that proves."

I picked up Hachi and took a small hammer and spike out of my waist pouch. I went to work, easing out the bone mekugi. The peg held the handle to the tang of the blade. Adam was experienced enough with blades to know what I was doing. I carefully went through the painstaking ritual of removing the habaki, then the seppa, all leading up to the tsuba.

"I named her Hachi because of her sting. She is an old blade, but not as old as the katana. However, she was forged by the same clan who forged the katana."

At last I revealed the tang, with its centuries of accumulated dirt and rust. I rubbed my finger gently over a small spot just below where the seppa would sit. I fed it more qì and a small shape of a bee emerged, symmetrical and unmistakable.

Adam tilted his head to study the bee but didn't say anything. I could guess what was going through his head. Sword aficionados did not clean the dirt and rust from the tang—it helped with verifying the age of the sword. Now Adam was wondering what was under the dirt and rust of the katana. Would he also find a small etched bee?

"The Changs started with forging jian and eventually settled on the tachi blade. They came through the Gate in the eighth century, finally ending up in the Yamato Province around 700 A.D. and taking on a new clan name. My clan came through the Gate roughly the same time. We were fleeing the Dragon Wars and this place was safer. None of the Júwàirén here had any dangerous talents."

Adam cleared his throat. "Dragon Wars?"

I nodded and I pointed at the katana. "If you remove the tsuka, and I light it with my qì, you will find this same bee engraved there. The bee is the hallmark of the Chang family and their forging talents. They can work with unearthly temperatures and fold the finest of layers. Their talent ensures that people like me can activate the jade inlay."

"People like you?"

"Lóng Jiārén. We have Gifts because we are descended from the Sons of the Dragon."

Adam shook his head, his eyes confused. "I'm not following you."

"Look at me, Adam. I'm telling you that I'm descended from dragons."

Adam dug the heels of his palms into his eye sockets. "Okay, look. I don't understand what you're saying. But I don't see what this proves."

I shook my head. "Its provenance is much rarer than a mere Kunimitsu. It's so coveted by my people that they will kill you, Tessa, and all of the Yamamoto family, to reclaim it and keep it secret."

Adam's voice grew hard. "Are you threatening me?"

Now I was getting frustrated. "No, Adam. I could have stolen the sword from you any number of times, including tonight. I didn't do that."

He didn't like that response. It didn't help that it was totally true. I had easily bypassed all of his security tonight. He would have woken to find the sword missing. I watched his jaw work for a moment while he reined in his emotions. His self-mastery impressed me.

Finally he leaned over me and snatched the katana off the counter. "I'm taking it to Professor Ōtsuka this week."

My teeth ground together and made my jaw ache. So far "kinder and gentler" hadn't worked with Tessa and it wasn't convincing Adam. It would be so much easier if I could solve this problem the old way. The hard way.

My father would approve.

I wasn't going down that road, but perhaps a little more stick, since the carrot wasn't enough. As Adam poured another drink, I pulled the photo off its hook on the wall.

"Are these the Yamamotos?"

"Yes."

"What are their names?"

Adam took a sip of whiskey, his eyes traveling over the photo. "I called them Ojisan and Obasan. The young guy is Kenji. He's at university now."

"Why do you have the sword instead of Kenji?"

Adam's eyes darkened. "He was still pretty young when his dad passed. I had gone to Japan an angry kid, mad about my dad dying and my mom shipping me off to some family friend in Japan. But Yamamoto-san treated me as his own, and taught me everything. When he was dying, he made me promise to take care of Kenji. So I do. I'm just the custodian for the sword until Kenji is older."

I might never figure out how Crimson Cloud Splitter had ended up with this family, but I focused on the important part.

"That sword puts Kenji and his mother at risk. You have to withdraw the sword from the exhibit."

Adam turned back to his drink. "I'll take it under advisement."

It was his executive voice, the one that said he had all the leverage with the museum and I was just an employee. I changed tactics.

"Did you really think that your lightning strike was an act of nature?"

He set down his whiskey, leaning forward. His entire body looked taut as a wire as he stared me down. "Now you're finally going to tell me? After you break into my place and threaten my extended family? Now you want to share?"

I pressed my palms flat on the table, bringing my face closer to his. "You paid two million for a fan to get into a Jiārén auction for the Lost Heart of Yázì. Do you remember that?"

His eyes lasered into mine. "Yes." He said it like a challenge.

"I activated this fan and a driver showed up to take us to the Palace of Fine Arts."

He nodded and I could smell the rich whiskey aroma on his breath.

"Once there, we found your inside man, but he had been brutally beaten by his clan." My recitation took on a dull note in remembering how that man had been severed from the Kohs.

"Haider . . ." he whispered.

I picked up Hachi's parts and gave him a humorless smile before I proceeded to narrate the sequence of events, from the undead kappas to unsuccessfully chasing the Lost Heart of Yázì. My hands moved on autopilot, reassembling Hachi with quick, sure movements. When I mentioned breaking out of an ice cage that Awang Koh had imprisoned us in, the muscles of Adam's throat worked, but he said nothing.

"That's when one of them aimed a lightning strike at me to settle an old score. You threw yourself over me and in order for me to get someone to heal you, I extended the protection of my clan over you. That is the only reason you are not a vegetable today. I'm now responsible for what you do."

Adam raked his fingers through his curls, then picked up his whiskey and drained it.

I sheathed Hachi with a firm movement. "And that is why you can never tell anyone what I have told you today. My clan duty requires me to kill you myself if you reveal our secrets."

His face went slack with shock. For once, his absolute certainty that his life should be the way he engineered it was gone. I showed him who I truly was and allowed him to see the conviction in my eyes. The hard resignation of my decision. And now when his eyes looked at me, he saw that I was a killer.

I found that I didn't like it.

"We are on borrowed time, Adam." I pointed at the katana. "This can't resurface and I will do everything in my power to prevent it. Do you understand?"

"What I understand is that you threatened me again." His voice took on an edge. "You'll excuse me if I don't walk you out."

"I told you what you wanted to know. My obligation to do that is fulfilled. After this, I won't be explaining my actions to you."

I spun on my heel and stalked to the door.

POSTMORTEM AT GRANDMA'S

The darkness that surrounds me is as deep as the ocean, and heavy with the scent of ginger and pepper. It is hungry and it breathes like an animal. I know it's hungry because the same hunger is a sharp stitch in my belly.

I run, but my legs are heavy, my steps as clumsy as a toddler. The darkness surrounds me and drapes over my shoulders like a cloak. The hunger spikes, intense enough to double me over. I check my belly, to be sure I haven't been stabbed. I twist and thrash, desperate to get away from the darkness. The inky blackness just clings closer to me and squeezes like a demented lover.

The pain shocks my system, and then the scream bursts from my lips.

"Emiko!" The boom of my mother's voice fills the world.

The shadows tighten again but now I stand strong. I will not cower. I strike out at the darkness.

The hunger is alive and it laughs at me. The air explodes with ginger and pepper and makes my eyes sting and water. The hunger fades a little but instead of being a relief, there is only crawling horror that makes me want to tear off my own skin.

Another scream escapes me.

"Emi-chan!" My mother's voice is equal parts terror and revulsion.

The darkness pulls away and I am in Golden Gate Park, just outside the tea garden. Fiona and Freddy are here, as well as Tessa and Andie, and countless others. Everyone is hunched over in pain and covered in bloody wounds. The wounds are ugly, the bites of a deranged animal. Freddy collapses to his knees, his arms held tight to his belly, useless as blood pours out of him like a waterfall. His face is pale, his eyes go distant, and then he is very, very still.

Before I can go to him the hunger in my belly roars again, and more of my people collapse in crimson pools.

"Emi-chan!"

I turn to the voice and my mother stands behind me but she is twenty feet tall, a nightmare clad in a fiery kimono. A dancing pattern of black flames plays at the hem of her garment. The flames are eating her alive.

The hunger spikes again and it is too much to bear. I crawl toward her. "Kaasan . . ."

Her eyes are glowing spheres of blood jade. Crimson tears run down her cheeks. My pain redoubles and ragged wounds appear on my mother's arms, belly, and legs. The scent of ginger is strong enough to make me gag.

My mother doesn't make a sound as the wounds open like mouths. I sob and curl into myself, but the pain, the hunger, it feels like it wants to explode out of me. If I let it go, it will consume my mother, my family, my friends.

A hand strokes my cheek. My mother's touch is cool against the heat of my skin. Her fingertips tremble as they caress my neck.

"Hontou ni gomen nasai . . ."

White smoke billows out of my mother's sleeves and rushes toward me. The smoke smells like dried leaves and damp earth, like old wood and winter spices. When it touches my skin, the black shadows shrink away.

When the hunger starts to fade I panic. Something is changing. I don't know what, but I know I have to fight it. I strike out again but my hands pass through the smoke with no effect. My mother holds me down as the smoke crawls up my neck and toward my mouth.

Her eyes glisten with tears. "Gomen ne . . ."

The smoke enters my mouth and my world becomes agony. I choke on the cloying scent of spice and earth, and through it all I can feel my mother's hands on me, holding me down.

There is no more hunger.

Only pain.

I awoke in a panic, heart hammering, my sheets drenched with sweat. The room was dark. Faint shadows reached across my floor from the moonlight, but quiet and motionless. Harmless. I shivered as the sweat cooled on my shoulders.

Dreams about my mother were never good, which was odd since I had so few memories of her from my childhood. As a member of Bā Shǒu, her work kept her away from home more often than not. But my mother seemed to have an outsized influence on my troubled sleep, one of the many things I held against her.

All I wanted was to wrap my arms around my friend, but Bāo was still only a jade pendant. I crawled out of bed and curled up inside my sound circle. I tapped the largest of my singing bowls and a low, resonant tone filled my room, masking the sound of my ragged breaths. I clung tight to Bāo, the familiar ridges pressed to my lips. I lay there and watched the sky slowly turn from indigo to pale gray.

Last night had been a cascade of failures—it was no wonder this dream had followed. My options were quickly whittling down to the kinds of things I'd spent two years avoiding. On top of everything else, the assassin had escaped and she'd said my name like she knew me. I'd spent an hour combing through my memories for a dark walker who might hold a grudge against me and come up empty.

Finally I gave up on sleep. I pocketed two handfuls of Kit Kats and made my way to Inner Sunset on autopilot. I jerked open the door to Popo's homeopathic spa and the normally pleasant bell that chimed with the door opening clanged like a broken gong, causing several clients to look toward the door in concern. The young man behind the counter raised one delicately arched eyebrow and slipped into a screened-off doorway without a word. I sighed and caught the door before it could slam back into the frame.

Popo's clients settled back into their spa loungers to continue receiving their custom herbal facial treatments. I had to be more careful, especially here. Most of the clientele were Wàirén, totally unaware of our dragon nature. Popo was one of the few Jiārén who managed to successfully straddle the line between our worlds. I envied her greatly for it. I was trying, but mostly I was failing.

The spa was decorated in something of a cross between a minimalist spaceship and an Apple flagship store. Massive spa loungers dotted the main room along the longest wall, each one next to a workstation stocked with custom herbs, creams, and other homemade remedies. It smelled wonderful—clean but not mediciney. Elegant potted plants accented the area, and, with the central water feature, artfully directed the qì flowing through the room.

Popo bustled out, her neat gray updo coming to my shoulders. She wasn't actually my grandmother, but tradition and our history dictated that she deserved the honorific. In truth, like many of the people attached to my clan, Popo was sometimes more like family than my family. Despite being over eighty, she was still spry, and the clarity in her eyes had never dimmed.

Those eyes took me in now, traveling up and down my body. With a sigh she took hold of my hand and pinched her thumb firmly into my wrist. The spot tingled for a moment and then the rest of the tension in my neck faded away.

She clucked as she released my wrist. "Aiya, Emiko. I thought being the Sentinel would clear your blockages."

I rubbed my wrist and cracked my neck. Instant relief. I really needed to learn whatever Popo had just done. "At least I heal faster now."

Popo nodded approvingly. "Lai, lai, your friends are waiting for us in the back."

"Um, I don't think we're exactly friends." Maybe Freddy. With

Fiona, it was a little more complicated. I guess I could count her as an ally, which in Jiārén currency was more valuable.

"They're close enough."

Thankfully, Grandma steered us away from the Door that led to her pocket of the Realm, instead taking us to one of her smaller offices. An earthenware pot sat in the center of the table on a small trivet, a tendril of steam rising from the spout. Fiona and Freddy sat, talking in low Vietnamese and drinking tea. From the look on Freddy's face, it wasn't a pleasant conversation. Not surprising given why we were all here.

Dark circles ringed Fiona's eyes, but they glittered with suppressed emotion. I'd seen this before, the deep and unyielding need to take action, to move. Some people shut down after the trauma of a death. Fiona was not that person. I doubted she'd gotten any sleep last night, either.

Despite her obvious fatigue, Fiona still cut an impressive figure, dressed in a white, sleeveless cashmere sweater dress and fringed white suede boots. Silver bangles rode high midway up her forearms. I wondered how hard it was for her to keep up appearances like this. With the Moks gone, Freddy had reverted to his staples, worn board shorts, a long-sleeved T-shirt, and his trademark leather sandals. They both stood when we entered.

Fiona bowed and smacked Freddy's hand when he didn't copy the gesture. Freddy sketched a bow as well, masking his discomfort with an embarrassed smile to me. The bowing made me uncomfortable but at least Fiona didn't call me Mimi.

Popo trundled into the room behind me. "Sit, sit, both of you. You're making her uncomfortable."

I sat at the table, grateful for her acute perceptions. Freddy poured tea for Popo, and then for me, before refilling his and Fiona's tiny cups. Jasmine pu-erh.

As I sipped the fragrant tea, Popo pulled a small glass vial from her pocket and set it in the center of the table. I lowered my cup and stared at it. A layer of what looked like soot or dust coated the bottom of the vial. "Is this . . . ?"

Popo nodded. "This is what killed the aegis."

I reached across the table, only to have Popo fend me off with a glare. She reached out and her qì kindled between her hands.

The dust in the vial jumped and went wild. In an instant the interior of the glass was filled with a whirlwind of jet-black dust, swirling so violently that the vial wobbled and nearly toppled. Grandma silenced her talent and snapped up the glass before it could fall and shatter. She placed it carefully back on the table. The dust inside was still moving, but much slower, and collapsed back into a thin film at the bottom.

Popo cleared her throat. "Final Breath. A rare poison. Distilled from tetrodotoxin from the torafugu puffer fish and modified to target the meridians. Once administered, the poison is particularly dangerous for Lóng Jiārén."

She definitely had my attention now. During my training with the Jōkōryūkai, I'd had plenty of poison lessons. Although I'd never told Grandma, I knew my way around most of her herbs and tinctures, but only for ill effects. I had never once heard of Final Breath, not even in terms of defensive measures should it be deployed against me.

Popo continued. "The toxin affects our qì and corrupts the meridians. In small quantities like we have here, the effects are only temporary, but quite painful. In larger doses, there have been cases of Jiārén losing their abilities for the remainder of their lives, and death."

She picked up the vial and shook it in her hand. The dust stirred a little but otherwise did not move. "You see? The elegance of it. It only activates in close proximity to qì and then it seeks the source. It follows your qì back through your meridians, closing off the channels as it enters your system."

Fiona's eyes widened and locked onto the vial, her hands clenching and unclenching on the table, her tea grown cold next to her.

Franklin truly had had no chance of survival. The only way he could have survived the sword strike was with his talent. But activating his qì had only signed his death warrant.

Popo set the vial back on the table. "I have not seen this since my training at Lóng Kǒu. The ingredients are nearly impossible to source and it is extremely difficult to concoct. Most who have tried were killed in the process."

I met her eyes. "But you know who could have made this."

Her eyes went from me, to Fiona, and back to me. "Yes. The fugu is found in the Sea of Japan. Ah Tong in Tokyo is the only Herbalist I know of who could safely make Final Breath, and have ready access to live puffer fish."

Fiona slapped her hand on the table. "We find this Herbalist, and we can track down whoever is behind the assassin."

I sat up, my eyes focused on the vial of poison. "We just need to wait. If the assassin has something like this at their disposal, then she's a pro."

Fiona sniffed. "Unacceptable. Lóng Yá is next week. I will not cower in my home because of some upstart assassin."

We were going around in circles. Time for another angle. "You asked me to help you find Franklin's killer. My Sentinel authority ends when you leave the city, Fiona. I can't help you if you go to Lóng Yá."

Freddy blinked at that.

Fiona sat up straight and brought her hands together on the table. "Very well then. The Tran Clan formally requests aid from the Soong Clan, as well as the Sentinel of San Francisco."

That was the last thing I would agree to.

I remained silent for a long moment while she drank her tea.

When Fiona set her cup down, Freddy moved in and poured more tea, first for me, then for his sister. Then he surprised everyone by speaking up.

"Emiko, do you remember what I told you about my Lóng Yá?"

I blinked at the shift in the conversation but nodded.

He leaned forward on his elbows, his expression earnest. "I lost a lot of friends that year. All of them due to their families trying to outplot the others."

Freddy pointed a finger at me and Fiona. His sister studied her manicured nails. "It's happening here. This is how it starts. Everyone trying to get an edge over everyone else."

Fiona huffed. "Freddy—"

Freddy cut her off. "No, Fiona. It doesn't have to be like this—all these deals and obligations."

Before I could say anything Freddy shot me a look, too, and I closed my mouth. I'd never seen such an intense look on his face before.

Freddy said, "We're friends. Let's act like it."

He locked eyes with me. "Emiko, I have to stay in San Francisco while Fiona goes to Lóng Yá. Attending Lóng Yá is important for her. Could you do me a solid and watch her back while she's there?"

Damn it.

I wouldn't have said Fiona and I were friends, but Freddy had grown on me in the last few weeks, recent kidnappings notwithstanding. Fiona met my eyes and I had the sneaking suspicion that she was just as uncomfortable about this as I was.

But Freddy was using my own playbook against me when I'd told him that maybe some Jiārén ways were wrong.

Freddy was asking me for a favor. As a friend.

Which meant I could cover for Fiona without involving my father and without generating bad blood between our clans. It wasn't exactly a fair trade, but that was Freddy's whole point. Friends didn't weigh things on some scale. They did things because they cared. I wanted to be that kind of friend.

I gave a small bow. "I'm glad to call you both friends."

As I said it, it rang true inside me, like I had spoken it into being. "In Tokyo, I'll do everything in my power to keep your sister safe when we are together."

Meaning, when we were together, I would keep an eye on her.

I wasn't going to be shadowing her, or bringing all the Soong resources to bear.

Fiona smiled and her eyes slid back and forth between me and her brother. "Thanks, Mimi. I appreciate it."

I let her have that one.

Popo scooped the vial off the table as Fiona and I gave each other shallow bows. Freddy smiled and punched me on the bicep. "Thanks, Emiko."

Fiona stood from the table and turned to Popo, putting her right fist in her left palm in front of her chest. "Popo, our clan thanks you for your services. I hope we can continue to do business in the future."

Irrational possessiveness stabbed at me when Fiona called her *Popo.* I wrestled it down, though. Having the Trans as an ally was good for Popo and would keep the Louie Claws away. Popo was moving forward. I had to do the same.

A bar of soft gold embossed with the Tran name slid discreetly across the table. Popo made it disappear with practiced efficiency. It was far more than Popo needed for this consultation, and I suspected Fiona was trying to move the boundaries of the coming conflict with the Louies. She might be playing nice with me, but everywhere else, just like my father, she always squeezed out maximum value.

Fiona turned to me. "We're leaving for Tokyo tomorrow. Do you have affairs you need to settle before leaving?"

I hadn't intended to leave for Tokyo so early, but it looked like it couldn't be helped. I had the distinct feeling that the next seven days would be a roller coaster. It was time to gear up. "I have some things to pick up. I'll meet you at the train station."

TRAIN STATION

I was running late, but the city seemed to be helping me out, and all the lights turned green for my rideshare. Traffic was also unusually light, and I made good time to the train station.

On the way I texted Leanna to apologize for missing our lesson. The little squirt took it pretty well. A waterfall of crying emojis blanketed my screen.

but i had new tricks to try on you

Sorry kiddo, duty calls

ya i guess so

send me pics from Lóng Yá pls? i wish i could go

With Uncle Jimmy as her benefactor there was no doubt she would attend Lóng Kǒu, but the idea of her competing in Lóng Yá made my guts twist. Freddy's voice was laced with unnatural bitterness whenever he spoke of it. I wished I could shelter my student from Jiārén schemes as long as possible.

I'll send you what I can, going to be busy, though.

Practice hard until I come back.

I chuckled as another wave of crying emojis covered my phone.

The Caltrain station at 4th and King Streets was a long, narrow building encased in glass. I pulled my bags from the car, two compact duffels expertly packed by Sally with my latest treasures from the Sun Emporium. I hated feeling unprepared, but I still had no idea what I might be facing in Tokyo. I'd purchased a little bit of nearly everything in the Sun Emporium, figuring that less was not more in this instance.

It was not lost on me at all, the irony of departing San Francisco via the same route that I had arrived. It had been two years. I had changed. I was not the same person who arrived covered in mud and blood two years ago. I was not going back to Tokyo to be that person again. My brother needed me and I was going to help him.

A gentle breeze rushed up behind me, giving me a gentle push toward the glass doors.

Right. I had a job to do. "Yeah, yeah. Get a move on. I got it."

The ticket lobby was a long, boxy building, walled in with floor-to-ceiling windows on all sides. Several train tracks terminated here at platforms beyond the opposite wall of windows. As I entered I passed a news kiosk on my right, selling newspapers and snacks. The young Asian man behind the counter met my eyes as I crossed the lobby. He had the distinctive eyes of the Zhao family, deep brown accented with flecks of gold, and was dressed in a fitted vest over a crisp white dress shirt. A neat row of tastefully understated polished onyx buttoned the vest closed. Their family spanned the world, literally, building and maintaining these transit stations with their Dragon talents. None of their elders sat on the Bā Tóu, our governing council, but all Jiārén held them in as much esteem for the work they did for all our people.

I gave him a slight bow with my head as I walked. It was always good form to greet your hosts when you entered their home. I drifted closer to the newsstand, slid my hand into my pocket, and pulled out a slim bar of Soong gold embossed with a rearing dragon. The bar rang with a high, clear note as I laid it on the counter in front of the young man. His clever hands flashed and made the bar disappear, as neatly as a magician's trick. The young man inclined his head to me and swept his arm out, indicating one of the ticket machines at the far end of the building.

The battered ticket machine at the end of the row had clearly seen better days. A sign hanging askew off one of the buttons proclaimed that a repairman was on the way. I brushed my fingers over the worn-out keypad buttons. The eight had just a bit more wear than the others, the engraved number eroded down to near smoothness.

I checked around me, making sure no Wàirén were headed in my direction. I still hadn't seen Fiona's group but assumed they had gone on without me. No sign of the dark walker, either. Satisfied, I took a breath, pressed the eight button, and winced as a small needle emerged and pricked the pad of my thumb.

Magic blossomed around me, reacting to the power in my blood. The air around me shimmered, and the hustle and bustle of the Caltrain station faded away, leaving me in a blank white void. This was only the first step on my return journey, a magic-powered step from San Francisco into a massive Realm Fragment controlled by the Zhao. Jiārén were stronger in these Fragments, our talents more potent, and each family that controlled a Fragment used it to enhance their standing. The Zhaos used their Realm Fragments to bend space to their will.

The sounds came back first, strident voices calling through the white light in a dozen different languages, from the clipped to the melodic. The smells came next, rich scents of roasting meats and syrupy sweets, and the musky stink of too many people in too little space. The shimmering air parted and I stood in the middle of the Glorious Emerald Pagoda, the Jiārén transportation hub of the United States. A massive central atrium stretched into the distance in all directions, large enough to swallow the entirety of the Caltrain station with room to spare. Vendors selling food and drink ringed the atrium, hawking almost every kind of meat imaginable, roasted on a stick.

People of all stripes crossed the space, dressed for all manner of weather, traveling to and from the far corners of the globe. Dozens of exits dotted the perimeter of the Pagoda, each one leading to a different location. Zhao power held the Pagoda steady as space folded around it as neatly as an origami crane. The pros of traveling this way meant I could transport all my weapons and gold. Also, it was almost instantaneous. The downside was that it affected me the same way as tunneling with Freddy did.

I held it in for just under a minute, enough time to determine that I wasn't in immediate danger, and then emptied my churning stomach into the nearest waste bin. Portal travel just wasn't my strength. Add in being cut off from San Francisco, and it almost made the twelve-hour flight seem worth it to avoid barfing.

My Sentinel powers would be gone for as long as I was away from my city. I took a moment to recalibrate, and drank a little water to calm my insides. As I centered my energy, I took in the crowds. It had been a long time since I'd been in the presence of so many Jiārén. If my adventures of the last week hadn't been enough, the cold grip of foreboding in my gut marked my return to my ancestral home.

A quick check of my surroundings confirmed that I had in fact gotten to the Emerald Pagoda ahead of Fiona and her contingent. I hoisted my bags and began a slow circuit of the atrium, looking for signs of trouble. Traffic seemed particularly heavy today, probably due to the oncoming Lóng Yá Tourney. A dense current of travelers pushed through the crowd toward the Tokyo exit.

Despite its earlier gymnastics, my stomach growled at the scent of so much familiar cuisine.

I made a beeline for the kiosk with a pink sign proclaiming it as Sugar Sugar House in curling script. A slim girl with perfect bangs and wearing a pink apron sorted colorful bags at the counter. This place had the one thing I had missed the most after leaving Japan.

Kit Kats.

Rows and rows of pastel-colored bags beckoned me. In San Francisco, I could score the matcha flavor at the local Nijiya. But here I could stock up on my beloved sakura flavor.

The pink and white flowers on the sakura package winked at me. I swept the entire basket onto the cashier's counter.

"I'll take these."

The clerk blinked, her eyebrows rising nearly to her bangs. "All of these?"

I studied my duffel bag. "You're right. I have room for more."

I went back to the basket with the Shinshu apple flavor. Between the apple and strawberry cheesecake, it was a tie. I couldn't decide. And, it would be nice to bring some back for Tessa and Andie. I brought both baskets up to the clerk. They didn't fit on the counter.

"These, too."

Her mouth fell open, but her fingers started ringing. Moments later, she had bagged them all and I stuffed five kilograms of Kit Kats into my duffel bag, backpack, and fanny pack. I'd eat some momentarily so it would be fine.

My bags were heavier now, but my heart was happy. I practically floated to the ring of hawkers and their parade of skewered and roasted, fried, or grilled goodness. One of the stalls at the end caught my eye with its flapping banner emblazoned with a comically bad drawing of a massive fish pinned beneath a heavy stone.

My inner carnivore salivated when I read the handwritten sign. NAMAZU. One of the rarer finds in the ocean, a gigantic, bottom-dwelling fish with the power to cause earthquakes and tsunamis. Sure enough, a quick scan of the people lined up for a taste showed auras leaning toward earth and water talents. Namazu were hard to find, and even rarer to catch alive. The flesh of this specimen was said to only be edible for one day after its death. This was a once-in-a-lifetime culinary opportunity.

I kept an eye out for Fiona as I waited in line and then gratefully paid for a taste of a fish I might never get to eat again. The hand-sized slab of fish was battered in airy tempura, threaded onto a jagged bamboo skewer, fried to golden perfection, and served in a clever cardboard tray with tiny compartments for a cup of spicy dipping sauce and a garnish of colorful pickles. I took the first bite without condiments to get the full effect.

My teeth crunched through paper-thin batter and into steaming hot, flaky fish that tasted of ocean brine and cloying umami. Wow. It was like unagi and oysters had a sexy, delicious love child. I dunked the next bite in the sauce which complemented the fish with the salty tang of fish sauce, lime, crushed garlic, and wafer-thin rings of vibrant crimson chilis. In seconds my stomach troubles were long forgotten as I licked the last bit of pickle brine from my fingers and tossed the tray in the garbage. My hunger sated, I dared to imagine that maybe this trip would go down as easily as the namazu.

Then I spotted Fiona.

In fact, I was sure that everyone in the Emerald Pagoda spotted her. Fiona's entourage materialized from the San Francisco station like an eighties hair band in a cloud of dry ice smoke. A small army of smartly dressed guards with mirrored sunglasses formed a tight circle around her and broke trail through the crowd. In the center of the circle, Fiona strolled along as easily as a Sunday walk in the park. Behind her circle of bodyguards, a group of Tran porters in nondescript gray suits followed with a small train of rolling Vuitton trunks.

Even in a crowded station populated entirely by Jiārén, Fiona managed to stand out like a peacock in a henhouse. Her face was obscured beneath a wide-brimmed, silver-and-black-checkered hat that belonged at the Kentucky Derby. A delicate Swiss-dotted veil hid the top half of her face. Only a Princess of Wales and Fiona could carry off a fascinator. Below that she was clad in a shimmering silver latex trench coat that screamed, *If any assassins are nearby, here I am.*

The flow and press of bodies carried me along and I let myself blend into the crowd. I nudged my way through, working my way toward what I pegged as the weakest link in her protection detail, a young man with a nervously bobbing Adam's apple and the wide eyes of someone who'd never been to the Emerald Pagoda. I got close enough to the swishing silver trench coat that I could have simply reached out and touched her through her fence of heavies.

Fiona wasn't taking the threat of the assassin seriously enough.

My steps slowed and I let the crowd move past me. Fiona's group passed me at a steady clip. I slowed until I was pushed back toward the train of baggage handlers and fell in step next to the last one, a woman with her hair tied into a severe bun and wearing mirrored aviators.

I kept my eyes on the ludicrous hat in the distance and pitched my voice low. "Not bad, but she doesn't walk like you do."

Fiona's perfectly glossy lips quirked under her aviator sunglasses. "No, I guess there isn't anyone quite like me, is there?"

Frustration reared up like an angry dog. "If I could spot Linh wearing a cheap hat and wig, you don't think the assassin could?"

"That hat is an Armani from the spring collection, Mimi." Fiona sounded offended.

"Don't call me Mimi." Guess now that I was out of my territory, I wasn't getting the Sentinel courtesy anymore from her.

Fiona kept her face forward, watching over her entourage. "Really, this is ideal. If the assassin shows up, Linh will draw her out and into our trap."

I grunted. "And if she shows up here, at the back of the line, where you have no protection?"

Fiona arched an eyebrow over her sunglasses. "If she shows up back here, then she'll have to deal with the both of us, won't she?"

I shot her my best stink eye, which did absolutely nothing, and melted back into the crowd, pacing the baggage train from a distance. We crossed the Pagoda without any drama and stopped before a set of wide doors.

TOKYO was spelled out in a dozen languages above the frame.

I was home. But it didn't feel like home anymore. Now it felt like traveling for work, and without the protection of my city's gifts.

An attendant at our door held a book in his hands. As he turned the pages the script morphed, the words changing as the Wàirén world moved around the Realm pocket. He held up his hand and waved us forward. The doors opened onto a formless gray void sprinkled with bright pinpoints of light. Stale air that smelled of concrete and car exhaust blew over us.

Linh said, "Let's go."

The entourage moved forward as one and stepped into the void.

KAGE

Nostalgia rolled over me in waves as we stepped through the door of the Glorious Emerald Pagoda and into Shinjuku Station, the largest train station in Japan, in the heart of Tokyo. Our group emerged on one of the lower platforms, well away from the more traveled areas of the station. From here we would have several decks to ascend before we made it to street level.

Even here, four levels below the main station, the smell of Tokyo trains and the musty air pushed through the subterranean tunnels brought back memories of my childhood and nearly getting lost in the mazelike station. The late spring temperature and humidity were similar to San Francisco, but somehow even the air felt different here in Tokyo. Heavier. Richer.

By force of will I kept down the fried namazu and saved myself the embarrassment of throwing up in front of Fiona's entire security detail. Making the crossing in the midst of so many powerful talents did have its uses.

Linh-Fiona gave a quick set of orders to her group, splitting them up in two. They would take separate routes out of the station and meet up later at their hotel. The main force of Fiona's security detail walked off in a protective pack around Linh. Two enforcers stayed with Fiona and the luggage, and they adopted the air of beaten-down travelers, the lowliest of Tran functionaries, saddled with moving their mistress's baggage. I had to admit, it was a pretty good plan.

The four of us set off in the opposite direction with Fiona's enforcers leading the way. Fiona glanced at me sidelong as we walked. "You must be very familiar with dark walkers."

I'd been dreading this conversation.

"Not really." Take Your Daughter to Work Day was not a common occurrence at Bā Shǒu. Bā Tóu, the governing body that my father sat on, set out the rules Jiārén lived by. Bā Shǒu was the complementary body to Bā Tóu, and how the ruling clans *interfaced* with Jiārén. Such interfacing was often carried out in unsubtle fashion. My mother was notorious for it and had more than earned her reputation as Bā Shǒu's most feared hatchet woman.

Eat your rice or the Walker of the Void will come for you!

Fiona smiled like a predator, all dazzling teeth and sly eyes. "You told Freddy you'd help me out here. My security detail needs to know what they are up against."

She had me there. I doled out the intel, cautious of how much I should reveal. "Píng talents need line of sight. Zhong talents need to have been to the destination before, to visualize the exit point."

Fiona nodded. "Gāo?"

I grimaced. "Gāo talents can learn to see and hear through the darkness, and search for their targets. Only the strongest wards can keep them out."

Fiona turned away, her expression smug. She'd gotten enough to satisfy her security needs and her own innate curiosity.

I wasn't giving away clan secrets but neither were these nuances of dark walking common knowledge. What I didn't tell Fiona was that with the proper training and enough reckless bravado, they could appear almost anywhere. They could also lose themselves in the dark place between worlds and slowly go insane in the endless dark void. To keep their minds intact, a dark walker used an anchor to keep them tethered to this world. But Fiona didn't need to know that.

We made our way up two platforms in relative calm. As we moved up, traveler density increased. We'd arrived in late afternoon, and the press of bodies on their way home after a long day at the office grew thick as weeds. Vast crowds of bored salarymen trudged home in identical white shirts and black ties, buttons undone at the neck, ties hanging loose. Students armed with backpacks and cell phones navigated the station on autopilot, eyes glued to their phones as they followed some invisible trail, threading the crowds and unerringly finding their destinations.

Our escorts kept a low, easy banter going between themselves, talking about nothing of consequence. It was just a cover, as they kept their eyes roving across the massive station, watching for threats from unseen corners. Was the assassin desperate enough to risk the First Law and attack us in the middle of Shinjuku? If she did, I hoped Fiona's team was as competent as they looked.

The third platform added shoppers to the crowd. Shinjuku Station housed shopping opportunities for anyone and anything at all hours of the day. The smell of fresh pastries and hot ramen competed with the musk of leather handbags and cosmetics. My stomach growled at the cloying scent of tonkotsu broth, thick and rich, with enough dissolved collagen to leave a residue in my nose. Gods, I'd missed the food here.

By the fourth platform, daylight started to trickle in from the far reaches of the station, through distant doors that led to the rest of the wonderful chaos that was Tokyo. The back of my neck also started to itch, and I scanned every dark corner twice before we passed, and twice after we passed.

As the sounds of the station increased, my ears began playing tricks on me, distorting the meaningless background noise. Bubblegum synth music from shops blended with overhead train announcements and restaurant hawkers, morphing into a wall of sound that faded in and out of focus. On several occasions the sound coalesced into a pinpoint just behind me, a whisper that called to me out of thin air.

A few more steps, and the whisper seemed to come from just behind me. But I couldn't make out the words.

I had turned around to try to spot the source of the whisper for the third time when Fiona asked me what I was doing.

Other than the throngs of commuters behind us, there didn't

seem to be anyone near enough to be responsible for the sound. My eyes scanned the shadows convulsively. Had the killer followed us to Tokyo? If it was the killer, how was she speaking to me? I had never heard of anything like this from my mother.

I shook my head to Fiona's question. Without knowing what was happening, it wouldn't do any good to spook her or her enforcers. Maybe my ears really were just playing tricks on me.

Which was comical optimism on my part. The closest thing I'd experienced to this was in San Francisco. At times the mantle of the city let me hear snatches of conversation from everyone in my city. It was maddening when it happened, and it definitely wasn't supposed to be happening in Tokyo.

We took the east exit from Shinjuku and stepped into the golden hour, early evening in Tokyo where the setting sun lit the streets like a warm fire. The itch on the back of my neck was turning into palpable pain but I still hadn't pinned it down. We were nearly to the parking lot with Fiona's armored Range Rover when I blew it. The growl of Tokyo street traffic combined with the raucous jangling of a pachinko parlor, melding into a voice composed of equal parts scraping metal and television static.

The voice rasped in my ear, "Emiko."

My head jerked around and I dropped the luggage handles, my hand gripping Hachi. I had her barely out of her scabbard when I realized my mistake.

I kicked out, planting my boot into the side of the trunk I'd just dropped. It rolled forward and slammed into the back of Fiona's knees, pitching her forward and away from a dark slash of shadow cast by the setting sun. Golden sunlight glinted off a short, wicked blade held in a slender hand that extended from the depths of the shadow. As Fiona fell, the tanto made a quick arc, passing through the space just vacated by her abdomen.

Fiona stumbled to her hands and knees. I leapt forward and grabbed the assassin's wrist, squeezing down brutally and forcing her to drop the weapon. I planted my feet and pulled. Forcing a dark walker to emerge was risky. If she wasn't trained, she might die in the process, her mind torn to splinters as I yanked her out of the void.

Too bad.

I squeezed harder, ready to break every bone in her body if I had to.

The assassin's hand flexed and her fingers curled around my wrist. She pulled away and I went down to one knee, my arm straining to keep my hand clear of the shadow. Dark walkers trained extensively to protect their minds from the chaos of the dark space between worlds. Getting pulled in there would flay my mind to shreds. My shoulder quivered as I leaned back. If I could pull her out, either Fiona would have her, or she'd be dead. Either way I considered it a win.

Sweat coursed down my back as I was dragged slowly toward the shadow. Frost crackled along the edges of the shadow, creeping out in crooked fingers of dirty ice. Bitter cold lanced up my arm as my fingertips brushed the darkness. I bit back a scream.

Arms wrapped around me from behind. Fiona's enforcer, a tall, lithe woman with the build of a swimmer, knelt behind me, her arms cradling my torso. A sharp ozone scent bloomed around me and the enforcer's arms shivered and morphed into cold granite. In seconds her stone limbs surrounded me and anchored me to the sidewalk.

I screamed as the assassin pulled again and my shoulder slowly gave way to the strain. A face swam out of the darkness, with brows like angry slashes and eyes bright with fury. She still wore the half mask with the bloodred, dead smile. The dark walker snarled and I could only stare in horror.

No one did this.

No one dallied between this world and the dark. The strain alone should be ripping her to pieces.

The assassin bared her teeth and dug her fingers into my wrist. "Welcome home, Emiko."

The shadows around the assassin's face boiled, reaching up and out like a mass of spasming tentacles. The stone limb talent yelped in surprise, her arms shifting back to flesh as her concentration broke. My mind stuttered, unable to comprehend what I was seeing. Dark walkers moved themselves through dark space, they didn't do . . . whatever this was.

Shadow tentacles whipped out, slamming into the street. One of them crashed through a streetlight. Where the shadow passed over it, the metal simply disappeared, the edges sheared through like a laser. The streetlight toppled to the ground and sprayed us with broken glass and concrete chips.

I flicked a kunai into my hand, ready to stab deep into the assassin's arm, just as Fiona barked out a cry and stomped her foot down, bringing her hands forward like she was throwing a spear. I flinched back on instinct, pulling the assassin with me. Fiona's enforcer leaned into it, dragging us both with her.

The assassin hissed and threw her shadow limbs at Fiona and the approaching blade of air, but the shadows did nothing but waver slightly as the wind passed through them. The young woman screamed, an inarticulate roar, and the shadow tentacles went wild. A wriggling mass of black shot toward me and I dropped to the sidewalk.

The stone limb wasn't so fast.

The shadow arced over my head and the darkness blotted out the sun. Fiona cried out and the enforcer screamed. The darkness swallowed the enforcer's scream and just . . . erased her from the shoulders up. Blood fountained and splattered over me as the stone limb toppled backward, her arms falling to the sidewalk.

Fiona and her last enforcer scrambled back, running now from the twisting shadows that grabbed at them and chased them across the street. I pushed myself back, feet slipping on the blood of the stone limb, and stumbling over her broken body. A half-dozen shadowy limbs twisted together and merged into one huge, bulbous limb that reared above my head. Bitter cold that had nothing to do with the weather gripped my chest like a fist.

What was this?

How was the assassin doing this? How could I fight shadows?

Purple light flared from the end of the alley and a deep, guttural voice rang out, low enough to make my teeth rattle in my head. "Ai!"

A blinding flash of light flooded the alley, tearing the twisting shadows to shreds of darkness that evaporated. The blast flattened everyone and Fiona gasped in distress. A huge figure stood at the end of the alley, carrying a massive naginata that glowed with violet neon light. Wait, no, there actually was a violet neon tube running parallel to the handle. As the shadows dissipated the glow of the neon tube slowly faded and I blinked against the ghost images in my eyes. The figure slowly came into focus, a massive man dressed in mismatched armor, radiating power like the naked core of a nuclear reactor.

The shadows retreated to the space around the assassin. Her fingernails dug into my forearm as she took in the new stranger. The man lowered his naginata, pointing the blade at the assassin. The purple neon tube brightened again, his power building in a wave of pressure that popped my ears.

Pain burned in bright lines down my arm as the assassin dragged her fingernails down my forearm. The shadow convulsed around her, swallowing her in darkness. She hissed at me as her face melted into shadow and disappeared.

"Say hello to your mother for me."

TOKYO

It was bad enough the assassin seemed to know me personally, but now my mother was somehow involved. Despite her best efforts to ignore me for the last two years, she was still popping up in my affairs with disturbing frequency. What had she done to antagonize this woman, and why did that anger translate to me? Unknown shadows from my family's past loomed over me like storm clouds, and the early evening sun seemed to dim a little.

Standing squarely in that sunlight was the mysterious man who had driven off the assassin. He was a bear of a man, barrel chest, beer belly, and stocky limbs like tree trunks. A wispy beard of tangled black hair hid a neck as thick as my thigh. His eyes shone with fever-bright heat and he wore a confused mishmash, track pants over his bulging legs, with sandals on his gnarled feet. A dirty haori strained to cover his massive chest. Topping off the garish dress, he wore mismatched armor over his clothes, bright red lacquered pauldrons covered his shoulders, and four panels of hardened black leather protected his hips.

At his side, his impressive naginata. The end of the blade topped at least eight feet at the end of a finely finished shaft of some dark wood I didn't recognize. Five metal rings clinked together where the tang of the blade attached to the pole. The lacquer on the handle was worn smooth and shiny and his hands were thick with callouses. Somehow a lit neon tube had been fastened parallel to the wood, flickering purple. And was that a Hello Kitty charm dangling from the tsuba?

He looked like a homeless, urban samurai. I almost expected to find a rusted shopping cart piled with belongings behind him.

But by far the most notable thing about him was his aura. It shone around him like the corona of a dying star about to go supernova, so bright it hurt to look at it. It stretched away from him in all directions and faded into the distance, pure, bright gold.

Like mine.

The Sentinel of Tokyo whipped his naginata around him, cleaving off another streetlamp and neatly slicing a row of bicycles in half. His eyes burned with furious light and searched the alley, seeming to gloss over me and Fiona.

The Pearl in my chest pulled toward him and pulsed in time with his aura. I pressed a hand against my chest, unnerved by the sensation.

This man was a Sentinel but he also appeared dangerously unhinged.

Unhinged or not, I couldn't let this chance pass me by. I inched closer, keeping my hand near Hachi's grip and making sure to stay outside the arc of Tokyo's massive polearm. His knuckles whitened as his hands clenched spastically on the naginata. Sweat rained off his bedraggled hair as he whipped his head back and forth, eyes darting up and down the alley.

I kept my eyes off his hands, and instead watched his hips and shoulders, waiting for him to make a move. With that naginata, his reach outstripped mine by at least a meter.

I pitched my voice low and soothing. "Thank you for your help."

"Help?"

Tokyo's eyes dimmed and his lips trembled. He began speaking in a droning monotone, a mush of sounds and words. I barely picked out one word in twenty. His eyes looked everywhere and nowhere. His arms went rigid, his massive hands clenched into fists nearly the size of my head, knuckles white with strain.

Tokyo's voice reduced to a bare whisper as if he was being choked off. A chill rolled down my back as I made out what he was saying.

". . . help help help help help . . ."

I leaned forward and a blast of power slammed me in the chest and threw me onto my back. Tokyo's eyes flashed fire bright, the shine of mania back again. He leapt to his feet and snatched his naginata up.

"You can't stop me!"

He slammed the butt of the naginata into the sidewalk. The neon tube exploded in light that bleached out every other light in the alley, turning early evening into an alien, purple high noon. When my eyes cleared I caught the flash of his armor disappearing around the corner at the end of the street.

Fiona grabbed my arm. "Was that . . . ?"

That was a rhetorical question. The Sentinel's aura had been a golden nimbus signaling to all Jiārén his status.

I hated to leave her, but she already had an entire entourage waiting at the rendezvous. I didn't think the assassin would make a reappearance now. "I'll catch up with you later."

I slung my bags across my back and bolted down the narrow street. I put on a burst of speed as I hit the main road. Tokyo was somewhere ahead of me. He had disappeared into the crowds of evening pedestrians, but the Pearl in my chest told me exactly what direction I needed to follow him.

After nearly having my head taken off by the assassin's shadow . . . things, a run was just the thing to burn off the excess adrenaline. The route took me roughly south through Shibuya. My muscles warmed to the run and I picked my way along the streets, dodging rush-hour traffic, running along row after row of high-rise apartment buildings. The urban perfume of car exhaust and sun-baked concrete hung thick in the humid air. If Tokyo knew I was following him, he wasn't giving any indication. He continued to head south, keeping up the brisk pace, but not speeding up.

I consulted my memories of the city and decided on a likely destination. It wasn't far. If my guess was right, I would catch him when he arrived. I picked up the pace and began cutting east. My route took me along the western edge of Aoyama cemetery. The faintest scent of cherry blossoms and cut grass wafted over the street from the cemetery.

The tug of the Pearl aimed me like an arrow to my destination just ahead. The Tokyo Metro Central Library. The Library was situated on a small hill, hidden behind a dense wall of cherry and plum trees. I sprinted the last two hundred meters and slammed through the outer glass doors. My Pearl thudded in time with my heart, pulling me further into the Library. There were very few people, and those who were here stared at me in disbelief.

I rushed past them and through the vaulted lobby, an open space with towering ceilings that reminded me quite a bit of the San Francisco Library. My instincts brought me to an alcove in the rear of the Library. A slender young woman dressed in a white Swiss-dot blouse tucked into a sleek black pencil skirt stood behind a small desk, tidying up. Her long brown hair was pulled back with a red leather headband.

At the sound of my footsteps, she spoke without looking up. "I'm sorry, but the Library is closing soon."

The woman's absent tone told me I needed to get her attention. I let my aura go big. "I think you'll find time for me. I need to follow the man who just entered."

I figured my aura wasn't solid gold, now that I'd left my city again. The Librarian's confused expression told me that my guess was correct. But it apparently had enough gold in it that after a moment, her eyes widened in shock as they traced an outline around my head. The book she'd been holding slipped out of her hand and crashed to the desk and she stammered.

Well, this was quite a bit different from the treatment I got back home. I decided to take pity on her. It wasn't every day that you ran into two Sentinels. Even if you were a Librarian.

"Just show me the door. I'll find my own way."

The woman lifted a trembling hand up, pointing to an ornate bookshelf on the back wall. "Mr. Tanaka went that way."

Was it a coincidence that Tokyo's Sentinel was a Tanaka? I thanked her and crossed the room. The bookshelf slid open as I approached, revealing a small metal gate, a twin to the one at San Francisco's public library. I waved to the stunned Librarian again as I opened the gate and stepped into the waiting elevator.

The elevator dropped like a stone, leaving my stomach in the lobby before mercifully opening on the sub-ninth level. Just like under the San Francisco Library, the elevator opened onto a dark tunnel. Instead of being hewn from rough bedrock, the tunnel I found myself in was the smooth bore of poured concrete. Graffiti decorated the walls in several languages. It took a moment to register that I was in an abandoned subway tunnel, with dim light at the far end. I followed the tunnel until it dead-ended in a widened space that held a round door set into the concrete. A round stone door that looked very similar to the one I could not open in San Francisco. But this door was ajar and light shone through the opening.

I edged through the door and into a library of dreams. The space was a massive half dome, the ceiling arcing up into the distance. Light shone from the stone floor just inside the open door. The room disappeared into darkness in all directions, the walls gently curving inward. More closed circular doors dotted the outer wall in long intervals. I sensed that somewhere along the wall, one of these doors led to San Francisco.

This had to be the Archive, the place I had failed to enter back home.

Waist-high bookshelves drew concentric circles that marched toward the center of the room. The closest shelves to me held volumes with arcane titles such as *Clan Power as a Function of Qì Density* and *Shēnzhèn's Compendium of Lost Artifacts, vol. 138.*

A break in the shelves provided a path through the Library. The ethereal glowing yellow light from the stone floor followed the path inward. I walked slowly along the lighted stone, looking for signs of the Tokyo Sentinel.

As I made my way farther into the Archive, the books began to show signs of wear and age. I spotted *Shēnzhèn's Compendium,* volumes 126 and 124, with an empty space marking the missing book. The shadows dimmed and I turned to find the lit stone fading behind me. I rushed forward to stay within the light.

I found Tokyo curled into a ball on the floor at the center of the brightest light. I had lost count of the number of shelves I had passed. The ones here were made of lacquered rosewood and carved with intricate designs of lotus blooms and rearing horses. The books were ancient, bound in animal hides, the pages yellowed with age. I squinted into the darkness at the center of the Archive, wondering how far it went, and what I would find there.

Tokyo clutched at his shoulders, his arms hugging his broad chest and his eyes shut. His red armor lay scattered on the floor, the naginata laid carefully across the tops of the nearest shelves. His ragged breathing echoed off the far walls and finally slowed and settled into a steady rhythm.

Lore of the Sentinels had been difficult to find, and most of what I found was dubious at best. Even after taking the mantle, I had not considered the possibility of meeting another Sentinel. I should have realized that stepping foot in another's city wouldn't go unnoticed.

The naginata drew my eyes like a magnet. The weapon was massive, the heavy blade worn and notched, but still bearing the gleam that spoke of proper care. My hand came up of its own volition and hovered over the dark wood. Even at a distance, the power of this weapon warmed my palm as surely as any fire. What would it be like to wield this beast? My senses crackled as I imagined feeling the heft of this blade in my hands.

A weary voice croaked from behind me. "Please don't touch it."

"Of course not. I would not want to offend."

Tokyo opened his eyes and levered himself up to sit seiza, his hands resting heavily on his thighs. He looked me up and down, taking in the space above my head and also the streak in my hair. "You're so young."

Outside the train station, his eyes had been wild, fever bright with the kind of panic I associated with trapped and wounded animals. Here he was calm, his gaze sharp and direct. Now he reminded me of Ogata-sensei, brimming with violence just beneath an outwardly undisturbed surface.

"I didn't realize there was an age limit to become a Sentinel."

"I'm not talking about you as a person. I'm talking about your city."

Shuffling footsteps crept toward us out of the dark and we both turned to look in that direction. A dull orange glow emerged from the darkness, moving our way in slow lurches. Gu Ma materialized from the gloom, shuffling behind her battered walker. A crooked cigarette dangled from her lips and a thin trail of smoke curled around her gray hair.

Gu Ma coughed, the sound thick and wet in her chest. "Yes, too young by far. And also not supposed to be in the Archive!"

Thick, smothering power burst from Gu Ma as she spoke, her voice rising with her anger. I fell back a step and stumbled against a bookshelf. A blast of force slammed into my back, throwing me to the floor. My head hit the flagstones and sunbursts exploded across my vision.

Tokyo's voice swam out of the ringing in my ears. "Gu Ma! She's my guest! I let her in!"

Gu Ma's stifling power faded and I gasped air into my lungs again. When had I stopped breathing? Tokyo's and Gu Ma's voices warbled, the words distorted into meaningless noise. I rolled onto my hands and knees and gagged.

The tennis ball–clad feet of Gu Ma's walker stopped in front of my hands. The old woman bent down, sticking her smoking cigarette in my face. She snapped her fingers and my ears popped, sound returning to normal. "Hmph. You're lucky Oda invited you. Don't think this gets you a pass when you return to San Francisco."

She put one bony finger on my forehead. "Do better."

My skin burned where her finger touched me. The scraping sound of the walker edged away from me. I looked up in time to see Gu Ma's feet, clad in threadbare pink house slippers, disappear into the darkness again.

Oda helped me to my feet. "Don't let her scare you. She likes you, you know."

I rubbed at my forehead. Whatever power Gu Ma had, it had done a number on my head, and she probably hadn't even hit me with all of it. "She's got a great way of showing it."

"Well, she didn't kill you."

"Funny, I had that same thought in San Francisco."

Oda's bushy eyebrows drew down in sharp lines. "You couldn't open the Archive."

"How did you know?"

"The books."

He pointed to the shelf behind me, where the books glowed with power, a faint line of green from floor to ceiling. The books I'd fallen against were dull, as if camouflaged for Wàirén eyes.

"The Archive has not recognized you yet because you have not opened your door. If you wish to return here on your own terms, and benefit from the knowledge stored here, you must open your door."

"Or Gu Ma will kill me."

He shrugged, the movement like a mountain shifting. "Possibly. But she never gave anyone else a second try. So she must favor you."

I had no idea what to say to that.

Oda held out a hand. "Maybe I can help."

I fought my gut instinct to pull away. The wreckage of my meridians and qì was not something I shared. The only person outside of my family who had ever done this was Popo, and she was family in every sense but name.

But I needed to open the Archive, and here was an actual Sentinel standing in front of me. Would I ever get this chance again?

His hand was twice the size of mine, with thick, calloused fingers that looked like they could punch through concrete. But when I put my hand in his, his touch was light and gentle, as if he were handling a dried flower. Tokyo turned my hand over and traced his fingertips along the inside of my wrist before pressing on my pulse. It took everything in me to not snatch my hand out of his.

Oda's qì brushed against mine and sent a thrill of electricity down my spine.

He grunted. "Why are you like that?"

"Like what?"

"Broken."

The old reflex kicked again. "I'm not broken."

He mumbled something unintelligible and continued to examine me.

"I. Am not. Broken."

I yanked my hand, but his grasp stayed firm. The Tokyo Sentinel's words stirred long-buried emotions deep in my belly that I failed to suppress. First Iron Serpent, and now this Sentinel ripping off my old scab, exhuming my anxiety and insecurity. Mother and Father's faces loomed up out of the depths of memory, their brows creased with worry and disappointment.

Old anger and hurt burst forth and sent a flash of heat over my body. I snarled and bared my teeth, dropping my weight into my knees.

Whatever Oda was looking for, my answer didn't seem to be it. He continued to study me, his head tipped to the side, one meaty paw still wrapped around my wrist as he started mumbling under his breath.

It was like he wasn't hearing me at all.

Well, I didn't need his assessment.

My other hand lashed out, ready to jab into a nerve strike to free my hand. I launched myself forward and I aimed low. He released my hand and took a step back to avoid my strike. With my hand free, I instinctively reached for Hachi, readying to slash my way free.

Steel rang out and my arm nearly jerked out of its socket as Hachi stopped in midswing. Oda's naginata had jumped to his hand from the bookshelf behind him. Hachi's blade bit into the dark wood of the handle a bare millimeter, the sword still vibrating from the impact.

In that split second of my shock, he closed the remaining distance between us.

His finger touched the scar on my chest where San Francisco had marked the Pearl inside me. Hachi dropped from my nerveless hands but I barely registered that as blinding light filled my vision and my world exploded.

My world is filled with gnawing hunger and white smoke. The hunger consumes me from within, and everywhere the while smoke touches me, there is sharp, cold pain. The only warmth I feel is two hands on my chest that push me to the ground, that keep me from twisting away from the pain.

My mother's voice pleads, "Gomen ne . . ."

The pain sinks through my skin, into my flesh. As it melds into me, the aching hunger in my belly fades. The pain is a part of me now, as essential as my bones and blood. I envelop the pain and hold it close.

Two more hands appear and brush away my mother's hands.

I can't fight them, the hands plunge into my belly and grasp at my pain, but it twists and writhes like a serpent. No! The pain is precious to me, it is a part of me!

The hands are relentless. They draw the pain from my body and all that is left of me is a hollow shell.

My eyes sprang open. The dark stone vault of the Archive roof was above me and the cold stone floor pressed into my shoulder blades. Moving as little as possible I reassessed my surroundings. I didn't understand how he had moved so fast, or how he'd called his naginata into his hand in time to block my strike.

The Archive was silent, except for the harsh sound of my breathing. As my heart settled, the faintest brush of movement nearby tickled my senses. It had to be Tokyo's Sentinel. I stretched my senses, trying to determine where he was before I made my move. My legs tensed, ready to kick me off the floor.

A new sensation derailed my thoughts of finding Oda. My arms and legs vibrated with energy, like I'd touched a live wire. I relaxed, and the sensation ebbed, flowing into my dantien where it pooled like cool water. When I readied myself again, my limbs lit up, energy flowing through them like warm water.

My breath hitched in surprise.

Impossible.

I levered myself up on an elbow and found Hachi at my side, cushioned on an old, but serviceable, cloth to protect her from the stone floor. There wasn't even an extra fingerprint on her. I picked her up and resheathed her.

Oda sat seiza a few feet from me, his naginata laid across his legs, his eyes closed. His lips moved soundlessly and his eyes darted back and forth under his lids. Small tremors shook his arms and hands and sweat beaded on his broad forehead.

I sat seiza as well, across from him, and tried to make sense of things. I hardly dared to consider what had happened.

I pulled out a trick from long ago and let my eyes relax, my lids coming down halfway. This way I could enter a more meditative state while still keeping an eye on Tokyo. I went back to the beginning and focused on my breathing, visualizing my qì flowing through me, and in and out of the world around me.

The differences were easy to spot, once I looked for them. My qì moved through me with an ease I had not thought possible. Using what little talent I possessed had always been hard work, a source of frustration when I watched others accomplish so much more with less effort.

Even my breathing was easier as I concentrated on it. Everything felt lighter. Constricting bands that had held me down before had been removed. I inhaled, and air and qì flowed to my core, lighting up my nerves with crackling energy. I followed the flow of energy and found myself plunging into a blazing sphere of fiery power.

His eyes snapped open. "Don't fight it. The Pearl is your conduit to your city's power."

My qì brushed against the Pearl, just the lightest touch, and my senses exploded again, sound and light crashing over me like a rogue wave of ice-cold sea water. I pulled back and normality slowly bled back into the world. I took a long, shuddering breath.

Oda grunted. "Yes, it can be a little overwhelming, the first time."

I approached the Pearl again, even more slowly. As my qì surrounded it, the same thrilling energy ignited, flushing my skin. I kept my qì at a distance, like staying just far enough from a roaring fire. My skin tingled from the alternating sensations of the gentle warmth of the San Francisco sunlight and the harsh rasp of the salty breeze off the bay.

It felt like home and pulled me in as surely as a magnet. As I drew closer, power surged through me like a bolt of lightning. When I had left San Francisco, it had been like a sheet was pulled over my senses, blunting my perception of the world. The Pearl ripped that away and returned everything to full color and stereo sound. I lunged toward the Pearl, eager to regain my Sentinel senses and power.

Oda put a hand on my shoulder. "Stop."

I opened my eyes and the extraordinary sensations ebbed like low tide.

"I have shown you a path, but you need to go back to your city to explore it. I don't know what Gu Ma was thinking. A Sentinel usually spends weeks in the Archive at first, learning to understand and control their powers."

At last, someone who had real information about Sentinels. "I'd appreciate whatever you can tell me."

"Not much. The Sentinel experience is defined not only by our city, but also by who we are. The city shapes us as much as we shape the city. I only know this because the woman who stood for Tokyo before me told me such."

He pointed at my chest again. "I can tell you this. Your Pearl is not mature. When ready, it is a store of your city's power, allowing you access to a limited amount of your authority outside of your city, to be drawn on if needed. Yours is not ready."

He was close enough that our knees nearly touched. His dark eyes focused on mine, the light behind them clear and steady. The eyes of a man in control of himself. His lips twisted into a bare grimace. A far cry from the way he looked at the station.

Embarrassment at my earlier behavior washed over me. He'd managed to find my weakness with uncanny precision. The same way Iron Serpent had. It made me wonder how I'd managed all those years as the Blade, with cool disdain in the face of so many Jiārén taunts. It was like becoming the Sentinel had robbed me of my old shields, reshaping me from the inside out. Leaving me raw and vulnerable.

And now this unexpected boon from the Tokyo Sentinel. I sat up slowly and bowed my head in gratitude.

"May I ask what you did?"

His brow creased. "There was an old pain inside you. It would have interfered with your duties as a Sentinel. That is all I will say."

My world spun. For the first time in my life, my qì flowed as easily as water flowing downhill. What would this feel like when I got back to San Francisco?

Thoughts of home brought me back to earth. I wasn't here on vacation, and I hadn't ended up at the Tokyo Metro Library on a whim.

"I have an assassin trying to kill me and mine, if you hadn't noticed. She followed me here from San Francisco."

Oda grunted. "I notice everything in my city. I wouldn't worry too much about the dark walker. At the rate she's using her blood jade, she'll be dead in a few days."

Well, that was interesting. If he was right, my job had just gotten a lot easier. Fiona still wanted the player behind the assassin, though. If the assassin was dead, then things got harder. "I need your help to find her. You don't want an assassin running around in your city any more than I did."

Oda got off his knees and bent to pick up his armor, setting the pieces on a nearby table in orderly fashion. He turned away from me and began wiping down the armor with an oiled cloth. "You're right. But I can't help you."

He put down the oil cloth and turned to look around the Archive as if seeing it for the first time. "You're so young. You don't understand . . . and I envy that. I must stay here in the Archive, if I am to help my city. Outside . . ."

His eyes darted toward the outer wall and the open door leading back to Tokyo. "Being a Sentinel is a burden you can never put down. And outside . . . I am not the person I used to be."

He took a long breath and returned to oiling his armor. "Today was the first time I've left the Archive in decades. I sensed your arrival and I had to know. Even if the worst were to happen, I had to know. It's been so long . . ."

He turned to me, his eyes full of pain and loss. Was this what I had to look forward to? What had happened to cause him to shut himself away?

"I still need to find the dark walker. I have people depending on me."

"That is the way of the Sentinel. Much responsibility," Oda mumbled.

I nodded in agreement, hoping he would change his mind.

Oda's face brightened. "Come. Let me show you this. I don't think Gu Ma would mind."

I scrambled to my feet to follow him.

He put down his armor and led me back to the circular door in the outer wall. Once we entered the abandoned subway tunnel Oda moved to the right-hand wall, gliding his hand over the graffitied concrete. He stopped at a black and red symbol. A black circle with a red center, with six black arms radiating out from the edge of the circle.

He pointed at the sun emblem. "Touch here."

I placed my hand on the sun and my skin tingled. The concrete of the wall sagged and flowed like water, revealing a small square room beyond the wall. Oda gestured for me to enter the room and I stepped in.

When I turned back, the concrete flowed back up, blocking my return. I bolted but Oda's qì flared, holding me in place. As he spoke the concrete closed off the room. "I must stay in the Archive. If you need me, invoke my emblem, and if I can, I will help you."

Darkness swallowed me as the room sealed shut. I felt a sickening moment of vertigo and then light reappeared. I was standing outside the Tokyo Metro Library next to a bus stop. On the wall in front of me, a six-pointed sun was spray-painted on the building.

I slapped my hand back onto the painted sun icon but this time I felt nothing. Pressing my hand harder into the wall only gave my skin a pebbly texture from the concrete. I'd finally met another Sentinel and he'd shooed me out of the Archive like a guest who'd overstayed her welcome.

There was no guarantee I would ever be allowed in the Archive again. This had been my chance to learn more about being a Sentinel, but nothing had ever come this easily in my life. Why would it start for me now? I held my hand to the wall for another moment before giving up on it. Whatever was going on in Tokyo's head, he wasn't going to let me back in until he was ready.

There was nothing else I could do for now. My meridians were clear for the first time in my life and a mysterious weight had been lifted from my shoulders. I felt as if I could float off the ground. I would take this as a win.

I shouldered my gear and called Fiona. When she picked up I heard soft J-pop music in the background over muffled road noise. She'd made it to her ride.

"Fiona, sorry about that. I couldn't let him get away."

It wasn't a great look, running out on her at the train station, but even if I never saw the Tokyo Sentinel again, I'd learned enough from him to make the snub worth it.

Fiona's voice lowered to a dramatic whisper. "Was that who I think it was?"

"Yeah . . ."

The extended silence was proof enough that even the Tran princess could be shocked. It was . . . nice. Her stunned silence reminded me that she was almost the same age as me, and clearly wore a lot of emotional armor to lead her clan the way she did.

I'd come with her to Tokyo to help protect her from the nameless assassin and instead Fiona's crew had been the ones to save my dumplings in the end.

"Fiona, I'm sorry about your bodyguard."

And just like that, the armor went back on. "Pia understood the risks. She did her job. She will be honored for it."

"Of course. I'm in your debt."

Debts were a dangerous thing among Jiārén. Dangerously close to Talons, blood debts between families that transcended generations. My mother had traded a Talon to the shinigami to save my life and my father's. That same Talon bound me to find the Ebony Gate. Whenever Talons appeared, lives hung in the balance.

Fiona's voice was tight. "Find the killer for me and we're even."

Yes, the killer who seemed to have an intensely personal bone to pick with me. Every instinct I'd honed over the years was screaming at me. Whatever this was, it was moments away from blowing up in my face.

"I'm working on it, Fiona. But this isn't going to end well."

"No, especially if you keep sticking me with cleanup."

It was my turn to be silent. Because she wasn't wrong; I'd left the scene of her bodyguard's brutal murder, in the middle of a huge population of Wàirén. I could only imagine the number of people needed to maintain the First Law in a situation like that. Luckily, Fiona wasn't in the mood to let me twist in the wind.

"My team sanitized the alley. All the Wàirén have been cleaned as well. But cleaning up after you is getting old, Mimi."

And yet she kept doing it for me. I wondered if I wasn't growing on her, the same way Freddy had grown on me.

It had to be tough for her, to have no peers within her clan. The face she wore to maintain order had to be like when I'd carried the Blade. The office forced a numbness on you, made you feel less, so you could do more, sacrificing your own life for the lives of others. With that kind of weight on her shoulders, there were only so many ways Fiona could express her gratitude.

"I appreciate it. And don't call me Mimi."

HOMECOMING

My parents had settled in Atami in Shizuoka prefecture, about an hour and half from Tokyo. Father missed Shanghai and liked the east-facing water view that reminded him of his childhood home.

The train ride down from Tokyo gave me plenty of time to ready myself for dealing with Father. I needed to prepare for this as surely as any physical conflict, and I was two years out of practice.

But first, I was starving. I ripped open the Kit Kats in my fanny pack. Sakura. Delicate pink chocolate. Thin crispy cookie wafers light as air. I bit down and let out a low moan of bliss. I looked around but everybody was wearing headphones and studiously ignoring me. I polished off the bag. It was so good. Some genmaicha to wash it down would have been nice. Tea always made everything better.

I should have bought more. This haul wouldn't last me my stay in Tokyo. I wouldn't have any left by the time I had to return to San Francisco.

This was all distraction, of course. I was only delaying the inevitable. Two years ago I ran out on my family and my duty, and shattered a priceless sword in the process. In retrospect it had been naive of me to assume that something as simple as the wide expanse of the Pacific Ocean would keep Father from keeping tabs on me.

My freedom had been a carefully crafted illusion. And now I was going back to clanhome to face the music.

Dealing with my father had been simple when I wore the mantle of the Blade. He gave orders and I carried them out. The relationship between the Head and the Blade was all-consuming. The ties had smoothed my emotions out into an even layer of textureless bean paste. After I broke away, years of pent-up emotions fell upon me, with interest. Even phone calls with my father were torturous.

Every interaction with him now was a delicate dance across a floor covered in broken glass. When he asked how I was doing, was he trying to manipulate me? Bend me to his will? I never doubted that Father had the clan's best interests at heart, just that his methods for pushing me in that direction weren't necessarily what I would have chosen.

Coming home now was especially fraught. With my brother's Lóng Yá, tension between Hoard Guardian families would be high as each family muscled for prominence. My father was sure to have plans within plans already laid out, and he would undoubtedly include me.

What would Father ask me to do?

The better question was: once I was standing before him, could I even say no?

I pressed my fingers to the Pearl in my chest and a cool rush of salt wind fluttered over my arms. It reminded me of standing on Highway 1 and looking out over the crashing waves. Whatever the Tokyo Sentinel had done, my connection to San Francisco felt awakened, despite being an ocean away. Oda had said I needed to spend more time in the Archive. Had that been his place of learning as well? Until he'd returned to the Archive, he had been wildly erratic, like someone enduring too much stimulation. Had he managed to temper it by finding refuge in the Archive?

Was Oda's current state my future?

Clinging to my sanity by exiling myself under the Library?

I recalled the times the city had bludgeoned me with its power. It had been something I endured. As I grew closer to my city, I found it easier to exert a measure of control. But what if that push and pull never ended?

What exactly was I paying to be the Sentinel?

What would Father say?

My limbs chilled and my mind ran in circles around these questions I couldn't answer. I leaned my head against the window and watched the countryside pass in a blur. My eyes lost focus and the gentle hum of the bullet train lulled me to sleep as it hurtled me back into the arms of my family.

The Soong estate boasted nearly two acres, its sleek modern architecture nestled tightly into the hillside. Visiting dignitaries, vendors, and other Wàirén saw the sprawling expanse of real estate with its meticulous gardens and never suspected that it was a mere shell that contained the true pearl of the Soong clanhome.

I walked up the hilly path to the front gate and punched in my keycode. The iron gate unlocked with a buzz and I stepped onto the Soong estate for the first time in over two years. Unlike the Tran château, there were no drones overhead, no cameras on the gates, and no staff milling about. Just elegant maples swaying in a gentle breeze to witness my homecoming. It was strangely anticlimactic.

Even without the magic of San Francisco humming through me, each step I took felt charged. My body, my blood, and even Hachi knew this place. It called me softly and grew steadily louder until it was a loud hum through my skull. The empty space at my shoulder felt naked and exposed to the judgment of my ancestors.

Red double doors with half-moon door pulls greeted me at the top of the path. I pushed forward on the right handle. Unlocked.

I shivered as I stepped into the chill of the entryway and slipped my sneakers off in the genkan. Rather than leave my shoes in the recessed flooring of the genkan, I hooked my fingers into them and carried them in.

The interior blended the austere edges of modern architecture with traditional Japanese touches. White Carrara marble floor tiles in the entryway gave way to woven tatami in the living room. Handmade windowpane shoji lanterns cast the house in soft illumination.

A sleek console table of petrified wood stood on my left, framed on both sides by shoji. Freshly cut pink peonies floated in a silver bowl filled with clear water. Mother's favorite flowers. I slid a shoji screen on the right wall to reveal the shoe shelving and tucked my sneakers there. The last row on the shoe shelf had uwabaki for guests. I pulled down the house slippers and of course, Fujita-san had made sure there was a pair my size there. Fujita-san managed the household like a precision watch.

I slid the shoji screen to the left of the console table to hang my haori. The spacious closet contained a single item. A charcoal-dyed samue. I pulled it out and ran my fingers over the intricate pink embroidery of the phoenix that spanned the back of the linen jacket. The silk thread gleamed in the low light. Again, Fujita-san remembered what I preferred to wear when home.

All at once the soft touches reminded me that chains were still chains, even when they were shaped from love and duty.

I wrapped the jacket around me, the smell of the crisp linen blend evoking a host of conflicting memories. Competitively eating dumplings for breakfast with my brother. Sparring in the courtyard with Kubota-san. Picking fat peaches in the garden with Lulu Āyí. Kneeling at Father's feet, taking orders.

Despite that conflict, everything felt familiar, and dangerous in its comfort. Even walking across the tatami was a welcome sensation, down to the soft sound of my slippers against the woven straw. The living room had little in the way of furniture but the walls sported dazzling displays of swords from the last several centuries. Adam would be envious. My father was the type of collector who felt no need to share his collection with a museum, not when they were so much more useful here, at the seat of his power.

The seating area had cushions and a low table with a hand-carved Go set on top of it, the black and white pieces like small soldiers awaiting their orders. Beyond the living room, the house opened to an entertainment area with sliding doors out to the balcony with a view of the ocean.

I dropped my bags onto the floor, the distressed canvas looking out of place among the elegant decor.

The showpiece of the lounge was the bar. To the left of the bar, two noren curtain panels emblazoned with a pink phoenix covered a hallway.

A tall water feature rose behind the bar, flowing from cut black bamboo recessed into the west wall. Above, a coffered ceiling housed a flock of bronze origami cranes dangled from wires, as if in midflight. The cranes were my mother's clan emblem. The cranes were all over our estate, a tribute to the Hiroto legacy and my mother's anchor.

I moved to the fountain, where a pair of stone turtles sat placidly at the base. I picked up the right one, which fit perfectly into the palm of my hand. Father imbued his animation talent into these carvings, and his power left behind the nose-twitching smell of pepper and sawdust. The familiar gesture made my throat tighten. This would let me cross over. Once I was in the Realm pocket, Father could replenish Bāo's animation magic. I missed Bāo terribly. I thought about the cost and closed my eyes. Nothing was free with Father. But it was worth it to have my foo lion back.

I turned away from the bar and the fountain to gaze out at the panoramic view of the ocean. Just one moment more and I'd be truly back in the Soong's seat of power.

A moment was all I got.

Sensing movement from behind me, I crouched low and spun. My attacker kicked out from the top of the bar, two feet aimed squarely at my head. Adrenaline electrified my limbs. I reached out and yanked his ankle with my left hand, readying the stone turtle with my right. He yelped and scrambled but I twisted the fabric of his joggers and brought my weight down, pinning him to the bar. My arm arced down, aiming to smash the stone into my attacker's kneecap when the scent of pepper stung my nose.

Skies grant me patience.

I grunted and dropped the turtle with a thud to the tatami. Releasing his pant leg I took a step back. "Tacchan, I could have hurt you."

Tatsuya dropped off the bar and yanked his waistband up. He was several inches taller than me now. When had that happened?

His round cheeks creased with dimples as he smiled.

"Could have hurt you back."

I looked up. The bronze cranes hung in the air around me, quivering, sharp beaks all pointing in my direction. I looked over my shoulder at the living room. Two of the swords floated in midair, aimed at my back. All of the black and white Go pieces hovered above the board, ready to fly at me like an angry swarm.

Always fun and games at the Soong House.

Any strong kinetic talent could do this. My father and Tatsuya's talent was a step beyond, animating objects to act independently. Even if Tacchan went down in combat, his animates would continue to attack.

His eyes were mirrors of mine, framed with sooty dark lashes and straight slashing brows. I could see now that he really took after our mother, but the round cheeks and square jaw were strictly from Father. Unlike our father who wore his hair high and tight, Tatsuya now had long waves on top, his inky hair as glossy as a K-pop boy band member.

I pulled him in for a tight hug. Skies, there was so much more of him in my arms now. But of all the people I could have run into first, I was glad it was my little brother. His arms squeezed down on me until I almost gasped for breath. I broke the hug and punched him in the shoulder. The hit was good, but my brother was a lot more solid than I remembered. He had the grace to wince.

"Tatsuya, you're not twelve anymore. You can't just sneak-attack me just to see how I'll react."

Tatsuya waved absently and the swords flew back to their mounts. The Go pieces clattered back to the board and the cranes resumed their previous random arrangement. "I needed to know if you still have it."

My lips thinned out as annoyance chased by embarrassment rose in my throat. "I'm rusty now. I don't train like I used to."

I hadn't seen the need to once I'd broken Truth. Also, on a more practical note, I didn't have Uncle Lau and his militia to train with anymore. I'd left all of that behind, or at least, I'd tried to. Yet here I was, dancing to my father's tune as well as Fiona's. And my little brother thought I needed testing.

That realization grated.

Tacchan shook his head. "No, you're still fast. Really fast."

He hadn't seen me barely hold my own against Fiona's assassin.

Tatsuya pointed at Hachi on my hip, his dark eyes intent. "That's why I wanted you to come home. I need you to help me get ready for Lóng Yá. No one else here is as fast as you are."

I had failed out of Lóng Kǒu after only one year, a powerless embarrassment to my family. And yet my brother felt that my years as the brutal Blade of Soong were merit enough to train him.

Tatsuya held my hand, so I put the stone turtle back on the fountain and slung my bags over my shoulder. He pushed aside the noren curtains and we stepped through. His aura flashed, the same cool blue-green of Father's talent, but with streaks of yellow. The room shimmered as we walked to our true clanhome. The hallway dissolved, giving way to tall bamboo reeds that shaded us, woven into a braided archway that obscured the sky. The tatami vanished and became a path of golden bricks from Suzhou.

My brother's talent warmed me, flowing from our joined hands and up through my arm to my chest. It shielded me from the normal nausea of a Crossing. Coming out in the Realm pocket here dialed up my senses to eleven, as if I had been sleepwalking before. The air smelled of peach blossoms, and even the bamboo was a vibrant green that shone like wet paint. It was oddly silent though, with only the sound of swaying bamboo and our own footsteps.

Stone rabbits peeked through the dense vegetation, and occasionally a steel fox. After fifty meters or so, a heavy fog rose and obscured everything but a massive ivory stag that cut across the pathway. The stag turned toward us, his crown of antlers sharp and menacing. Father's welcome committee.

Tatsuya went to the left and I headed right, each of us raising a hand to one of the stag's sharp points. Blood welled from my palm and ran down the ivory antler. Red stained the ivory for a moment then faded. The bamboo reeds fell away and the stag leapt up and vanished into the darkening sky.

The Soong clanhome was revealed, an enormous structure rising three stories from the mist, the impossible sun setting behind it in a vivid splash of pink against a sky of deep violet.

Before us loomed a pair of enormous white marble foo lions on either side of the stairs. The female foo lion had a pup with her. The male foo lion on the right was newer and less worn by the elements. It was a more recent installation, a replacement for the one I now wore around my neck. They didn't move, but it felt like their eyes watched us. Knowing Father, that was probably the case.

Suddenly I wasn't so eager to go inside.

"Tacchan, tell me what you're dealing with at Lóng Yá."

He stopped and ran a nervous hand through his fluffy mop. "I've got no issues with making top eight. But at least five other students to worry about after running the maze."

I picked up a stick and drew two bisecting lines into the dirt. I labeled the quadrants clockwise, from the upper left: Tiger, Tortoise, Dragon, Bird. "Okay, group their talent class."

Tatsuya and Father's talent placed them into the overlap between Vermillion Bird and the bigger class of Azure Dragon talents. Jiārén with a Dragon talent manifested early, their simple kinetics easily demonstrable. Most combat houses like ours had a disproportionate number of Dragon talents. They used their qì to push the world around them, either as element control or, like my mother, to rip the very fabric of the world apart.

Bird talents sent their qì out into the world and altered the very fabric of reality. The rarest Bird talents of all had been the Jin Clan. The Jins could transmute base metals into the unique gold we used for our Talons and so many Hoard pieces. The entire clan, loyal to the Dragons to the end, had stayed behind as the Realm had descended into chaos and fire. Not one was believed to have survived.

White Tiger talents were second in number to Dragon talents, with the power to augment or control their bodies. Commonly Dragon Limbs, Steel Fists, or Dragon Sight. Regardless of their talent, they would all lean on it to amplify some form of physical attack. It was hard to argue against pounding your opponent into the dirt if your fists could punch through walls. However, these were the easiest group to counter. Focusing their training to maximize a narrow talent just ensured that they were vulnerable in a myriad of ways.

Black Tortoise talents were the most frightening to me because they could manipulate the minds or perceptions of others. The Louies were a good example of that. Advocate Leung was a unique intersection of Tiger and Tortoise, and had used her mind to render my body into a receptive state where my memories could be unlocked and shared. It was a deeply invasive and disturbing talent.

He marked the quadrants. "Here, here, here, and here."

I nodded. "Okay, we'll have to work on your strategies for defense and offense with these specific opponents."

He frowned. "I wish you didn't call them that."

"That's what they are now. You aren't friends for this tourney." And I didn't know if they would be afterward, either. My heart broke a little for him. There would be no going back after Lóng Yá.

And looking at the Soong mansion before us, and my father within, I didn't think there was any going back for me, either.

"Can we go to the courtyard?"

Tatsuya shrugged and we deposited my bags onto the porch, then veered north to the garden gates. Tall peach trees heavy with lush blossoms lined the walkway through the side yard. I breathed in deeply, enjoying the light fragrance that I hadn't realized I'd missed.

Lulu Āyí's talent meant that the fruit trees bloomed regardless of season and heart-shaped hachiya persimmons hung heavy from the trees closest to the courtyard. Father's head chef, Huang si-fu, had learned to make hoshigaki for Mother, hanging and drying the persimmons, then massaging them each day, breaking down the fruit until it was a velvety texture and sugar bloomed over the skin a month later. Just thinking about it made my teeth ache.

As we walked, a chorus of banging and clashing reached us, along with shouted orders. Though night was falling, Uncle Lau hadn't excused his soldiers. My blood quickened at the familiar, dissonant music of weapons training.

We came around the side of the house and the rear courtyard opened wide before us, an expanse of golden stone and fat round lanterns lighting the way. Tall píxiū guardians loomed over all four corners of the courtyard, their stone wingspans as wide as a truck. I'd always loved the way they looked, like massive versions of Bāo but with antlers, wings, and a much more ferocious aspect.

Soldiers wearing jackets like mine and loose black pants sparred in the courtyard. I counted twenty, with the smooth movements and precision of Father's elite soldiers. These were the Iron Fists, early strikers who smoothed the way for the Pearl Guard. Uncle Lau led the Iron Fists and Kubota-san led the Pearl Guard battalion.

This wasn't wartime, but Soongs always trained to be combat ready. We were a small house and couldn't afford to be seen as anything less than a strong one.

Uncle Lau bounded up above the soldiers, his rotund frame defying gravity as he issued commands from the air. His amber aura was tinged with red, brilliant in the light of the paper lanterns.

His grasshopper limb talent kept him constantly aloft and when he spotted us, his broad face lit up in mischievous glee.

"Sha!" Uncle Lau's meaty arm pointed at me and Tacchan.

The Iron Fists lived up to their reputation and didn't miss a beat. In unison, twenty soldiers charged us, a dizzying array of pikes, staffs, broadswords, and pudao.

Tacchan and I put our backs together, instinctively turning as we were surrounded. Above us, Uncle Lau grinned and rubbed his hands together. For him, there was nothing quite as invigorating as a good fight. In this we agreed.

Some people got a welcome-home banner and balloons. I got a welcome-home melee round with twenty seasoned soldiers. Perfect. I usually trained with the Pearl Guard so this would be a new experience. How serious of a fight was this going to be?

I looked for the biggest soldier. He was hard to miss, nearly a foot taller than me and wielding a pudao with a wickedly sharp blade. The broadsword attachment to the long staff had earned it the nickname of "horse cutter."

This skirmish was exactly what I needed. Anticipation licked through my skin like fire. I met his eyes and lifted my hand. His eyebrows crawled up in disbelief when I beckoned to him with my fingers.

Try me.

The giant's eyes blazed with indignation and he charged straight at me. Too easy. He took two steps before Tacchan ripped up the courtyard flagstones in a circle twenty feet wide. The stones whirled around us, slamming into each other and breaking apart into smaller stones. My brother's talent created a grinding whirlwind of jagged debris, a protective cylinder around the two of us.

Well, the two of us and the giant with the pudao.

I whipped out two shurikens, one for each leg. The ceramic blades skimmed in a blur until their edges cut across the meatiest part of his thighs. Just enough to slow him down. The giant grunted, blood gleaming through his trousers before ice crystals formed and sealed the wounds.

Ice talents were the worst.

My little brother had gotten better since I'd last seen him. His whirling shield of rocks kept the rest of the Iron Fists at bay. I saw a lot of wary eyes that spoke of experience with my brother's tactics. They were out of the equation for now, but they would find a way in.

I turned my attention back to the giant. Tatsuya claimed I still had it.

Did I?

I drew Hachi but left her sheathed. As he swung with the pudao, I dashed inside his reach, turned, and slammed Hachi's pommel into his gut.

He barely moved.

Plan B, then. I slammed my fist into the wound on his right thigh, crunching through the ice. He grunted from the impact and I followed up by smashing his other leg. He took one beefy hand off the pudao and backhanded me. Unfortunately for me, he'd hardened a coating of ice around his fist.

Stars exploded across my vision and I staggered back. I moved my jaw around, relieved to find it wasn't broken. Blood came away on my fingers where all the ice had cut my cheek and neck. I was lucky he hadn't sliced my ear off. Ugh. I hated ice talents.

The big man with the pudao smiled grimly at me. He raised his hand and threw my taunt back in my face. I smiled in return, eager for a real fight. Shouts went up all around us as the Iron Fists barreled into our position from several directions. They carried improvised shields to break through my brother's rock storm.

Tacchan pivoted his strategy and the world turned orange. Persimmons dive-bombed the soldiers, a pelting rain of fruit. More yelps of surprise as the Iron Fists broke through the rocks only to get fragrant fruit smashed in their faces. The giant took one in the nose, the ripe flesh splattering across his cheeks and eyes. He swiped frantically with his free hand and I jumped into the opening.

I swatted his wrist with Hachi's scabbard. His fingers released the pudao and I caught it before it hit the ground. Mine now. The staff was so bitterly cold I nearly let go. I whirled and used the momentum to snap the hefty staff of the horse cutter against the giant's knee. He crashed to the ground with a satisfying thunk and I hit his face with the flat of the pudao blade to make sure he stayed down. Blood sprayed from his nose.

Tatsuya carried no weapons but his talent made him dangerous enough. His first line of defense broken, he'd fallen back to a smaller shield of animated pebbles and rocks swirling around him like a tornado. The larger stones moved independently, knocking out the closest soldiers. A couple would likely wake with a concussion. But we were still outnumbered and needed something big to level the field.

Before I could jump in, Tatsuya pulled the lanterns into play and streamers of flaming paper flew in chaotic disarray, igniting the clothing of the remaining soldiers. They stopped to beat out the flames, leaving me free to take them out at the knees with the pudao. Men and women tumbled to the unforgiving stones of the courtyard, rolling out the flames while Uncle Lau bounced and laughed, his glee echoing off the back of the house.

Ironically, he yelled, "Jiāyóu!"

The classic term of encouragement to cheer one on could also be interpreted to add fuel to the fire. With Uncle Lau, I wouldn't put it past him not to pour the oil himself.

Full darkness fell on us as the paper lanterns burnt to ash and the fires extinguished. I fought in grim exhilaration, the heavy pudao making me work for every soldier I felled. But Tacchan's tactic had turned the tide and there was only one way this fight was going now. Even so, I knew the Iron Fists would make me pay for every bit of it.

Only a handful of soldiers remained and the shortest one slammed her two fists together. Oh no. I'd seen this pose at Fiona's house just yesterday. Somehow Father had managed to enlist a Disciple of Raijin. Who knew they were so thick on the ground?

Lightning forked through the cloudless night sky, improbable and stunning. On the other side of the courtyard, a blue-white bolt of electricity annihilated Tatsuya's shield of flying rocks, leaving him open to direct attack.

The last two soldiers were between me and Tatsuya. But I had to take out that lightning rod before she charged up again.

As she rubbed her palms together, I threw my last shuriken and ran.

My aim was true as the sharp ceramic star struck her in the meat of her right palm. She grunted and then yanked the star out, blood running down her hand.

Tatsuya dropped low and swept her, his long leg catching her from behind. She fell hard, her shoulder smacking the stones. I winced. Possible broken collarbone.

Behind me, a cold wind buffeted my back. I heard the heavy scrape of stone and knew what Tatsuya had done. It would be his last gambit because animating something the size of the píxiū would drain his qì to the dregs, especially if he'd imbued it with enough restraint to not kill anyone.

The last two soldiers between us put on a burst of speed, twin blurs in the confusion of darkness and ash. I smelled the crisp mint scent of their Dragon speed talent, saw the pale green flares of their auras. I was too far away. There was no way to reach them, even with the considerable length of the pudao.

The píxiū crashed between us, its enormous lion head rearing. Outstretched wings lashed out and both soldiers bounced off the stone wings and crashed senseless to the ground.

Tatsuya swayed, then leaned against the massive beast. The píxiū let out a rumble before wrapping its other wing protectively around my brother.

I exhaled in relief and dropped the pudao.

"Three minutes and nineteen seconds!" yelled Uncle Lau, his voice positively merry. He reached into his sleeve and pulled out a small gourd, uncapped it, and took a big swig. The heady scent of rice wine tickled my nose. I had a sudden craving for steamed drunken chicken and a bowl of rice. I was starving; all I'd eaten before the fight were Kit Kats.

The Disciple of Raijin groaned and rubbed her shoulder, getting to her feet. Blood dripped from her hand. She eyed me warily as I mounted my pudao on the wall rack. She looked like she wanted to say something, but she turned away and the moment passed. I stepped aside as the rest of the soldiers gathered their weapons and cleaned up. More than a few of them gave me the side-eye while they assessed their wounds.

I didn't blame them. I had broken my blade and abandoned them, bringing a shadow over our good name. No doubt they wondered why my father hadn't severed me from the clan. I had wondered myself. But now I was back. I couldn't expect to be welcomed by everyone with open arms.

But I was only here for Tacchan, and assessing this skirmish I wondered if they'd been training him properly for Lóng Yá. Were they pulling their punches?

I made a mental note to talk to Uncle Lau about it. Maybe Tacchan was right to ask me to come back.

The enormous píxiū let out a gust of wind and blew the remnants of Tatsuya's rock shield back to the garden. I winced. Lulu Āyí was going to have a fit when she saw the garden tomorrow morning.

Uncle Lau landed next to me, his girth even larger than I remembered. He pointed at my bloody neck and clucked in disapproval. "Mimi! You have to duck when someone's about to hit you."

I'd have to remember that next time.

FAMILY BUSINESS

Fujita-san slid open the house doors to the courtyard. He looked neat as always, his white button-down shirt crisp and tucked into gray wool slacks. Seed pearls studded his leather belt and he wore a tailored charcoal vest with the chain of his pocket watch dangling out.

He stepped out into the dark, the air heavy with smoke and the scent of crushed fruit and turned earth. He sighed and his shoulders slumped a little. Uncle Lau did frequently make a mess of the courtyard and garden.

Fujita-san straightened and clapped his hands twice, a sharp staccato.

A faint hum arose around the garden, and then sparks of light streamed toward the house to dance around the courtyard.

Hotaru!

I smiled in delight and watched the fireflies with their soft greenish glow as they flew above us. Tatsuya and I walked over to Fujita-san and bowed. The older gentleman retained an ageless look, his tan skin smooth and unlined, but his eyes seemed to hold a century of wisdom. His summoning talent was gentle and nature-based, making him an odd complement to our combat-focused household, but I also couldn't imagine clanhome without him. His talent smelled like crushed juniper and pine, comforting and welcome after the years away. Where Father was the head of this clan, Fujita-san was its heart.

Fujita-san greeted me, but his smile wavered as he took in the sad state of my attire. I looked down at myself. Persimmon guts mixed with ash smeared my jacket. My hands were bloody. I swiped quickly at my chin and dried blood flaked off.

"Emi-chan." His face took on a familiar expression, that of resignation. "Clean clothes are laid out for this evening's dinner."

I leaned in and wrapped my arms around him for a quick hug, careful not to mess up his vest. He startled and then patted my shoulder awkwardly. "Go."

Uncle Lau strode up behind us and smacked Tatsuya firmly on his back. "Not bad. You almost didn't need the píxiū."

I left them to their battle discussion and strode into the house. The closer I got to the center of the house, the more the Soong Hoard pulled at me. The power of the Hoard was embedded in every floorboard and wall hanging in this house. Hoard power was old, power that pre-dated our presence in this world. When Jiārén had fled the Realm we had taken as much Hoard as we could carry, treasures soaked in the devastating power of ancient Dragon gods.

For two years I had stayed away, and now I was walking straight into the heart of my father's power. An empire built on a mountain of treasure, drenched in Dragon magic. The weight of it, the call of it, was a lure hooked into my chest. I told myself that I had moved on, but like an addict taking another hit, I knew how much I craved it. The Hoard reminded me of my place in the family, my place in the Jiārén world. Like a dog to its master, I wanted to heel at the foot of the Hoard and feel at peace.

That image jarred me out of the madness.

The Pearl in my chest pulsed once, out of tune with the Hoard's song, a balm of soothing energy. I focused on that and took a long breath. Perhaps I'd traded one master for another, but the city's gift was honest and I'd taken it with my eyes wide open. The Hoard's power wove illusions of trust and power. I liked my new vision better. Raw and untried it may be, but I appreciated its honesty.

Two flights of rosewood stairs brought me to the bedrooms where

Tatsuya and I slept. Our parents had the third floor, but Mother was seldom home so it was largely Father's domain with the exception of her private chambers.

With each step, I became aware of the bruises and cuts I'd sustained from the fight in the courtyard. Making it to my room was a sweet relief.

My room looked the same as when I'd left it, the furnishings austere and the decorations minimal. No softness for the Blade.

I unstrapped Hachi and checked the blade. It was clean—no blood on the blade for once. Instead, just dried blood on the pommel. I opened drawers to find my supplies and cleaned Hachi. The stool I sat on was the one I'd had since I was little. It was too short for me now but I had kept it. I put the oil away next to my sandalwood comb and hairbrush.

The woody scent of the comb tickled my nose and a memory flashed through my mind. I was small, maybe seven, and sitting on this very stool as my mother brushed my hair with the sandalwood comb. I had only a few vivid memories of my mother. For most of my life she was an ethereal wraith who flitted in and out of my world like Fujita-san's fireflies.

I traced my fingers over the delicate tines of the comb. Between the assassin's parting words and the comb, my mother's presence was an anvil, full of dread and ready to fall on me. I held my breath, listening hard to the sounds of the house, but I only determined what I'd known when I stepped foot in clanhome. My mother wasn't here. Why would she be? She'd never been here much, only showing up at my moments of failure.

No.

The silence broke as I slid the drawer shut with a little too much force. Even if my mother couldn't be bothered to cross the Void for her family, I knew where I was needed. The Iron Fists' measured welcome had sealed it. Tatsuya needed me, so I was here for him.

My bags and backpack were waiting for me and I unzipped them to put away my things in the tansu cabinet. I admired the soft slide of the drawers and the heavy iron pulls. It smelled faintly of orange oil and old wood. I would use the largest shelf for my Kit Kat stash. But when I pulled the door open, a small basket was already there. I slid it out and found a bag of beni imo–flavored Kit Kat within. It had to be from Fujita-san. He knew I liked the purple sweet potato flavor. Fujita-san's thoughtful gesture swept away my dark thoughts and I got on with settling into my room. I would only be here a week, then I would be back in San Francisco. I'd survived worse.

My western clothing looked absurdly out of place in the Meiji-era cabinet. Just another reminder that I was only a visitor this time. Once my things were put away I piled in my Kit Kat haul from Sugar Sugar House. I placed the sakura flavor closest to the front.

Life was short.

I would eat my favorites first.

As Fujita-san had noted, he'd laid out clothing for me on the futon. The kakebuton was unfurled, the beautiful silk quilt in cherry-blossom pink. It was the one soft thing I'd permitted myself when I'd lived here. Atop the kakebuton, he'd draped a sleeveless silk blouse and flowing silk trousers. The fabric had been hand painted in a shimmering gray that transitioned to black at the hems. Hopefully the dinner entrees wouldn't have much sauce or that blouse was a goner.

On the nightstand my jewelry box was open, displaying row after row of pearls—freshwater, saltwater, seed, cultured. Flawless or deeply flawed, they were strung together in twists of gleaming clusters. For tonight, Father would expect me to wear the ones with that subtle red sheen that proclaimed to Jiārén that these were Hoard pieces.

I stripped down, leaving my grimy clothes in the basket in the corner. I stepped into the shower and the water stung the cuts on my face and neck. My encounters with ice talents always went badly.

I looked longingly at the ofuro. A cold plunge in the wooden soaking tub was probably a good idea, but I was running out of time. Any minute now, Fujita-san would send someone up to harangue me under the auspices of helping me get ready. My stomach growled, reminding me I hadn't eaten anything all day other than that skewer of delicious deep-fried namazu and a bag of Kit Kats.

The sooner I got dressed, the sooner I could eat.

I wiped the steam from the mirror and surveyed the damage. Lacerations on my shoulder, neck, and cheek on the left side of my body. The blood had washed away but the welts remained, red and angry against my fair skin. It hadn't even been a month and I was already missing the enhanced healing I enjoyed as the Sentinel. I towel-dried my hair and wound it into one long braid.

The silk clothing fluttered over me soft as a whisper and I walked over to the jewelry case. I pulled the heavy kumihimo-stranded seed beads and clasped them around my neck. I slipped on white-gold wrist cuffs studded with pink saltwater pearls. The weight of all the jewelry felt cool and comforting against my skin. As the pearls settled against my neck, an unfamiliar warmth and tingling spread across my skin. The sensation nearly knocked me off-balance, the increased intensity of my qì flow something I had never felt before. I sat down heavily on my bed, wondering at the sensation when a soft knock sounded at my door, followed by a familiar voice.

"Emi-chan?"

I was across the room in two steps. When I opened the door I grabbed the woman outside my door and unceremoniously pulled her in for a tight hug. She was my height, and she'd put on some weight in the two years I was gone, but she still smelled like eucalyptus and camphor, and she still wore her gray hair in a tight perm. Yoko-obaachan was clanhome's official house nurse and field medic. Like Fujita-san, her talent was complementary to the rest of our staff. Her Dragon healing talent was vital to keeping our soldiers patched up.

Over my years as Blade, she had restored me on numerous occasions. Her ability to do so despite the tangle of my meridians was testament to the strength of her talent.

Yoko-obaachan hugged me back, squeezing me tight. Our hug broke and she held me at arm's length to look at me. Her eyes wandered around my head, her keen gaze taking everything in, much the same way Popo's did.

She smiled and nodded with approval. "Whatever you're doing, it's been good for you."

When her hands trailed down my arms, she jerked back like she'd touched a live wire. Eyes wide, she reached for my arms again and childlike wonder suffused her face.

"Emi-chan. What happened?"

Before I could answer, Yoko's talent flared and cool relief flowed up my arms from her hands. Finally corrected, my meridians and qì flow didn't fight her anymore. Yoko's power surged through me, and the cuts and bruises on my arms faded in moments. It felt like the shower I'd just taken, but washing away the pain. It was wonderful. Yoko-obaachan's eyes shone with unshed tears.

"There. Now you look perfect for your dinner. Just as your mother would have wanted."

That wasn't quite what I was aiming for, but clearly Yoko was attributing more maternal instincts to my mother than I did. Yoko seemed to take my hesitation as nerves and she pushed me out the door.

"Well, go on, don't keep your father waiting. We can catch up later."

With bare feet I padded across the rosewood floors and made my way down to dinner. On the main floor, the portraits of Soong ancestors glared down at me. As always, the weight of their expectations made me walk faster to escape.

The heavy double doors to Father's office opened. "Mimi, bǎobèi. Lai, lai."

Elation and dread pooled in my stomach at his summons. I had hoped to have the buffer of Tatsuya and Fujita-san when greeting my father. That ever-present guilt that I had gotten pretty good at suppressing rose to the fore, tightening my throat. My appetite for dinner died as I crossed the threshold into Father's domain.

His office didn't have a desk or bookshelves, things you would normally expect to see in an office. Instead, figurines of carved jade lined the walls. Each one sat on a pedestal of dark lacquered wood, each one carved from the finest jade, a pale green color so milky it was nearly white. Hawks and ravens with wings stretched in mid-flight alternated with foxes and badgers with cunning eyes and sharp claws. Along the far wall, behind my father, stood a massive bull, nearly life-size, with rippling muscles carved in exquisite detail and horns that came to deadly sharp points.

I'd visited this room many times during my tenure as the Blade. Father always preferred to govern and negotiate from a position of strength.

Some men displayed their wealth or trophies to establish dominance. The carvings in his office were neither. My father could imbue his qì into each one of the carvings with just a thought. They were weapons, pure and simple, a wordless proclamation of his power. To sit in this room was to sit with your neck exposed, a knife hanging heavy over your life. The man who held that knife was my father.

I froze as I entered. There was an actual blade in the room tonight, jarringly out of place amongst Father's menagerie. A low, wide chest of lacquered wood sat just behind Father's right shoulder. The top of the chest was covered with a sheet of pale gray silk, to protect the finish from the jian that lay on it.

My back suddenly felt naked and exposed. The jian was longer than Truth, perhaps by two hands. The handle was proportionally longer, easily a hand and a half for me. Tiny seed pearls had been worked into the stingray skin on the scabbard, outlining a pale pink chrysanthemum. A large white pearl was set in the center of the flower.

I held my arms at my sides, willing them not to move, even as my hand ached to test the weight of the blade, to feel the new cords wrapping the handle biting into the skin of my palm. Of course, my father knew I would be tempted by a sword like this. And because I knew he knew, I held my tongue. I hadn't even breathed a word to him of relinquishing Truth to anchor the Ebony Gate, and he was already testing me with this replacement.

But nothing could replace Truth. This blade looked deadly and perfect, and soulless. Truth held the souls of the Soong Blades before me and I would forever mourn that loss.

My father knelt on the tatami in front of the bull statue, his face as unreadable as ever. Though we were the same height, he still felt larger than life to me. His every feature looked like it had been hewn from rough stone—his square frame, his leonine head, and his unyielding jaw. He held a scroll in his hand and his sharp eyes scanned the delicate paper.

His favorite animate was at his side today, a gray and green wolf constructed out of interlocking wooden tiles. Sugi was a gift from my mother, and the only construct that my father kept continuously animated. The wolf's head came up as I entered and her shining black eyes tracked my movement. Whenever Sugi moved, her wooden tiles slid over each other with a soft clicking sound that followed my father wherever he went in the house.

My father did not acknowledge my entrance.

He was dressed much more formally than I would have expected for a family dinner. He always wore tangzhuang, but instead of a cotton-linen blend, today his jacket was silk. The dark silk shimmered, embroidered with threads of silver. The Soong family fènghuáng was sewn on each sleeve, a dazzling work of the smallest seed pearls. A crisp white cuff with large freshwater pearl frog buttons finished the formal attire. Was my coming home some sort of special occasion?

Immediately I discarded the notion. He hadn't even bothered to come out to greet me.

A jade monkey closed the doors behind me and scampered across the tatami to clamber up the bull and take a seat on its back. The monkey's hard green eyes bored into me as it stilled, and then the spark of life faded and the monkey was dull stone again, its purpose served.

Father shifted the scroll, reading a bit farther. His eyes did not leave the paper. "Sit, Mimi."

I knelt opposite him and waited in silence. From this position, the bull looked as if it were charging at me, horns lowered to gore me through the neck. The hawks hung frozen in space, aimed at me in hunting dives. Two years of living on my own in America made me want to reach for my voice and speak into the silence.

But an entire lifetime of living under Father's rule stilled my voice and made me wait.

The rules of decorum permeated my being, much as the power of our Hoard hung thick in the air. I sat straight, my shoulders back, chin high, and calmly waited for my father's attention. His power swirled around the room like an errant wind. I kept my eyes forward and my body still. If I fidgeted, my legs would shift against the tatami, and Father would hear it.

Father's qì circled around me, flitting in and out of the carved figures. Their eyes lit up in sequence, going liquid for just a moment, each animal examining me in turn. I let my eyes unfocus into the middle space and stilled my qì. A childlike instinct in my heart longed to stretch out for my father's talent, like a child reaching for a parent's hand. I quashed it and sat, immobile.

Father finally put down the scroll, rolling it up and securing it in a traveling tube made of hammered silver. He turned to me and looked me in the eyes for the first time in two years.

He grunted. It sounded like a satisfied grunt.

His eyes traveled over my head. I fought down the urge to apologize for the absence of Truth. His eyes then traced the length of my braid with the haphazard streak of white running through it. The corner of his mouth twitched a micrometer. "It suits you."

I couldn't tell if he was talking about the missing sword, the gold-tinged aura, my white-striped hair, or the crazy tattoo, and it wouldn't do me any good to ask. I bowed my head, dropping my eyes to the tatami between us. "Father, you know what Mother gave the shiniga—"

His deep voice cut me off smoothly. "Your mother traded a Talon for the good of the clan."

A tiny spark of anger flared to life, deep in my gut, and I scrambled to smother it. Since the trade to the shinigami had saved both my father and me from death it was hard to argue that point. But finding myself in debt to a death god had felt like my mother playing fast and loose with our lives. I kept my face a mask and still felt like Father read every line of me like a book.

"Your mother was faced with an impossible situation. As I said, it was a good trade."

"It nearly killed me, Father."

"And yet you are here. A survivor."

"The shinigami took Truth." My voice broke a little.

"This is a great loss to the clan. But we will always be grateful to the Blades before us. Their legacy is your legacy." His eyes shone like river stones, cold and hard. "You redeemed a Hiroto Talon and upheld our family's honor. And it made you a Sentinel."

This was my father's twisted way of finding a silver lining. I changed tactics, trying to redirect him.

"The Louies and the Trans are on the precipice. The Louies will break the peace soon, and it will be clan war in San Francisco."

He reached down to the silver tube and straightened it, lining it up exactly with the borders of the tatami. "And you have brought the Tran Clan head to me, to treat with our clan. In times of strife, it is always best to have strong allies."

What? I didn't like the idea that I was doing my father's bidding again. "I didn't bring the Trans here for you."

"You have done well, daughter. The Trans and the Louies were ever going to return to war. I had thought to align with Dai Lou, but if you feel the Trans are the better play, I will back you. In any case, with you as the Sentinel, our clan is now well placed to advance, regardless of the war's outcome."

He paused. "You have fulfilled my expectations."

The spark in my gut flared hot and spiky. I wasn't his dog anymore.

I wasn't doing any of this for him. I clamped my mouth shut, unable to trust myself if I spoke.

Father picked an invisible speck of lint from his trousers and his eyes gleamed with fierce pride. "No, you are so much more now. You have established your own power, made your own allies. And you have brought them home, to forge an alliance with your clan. I expected nothing less from you."

My thoughts stalled on my father's words. In a way, he was—aggravatingly—right. Looking back on the last month, through his eyes, I was being his ideal daughter, stretching Soong power and influence into San Francisco. The fact that I'd been making my own decisions, for my own reasons, meant nothing to him. I was bringing honor and glory to our clan. That was all that mattered to him. Arguing anything else was futile.

Father stood, his movements fluid and precise. He picked up the scroll tube as he rose and a spark of his qì animated one of the jade foxes. The fox scampered up his legs and rested atop his shoulder. He lifted the silver case and the fox grabbed it in its jaws and leapt to the floor, running out of the room on nimble feet.

"Now, when will you bring your Adam Jørgensen to swear to the Hoard?"

My lips tightened. Father's emphasis on *your* disturbed me. I wanted to reject this designation, but truthfully, I had made Adam *ours* when I'd extended the Soong protection over him.

I stood and brushed off the knees of my trousers. "Father, I tried to tell—"

He made a chopping motion with his hand, cutting off my words. "No excuses. He will be brought before our Hoard to swear to uphold the First Law."

I nodded tightly. "Yes, of course."

"See that you take care of it, or I will."

My stomach clenched but I kept my tone bland. "Yes, Father."

"Have you considered what the Trans would need to formally ally our clans?"

I inhaled a sharp breath, the change of subject giving me whiplash. After a moment of consideration, I responded, "I've already agreed to help them with something."

I outlined the problem of the assassin as quickly as I could. Father's face remained an impassive mask throughout, even when I detailed the dark walker's unusual abilities. When I got to Popo's assessment of the poison his eyes took on the calculating air I knew so well. He was finding the angles, considering what leverage to apply to create the most movement for the least effort.

Father stared out into the middle distance for a moment before his gaze snapped back to mine, his decision made. Whatever course he had landed on, we were now moving forward with no hesitation.

He brushed past me and strode for the door. "Ah Tong is a recluse. He won't see anyone without some incentive. We can deal with the poisoner later. Go get Tatsuya from the Bǎowù hé. We are meeting guests for dinner in Shinjuku Golden Gai."

BǍOWÙ HÉ

On the top floor of clanhome, my parents' rooms faced east, and my mother's private office faced west. Between them stood our Bǎowù hé, the entirety of the Soong Hoard. With my repaired meridians, that much concentrated Dragon power was a nearly irresistible lure. I could find it even with my eyes closed, drawing me like a lodestone.

My steps slowed as I reached the third floor. Meeting with Father always resembled running a gauntlet of hidden traps. Even after two years away, the instinct to obey him was difficult to resist. Had I offered too much for what I'd received from him? Would any of my interactions with him not be measured for efficiency? I envied Tessa when she spoke of going fishing and camping with her father. Not that I had any desire to do any of those things, let alone do them with Father, but just the easy way Tessa could spend time with her parent seemed like utter fantasy.

My thoughts gave way to amusement as I tried to imagine my father fishing. His approach would be to animate the hooks to do the fishing for him. The unexpected mirth helped me put the last few minutes behind me. He wasn't going to change, and I knew better than to expect anything different.

Since Mother's offices were here, portraits of the Hiroto Clan decorated the walls. Mother didn't speak of her family much, but I remembered meeting one of her younger brothers when I was very young. Both her brothers were dead now. The photos were old and Mother looked very different in them, almost casual. Her brothers,

Shota and Jiro, were in the photos so these had to be more than ten years old.

Tatsuya looked a lot like Mother's youngest brother, Jiro. Maybe that was why she favored Tatsuya? No, nothing so sentimental. Tatsuya would be the head of the Soong Clan, a position I'd failed to live up to. He was simply more valuable than I was.

The photo closest to the door to the Bǎowù hé made me stop. Uncle Jiro held a young girl in his arms, next to me, Tatsuya, and Mother. She was younger than me, but older than my brother. Uncle Jiro never had children of his own, but he did take in Shota's daughter after Shota and his wife passed. Her name was Kaida.

Shota had also been a dark walker. Not my mother's caliber, but at least a píng-class talent. What about his daughter? Mother's extended family had been absent for the last decade or more. Where was Kaida?

I might have forgotten about Kaida's talent but I doubted my father had. He must have considered her when I told him about the assassin. He hadn't brought her up, though, so perhaps she wasn't someone I needed to worry about.

And maybe if I kept telling myself that, I would even believe it.

I grasped the iron handles on the double doors to the Bǎowù hé. The handles twisted and a micro needle released to taste my blood. After a moment, the heavy doors swung open, pulled by two stone guardian baboons. The baboons were nearly as tall as I was, and their arms hung nearly to the floor. When I was a child, I rode on their shoulders. Father didn't name his guardians but I called them Shāobǐng and Yóutiáo, which had been my favorite breakfast foods when I was three.

I inhaled deeply, the scent of all this Hoard power irresistible to my senses. Leaving Tokyo had been devastating, and coming back was equally hard. I would have to leave all this behind again. For the first time, I thought about other Jiārén families without this massive amount of Hoard. Were their lives more normal? Or did they feel like their talents wore thin without the rapid recharge of the Dragon power that radiated from a Hoard?

Tatsuya lay curled on his side within the sound circle. Unlike the polished metal Tibetan bowls I used in my house, these ones were white jade bowls of various sizes, their surfaces so thin that they glowed with inner light.

The circle was the only orderly thing in the room. A menagerie of stone, bone, or metal animals rested in the Bǎowù hé, the Hoard pieces nested in their paws or around their necks, horns, beaks, or antlers. The largest was the steel elephant, who topped out at twice my height, and three times longer. The elephant was constructed of chain links, and every part of it could articulate the smallest motion. I had named him Dòu jiāng and he carried an ornate closed box on his back. That's where Father stored the largest single item of the Hoard and the blood jade.

It wasn't particularly neat, but Father was old-school in how he viewed the Hoard. This wasn't a museum, and he didn't require order—he required power and he stowed the pieces accordingly.

For now, Tatsuya had guardians arranged to watch over him while he rested. Their heads swiveled in unison at my arrival. The spiky bone crocodile was particularly alarming.

"Tacchan, we need to leave for dinner."

He groaned and rolled over. "I thought we were staying home."

I shrugged. I, too, would have preferred to stay home and enjoy Huang si-fu's excellent cooking. "Apparently Father had other plans. We're headed to Golden Gai."

Tatsuya popped up, suddenly as alert as the jade hunting dog in the corner. "Really? Maybe we could hit a bar after."

I rolled my eyes. I did not want to go barhopping with my little brother.

He had a strand of blood jade beads wound around his hands the way a Buddhist would use prayer beads. Animating the píxiū must have really drained his qì. In the past blood jade had held as much utility for me as any other Hoard gem, which was to say, none. Now, though, there was a subtle warmth like a roaring fire at this distance.

By wearing the beads, Tatsuya got a boost as he restored his qì. Blood jade could be beneficial in short doses, but addictive and unstable after overuse—leading to palsy and, ultimately, blood jade madness. His color already seemed better now.

I'd seen blood jade madness before. It wasn't pretty. I pointed at the beads. "Do you need to wear those much longer?"

He shrugged. "I'm nearly done. These aren't even the big pieces." My little brother twisted the beads around his fingers. "I can handle these, been using them pretty regularly now. It's a lot faster than without them."

His casual tone alarmed me. "You shouldn't rely on blood jade to restore yourself, Tatsuya."

He groaned theatrically and lay back down, his arm over his eyes. "Oh skies, you and Yoko-obaachan both, please, stop! I know what I'm doing, I know my limits."

I ignored his outburst. "You've been trained better than this. You don't need to rely on blood jade."

"And you think all the other kids aren't doing the same?"

Of course, he was right. Everyone would be using whatever edge they could to improve their chances. I did it all the time. But that didn't mean I wanted to see my little brother doing it with blood jade. It was the same sensation I'd had when thinking about Leanna going through the brutal social dynamics of Lóng Kǒu.

"It's never a sure thing, Tacchan."

"Nothing in our lives ever is. Father said it would be fine. I believe him."

I relaxed a little. My father would not be cavalier with my brother's life. Tatsuya was the future of our family, and that future depended on his performance in the tournament. To me, though, it seemed like an unnecessary risk for little reward.

"Fine. But you're done for now, right?"

Tatsuya sat up and unwound the blood jade beads from his hands. The elephant stepped over, the floor flexing beneath its cumbersome weight. The elephant's trunk unfurled, the smooth links making a soft sound as the metal mesh slid. Tatsuya looped the blood jade beads onto its trunk and the elephant tilted its head, using its trunk to deposit the beads back into the box on its back.

"Happy?"

I eyed him for a moment. "I'll be happier when I see what else you can do in a fight. You did well in the courtyard, but you can't hide behind your shields forever."

He scowled. "Really? We wiped the floor with them!"

I replayed the fight in my head. "I think you've gotten too used to fighting the Iron Fists. Let's see how you handle my version of training."

He started to groan again and I cut him off. "Did you or did you not ask me to come home to train you?"

"Yeah, I did."

I crouched down so our eyes were level and gave him a beaming smile. "Then you will be happy to receive my instruction."

He rolled his eyes. "Thrilled."

I laughed and tousled his hair to defuse the tension. He batted my hand away but the air between us cleared.

He was big now but he looked so young. The assassin might only be a few years older than my brother.

"Hey, do you recall any dark walkers in the classes above you?"

Tatsuya looked up, his face scrunched in a slight frown. "Mmm. Not last year's. A few years back Amisha Kwik completed the last two rounds of Lóng Yá."

That meant she'd ranked in the top eight. I helped him up off the floor. "How tall is she?"

Tatsuya tilted his head and held his hand just above his head. "Here, maybe? She's really tall."

Scratch one suspect.

"What's this about?"

Even if Amisha was a possibility, there was nothing Tatsuya could do for me. And he had enough on his plate already. I waved him off. "Go change."

Tatsuya dashed out. Some of the menagerie hopped to the edges of the room and resumed their prior watchful state. The bronze tiger was last, giving me a dismissive swish of his tail. Unbidden, an image of Kamon rose in my mind. I squashed it. I'd left all that behind and Kamon as well.

I thought I had needed to change everything and sever all ties. But deep in my heart, I regretted losing Kamon the most. He'd expected too much of me then, but I would never know if we could have made it work, and now it was too late.

The double doors closed with a soft click as the baboons shuffled behind me.

Father was waiting but I lingered in the hallway. I made my way to the west suite and studied the photos along the way. There were more photos of my mother with Jiro, and Shota's daughter. Her resemblance to my mother was striking as she lost her baby fat and even began to style her hair the same way. We all had the same intense inky eyes and thick lashes. I saw it every time I looked in the mirror. I realized with a start that Kaida looked more like my mother than I did.

Without stopping to wonder why, I took the last photo of Kaida and Jiro off the wall and rushed down the stairs to stash it in my room.

DINNER PLANS

I put the photo face down in the drawer with my hairbrush and the oil I used on my blades. Strapping on Hachi and then putting on a long trench coat for Tokyo's capricious spring weather seemed prudent so I took care of those things and stepped into soft low-heeled black leather boots.

Golden Gai had a lot of bars. A lot of bars meant people drank too much and then barfed on the street. No way would I wear sandals or heels tonight.

I managed to beat Tatsuya to the ground floor. Father and Fujita-san were waiting. Apparently the Disciple of Raijin would be joining us this evening as well. She'd changed out of her loose training gear into an inky silk pantsuit with a long lightweight duster jacket. Her short hair was slicked back behind her ears. A stickpin of three large pearls gleamed on the front of her blazer. She wasn't tall but she looked polished and dangerous.

Fujita-san greeted me. "Emi-chan, have you met Nami?"

The Disciple of Raijin gave me a small bow. I bowed in return. "How's your shoulder?"

"It's nothing."

"Glad to hear it. Sometimes Uncle Lau can get carried away."

She flexed her hand against her side, an involuntary motion, and I saw that the cut from my shuriken was already nothing more than a faded scar. "A little variety is good for the Iron Fists."

"Some may be sore tomorrow."

Nami shrugged, the movement surprisingly fluid under her jacket given the fall she'd taken earlier during our melee. It seemed the Disciples of Raijin were exceptionally hardy. A coveted member to any clan, for sure, and another sign that my father and Fiona were two of a kind.

Tatsuya rushed down the stairs and I blinked in astonishment at his transformation. Gone were the casual sweater and joggers. He wore a silky pink tab-collar shirt under a shiny gray suit so tight that a European golfer would have winced. Tatsuya had styled his hair into fluffy tousled locks and finished the look with a pearly pink lip tint. Tatsuya's fashion sense was clearly more developed than mine. No wonder Fujita-san felt the need to pick out my clothes. Left to my own devices I would have looked like a slob next to my little brother.

Father stepped aside, taking a polished wooden box from Fujita-san. He opened the box to reveal a pair of wide bracelets carved from blood jade. The jade was a deep crimson that caught the evening light like fire. A phoenix was carved in relief on both bracelets, winding around the band.

My father pulled the bracelets out of the velvet interior. "For you both to wear, just for tonight."

Tatsuya had already worn the blood jade beads for at least an hour. I opened my mouth to protest but old habits held me back. My father had a plan. He always had a plan.

Father saw the look on my face and seemed to sense my skepticism. "Indulge me."

I traded a quick glance with Tatsuya but he was already putting his on. I reached for the remaining bracelet and flinched a little inside as my skin touched it.

Heat radiated from the stone band and it coursed through my meridians, scorching a path through my body. I clenched my teeth against the unfamiliar sensation, willing my body to stay still. I swallowed hard with the effort of keeping my aura tightly furled, something I had taken for granted for decades. A gnawing ache rose in my gut, reaching outward for . . . something. Anything.

It was as if the blood jade wanted me to reveal my talent, as nonexistent as it was.

Instinctively, my fingers touched my chest where the Pearl beat within. The fire of the blood jade receded, and the ache in my gut subsided. My fingers trembled before I clenched them into a fist and brought it down to my side. When I looked up, my father was watching me, a quizzical expression on his face, immediately followed by speculation.

That didn't bode well.

Tacchan labored under the blood jade as well. A thin sheen of sweat broke out on his face that had nothing to do with the early evening humidity. I wanted to protest, but this was Tatsuya's decision.

Fujita-san made the jewelry box disappear without a word. Blood jade of any kind was the crown jewel of any Hoard. It was the kind of thing you took out of safekeeping for meeting emperors and kings. This felt like we were taking the Bentley down to the corner for boba tea. Just another day for a Hoard Custodian family.

Fujita-san and Father donned soft gray fedora hats, which signaled our departure.

Golden Gai was tucked away in Kabukicho. It had been years since I'd eaten at Father's favorite restaurant, Shanghai Lotus, which was nestled behind the more popular bars that fronted the street. The alleys in Golden Gai were ancient narrow spaces that were single file only. Great from a fighting perspective but terrible for security. We were strolling along with priceless Hoard artifacts wrapped all over our bodies and all I had was a short sword.

My nerves were on edge by the time the maître d' and the owner, Bīng Xiānshēng, greeted us. There was the exchange of bows, and they took our hats and coats. When we rolled in, the maître d' casually flipped over a sign on the door that said PRIVATE PARTY.

Bīng Xiānshēng swung open the double doors to the banquet room. "Enjoy."

The owner's voice rang hollowly across the vast open space. Father had booked out the entire venue, and the staff had cleared all the tables except one.

Gauzy ivory silk drapes covered the walls, backlit by soft ground lights. The effect cast the room in an ethereal light that seemed to glow from everywhere. A long rectangular table was set well away from the kitchen for privacy, and a waiter walked briskly ahead of us with a crystal decanter of cognac. A large saltwater aquarium, as long as a stretch limo, accented the wall behind the table. Schools of vibrant lionfish swam in lazy loops, darting in an out of large rocks decorating the tank.

Two figures sat on the opposite side of the table and watched as we approached. Koh Lǐ Qiáng, the patriarch of the Koh Clan, sat in the center seat. His bloodshot eyes and ruddy complexion contrasted against the dark blue of his suit jacket. A crown of wispy white hair circled a bald pate dotted with age spots. He had to be older than my father by at least twenty years. Despite his age, his eyes were bright and his hands steady as he took the decanter and dismissed the waitstaff with a negligent wave. Sapphire cuff links winked from the ends of his coat sleeves, and cabochon stones caught the light on both pinkies.

To his right, Sabine Koh Daiyu sat in a dazzling gown of deepest blue, sipping on a bottle of sparking water. I recognized her from my research into the Singapore clans. She was five years younger than me and every bit as regal as her reputation. Her dress was elegant and understated, and she looked like she would be at equal ease serving in a soup kitchen or fighting for her life. A necklace of rough-cut sapphires accented the neckline of her dress. Her dark eyes followed my father intently as we crossed the room.

If Old Li ever decided to retire or die, Sabine was his obvious choice as a successor. Sabine was Lǐ Qiáng's only child by his youngest wife, and a prize graduate of Lóng Kǒu. Old Li had children and grandchildren to spare, but Sabine was his jewel. She had entered school as a gāo talent and gotten stronger every year. No small feat.

Her ability to control water was the standard all others worked toward, with no hope of even coming close. An impressive, and predictable, showing at her Lóng Yá had shot her to the top of the Koh family hierarchy, hopping over several siblings.

In fact, the chair to Old Li's left was conspicuously empty. His eldest son, Awang, head of the Ice Tsunami Trio, had made a visit to my fair city a few weeks ago. It hadn't gone well for them. Perhaps Awang had finally lost his last little bit of Old Li's approval?

Not that Old Li even needed his son here. The aquarium was a definite factor if things got hairy. Lǐ Qiáng was a legendary water talent. Adding Sabine to the mix turned the room into an even more lethal death trap. If I had hackles, they would be standing straight up.

Old Li rose as we reached the table and uncorked the bottle, pointing to the empty seats across from him. He poured cognac generously into all of our glasses. "Sit, sit. You're just in time, food's nearly here. I took the liberty of ordering."

"You're too kind, my friend."

"It's been too long, and now both of your children are home."

Father waved a dismissive hand. "Tatsuya is so busy at Lóng Kǒu. Emiko is so busy in San Francisco, too busy being the Sentinel to visit her old father."

Old Li grunted in acknowledgment and eyeballed my Sentinel aura and the way the city had marked my right shoulder.

My father's classic and ruthless efficiency. In one sentence he'd managed to chastise me for not being more attentive, brag about my status, and insult Old Li for siring only one powerful child while he had both me and Tatsuya.

With a pang, I realized for the first time that my father thought I was a credit to him. No matter my many failings.

My father picked up his glass and lifted it in a toast. "Thank you, Old Li. To your health."

I touched the glass to my lips but did not drink. The fumes from the alcohol burned in my nose. Old Li wasn't wasting any time tonight. We sat after my father took his seat. Fujita-san pulled out the chair directly across from Old Li and got my father seated, then retreated to a respectful distance, standing at parade rest and blending in with the background. Nami took up station on the opposite wall. Tatsuya sat on Father's right, and I took the seat on his left, directly across from Sabine. She inclined her head to me in a small bow as I sat, her eyes going first to my shoulders and then to Hachi at my hip. The missing weight across my back burned like severed nerves. Sabine's gaze returned to my father, her luminous eyes missing nothing.

I let my vision expand around me, taking in the details of our surroundings as Father and Old Li made small talk and reminisced about past Tourneys. The first courses arrived and Old Li dug into his food with gusto, spoons clattering against the serving plates as he served himself and then my father. Seemingly satisfied that I was not a threat, Sabine moved on, speaking to Tatsuya across the table and making polite talk about the upcoming Lóng Yá.

This was an odd dinner pairing. The Kohs weren't exactly friends of ours, but not enemies, either. Our territory had little overlap, both in business and geography, so there was little tension between our clans. The Kohs were an old clan, with old money and Hoard. Goodwill between our clans could be beneficial to us both.

The venue was odd as well. The Shanghai Lotus was an established restaurant, but hardly a destination. Their food, while good, was nothing like the more adventurous fare to be found in newer eateries. Choosing this old restaurant was possibly just habit, given that Father enjoyed the food here, but my father was one to consider all the angles for even the simplest things. I was positive he'd considered at least three different ways to display the jian in his office to tempt me. No, this was deliberate. If not as an obvious slight against our guests, I didn't see the angle. And experience had taught me to be wary when I couldn't anticipate my father's next moves.

Massive platters of appetizers arrived, pickled jellyfish mounded high, next to thinly sliced cold beef, and boiled peanuts. Tatsuya loaded his plate with food and ate like there was no tomorrow. He had to be hungry after all the power we'd expended this afternoon.

He was also used to being ornamental at Father's meetings, and, like any teenaged boy, had learned to take advantage of any food presented to him.

I helped myself to enough of each plate to be polite and pushed my food around, pretending to eat. Just enough was wrong here that my appetite had disappeared. Sabine wasn't really eating, either, and her gaze kept moving between her father, my father, and me. She looked at me enough times that I began to wonder if we'd met before and I'd forgotten.

Old Li drained his glass with the appetizers and Father poured more. Old Li's hands shook now as he tipped glass after glass. Gods but this dinner was going to drag on all night. I couldn't believe Father had dragged Tatsuya away from his training for . . . this. I had come back to Tokyo ostensibly at Tatsuya's request and I should've been with him now, prepping for Lóng Yá. Instead we were being paraded about with people we rarely saw . . . but for what?

The main course arrived, a whole suckling pig covered in crispy skin. Old Li took the cleaver from the waiter and waved him off. The elder Koh seemed to settle down, but not before he topped off his and my father's glasses.

Old Li offered a clumsy toast and sloshed a good quarter of his glass onto his cuffs and the tabletop. "On to business, then?" He propped his elbows on the table and looked at me and my brother for the first time the entire dinner.

His fingers trembled as he pointed at me with his half-empty glass. "Not her. I won't have her. Doubt any of my sons are desperate enough to have her, either."

Oh, dear. Is that what this dinner was about? I turned to look at Tatsuya as Old Li swiveled his arm to my brother. "Him. I can find a good match for him."

Old Li wiped sweat off his forehead and took off his jacket, revealing darkened patches under his arms. He leaned back in his chair and elbowed Sabine. "Which one of your sisters would make the best match, eh?"

Heat flushed down my arms and legs and I fought down the urge to kick back my chair and smash the table in half. Tatsuya, already pale from our impromptu exercise, seemed to go another shade lighter. Based on the shell shock on Tatsuya's face, this was a complete surprise to him as well. In the silence as Sabine considered the question, my knuckles popped like firecrackers under the table.

For all my father's domineering ways, I had never once considered that he would try to arrange a marriage for us. It wasn't unheard of amongst Hoard Custodian families but it wasn't customary in our family. I had very little insight into my father's feelings but when my mother was around, he looked at her like she was the only star in his sky. I had never questioned that for him, theirs had been a love match. Of course, my father, from one of the oldest combat clans, would fall head over heels for a woman with one of the least understood, most dangerous branches of Jiārén talent.

Father put down his drink and folded his napkin alongside his plate. "Old Li, my friend, I'm afraid there's been some kind of misunderstanding."

His hard, dark eyes tracked from Lǐ Qiáng to Sabine. The eyes of a predator. "I'm not shopping for second best. We're here to talk about Tatsuya and Sabine."

Old Li's glass dropped to the table and shattered. His dark yellow aura flashed. His eyes, now bloodred, widened in shock and his lips curled in disgust. "Insolent! I did not come here to be insulted!"

The saltwater tank rocked on its base as waves formed, frothing the water and pushing the fish back and forth. The tang of brine filled the air as water sloshed over the sides of the tank. Old Li's water talent drenched my senses in a thick carpet of cloying lemon and mint, with a distinct undertone of rot. I nearly gagged on the odor and thanked the Old Dragons that I hadn't eaten anything.

Sabine had gone pale as a ghost but she remained in her seat and did nothing to calm her father. As far as I could tell, she wasn't even trying to use her talent.

My stomach went cold as Old Li rambled on, his speech slurred and stuttering now, pink-flecked spittle landing on the roast duck. The scent of his talent morphed as he grew angrier, the stink of rot and corruption coming to the fore. More spittle landed on the ivory tablecloth and spread into little gory rosettes. I focused on his eyes, his red, red eyes and the cold, dead weight of the blood jade on my wrist. The weight in my gut grew heavier. I recognized and despised this sensation, the belated understanding of my father's schemes.

Father remained in his chair. He'd dropped one hand to his side and held Tatsuya from getting up. He had not extended an arm in my direction. "Honestly, Old Li. Did you expect I was here for anything less?"

Lǐ Qiáng clawed at his collar, sweat now beading up on his skin like rain. "Sabine is worth ten of each of you! None of you deserve to even breathe the same air!"

He tore at his shirt and the buttons popped, tearing open down to midchest. I knew what I would see before it appeared. A mazelike pattern of bloodred lines tracked outward from his heart, reaching for his limbs and head. Old Li had maybe two minutes to live, but until the blood jade destroyed him he would be both insanely powerful, and insane.

The aquarium exploded like a bomb, the glass bursting and showering us with shrapnel. Red lines appeared on everyone's exposed skin except my father, sitting in Old Li's shadow. Fujita-san and Nami dropped into combat poses, arms up. Nami called up a whirling ball of blue lightning between her hands.

Behind Old Li, a thousand gallons of salt water coalesced into a wall of water that flexed and moved with Old Li's labored breathing.

The Disciple shouted and launched a hammer of electricity across the room. The jagged blue streak lifted the hair on my arms as it crossed. Old Li met the bolt with a tide of water that swallowed the energy. The lionfish trapped in the water died instantly.

Father still hadn't moved from his seat. He took a small sip from his snifter. “Really, I think you’re not seeing the benefits of this arrangement. You should be thinking about your clan’s future.”

Blood ran like tears from Old Li’s eyes as his power pulsed again and the water morphed into hundreds of deadly spears aimed at all of us.

We had driven Old Li to blood jade madness.

What was Father’s endgame here?

Old Li grabbed the cleaver and lunged across the banquet table. His eyes were solid red, the crimson lines on his neck creeping up behind his ears.

The water spears jumped forward.

My father sat calmly in his chair and watched certain doom fall upon him.

Instinct and muscle memory took over. The blood jade pulsed against my skin and qì coursed through my meridians like a tsunami. I surged forward, knocking my chair back with my knees. My hand flew to Hachi’s grip and I drew in the same instant, pushing my weight forward. My wakizashi snapped out, the perfect weapon for close conditions like this, and drew a precise line across Old Li’s throat, just above his Adam’s apple. Blood sprayed in an arc, coating my forearm and hitting Tatsuya’s face. I had Hachi back in her scabbard before Old Li hit the table.

The water spears collapsed, drenching the floor and scattering dead lionfish over the entire restaurant. Father put down his glass and finally stood. He grabbed Old Li by the shoulders and turned him face up. Old Li’s eyes tracked blindly and his neck gaped open, wet, white bone glistening. A long, rattling breath wheezed through the gaping ruin of his throat.

Old Li’s crimson eyes seemed to find my father. The old man groaned as the pool of blood expanded across the table. Father cradled Old Li’s face, not shying away from the blood, his hands gentle. “Shh. This is your end, old friend. Rest content in the knowledge that your clan lives on.”

With surprising care, Father closed Old Li's eyes and arranged his body into a peaceful pose. Father closed his eyes for a moment, then snapped his fingers. Two waitstaff hurried to the table and carried away Old Li's body. More staff emerged and cleared the bloody table linens and ruined food. In seconds the restaurant was quiet again.

Sabine, who had remained as motionless as a statue, now stood, every inch regal and commanding, despite her young age. With a flick of her wrist the salt water jumped from her clothes, leaving her gown in immaculate condition. The tiny lines of blood on her pale cheeks faded and disappeared. She picked up the seat her father had occupied and slowly sat, opposite my father. When she spoke, the words had the cadence of a memorized script. "I apologize for my father's behavior. His descent into blood jade madness has been well documented by our family physicians. I hope this will not alter the terms of our alliance."

Father nodded once, his eyes steady on Sabine. "Of course not. Your father was sick, and not in control of himself. I hope Emiko's decisive action will not be seen as an overreach."

Sabine turned to me, her face placid, if maybe a little paler than before. "Of course not. It was in your defense, and an ease to my father's suffering. The Koh family does not view this as a violation of the Second Law."

Father turned to me now as well, his dark eyes cold river rocks again, wielding his absolute authority over our family. There was only one thing he wanted me to say.

My lips twisted bitterly as I uttered the opening call. "Witness."

Sabine nodded once and took a shaky breath. "So witnessed."

Father turned back to Sabine. "You will let us know when the arrangements are made. I knew your father for many years. I will come to pay my respects."

I was unsure what kind of respects you could pay to a man when you had conspired with his own daughter to kill him, but that thorny issue was set aside when Father's demeanor shifted. I felt it as surely as if the thermostat had been turned down suddenly. The dinner was over. It was time for business.

Father spoke without turning to look at me or my brother. "Tatsuya. Emiko. Wait outside."

I was happy to be dismissed.

Bīng Xiānshēng looked understandably concerned when we stepped out of the banquet room. Nami immediately took a defensible position near the front doors as Fujita-san took the restaurant owner to a quiet corner and spoke with him. I recognized all the body language, the grip on the upper arm, the nods, moving the grip from the arm up to the shoulder, establishing dominance. It all said, *We're terribly sorry about the mess, but business is business, yes?*

And right on cue, gold glinted, slim bars appearing out of nowhere between Fujita-san's fingers. Bīng Xiānshēng only hesitated a moment before taking the gold with both hands and bowing deeply.

The Shanghai Lotus's banquet room could be repaired, the tanks replaced as if nothing had ever occurred. That wasn't true of Old Li's life and my throat tightened with remorse. Resentment soured in my belly, familiar and unwelcome. First day back, body count: one. I didn't like that trend.

Mitsugo no tamashi hyaku made.

What I had learned at age three would still be true when I was a hundred and that was the same for my father. He would never change. He was a relentless river breaking down the rocks and the earth in its path and I'd gotten pulled back into the stream. Being angry with Father was like being angry at the river. Pointless. That left me with another target—Sabine Koh.

Patricide was generally frowned upon, so I could understand why she couldn't off Old Li herself. But she'd done a side deal with my father that had roped me into it and I wasn't going to forget it.

Tatsuya nearly bumped into me from behind, engrossed with his phone as he walked out of the dining room. Smears of blood ran down the left side of his face, some of it his, some Old Li's. I grabbed a towel from the busboy station and got to cleaning him up.

"We can't have you going into Lóng Yá looking like you just lost a fight."

He shrugged and let me clean up the blood, still focused on his phone. I leaned down to get into his eyeline. "Did you know what Father had planned tonight?"

"Would it matter if I did?"

I grimaced.

I was still considering that question when Fujita-san walked up behind us with the velvet-lined box open in his hands. Tatsuya and I removed the bracelets and placed them back in the box. His shoulders visibly relaxed after relinquishing the blood jade. Mine did as well. Our role for the night was complete.

Tatsuya's phone chirped and his eyes lit up. "Well, since this night is a bit of a wash, I'm going to blow off some steam."

I marveled at his quick recovery from the violence of moments ago. Two years away from Father had made me soft.

"The guys are meeting here in Golden Gai. Five-hundred-yen sake shots."

"You know I don't drink."

"If the Blade shows up with me they'll be buying me drinks all night."

"You can afford to buy your own drinks, Tatsuya."

"Help a brother out."

I tried to imagine an activity I wanted to do less than go drinking with a bunch of teen boys. A hot shower followed by a steady inhalation of Kit Kats sounded pretty good. But I didn't want to be alone in the house with Father after this stunt. Grudgingly, I concluded that even a ridiculous outing with Tatsuya was better than stewing alone, or worse, having it out with Father if I lost my composure.

"Fine. Let me clean my sword first."

I made my way to the ladies' room. Probably best to wash the dried blood off my arms, too, before going out for drinks.

GOLDEN GAI

When I stepped outside of the restaurant, Fujita-san was putting on his hat. He walked over to me and put a hand on my shoulder. His gaze looked at my neck and cheek and then finally he met my eyes.

"You are healing faster now."

Those were just on the surface. I wondered how long the wounds on the inside would take.

He patted my shoulder gently. "Your father knows you will always put the family first."

His words were the typical party line but his eyes looked sad. I nodded. Just as Father wouldn't change, I wouldn't, either. I *did* always put the family first and I didn't know any other way to do things. These last two years had only been a brief reprieve, and the last bit of that illusion had been ripped away tonight.

I wrapped my hand over Fujita-san's and gave it a squeeze to tell him I understood. He had patched me up many times over the years, and I knew his concern was genuine. His words said one thing, but the sadness in his eyes told me that he didn't want this for me, either.

I needed a new way of responding. One that didn't require me to leave bodies everywhere I went when I was taking care of my family. I might always be known as the Butcher, but I didn't have to act like one.

As if the heavens heard me, a splat of rain landed on my nose. I closed my eyes and tilted my face up to let the rain cool my hot cheeks. I vowed to leave the Butcher in the past where she belonged. No more half measures.

I was done.

After a long moment, I opened my eyes again to face Fujita-san.

Fujita-san reached into his pocket and pulled out a folded square of paper and a small corked glass vial about as big as my thumb. "Your father asked me to give you this. After the dinner."

He held the vial up to the light. The vial contained a few gleaming pebbles of jade. As I looked closer I noted that the pebbles moved through the vial on their own, bumping into each other like tiny bumper cars. I caught the faintest whiff of white pepper on the cork.

I unfolded the paper to find an address in Tokyo's Chinatown.

Fujita-san said, "Ah Tong will be there tomorrow during normal business hours. The contents of the vial should produce whatever cooperation you need."

As much as I needed access to the Herbalist, taking my father's help now, after that farce of a dinner, was about as palatable as eating the food that had been ruined.

Fujita-san sensed my hesitation. He took my hand and pressed the vial into my palm. "Emi-chan. You may not like it, but you earned this tonight. Do not throw away your father's assistance."

"I don't want his help. Not like this."

"This is the only way he knows."

And he wasn't going to change. I closed my hand around the vial, hating the necessity. Damn Fiona for putting me in this position. But even as I cursed her, I knew if it hadn't been her request for an alliance, it would have been something else. Father had merely bided his time. I shoved the vial in the pocket of my trench and cinched my jacket tighter.

Fujita-san smiled but I just turned my back on him before I could say anything else. I'd spent two years in San Francisco, only to return home to find out that my father's leash had indeed extended across the Pacific. While I could voice my opinion to Fujita-san, he didn't deserve my wrath. Just like me, he was tethered to his path. Unlike me, he had made peace with it.

I picked up my pace to catch up to Tatsuya. Maybe the old gods would smile upon me tonight and bring some belligerent drunks into my path. If Tatsuya needed a drink, I needed a fight.

Standing in front of the ominously named Hell's Bite bar, I eyed the stream of revelers cruising the narrow alley. The rain had not deterred them as they dashed in and out of the colorful bars.

Two young men high-fived Tatsuya while I stood a few steps back. If I thought Tatsuya was pretty with his tousled locks and tailored clothes, his friends put him to shame. One was a head taller than all of us, his big frame filling out a lavender cashmere coat over a snowy-white fitted T-shirt, shredded gray jeans, and purple Converse. A flashy belt buckle studded with amethyst completed the outfit. He should've looked underdressed next to Tatsuya's sharkskin suit but somehow his look screamed casual but obscenely wealthy. The other guy was only a few inches taller than me, his hair tinted a soft peach. He wore a fuzzy orange turtleneck sweater under a black Burberry trench coat and managed to look like a cover model instead of a Halloween decoration.

Tatsuya introduced us.

The tall one was Minjae Byun. He glanced at my aura and at Hachi before giving me a nervous smile. If he was also getting ready for Lóng Yá then this would be a banner year with another Hoard Custodian family claiming a berth in the rankings. The Byuns were an old clan, a powerful mix of psionics and shriekers. Theirs was a complicated set of talents. Some manifested as empaths and intuitives, making them good intelligence gatherers. But some in the clan had a combat-grade talent. No wonder it was becoming such a spectacle on Yíchǎn with everyone coming to check out this year's class.

The guy with the pretty peach hair and deep tan was Colin Aung. When he smiled, two dimples flashed against his brown skin and his eyes curved like half moons. His clan was from Myanmar but I'd never dealt with them. I also didn't have anything in my dossiers about the Aungs. Perhaps they were aligned with the Moks.

The three of them immediately wanted to take selfies for Yíchǎn. I threatened to smash Colin's phone when he tried to get me in the photo. They all made puppy dog eyes at me. My brother's friends were outrageously appealing. I would have to beat off interested parties with a stick.

We went inside Hell's Bite and my spirits perked up slightly at the thought of a little healthy altercation with overly exuberant drunks who stepped out of line.

By the third bar of the night, I was despairing that the old gods had completely forsaken me to a life of utter misery. Tatsuya and his mates screamed at the tops of their lungs, belting out some C-pop tune, committing what had to amount to a felony crime against the arts. The crowded interior of the karaoke lounge was littered with empty plates of bar food and crushed beer cans, and packed with a gaggle of Tatsuya's classmates, each of them in various states of inebriation.

I stood alone in the back corner, sipping a bottle of sparkling water, keeping a wary eye on the one exit we had from this room. I had positioned myself to see out the door and down the narrow hallway that led to the exit from the building. The hallway was narrow enough for me to defend on my own. In a pinch, the small windows in the lounge could be broken out and we were only on the second floor.

My hopes for a proper brawl with a bunch of anonymous drunks had been dashed after the first bar. As it turned out, I was part of the group of anonymous drunks. Tatsuya's group was big enough, and my warning glares were harsh enough, that we'd spent the night unmolested.

This was turning into a terrible night for me. I could have downed two bags of strawberry Kit Kats by now. Instead, I was enduring this torment. My only solace were the Kit Kats I'd stuffed in my pockets. I pulled out the cheery pink package, tearing the foil and biting across the bar. Some people liked to snap each stick off. I found it more satisfying to just chomp straight down. Two packages later, I was still stuck in this lousy bar with this lousy music but I was feeling a little more magnanimous.

At least Tatsuya was getting a chance to blow off some steam before Lóng Yá. As Freddy had warned me, my brother might face some of these kids in competition, and the bonds of their friendship would truly be tested. It was good for them to have this one last night with the illusion of their friendship.

Minjae lumbered over, folding his tall frame into the bench across from me. I signaled the waiter and asked for tea. Maybe I could get some down his gullet so that he could actually walk back home in a somewhat straight line. Drunk as he was, he managed to keep his aura locked down tight, second nature for a Byun.

He blinked slowly, looking like a drunk baby owl. His eyes seemed to have a hard time focusing. He swallowed and mustered up the words that I'd sensed were coming.

"Are you still the Blade?"

"No."

He blinked again, my curt response apparently derailing his train of thought.

"Did you really get kicked out of Lóng Kǒu?"

"Yes."

The tea arrived and I pushed it in front of him. "Drink this."

He obliged, wiped his lips with the back of his wrist, then set the teacup back down.

"What do you do if you're not the Blade and you didn't get ranked during Lóng Yá?"

If it were anyone else than a kid about to go through Lóng Yá, I probably would have been offended. But he seemed genuinely confused. I understood that, too. Growing up in a Hoard Custodian family, you had no real choices. Your *only* choice was Lóng Yá.

I had defied those traditions. My history was well known, and to outsiders, it looked strange. How did one fail out of Lóng Kǒu due to weakness, and yet still inherit a Blade?

By my parents' scheming, the use of a Talon, and Ogata-sensei's training, I'd been reshaped. Forged anew to suit a new purpose. As part of Jōkōryūkai, I had existed outside of my family. But failing to take the final oath to the Association and formally renouncing my clan ties had resulted in yet another failure. My father found another role for me. And once again, I had purpose to serve the family.

I boiled it down for Minjae, who wanted to know what would happen if he didn't make it through Lóng Yá. In the end, there was only one answer.

"One can still be of service to the clan."

This was the inescapable truth I had spent two years trying to deny. I had put an ocean between me and the rest of the clan, but it didn't matter. When the Jōkōryūkai had demanded my last vow, I couldn't do it. Even after breaking Truth, I couldn't sever ties with my clan. I was the Sentinel of San Francisco now, but cut me and Soong blood would spill forth.

Minjae scrubbed a big palm over his face, his skin ghostly under the neon lighting of the bar. The smiles and goofy poses of earlier were gone as he slumped lower into the bench. Finally he nodded and said, "Yes, family first."

My chest tightened in sympathy. He did not look like the confident young man from hours earlier. He looked like someone who understood he had a major trial ahead of him and was dreading it. I would be seeing this same thing in Tatsuya. If not tonight, very soon.

Colin bopped over and scooted in next to me on my bench. "Can I buy you a drink?"

"No."

"How do you feel about younger men?"

"I find they bleed faster when I cut them."

I lit up the pommel on Hachi, the blood jade glittering there. Colin's eyes went big and he placed a hand on his heart. "Please take me under your wing and show me the ways of the Blade."

I rolled my eyes and cuffed him on the back of his head. "Get Tatsuya, we need to leave."

With a gratifying show of speed, Colin rushed off to track down my gregarious brother.

A subjective eon later, the boys lurched out of the bar, still belting the chorus from the last song. Maybe the cool night air and drizzling rain would sober them up. Despite his size, Minjae was the clear lightweight of the trio, his lanky form propped on either side by Tatsuya and Colin. The crowds from earlier had thinned out and only the most determined partygoers were still out at this hour. With Lóng Yá starting soon, the rest of the students chose to retire as well, dispersing in different directions. That left me with just Tatsuya and his two friends.

The streetlamps glowed weakly and night seemed to swallow us as we left Golden Gai. With no further plans, I steered the boys to a street where we could hail a cab. The music of the bars faded and now the only sounds were the murmurs and laughs of the boys and our footsteps in the rain. I stayed behind the wobbling gait of the boys but close, my eyes sweeping the twisty streets out of habit.

As we turned down a narrow street, a raspy laugh drifted out of the darkness. I whirled to find nothing but flickering shadows. Red and blue tinted light from storefront neons and a lone vending machine lit the rain-splattered pavement in jittering rings of color. A bolt of lightning crackled across the sky, lighting the street from end to end. Thunder boomed and the light rain turned into a torrent, smearing the colors of the streetlamps and neons and filling the world with the hammering drone of rain. Tension clawed its way up my spine even as rainwater crept down the back of my neck.

I unbuttoned the trench coat to let it hang open, giving me more freedom of movement, and drew Hachi. The rain soaked my silk blouse and trousers instantly, but I paid the cold and wet little mind. Water beaded and ran along Hachi's blade, little glittering pearls sparkling in the flickering neon light. I searched the darkness. She was here.

"Tatsuya!"

"Yeah?"

He froze when he saw Hachi, the drunken ease wiped off his face. I wasted precious seconds shucking my jewelry and threw all the pearls at him. They wouldn't do me any good, and he might need them. Tatsuya ducked out from under Minjae's arm to catch the pearls before they fell to the street. Minjae and Colin went down in a puddle of water, laughing as they landed.

Lightning flashed again and I whirled, searching the opposite end of the street in the brief glare. The two boys continued to howl with laughter even as Tatsuya struggled to don the extra pearls and get his friends to his feet. He turned to me, his eyes wide as saucers.

The odor of rotting ginger assaulted me. I looked up behind Tatsuya to the second story where a large, dilapidated air conditioner unit sat in shadow. I lunged for him as the dark walker melted out of the darkness, her eyes burning bright above the broken Noh mask. Her katana was already drawn and pulled back to strike.

My boots splashed through ankle-deep water. "Get down!"

Tatsuya spun to look behind him, his hands still busy trying to wrangle his friends. The assassin landed softly on the sidewalk and sprang forward, eyes intent on the boys.

My brother screamed and his power ignited, filling the alleyway with the stinging scent of pepper. He clenched a fist and ripped a backpack-sized chunk of asphalt up from the street and threw it at the assassin. Gods, he was panicking, not even using his talent like he'd been trained.

The dark walker swerved to the side, evading Tatsuya's attack with ease. I juked to my right to meet her head-on, but now we were running straight at Colin and Minjae.

I screamed at them to get away as the assassin tucked into a slide and took them both out at the knees. They tumbled into my path and I was forced to put up Hachi and jump to clear them both. The assassin came up from her slide again on the opposite side of my brother. Her sword came slashing up as I landed from my jump.

Tatsuya yelped and fell back, narrowly avoiding the strike. The assassin pressed, lunging into my brother as he landed on the pavement. He was beyond my reach. I wasn't going to make it.

Colin untangled himself from Minjae and slammed into Tatsuya, taking him down like a rugby tackle. The katana flicked out and across Colin's shoulder. His soaked trench coat parted like wet paper-mache and blood fountained from a gaping wound in his arm. The young man screamed as he and Tatsuya rolled away from the assassin.

My voice boomed, pitched like Uncle Lau's. "Tatsuya! Defend!"

That snapped him out of it. He grunted and the blacktop around him and his friends shattered in a ten-foot circle. Marble-sized rocks whirled into the air, forming a column of grinding rubble around the boys. Colin's moaning cries broke through the crush of rocks and gravel. I had to leave Tatsuya to take care of his friend.

"Tatsuya! Don't let Colin use his talent! Her sword is poisoned!"

The assassin stopped, considering the protective cyclone Tatsuya had created, and then turned to me.

Her voice was a low growl. "The job is your brother. But you I'll do for free."

With the mask I couldn't see her mouth moving. But her eyes burned hotter as she spoke, widening until the whites were exposed.

The stench of her talent hit me again. "Tatsuya! Go to the safe house!"

"But—"

"Go!"

The shadows up and down the alley exploded and I charged straight for the dark walker. I had to keep her focused on me while Tatsuya and his friends got away. She met my strike with her blade and we traded blows as I pushed her back a step. Rain flew from our swords as we clashed, the sound of ringing metal echoing off the stone walls.

Her katana flashed at my eyes. I ducked and put Hachi up. The edge of her blade met the flat of mine and slid past me. I spun and aimed a kick at her back as her momentum carried her behind me.

My boot landed in empty space and the cold of the dark dimension gripped my leg, pain lancing up to my hip. She'd opened a hole in the folds of her jacket. I jumped back, favoring the leg, and we squared off again.

Tatsuya and his friends had cleared the alley. At least I'd done that much. The assassin and I circled each other, slow steps to the left, taking a pause to size the other up while staying out of striking distance. Her hood was thrown back, revealing dark hair tied back into a functional ponytail. The flickering neons cast her Noh mask in mottled shades of blue, her eyes glittering beneath severe brows.

The assassin made a strange, hacking sound. Was she laughing? "You know, I used to be so scared of you."

"You should be. If you know me, you know what I've done."

"Your stories are legend, true. But it's also true that the legends are bigger."

Her head tilted to the side. "And you're so . . . small."

A bright line of pain sizzled across the back of my left thigh. I spun, Hachi flashing out, but there was nothing there. I tried my weight on the leg and my knee nearly buckled. A rush of heat drenched the back of my thigh. The dark walker made her low, hacking sound again. The stench of rotting ginger filled the alley like a fog.

"To think, I once thought I had to be as good as you."

She twirled her katana and a flash of dull red caught my eye. "The amount of time and respect I wasted on your whole family."

The assassin didn't move from her spot but something cut into my right calf. I spun again, my trench coat flaring around me, spraying water in all directions. Still there was nothing to be seen. No other opponents. Not even the glint of metal. Hot blood seeped into my boot.

The dark walker sheathed her katana, her eyes brimming with hatred. "Ogata-sensei was right. You really are a one-trick pony."

The cold of the rainwater shot through me like a spear. The assassin laughed as she saw the dawning realization on my face.

This time I caught the motion out of the corner of my eye and spun to face it. The shadows from a doorway reached out to me. Unlike the ones at the train station, this one was narrow and shaped like a blade. I screamed and brought up Hachi to smash it away.

My sword passed through the shadow with no effect. My swing carried me around and the shadow blade shot past me, piercing my trench and carving a white-hot arc of pain across my ribs. I fell to the wet street and curled around my wounded side.

The assassin walked toward me, her black boots splashing water as she came. I tried to lift Hachi but she stepped on my hand, crushing my fingers against the grip. I bit back a whimper of pain.

I'd lived a dangerous life. I knew my career would invariably lead me to a messy end. There was a certain irony that it would be at the hand of the Jōkōryūkai, the ones who had forged me. And there would be no honor for me, bleeding out on a rain-soaked street in Tokyo like so much trash. I sent a silent prayer to the Old Dragons to watch over Tatsuya for me. Freddy and Fiona, too. It couldn't hurt.

The dark walker squatted down, keeping her foot on my hand. One of my finger joints popped out, sending a white-hot star of pain up my arm. Her voice was a bare rumble over the pattering rain on the blacktop. "This has been fun. Everything I always dreamed it would be."

She raised a hand to her face and pulled away the Noh mask. Gooseflesh prickled over my already frozen skin as Kaida's face emerged, the slashing eyebrows over the straight Hiroto nose. The spitting image of my mother. She smiled at me as rainwater dripped off her chin.

"Poor pampered Emiko. Your mother didn't tell you, did she?"

Kaida jammed the handle of her katana under my chin and forced my head up. With my hand pinned I strained to keep my shoulder from popping out.

"Perfect little Emiko. Sara's favorite. I still can't believe she kept coming back to clean up your messes."

She leaned forward and something went loose and hot in my elbow. "Forcing *me* to clean up your mess!"

I had no idea what she was talking about but I was finding it hard to pay attention to her words because my eyes were locked on her sword and the carved blood jade phoenix set into the tsuba.

A perfect match to Hachi's.

Kaida smiled, the expression wide and manic. "Ah, you noticed you're holding onto my sword, did you?"

She pulled her sword away from my neck and brought the tsuba close to her face. The blood jade lit up, casting her features in hellish shadows.

"I'm going to let you keep Hachi, for now. I just wanted you to know that I can beat you, anytime I want to. I'll get to your little brother in time. And there's nothing you can do about it. Once I'm done, I'll be back for Hachi."

She stood and stepped over me. After a few more footsteps she simply vanished, taking the scent of ginger with her. I stared at the oily stains of her power until there was nothing but the torrent of rain washing down.

JŌKŌRYŪKAI

Father was nowhere to be found as Tatsuya and I limped home in the dark hours before dawn. I'd abandoned my dignity and shredded my silk trousers into very serviceable bandages across my torso and around both legs. Tatsuya had a lot of questions, but I had no answers for him. Or at least, none that I wanted to speak out loud.

My time at Jōkōryūkai was something my family kept under wraps. I didn't talk about it and everyone knew not to ask me about it. Aside from Uncle Lau and Fujita-san, it wasn't clear to me that anyone else even knew where I spent those six years. I'd once heard Father tell someone I'd been away at a very remote boarding school in Switzerland.

Not even close. Instead, I'd been hidden away at one of the most shadowy organizations that lurked at the Jiārén outskirts. I'd trained with the best and I'd become very good at eliminating Wàirén threats to the First Law.

But I'd fallen short and disappointed Ogata-sensei, and my prospects at Jōkōryūkai terminated at year six. Was my failure coming back to haunt me?

Maybe it wasn't about me.

Kaida had targeted Fiona, not me. But her grudge with me seemed personal. And now she'd targeted Tatsuya.

But why? As much as I hated to admit it, I needed to think like my father, and look past the surface. My father's plans always had layers within layers, all concealing and protecting each other.

My brother was too young to have gained an enemy like this. A strike at him could only be a strike at my father, at our family. We were a small clan, and there was no heir in waiting after Tatsuya. We kept an outsized fighting force to guard against threats, but clearly Tacchan was our weak point. If something were to happen to him, who would the clan follow? Certainly not me.

The looks on the faces of the Iron Fists swam up out of memory. No, I could not lead the clan the way my brother could. Taking my brother out would rob our clan of its future.

It occurred to me then that an outsider might consider Fiona to be in a similar situation. Freddy had stepped aside for his sister and kept himself conspicuously away from clan operations. I knew the truth behind Freddy's quasi-exile, but who else? Did Freddy's laid-back temperament make his sister appear vulnerable?

I closed my eyes in despair. Someone was trying to take out two Bā Tóu families, and they were using Jōkōryūkai to do it. What had started with me doing a favor for Fiona was now so intensely personal I couldn't see my way out of this. I thought about my vow to leave the Butcher behind.

Could I do it?

Or would I renounce my new vow in order to protect Tatsuya? Bitterness rose in my throat. I might as well take Father's sword tonight. What was the point in me pretending to be different?

I stared up at the coffered ceiling as I lay in the circle in the Bǎowù hé and Tatsuya tapped softly on the sound bowls. The cut on my calf was a thin pink line now, nearly healed. I didn't even need Yoko this time. The ringing of the bowls rose and fell, and I felt my qì cycle faster, resonating with the waves. Exhaustion caught up to me and dragged me down to sleep.

I am lost in a world of twisting shadows, shifting bands of darkness that confuse my perspective and make me dizzy. A knot of anxiety sits heavy on my heart and I know I have to move. When I try to run the moving shadows trip up my feet and send me crashing down.

Tatsuya's voice comes to me out of the darkness. "Emi?"

"Tacchan!"

His voice seems to come from everywhere. I crawl on hands and knees and stop when my hand lands on something cold and sticky. Light flashes briefly and I gag. My hand is covered in old blood, pooled around Freddy's body. He's been ravaged by blades, his body opened a dozen times, and his eyes stare unseeing into the dark.

I jerk away from his body and the shifting shadows spin me around again.

Light blinks again and this time I see Tacchan in the distance. I scramble to my feet and run to him. Where is my sword? Where are my weapons?

Tacchan is standing half in shadow, his eyes pleading, his hand reaching for me.

No, not half in shadow. The darkness behind him shifts and distorts until Kaida's face emerges from the inky black. Her eyes are black and her mouth is a cruel smile.

She laughs, mocking. "Too late!"

Kaida erupts into a writhing mass of shadow. I run faster but can't get any closer. The shadows turn into blades and descend on my brother, impaling him. His screams drive a dagger of fear through my heart.

I awoke with a start, my heart pounding in my ears. After a moment I recognized the ceiling of our Bǎowù hé. The ringing bowls had gone silent. I scrubbed at my face to erase the last wisps of the nightmare and sat up.

Tacchan was asleep on the floor next to me, his breathing slow and regular. At least he seemed to be having a peaceful rest. I tapped the bowls again and lay down, hoping the sound would soothe me back to sleep. I stared at the ceiling, but sleep eluded me.

Kaida's face kept coming back to me, filling my vision even with my eyes open. The naked hatred in her eyes haunted me. I'd made a lot of enemies as the Blade, but I had never felt anything so intensely personal.

Tacchan stirred and I tapped his shoulder. "When was the last time you saw Uncle Jiro?"

He groaned and turned on his side. "Um . . . maybe ten years ago?"

"Have you seen Kaida since Uncle Jiro died?"

"Yeah. Uh, Mother had her over a lot before I started at Lóng Kǒu."

"How long before?"

He blinked and his eyebrows drew together as he thought for a while. "Maybe within the year before I went to Lóng Kǒu."

So that had been almost seven years ago. Long enough for Kaida to train at Jōkōryūkai.

Tacchan rubbed his face. "You going to tell me why someone tried to kill us tonight and why you're asking me questions about our cousin?"

I sighed. I didn't want to have this talk. But Tatsuya's life was in danger and anything I gave him could be the edge he needed to save his life.

"It's Kaida. She's after Fiona. And apparently, she's after you as well."

Tatsuya's eyes widened. "But, you beat her tonight, right?"

I clenched my hand into a fist. The dislocated finger was nearly healed but still tender. "No, Tacchan. She let me off with a warning tonight. She's toying with us, like a cat playing with its food."

My brother's voice was a whisper, barely audible.

"What?"

Tatsuya said, "I didn't think she was mad at all of us."

"Kaida? Who was she mad at?"

Tatsuya scrubbed his hands over his face. "I don't know. I just remember her fighting with Mother. All the time. I thought she was just mad that Mother was so strict with her. I never thought she would come back and attack us."

After I was shipped off to Jōkō I had very little contact with my family. "What happened to her?"

Tatsuya shook his head. "I don't know. All I know is, one day you were back, and then Kaida was gone."

Gooseflesh puckered up and down my arms and I rubbed the sensation away. Skies above, what had my mother done this time? A dark suspicion surfaced. Had she sent Kaida to Jōkō in my place?

Was that even possible?

This was not my forte. Send me to take out threats. I knew how to do that. Clan treachery and scheming, though, were beyond my abilities. I focused on learning my opponents' fighting strengths and weaknesses, opportunities for me to exploit in combat or assassination. I had nothing significant in my research about clan relationships. I inhaled deeply, considering what I could do.

I needed to protect my brother and Fiona. My father would take care of the rest.

Tacchan sighed, the sound long and piteous. "I can't believe Colin's out."

It would take days to purge the toxin from the young man's system. Days during which he would have to be very careful about moving his qì. Not something he could do and still participate in Lóng Yá.

Tacchan threw an arm over his eyes. "His parents are going to be beyond angry. Their sponsor was going to put up a Hoard piece for him if he made the top eight. This was supposed to be the year his family made a big move."

Every family that competed in the final rounds of Lóng Yá put one piece of their Hoard into a Winner's Pot. It was not unheard of for an underdog talent to win the Tourney and propel their family into top-tier Jiārén status. Unlikely, but not unheard of.

"At least he's still alive. And he saved your life doing it."

My brother turned to look at me and the expression on his face added ten years. "Ask him in a few days if he still thinks it was worth it."

"Lóng Yá isn't everything, Tacchan."

"That's easy for you to say."

"What's that supposed to mean?"

My brother groaned. "I don't know. It means not everyone that fails out of Lóng Kǒu gets a magic sword, Emiko."

"What, are you mad that I became the Blade? You know what that cost me."

"No, I'm not mad, it's just . . . Lóng Yá really is everything. For a lot of people, it's the only thing."

"What are you talking about? Father is going—"

"Gods, I'm not talking about just me, Emi. Look at Colin. He's been working his butt off to do well in the maze. He didn't even need to compete beyond that. He would've made top eight, and earned a sponsor for his family. Even without winning the Pot, his family would take a step up in status. New friends, new connections, everything!"

My brother sat up and buried his face in his hands. "And now because of me, he's out of Lóng Yá. Do you know what happens to bottom-tier students? His parents might even decide to pull his sister out. She's supposed to start next year, but if she starts with that albatross around her neck . . ."

I put my hands on my brother's shoulders until he raised his head. "It's not your fault, Tatsuya. And Colin did a good thing. Our family is not going to forget that. I'm not going to forget that."

Father seemed inordinately happy that I'd taken the Sentinel mantle. Perhaps it was time I tried to sway some of that goodwill. "I'll talk to Father, ask him to take Colin on this year. The family owes him for saving your life."

My brother scrunched up his face, his skepticism clear. "Really? You think Father will go for that?"

He had to. The thought of Colin losing his way because of a service he'd done for our family was a twisting cold knot in my gut now. Tacchan was right to be upset. We had to make this right.

His eyes drifted up to the box on the steel elephant's back. Where the blood jade was secured.

I thumped him on the sternum with my fist. "Absolutely not."

"What? I didn't do anything."

"You saw what happened to Old Li tonight. You're in no shape to absorb any more blood jade. You're just going to have to prepare for Lóng Yá the hard way."

His eyes met mine, annoyed. "Your way?"

"My way."

I rolled up onto my knees and looked down at Tatsuya. His face was pale, the alcohol and the attack all catching up with him. I, on the other hand, would not be getting any more sleep. Too many pieces were falling into places that I didn't like. I needed answers. "Get some rest. We'll train later."

Sleep pulled at his eyes. "Where are you going?"

"I need to follow up on something." It wasn't a lie, but it was nowhere near the truth, either. But Tacchan didn't need to hear the truth right now. Right now he needed rest.

He nodded and his head fell back with a thunk. Dark lashes fanned across his high cheeks and it struck me how very young he was. Not just him, but his friends as well. And at this moment, they were all training for the most brutal fight of their lives. I'd never participated in Lóng Yá, and the closer we got to Tacchan's, the less I liked it. I picked up the mallet and struck the singing bowls to set them cascading while Tatsuya cycled his qì.

Whatever happened, I would make sure my brother survived.

Clanhome was never fully quiet, but the small hours between the darkest night and dawn was as close as it ever came to full sleep. After a change of clothes, I walked slowly through the house, keeping my steps light and staying near the walls. I knew every foot of this house, and long ago memorized where all the squeaks in the floor were. So it wasn't difficult to make it to my father's office without making a sound.

I pulled open the door and peered in through the tiny crack.

Father's animals were all quiet, their eyes dull and dark. Wherever he was, my father was asleep. The jian he had laid out to tempt me was in the same place, atop the silk cloth. My fingers itched to hold it, to feel the weight in my palm, to once again have that deadly extension of my arm.

There was only one place I could go to get answers about Kaida and Jōkōryūkai, but it should be a death sentence to go there. The idea of having a blade with longer reach was a siren song in my heart. The heft of a new jian across my back would go a long way to making me feel better about my plan.

I stood there for a full minute, my eyes drinking in the sword through the crack in the doorway. It took every bit of my will to slowly shut the door. I held the latch and allowed the door to lock silently.

A second sword wasn't going to help me much if things went badly. And nothing from my father was a gift. Taking the sword would mean consequences I hadn't planned for, and I had promised myself that I was done submitting myself to his will.

I needed to do this without his help.

The trip from Atami to Fuji-Hakone-Izu was a short train ride that took me into the pastoral Japanese countryside. Long before I'd left my place at my father's side as the Blade, I'd already abandoned another. The train sped north, taking me closer to another failure I'd been running from. Kaida's appearance had opened an old door that I'd spent a long time trying to close. Now it was open again, and I wondered what it would cost me to close it.

Ogata-sensei's granite jawline loomed out of memory, disappointment and anger clear in the tight line of the scar along his neck.

I kneel in the same small dojo where we first met, the year I left Lóng Kǒu. Much has changed. Gone is the silly girl who despaired of finding her talent to please her parents. The Jōkōryūkai has molded the soft clay of that girl into a sharp implement, ready to be tested.

I bow until my forehead touches the old straw, anguish thick in my throat. My belly roils, threatening to eject my breakfast onto the tatami, only furthering my shame. It is the last day of six years of training. Ogata-sensei has been a harsh, demanding, and yet generous master, giving me purpose and drive. He has been more than a teacher to me. I have come to respect him as much as my own father.

And so the pain of betraying his trust is like the thrust of cold steel into my belly. In my first test, Ogata-sensei's newest weapon is revealed to be brittle, shattering on impact.

Ogata-sensei's voice is a harsh whisper. "Say the words!"

I press my forehead into the mat, trying to push myself through the floor and into the depths of hell. Hot tears sting my eyes. "I cannot."

Rare emotion thickens my sensei's voice. "Emi-chan."

I close my eyes and shut out his voice. If I had known the path would end here, I would have fought my parents the day they left me here. I would have died before I let them leave me. Ogata-sensei trained me for many things, but not for this.

The air stirs, and steel hisses. My arms move with speed born of relentless training, drawing my sword. I bring my sword up as I roll up to my knees. Ogata-sensei stands above me, his hands bringing his sword down upon my head. My own sword comes up and our blades meet between us with a ringing clash.

My shame knows no bounds. A dutiful student would have accepted her failure and allowed Ogata-sensei to strike her head off. I flaunt my shame and insist that I live, further defying my sensei.

Unthinkable.

Ogata-sensei's eyes are rimmed with red and dark with emotion. His arms strain against me, levering his weight against me and bringing the edge of his sword closer to my exposed neck. I push and twist, sending my teacher falling past me as our swords part. His bare foot slams onto the tatami, the sound heavy with ruin. He stands and sheaths his sword, his face averted from mine. Without a word he steps to the door and slides it aside, letting in the cool autumn breeze. He walks out of the dojo and crosses the courtyard, his shoulders stiff, his usual rolling gait altered, like he is walking with a terrible wound.

I never spoke to him again. I fled the grounds with nothing more than the clothes and swords on my back. I fought a gauntlet of others to escape and crawled home, leaving behind a trail of my blood. Once in the sanctuary of clanhome, Yoko had worked on me for weeks until I healed.

Ogata-sensei had let me off easy.

There was no guarantee that the reprieve Ogata-sensei had given me would last any longer than the time it took him to leave my sight.

Returning to the Jōkōryūkai was madness. Suicide. And yet, what choice did I have? I needed to know more about Kaida, and we clearly had shared history with Ogata-sensei. This was the only place to find answers.

The memory of my last words with my sensei was a raw wound that had never quite scabbed over. Going to the Jōkōryūkai grounds today would pour a bowl of salt over that wound. They'd taken me in after I'd failed out of Lóng Kǒu and forged me into the weapon. I'd repaid them by betraying the core of the Association. If I was lucky, they would kill me quickly when I stepped foot on the grounds.

If I wasn't lucky, they would use me as a training exercise.

While the pocket Realm for Lóng Kǒu was presently anchored at Todai University, the Jōkōryūkai grounds had been hidden deep in Fuji-Hakone-Izu National Park. The park's constant foot traffic was the perfect place to hide in plain sight.

I had walked this path to the torii shrine countless times. I let the tourists and shrine visitors pass by me then knelt to study the rocks on the northern patch. To passersby, they just looked like rocks. To Jōkōryūkai members, they pointed to the place for the Crossing.

When the path was clear, I stepped through the clearing to the dense cluster of ginkgo trees. I found the hidden carving and brought out the stone turtle in my pocket. In a breath and another heartbeat, I had crossed through to the grounds.

Unlike some Jiārén institutions that were more security conscious, Jōkōryūkai didn't worry overly about security. After all, every person there had extensive knowledge in how to kill or disable another with ease. And if you couldn't, then you weren't worthy to be a member of the Association.

Outsiders would be first confounded by the twisty and narrow roads, designed to funnel invaders into unfavorable battlegrounds.

The hilly terrain was shaded by beautiful trees, the ginkgos and maples offering a soft palette of color against the warriors' stark quarters. To the east was the tearoom, because even warrior monks needed to sit down for tea on occasion. I had loved that room, with its zen fusuma, the delicately painted paper panels offering me respite from the grueling rigors of training. My other refuge had been the koi garden behind the main hall. As a trainee, I'd gathered with the others at the main hall for recitations on the Way of the Jōkōryūkai, but despite being in the crowd, I'd always been alone.

My brain knew the path to Ogata-sensei's quarters like a bird returning to its nest. I heard the distinctive sounds of the bō strikes and a part of me wanted to stop and observe everyone staff fighting. I wondered if it would be different now to look at it as an instructor, the way I worked with Leanna on the staff, or if I'd get sucked back into the mental desperation I'd fought with before when I'd been so anxious to prove to Ogata-sensei that I was worth his attention.

I caught the scent of baked bread and I whirled with Hachi unsheathed in a single motion. My wakizashi struck steel with a ringing note. My opponent was dressed in the simple attire all Jōkōryūkai used for sparring—loose pants and a gi shirt that might have been black at some time in the past decades. None of that was a surprise. No, the surprise was that I knew him. Saburo's tanned face had the lean cheeks and hard planes of someone who worked hard every day. His salt-and-pepper hair was shaved down to an even stubble.

The last time I'd seen him, he'd been in my town, bleeding from the blow I'd dealt him.

Saburo leaned in to me and I leaned in as well, to keep him from taking the advantageous position. His dark eyes were flat, devoid of malice, and also absent any warmth. When we first met, he had the unenviable task of guarding Ray Ray Louie. We'd fought, and I'd spared his life. He didn't look like someone bent on revenge, but I still might live to regret my mercy.

With our swords locked we both pressed for dominance. I heard the others when they came through the trees, which meant they must have been trainees. Jōkōryūkai moved on silent feet. Saburo sighed and broke away from me. I backed up a step and found myself surrounded by six people in white trainee garb, each carrying a very real sword.

There was no time for kid gloves at Jōkōryūkai.

Saburo barked at the new arrivals. "That was abysmal. You make more noise than a herd of water buffalo. Back to the training room, all of you."

The trainees turned to go but one, a young man, hesitated. "Sensei?" The young man's eyes lingered on me, but lacked recognition. I was just a stranger to them then, not as notorious as I had feared.

Saburo waved him on. "This one is . . . my guest. I will see to her."

When the trainees were gone, Saburo gave me a small bow. "Our scales are balanced, Sentinel."

I returned the bow and Saburo turned on his heel, leading me up the gravel path, to the small square building that was Ogata-sensei's office. He tapped lightly on the wooden doorframe.

"Sensei. A visitor is here for you."

OGATA-SENSEI

At a grunt from inside the little house, Saburo slid the wooden door open and stood respectfully to the side to allow me to enter. I had returned to Jōkōryūkai and was lucky enough to have made it to my sensei's office. And now, standing on the threshold, I was more nervous than when I had been facing almost certain death. I forced my shoulders to relax and stepped into his domain.

Ogata-sensei knelt on the small square of tatami that made up the entire floor of the little building. He faced away from the door, with a low table before him. A small window offered a view of the training grounds, still empty in the early morning light. The table held a small clay teapot and cup, and a breakfast tray that had been pushed to the side, ready for someone to take away. A ledger lay open on the table before him. Ogata-sensei made no notice of my entrance other than the slight pause in the soft scratching of his pencil.

I knelt on the tatami, pressed my forehead to the mat, and stayed there.

The pencil scratched for a moment longer before it was put down and my sensei spoke. "Saburo?"

"Yes, sensei." From the muffled sound of his voice, I could tell Saburo was also bowed to the floor, just outside the door.

"Why?"

"The student apologizes to his master. I owed your visitor a life debt. Had I ended her life, I would have carried that debt into the afterlife."

"Hmm."

I hadn't moved since bowing. I sensed that Saburo hadn't moved, either. We both waited on Ogata-sensei's judgment. The irony that I had last left after refusing his judgment was not lost on me.

The pencil scratching resumed for a moment and then the ledger was closed.

"Saburo. You may go."

"Hai."

I kept my head down as Saburo's shuffling feet departed.

Cloth rustled across the tatami. From the shifting shadows I guessed that Ogata-sensei had turned to face me. I still dared not lift my head. My old master slurped the last of his tea and placed the clay cup back on the low table.

After a moment Ogata-sensei stood and moved about the small room, with more rustling cloth. He stepped over to me and stopped next to my head. From the corner of my eye I saw his feet clad in worn geta sandals.

"Come, Emi-chan. Let us talk."

I followed my old master at a respectful distance as we descended the small hill and followed a well-worn path that led to the sparring grounds. The sounds of students at work beating each other senseless drifted up to us as we walked through a grove of ginkgo trees.

Ogata-sensei walked with his hands behind his back, his wooden slippers clicking on the hard-packed path. He stopped to admire a particularly large ginkgo tree, a small smile on his face. His hair had considerably more gray in it than I remembered but was still cut neat and short. The scar along his neck flexed as he worked his jaw.

"Thank you for what happened in San Francisco. Saburo is a good man, and the task was unworthy of him."

That was not the opening I had expected from the master who I had betrayed when last I saw him. I opened my mouth and then closed it, uncertain how to respond.

His eyebrows went up, as if a thought had just occurred to him.

"Walk with me."

He strode off through the trees, not bothering to wait for me or even check if I was following. After a moment I hurried to catch up with him, my guts writhing with unspent tension. Even after all my years away, I still yearned for my teacher's approval. I was a disgraced student. I had expected trial by combat, facing down a team of screaming assassins. The last thing I had expected from Ogata-sensei was . . . a tour.

I followed him across the small valley to a low building set in the shade of towering trees. The shoji had been opened along the longest walls, allowing the building to warm in the morning air. We approached from the rear to find a dozen young men and women in practice gis shuffling to find their places on the tatami. On the opposite side of the building an iron bell large enough to engulf a man hung from one of the trees. One of my old instructors, Ito-sensei, a whip-thin woman with stern eyes and brutally short gray hair, stood beside the bell, holding a short length of wood in her hand. She had to be at least eighty years old by now, and still capable of breaking any of these students in half.

On some unheard signal the students came to order, facing Ito-sensei and knelt seiza in one smooth motion. Ito-sensei struck the bell and a low, resonant tone filled the little valley. My chest vibrated gently in response to the bell.

Oh, no.

Ogata-sensei's gaze was a physical weight on my shoulders. I kept my eyes forward, unable to bring myself to turn and face him, not in this context, in front of so many students who demonstrated their loyalty every day.

In unison, the students bowed their heads to the tatami. "We are Jōkōryūkai."

My chest seized up and my breath whistled through my nose, high and thin. I'd said these words, many years ago, but I did not complete the oath.

The students lifted their heads but kept their hands on the floor.

Ito-sensei struck the bell again and the students bowed again. "We are the sword and armor."

Another gong. Another bow. "Our life is service."

Tears stung the backs of my eyes and the scene wavered before me. The bell rang again and the students bowed. "I have no mother, no father."

The bell intoned one last time. "My family are Jōkōryūkai, my brothers and sisters."

Ito-sensei stepped into the dojo, her calloused feet scraping across the straw. Her dark eyes traveled over the bowed heads of her students. "Ai!"

Her voice was as I remembered, a biting snap that cleared the air. Her charges leapt to their feet at her cry, voices bellowing in response. As the students cleared the center of the dojo for sparring, Ogata-sensei took hold of my elbow and turned me down another path that led us deeper into the grounds.

His grip on my elbow tightened. "You have changed, Emiko."

My senses concentrated onto my elbow where his gnarled fingers held my arm in a viselike grip. What was he referring to? My golden Sentinel aura? But Ogata-sensei said nothing else and led me through the trees to a small clearing by a small creek. We stopped in the clearing on the soft grass and Ogata-sensei turned me to face him, his hand still gripping my arm.

"You are not the same woman I knew when you left."

"Yes, sensei. Much has changed."

"You came to us as a flawed stone. I recut that stone and made you into something useful."

His words cut me to my core.

It reminded me that everyone thought I was broken. Useless.

My teacher's hard eyes looked me up and down. "Who are you?"

Without warning, Ogata-sensei dropped my elbow and thrust his other palm at me, an open-handed strike at my chest. His qì exploded from him, an invisible wall of force set to batter me to pieces.

My hand came up to meet Ogata-sensei's strike, my fingers

straight and rigid. Qì coursed through my body, swirled around the Pearl, and flew from my hand as a razor-tipped lance of power.

Our energies collided in the small space between us, my qì fracturing and dissipating Ogata-sensei's attack with the precision of a jeweler's hammer on a stone. My teacher's face was stoic, even as his eyes widened the tiniest bit.

Our clothes rustled with the passing energy. He took a step back from me and set his feet, his hands held at chest level. Anxiety bloomed like a ball of thorns in my gut as Ogata-sensei settled his weight into his hips and waited.

I knew what was coming. It had been drilled into me as a girl. It was the First Steps of the Dragon, the first lesson in every Jiārén's training. Parents taught their children from a young age to move their qì, to prepare them for life in our unyielding society, where we always had to be on our guard. Old, forgotten shame made my hands clammy with sweat. Mother, frustrated and angry as I failed again and again.

Father took over my lessons after Mother gave up on me. He taught me the motions, without the flow of qì, so that I would at least have that. But it was like being taught how to cook, without taste or smell, devoid of truth and joy.

I took up position opposite my teacher and lifted my hands. My fingers trembled just the slightest bit. I knew in my head that Oda had fixed my meridians. I had seen the results. But even holding this position triggered enough of my old fear to make my breath quicken.

Ogata-sensei held the opening pose for a moment and stepped forward. I stepped in as well, bringing my hands up. My left hand on his right forearm, and his left on my right. I took a deep breath, willing my jittering nerves to calm down.

My teacher stepped forward, pressing his weight into mine, his qì swelling like a wave and flowing into me. I mirrored his movement and stepped back. Energy moved through his right arm and into my left hand, where I was supposed to catch it, bring it into my body, and then push it out through my other arm.

I flinched as Ogata-sensei's qì washed over my left hand, the sensation tingling like a thousand cool needles. I completed the step back and visualized the energy moving through me in a circle, blending with my qì, and pushing through my right arm. I shifted my weight forward and pushed, my qì moving with it.

Ogata-sensei's brow creased as he leaned back, completing the cycle. Was my qì too weak?

He pushed forward. "Again."

I blinked back the sting in my eyes as we pushed back and forth, nurturing this tiny eddy of our life energy between us. The rush of qì through my body was an exhilarating feeling I had never imagined I would experience. After a few cycles my breathing loosened and my meridians relaxed, allowing the movement to produce the flow almost effortlessly. Ogata-sensei shifted his feet as the cycle returned to him, moving into the Second Step. My arms changed position by habit, mirroring his, and we continued, swirling qì between us.

My sensei's voice had an odd hoarseness to it that I had not heard before. "When you came to us, your qì was weak. Broken."

The words fell out of my mouth. "I'm not broken."

"Broken. But you were not born with the blocked meridians that obstructed your qì. Something happened to you, but your parents did not share those details with me."

A yawning chasm of horror threatened to open in my gut and swallow me from the inside. I nearly stumbled at Ogata-sensei's words until he squeezed my arm and pulled me back into the flow of our movements. I concentrated on my breath, realigning my intake of air with the intake of qì, and my mind quieted.

I shied away from the topic Ogata-sensei had broached, like a child avoiding a hot pan. I was here for a different reason. "Why is Kaida trying to kill my brother?"

We moved into the Third Step, the form proceeding without need for cues. With this Step, the amount of qì we cycled between us increased to a small storm.

My teacher continued as if I hadn't spoken. "You have a Hoard Gift, Emiko. You just have never been able to access it."

This time I did stumble, my hand slipping off Ogata-sensei's shoulder. With a grunt he put my hand back in place and we continued. Our qì wobbled like an off-balance top until we had recentered ourselves.

"Why was Kaida trained by the Jōkōryūkai?"

"Now that your meridians are repaired, your Hoard Gift will manifest. This is an uncertain time for you, Emiko. You will go through what most Jiārén go through in their youth. Some will see you as vulnerable."

We slid into the Fourth Step, our actions becoming more dramatic and our qì growing into a tightly contained hurricane rushing between us.

"Why does she hate me?"

"Your Gift is unique, Emiko. Dangerous."

I'd been kicked out of Lóng Kǒu because I had no Gift. I was the Broken Tooth of Soong. This one-sided conversation with Ogata-sensei churned up a lot of old resentment. White-hot heat blazed in my belly and the thrashing storm of qì bucked and reared like a wild horse. I struggled to hold on to the wild energy, my voice rising to a shout. "Why won't you answer me?"

Ogata-sensei, calm and stoic as ever, pushed and this time instead of a harmonious sharing of power, he barreled into me. It was the slightest motion on his part, but it threw me off-balance, making me windmill my arms. His left hand shot out and grabbed my right hand, his bigger hand capturing mine in his fist. The flowing qì stuttered, the exit through my right arm cut off, and sloshed back into my center, making my head swim. I fell back and Ogata-sensei grabbed my other hand, forcing me to my knees.

His voice didn't rise above a whisper. "Because the answer is inside you."

The coursing power inside me coalesced into a shining point in my chest that ripped me open from front to back. My arms went rigid and power vented from me like steam escaping a boiler. My Gift blossomed like a burning ingot of molten metal in my bare hands. It had happened with Iron Serpent, and again with Oda Tanaka.

Something deep within me awoke and flared hot.

It took me a split second to realize that the scream was coming from my own mouth and another to comprehend what was going on. A bottomless pit opened inside me as my Gift leapt from my body, searching.

Searching for . . . what? It was hungry, finally loosed after decades of being chained. The hunger subsumed my will, leaving me limp in Ogata-sensei's hands, my arms hanging from his fists. My Gift twisted free of its shackles and leapt forward, latching onto the only target in range. Ogata-sensei.

In my entire tenure at Jōkōryūkai I had never seen my teacher show any outward expression of pain or discomfort, no matter how hard we trained. Now his heavy-lidded eyes widened enough to show the whites all the way around his dark irises. The creases on his brow, and the downward turn of his mouth, transformed him from my immutable teacher into any other Jiārén. A pained grunt escaped his lips and he went to one knee.

My Gift dug its teeth into Ogata-sensei's talent, a sensation both deeply scary and satisfying. Qì filled my limbs to bursting and I pushed to my feet, bringing my teacher with me. Ogata-sensei cried out and his hands let go of mine. Without thinking I grabbed his wrists, clamping my fingers down and tapping into the meridians along his forearms. Now that my Gift had a taste of him, there was no stopping it. Qì flowed out from my arms and barreled into Ogata-sensei, running up his arm and into his core. My sensei's Gift exploded before me, his aura pale red and filling my nose with the scent of herbs.

No!

I couldn't stop even as I struggled to backpedal. This was wrong, a violation.

But my Gift had thrown off its leash and rampaged over my will.

As qì flowed down my right arm and into Ogata-sensei, the cycle completed and returned to me through my left. The power returning to me *was* Ogata-sensei. It was his mannerisms, his demeanor, his very being. Horror dawned in my chest as my left arm . . . changed. My flesh writhed under my skin, muscles shifting and swelling as I drew my teacher's Gift of Dragon Limbs into my body. My eyes widened as jewel-bright, overlapping scales of deep blue-green erupted from my skin, sheathing my forearm in immaculate dragon hide.

The small clearing by the creek disappeared, my vision clouding over in a riot of swirling color. I fell to my knees, my hands still locked on Ogata-sensei's wrists. Qì continued to pour into my left arm and Ogata-sensei's presence rolled over me like a tide.

I am kneeling in the dojo. The tatami is like a dear friend. I know every ridge and contour and can determine my position in the room in the dark using only the soles of my feet. I come here often to meditate and think on the future. Today, however, I am not alone.

The woman who kneels on the tatami across from me is a striking woman, with dark eyes and brows painted by a master calligrapher. Elegant simplicity that speaks volumes. Sara Hiroto is the most powerful woman I have ever met.

Today she kneels before me in contrition, a position I know she is unused to. I consider pressing the issue, but decide that her contrition is adequate. The debts between us are muddled by my own inability to punish Emiko for her defection. It is only fitting that Emiko's mother find an acceptable solution. I would expect no less of a senior member of the Bā Shǒu.

A young woman who bears a striking resemblance to Sara kneels just behind her. At a word from Sara the younger woman comes forward, but stops just short of bringing her knees even with Sara's. She keeps her eyes cast down to the tatami, but even without seeing her face I can tell she is seething with anger. She unfolds her aura, revealing her Gift like an act of defiance.

I can see now, how this act of contrition is meant to appease me. Time has been spent to little effect, but in the larger picture, the past five years have been hardly more than a passing moment. There is still time. This young woman will succeed where Emiko did not. Her Gift will be a fine addition to the Jōkōryūkai.

A Talon sits on the tatami before me, a dark stain of blood swiped across the name engraved into the rich gold. I had not expected to use this Talon so soon, but there is little else to be done. My hand grips the Talon. The gold is warm and stirs my qì like a pebble thrown into still water.

I slide the Talon into the space between us. "Witness."

Sara bows to me.

The young one echoes, "So witnessed."

Sara Hiroto picks up her Talon and stands. She leaves without another word to the young woman.

"What is your name, girl?"

The young woman lifts her head for the first time, and I look into eyes that are the mirror of her aunt's. A raging inferno of emotion burns behind her eyes. "Kaida, sensei."

I threw my will out, clawing, scratching, gouging, fighting to rein in my Gift. This was too much, my master's Gift, his memories flowing into me. It shredded my soul to know that this . . . this abomination . . . was my Gift. With a scream I opened my hands. My joints creaked and popped, my fingers still hooked into claws. Bloody crescents lined the inside of Ogata-sensei's arms. As I broke contact, my Gift fought back, it wanted more, more power, more memories. I wielded my qì like a club and I beat it senseless. A cool balm swept across me, radiating from my chest. Tears streamed down my face as I raged against my Gift and the scent of ocean washed over me. Power from my Pearl bathed me in the sensations of sky and sand, calming the inferno with me. When it quieted, I strapped the hunger down under layers of my will, locking it deep inside me.

Ogata-sensei fell first, his eyes rolled up into the back of his head, collapsing onto me and taking us both to the soft, sweet grass. A sheen of sweat covered both of us. I lifted my sensei's dead weight off my chest and gasped for air. My arms slowly faded back to normal as the foreign qì dissipated from my system. But the memories remained and tore at my soul like rending teeth. The vision of my mother through my teacher's eyes, and the day Kaida paid the price for my weakness.

"No wonder she hates me."

Ogata-sensei had recovered enough to sit up, but both of us were still a ways off from walking around. "Kaida may despise you, but that was not her mission."

"What is her mission, exactly?"

My sensei's eyebrows furrowed. "I cannot say."

I frowned. He knew that I was no longer part of the Association and he couldn't tell me, which meant the Association was part of it.

My heart sank.

I had already been outmatched by the younger, more ruthless dark walker. To know that my family and the Trans were going to be the target of endless Jōkōryūkai members was beyond my worst nightmares.

"What can you tell me about my talent?"

Now Ogata-sensei's eyes became sad. "I think you know the answer to that."

He was right. I was going to have to ask my father.

Ogata-sensei looked away and studied the little creek for a time, and the only noise between us was the laughing water as it tumbled over river stones. My return to Jōkōryūkai was nothing like I'd expected. Strange emotions rolled in my gut as I tried to make sense out of these new truths in my life.

My old teacher stood and his posture was again straight and strong. He didn't look at me. "You can find your way out?"

"Yes."

He nodded. "No one will disturb you as you leave."

I got to my feet and bowed deeply. "The student thanks her master for today's lesson."

When I rose, Ogata-sensei still hadn't turned to face me. My chest ached as I realized this was the best he could do. My talent was a horror, a power so reviled because it went against everything we were as Jiārén.

I knelt and bowed, touching my forehead to the soft grass. My throat thickened and made the words catch. "Goodbye, sensei."

Tears stung the backs of my eyes as I turned to go. I had feared death upon returning to Jōkōryūkai. It might have been the preferred outcome.

HOME IS WHERE THE BUNS ARE

My sleep was restless on the return train to Atami. My insides churned, alternating between the gut-dropping feeling when Ogata-sensei confirmed my talent had been blocked, and the sense memory of the bottomless well of hunger that seemed to be my talent. My abomination of a talent.

In between waves of emotional nausea came raging spikes of anger at my father and mother. How could they hide this from me? How could they look me in the face and lie to me for so many years?

Fatigue eventually won out over outrage, and I spent the last hour of the ride in blessed unconsciousness. When I returned the sun was arcing high in the sky and clanhome was buzzing with its usual frenetic pace. I was a little late, but would be able to catch something sure to ease the discord in my heart: Uncle Jake's breakfast.

My heart lightened as I made my way down the stairs to the kitchen. The scent of mantou greeted me and set my stomach rumbling. I came around the corner and sure enough, the industrial kitchen was still humming but mostly empty. I must have arrived between the breakfast shifts.

Uncle Jake poured boiling pots of soybeans into strainers lined with cheesecloth. Trays of proofing dough lined up on the steel countertops. He was a kinetic with exquisite control, but he didn't serve in the Pearl Guard. Instead, he used his talents to make feasts for all of us. His vibrant red aura was on full display, the color shot through with silvery streaks.

As I watched, the cheesecloths squeezed themselves, straining steaming opaque soy milk into large white ceramic bowls. Small bowls of minced pickled turnip and dried shrimp floating in sesame oil waited to be added to the savory soy milk. The tart scent of Uncle Jake's talent seemed the perfect accompaniment to the scents and sounds of his kitchen.

On the stove, pots of oil heated and a dozen yóutiáo floated through the air to dip into the frying oil. My mouth watered. If there was anything better than baked dough, it was fried dough.

"Good morning, Uncle Jake."

"Mimi! You're home!"

Everything about Uncle Jake was shaped like a square. His block-shaped head was enhanced by his buzzed salt-and-pepper hair. He came around the counter and his rough-hewn face broadened with a big smile and his eyes twinkled with pleasure. He wiped a hand off on his red plaid apron and squeezed my arm. "So skinny. Food must be terrible in San Francisco."

I laughed and my chest loosened. The food was excellent in San Francisco. I was just terrible at eating real meals.

"Sit, sit." Uncle Jake waved me over to the barstools.

A thick ceramic mug floated over and set itself on the counter, along with a metal pot of jasmine tea. It poured a fragrant stream of the jasmine pu-erh blend I loved.

When Uncle Jake made bāo, he made bāo. The man tended an army and he believed a well-fed army was a strong army. Round bamboo steamers were stacked almost to the ceiling. Inside them I'd find ginger pork enrobed in fluffy white buns. There would also be minced tofu and spinach, and, of course, sweet buns filled with red bean paste or black sesame. If I asked nicely, Uncle Jake might even make me nai wong bāo, filled with a rich yellow custard that no restaurant version could hope to match.

Uncle Jake sent me a plate laden with all my favorites. The dish settled in front of me, next to the empty plate at my side. It pleased me to no end that he remembered. But of course, that was what made Uncle Jake so special, beyond his talent and skill.

In addition to remembering which bāo I loved, he always remembered to set a place at the table for my mother. Wherever she might be, on this side of the Void or the other, she could decide to come home at the drop of a hat. Uncle Jake never wanted my mother to feel that clanhome was anything less than her true home. A small, petty voice in my gut wondered if Uncle Jake had put out a plate for me, the long years I'd spent at Jōkō.

The first bite of bāo swept the dark thoughts from my mind and I lost myself in pillowy dough and seasoned pork. I stuffed myself and watched as Uncle Jake set up the rice and miso soup station, mincing scallions for the soup and setting down platter after platter of perfectly grilled mackerel. He set out bowls mounded high with hard-boiled eggs, little plates of sticky nattō, and tiny bowls with sliced takuwan, the cheerful yellow daikon brightening the table.

As the day wore on, the soldiers would arrive to eat, but for now, the kitchen was all mine, just the late-morning quiet accented with the clatter of dishes and pans. It was the closest thing to peaceful in this household.

The sliding glass door opened and Lulu Āyí walked in from the garden, her arms burdened with two large bushels. She wore a giant woven visor and a well-worn gardening apron. The petite woman slipped off her gray gardening clogs and set the heavy baskets down. She removed her enormous visor and pulled off her gloves. "Jake, the Iron Fists are headed over soon."

She looked up and spotted me. "Mimi!"

I hugged her slim frame and inhaled the sweet, honeyed scent of her talent.

Where Jake was wide, Lulu was spare. Her pixie-cut hair framed a delicate face with a sharp chin. Where Jake let the sun brown his skin to a deep hue, Lulu religiously protected her fair skin with hats and gloves. Lulu and Jake had grown up in Hong Kong, married, and moved in with us when Tatsuya was born. Together with Fujita-san they'd made this vast estate feel like a home, making sure we were all well taken care of.

She patted my cheek. "You should eat more."

I ate plenty but apparently Jake and Lulu didn't agree. To be fair, they'd always said the same thing to me the rare times I'd come back from Jōkōryūkai. Just thinking of those days tempered my appetite. I took a sip of tea and let the warmth spread through my chest.

Lulu Āyí reached down and pulled out a giant snow peach, setting it next to my tea. From the other bushel she pulled out a spiky lychee the size of a cantaloupe. Wow. Those were new. I'd have to try them at lunch.

The morning quiet was broken by the unmistakable sound of hundreds of hungry soldiers running toward us. The door burst open and a line of my father's best men and women marched in. The fragile bubble of intimacy that had surrounded me shattered under the weight of laughing voices and rattling armor.

Nami led her crew to breakfast. She spared me a cool glance before getting down to the business of grabbing her share of the food. I really should have left then, but something made me stay, and I dallied over the dregs of my tea.

When the soldiers were seated and noisily eating I noticed Nami giving me quick glances out of the corner of her eye when she thought I wasn't looking. She leaned over to the young man next to her and whispered something that made him shake his head and laugh. They didn't look back at me, but I had the distinct feeling that I was the topic of discussion.

I'd been gone for two years, and it showed. My father's soldiers didn't know me and certainly didn't trust me. I wondered if they treated my mother this way.

Maybe it didn't matter because Mother was never here. While Father certainly had a significant hand in raising me, I'd spent most of my time with Uncle Jake and Lulu Āyí, and an endless parade of tutors. I suddenly felt a kind of kinship with Leanna, being raised by her uncle.

I stood up and downed my tea. It scalded the lining of my throat, but at least it shook me out of my doldrums. I needed to be alert to deal with my father. He and I had a lot to talk about.

HEIR AND THE SPARE

The buns that had tasted so good earlier now sat heavy in my gut. I stopped in front of the imposing double doors to my father's office to compose myself. I squeezed Bāo's pendant for comfort and took a deep breath. I knocked twice and waited.

The doors pulled back and revealed Fujita-san. As usual, he was smartly attired, a crisp white shirt under a gray silk brocade vest embroidered with pink dots.

"Ah, Emi-chan. Your father and I were about to head over for breakfast."

"I just need to speak with Father a moment."

Fujita-san nodded and stepped back as I walked into Father's den. Against my will, my eyes went to the cabinet and the jian displayed there. I curled my fingers against my sides, crumpling the silk of my trousers.

I wrenched my gaze away and approached Father.

Father's dark eyes roamed over me, but all he said was, "Mimi. Can this wait until after breakfast?"

I shook my head and knelt across from him. He valued his time, so I started with the most pressing issue. "Father, Tatsuya and I were attacked last night."

He leaned forward, his gaze steady. "Did you kill them?"

I shook my head and gave him what details I could recall of the attack. He drummed his fingers on his thigh.

Tatsuya didn't know, but Father might. But would he tell me? Did he know I'd already gone to Jōkōryūkai this morning? I phrased my question carefully. "Why has Kaida been sent to kill Tacchan?"

Instead of answering, my father's hand flexed and his fingers performed a little magic trick, producing an acorn between his knuckles. Sugi's eyes locked on the nut. The acorn rolled across Father's knuckles. Another trick. Sugi tracked the treat left and right, the massive wolf otherwise utterly still.

Father only fed Sugi when he was plotting, calculating angles and trajectories of violence and anticipating the blast radius of his schemes.

Father stood up. "Come, let us take care of your pendant."

It was always like this with him. If I wanted his help to animate Bāo, I would have to drop the subject of Kaida. Have another losing skirmish with my father or have my dear companion back? Not a contest.

I bowed my head and removed my pendant to hand to Father. He palmed the jade, running his thumb over it before holding out his other hand to me. I stretched out my hand, palm up. We had done this many times before to recharge my lion.

Father placed the pendant in my palm, then slid his hand under mine, and closed my hand over it in a fist with his larger hand wrapped around mine. I looked at our wrapped hands, Father's calloused palm scraping my skin, and his knuckles, crisscrossed with numerous white scars. He ruled my life like this, a powerful hand wrapped around me—at turns protective and menacing.

The scent of white pepper and sawdust filled the room as Father channeled his talent through our joined hands. As always, the feel of the Soong Gift comforted me, warming the empty places within me. My qì cycled slowly at first and then faster as I concentrated on Bāo. It rushed within me, a broad river where once I'd had only a dry creek bed.

Deep inside my core, the hunger stirred again, awakened by the shared movement of energy between us. Pinpricks of sweat broke out on my neck as I clamped down on the sensation, but like an animal that has scented familiar prey, it lunged forward, battering through my restraints.

I snatched my hand back, breaking contact with my father and his talent. A wisp of his talent still flowed around my closed fist and I nurtured the energy like a tiny flame until it permeated my pendant.

The next moment my foo lion burst free from my hands. I knelt to wrap my arms around Bāo's neck and tangle my fingers in his golden mane. I buried my face in his fur and his answering purr made my whole chest vibrate. The warmth of my lion chased away the hunger inside me.

Father managed a small smile. If he was at all perturbed by my actions, it didn't show.

"Emiko, your qì is flowing much faster. San Francisco has been good to you."

Had Father felt the thing inside me? How much was he still trying to hide from me? "The Tokyo Sentinel repaired my meridians."

"Really?" His voice was casual, as if it was completely normal to run into Sentinels on the street.

Father clearly wanted to know more but I found myself reluctant to share the exchange that had occurred. I had skirted close to my real questions, close enough that I knew Father would infer my true meaning. If he wasn't already offering me answers, they weren't going to come. I pushed down the familiar frustration and I made my last ask instead.

"Father, we have to do something for Colin."

Father grunted and placed his hands behind his back, his chin rising as he contemplated my request.

"Fujita-san and Yoko can call upon young Aung and bring an elixir to speed his healing."

That was a good start but I was worried about what Tatsuya had said about Colin's family losing their sponsor.

"I think we should invite Colin to join the Soong cohort. We owe him."

My father's mouth twitched and he took a long moment before responding. "That is an admirable idea, Mimi."

I pressed my lips together. That sounded like a no.

"Now, tell me, in what capacity would it be best for us to take Colin on?"

"We could . . ." My mind stalled out, as I had failed to plan for this exercise.

"A member of the Pearl Guard, perhaps? Or the Iron Fists? Or in the kitchen with Jake and Lulu?"

My surprise turned to bitter ashes. Fujita-san studied the tatami mats and didn't say a word.

Father's eyes were hard, glinting stones. "What position can Colin hold in our cohort that will not be seen as either below his station or given out of pity? Colin's father is a proud man from an old family, trying to reestablish their strength. How will he see this as anything but a slight against his clan?"

"It's not fair." I hated the pleading tone in my voice almost as much as the fact that Father's cold words made sense. "He had no idea Kaida's sword was poisoned."

"Do you value Colin's bravery less for it?"

It was like a switch flipped, and the despair inside me turned into anger. I raised my head to meet my father's eyes. "No. Of course not."

His look softened. "Then do not cheapen his sacrifice. As I said, your intentions are admirable. But you have lived apart from Jiārén for some time now, and that has changed you. What you are proposing is not our way."

I wrestled down the roiling emotion in my gut. Cursed Jiārén ways—Colin had saved Tacchan! After a deep breath I contained my anger, but it felt like a half-defused bomb stored in flimsy cardboard.

My father gripped my shoulder and held my gaze. "Your anger is justified, but ensure that it is directed wisely. Someone tried to kill Tacchan. You will find them."

There was a time when his voice rang through my body like a

god's, supplanting my will with his. This time, it simply reminded me that someone had tried to hurt my brother, and they were going to pay for it. I backed away from my boxed-up emotions and gave my father a curt nod.

Father straightened. "It's a little early for those kinds of decisions but I will have Fujita-san keep an eye on Colin. Let us go to breakfast."

I knew that tone. It was as much as I would get for now but it was more than I had expected.

We went down to the kitchen. Many of the Iron Fists were done, heading out and stuffing bāo into their pockets. The Pearl Guard strode in and Jake floated giant steaming bowls of savory soybean milk and freshly fried yóutiáo to the tables.

Bāo butted his giant head against Uncle Jake's chest. The cook laughed and floated another bowl of soybean milk for the foo lion. The gesture soothed the jagged edges around my heart.

I sighed. "Uncle Jake, you don't have to feed him."

Technically, animates didn't need to eat, but somehow Bāo hadn't gotten the memo.

Jake waved a dismissive hand at me. "He's hungry."

I rolled my eyes. My appetite also revived, earlier buns forgotten. I sat down next to my brother and started eating the rice noodle–wrapped yóutiáo off his plate.

"Hey, get your own."

"Yours is right here though."

He pushed my food-raiding hand away and I smacked the back of his head.

"Ow! Quit it."

"Oh, yeah? Make me."

Uncle Lau sat down next to us and laughed. "Still the same, you two. Go outside and play."

I snorted. Some light exercise was exactly the distraction I needed. "Yeah, Tacchan, let's go outside and play."

"So eager for another beating?" Tatsuya threw down his napkin.

"I'm more worried about making sure you don't soil yourself like you nearly did last night."

At least he had the humility to blush at that. "I wasn't exactly ready—"

I cuffed him across the ear. "Weren't ready for that one, either. You're either ready, or you're dead."

Tatsuya yelped and rubbed at his head and I marveled at having to teach him the same lessons I gave Leanna. Leanna was probably glued to her phone, checking Yíchǎn for updates and wishing she was here. Preparing Tatsuya for Lóng Yá was not something I wanted to do. I didn't want my little brother to have to endure it. But I had promised myself that he would survive it.

I turned and pulled Tatsuya to leave the kitchen. "Uncle Lau is right. The courtyard will be empty for the next few hours. You have until then to prove to me that you're ready for Lóng Yá."

My brother was not ready for Lóng Yá.

At least, not by my standards. Trained from a young age, he had excellent qì control and mastery of his talent. I was sure he would do well in the maze and easily qualify for top eight. After that, his placement in the combat talent pool would be the toughest test of his life.

Sparring at Lóng Kǒu was an interesting affair, nothing like my training at Jōkōryūkai where I fought for my life every day. Students balanced doing well enough to impress the instructors, and place well in class rankings, against hiding enough talent to hold in reserve for Lóng Yá and beyond. No one wanted to go into Lóng Yá with every other student completely versed in their repertoire. Lóng Kǒu was also densely populated with the privileged heirs to the most powerful Jiārén clans. It was generally bad form to spar too enthusiastically with the sons and daughters of dangerous people. Tatsuya had spent the last six years sparring with the magical equivalent of kid gloves and thinking he was some kind of special.

I spent the first hour tearing that notion to shreds. In the dawn light, I hit my brother with everything I had. I pulled out my case of canned magic and played every dirty trick in the book, keeping him off-balance and on the defensive. I drilled him over and over until he was deflecting my attacks almost without looking.

My improved qì flow was immensely helpful as it gave me a lot more bang for my buck with my canned magic. While Tatsuya dodged gouts of dragon flame, I pulled in close and went to work in my preferred zone: the down and dirty.

He yelped and dodged a jab to his face. "Hey! No one fights like this!"

I swept Hachi at his ankles, forcing him to dance away. "Correction, no one has ever fought you like this until today."

I pushed forward, making sure to stay inside what I understood to be his effective range for his shield. It was painfully obvious that my proximity was freaking him out and throwing him out of his practiced routines. I grimly pressed the advantage and got close enough to take him down with a leg sweep. By the time he found his bearings I was on top of him with my finger on his forehead.

"Got you."

He groaned and lay back down in the dirt. "Aw, come on, Emi. Lóng Yá isn't going to be like this."

"Do you really think you've seen everything your classmates have to offer?"

That seemed to make an impression. He shook his head.

"That's right. Just like you haven't shown them everything you can do."

We stared at each other in grim understanding.

Everyone knew he could animate objects like Father. Fewer knew he could animate organic matter too. He could render living beings into his puppets.

This was a talent that would make Tacchan as feared as our mother. And yet, mine was still worse.

But this wasn't about me. My lips flattened as I laid out the facts for my brother. "You asked me to come home and train you. That's what I'm doing. I'm going to find your weak spots and keep hitting them until you get better. Or did you think I was just going to pat you on the head and tell you how good you're doing?"

He scowled but didn't argue, which was promising. I offered him a hand and pulled him to his feet.

Tatsuya dusted himself off and his eyes hardened. "Okay, let's go again."

By the time the sun peaked we were both drenched in sweat. Bāo had given up on us and was taking a nap. I chased my brother across the courtyard, Hachi winking in the morning light. Half a dozen baseball-sized stones circled my brother at speed, making it difficult to approach too close without getting brained.

I had to give it to him, he was improving quickly. His defensive circle was tighter now, and he refined his tactics based on how close I got to him, instead of sticking to a single playbook. He still wasn't fighting for his life though. I couldn't blame him, since his path to clan leadership was already set. But I knew some of his classmates might fight with more desperation, which was dangerous.

At odd intervals, Tatsuya would hurl one of the stones at me, forcing me to duck and retreat. I forbade him from animating the píxiū again. He didn't have the juice for it right now, and it wasn't like the terrain was going to be so favorable during his fights. No, better to work with the basics.

As Tatsuya backed up, I pulled a ceramic tile from my pocket, the symbol for water etched on its surface. I cracked the little tile between my fingers and skipped it across the courtyard and under my brother's whirling defenses. The tile tumbled to a stop behind him and a pool of water welled up from the earth, creating a sprawling expanse of mud.

Tatsuya's heel hit the mud and he slipped, arms windmilling. The stones dropped to the ground and I jumped into the opening, sword held high. My brother's eyes went wide as I fell onto him. He raised his hands and his talent surged, black pepper and the burn of horseradish.

I jerked to a stop, my shoulders screaming as my arms locked and refused to move forward. I collapsed to my knees and continued my advance, backing my brother into a corner. My right leg froze next and, overbalanced, I fell to my side.

My brother collapsed, breathing heavy. His qì twisted through my meridians, holding my limbs in place as surely as iron clamps. I strained against his puppetry talent but my limbs were just dead wood, completely numb. So far, this aspect of his Hoard Gift was strictly close range and I didn't know he had developed it even this far. Perhaps I would have more of a chance to resist if I knew it was coming. I'd have to take this into consideration next time. Tatsuya wiped the sweat from his eyes and scooted back on his butt a few feet before releasing me.

"Gods, Emi. It looked like you were really coming for me."

"I was." A little fear would go a long way to tempering his ego.

With my limbs back under my control, I put Hachi back in her sheath. That had been interesting. I'd never felt my brother's puppetry talent before. He was only allowed to practice it under strictly controlled conditions, here in our Realm pocket. I flexed my arms, the strange sensation falling away.

"You're going to keep that hidden."

"That's what Father said."

"He's right. You're not trying to impress some Hoard family to earn a sponsor. Keep it under wraps unless you have no other options left."

I turned toward the sound of marching feet. Uncle Lau and his Iron Fists, now well fed, entered the courtyard, ready for a day of training. Excellent.

Uncle Lau ambled over. "Xiǎo Mimi! Training your little brother?"

Only Uncle Lau could get away with calling me kitten.

"Yes. I just got him warmed up for you, in fact. If you could take over for the rest of the day, I would appreciate it."

Uncle Lau bowed. "The Iron Fists would be delighted."

I bet they would. Anything to redeem themselves from our courtyard melee. My brother glared daggers at me over our uncle's back. I gave him a cheery wave and turned to head up to my room. A hot shower and a visit to the Yokohama poisoner were next on my agenda.

YOKOHAMA

The largest Chinatown in Japan was a great place for a poisoner to hide. There were over two hundred and fifty colorful stores and restaurants packed into these few blocks and the streets teemed with busy shoppers. I kept my head down as I looked for the innocuously named Yook Bo storefront.

The vial from my father felt heavy in my pocket. It was very rare for anything like this to go outside the family. Which only impressed upon me how important this had to be to him. And if it was important to him, then I'd better pay sharp attention to everything.

I leaned against a lamp pole and pretended to scroll my phone while keeping an eye on the Yook Bo. To kill time I tore into my stash of Kit Kats. Mmm. Shinsu apple. I should have bought more. After twenty minutes, no one went in or came out. Popular place.

I pushed the door inward and a jangle of bells alerted the shopkeeper to my arrival. A young woman with short dark hair looked up from the crates she was unpacking. She looked me up and down with an appraising eye. "Can I help you?"

Behind a glass display case, the back wall of the shop was a floor-to-ceiling bookshelf crammed with tomes of various thickness. They didn't look like books you would pick up to read by a poolside while sipping a fruity beverage. Most looked aged and worn, bits of leather and string holding the yellowed papers together. The rest of the interior looked like any other Herbalist's shop I'd been in. Glass jars of tea leaves stacked in tight cubbies lined the right wall. Behind the woman, the left wall was a uniform pattern of drawers, each one labeled in precise handwriting.

Most people wouldn't even register the books, but they stood out to me. They told me Jiārén business was conducted here.

I let the door close behind me and walked in. "I'd like to speak with Tony."

The young woman's eyes went flat. Not much of a poker face. "He's busy and can't be disturbed."

I let my gaze roam over the wall of tea. A pair of small security cameras had been hung from the ceiling, in excellent locations to see the whole interior of the shop. I stared directly at the camera. Was Tony in the back, watching right now? That was my guess.

With a little burst of qì, I ignited Hachi's tsuba. Between the sword and the fènghuáng on my sleeves, any Jiārén should know instantly who I was. "I think he'll want to see me."

I took the vial out of my pocket and rattled it, stirring up the jade chips. The woman's eyes widened a fraction before she clamped down her reaction.

"He's busy."

I turned so I was facing one of the cameras and opened the vial. One of the jade chips floated out and I caught it between my fingers.

There was a sudden flurry of movement and sound from behind the bookcase and a hidden door off to the side opened. An absurdly pretty man came through the door, his eyes wide behind thick glasses. His hair stuck at angles as he rubbed his head. Ah Tong had round eyes, and he blinked at me like a bewildered owl. I took in his gingham plaid button-down shirt and khaki pants. I made him out to be my age. He had the studious look of a chemistry lab aide moonlighting as a pop idol.

He cleared his throat and adjusted the items on the counter. "Hello. I'm Tony. Can I see that?"

His English had that soft cadence that told me he probably spoke many languages, with English not even making it into the top three. I put the escaped chip back in the vial and closed it. "Not before you answer some questions."

Tony blanched a little and the young woman scowled. His eyes didn't move from the vial in my hand.

"Sure, sure. What are you looking for?" His voice shook a little.

The young woman by the crates stood up and wiped her hands on her apron. She stalked over to the door and locked it shut. Helpful. That would keep customers out. And it would also keep the poisoner locked in with me.

I bared my teeth at her. She crossed her arms and leaned against the door, her eyes watchful. The hard ball of prickling anger in my chest started to unfurl.

"You'd best come to the counter. I don't like strangers at my back."

She glared at me.

Tony laughed nervously. "Mèimei, please."

Mèimei returned to the crates and went back to unwrapping the clay bowls, her resentment evident in each heavy clink of the earthenware. They were an interesting pair. They looked alike but where the features were delicate on Tony, Mèimei had a solid look to her. Mèimei had the same large round eyes, but instead of the flustered expressions, her eyes were hard like marbles.

I turned my attention back to Tony. I had expected Ah Tong to be a wizened old man, even older than Grandma Chen. Instead I got this flustered young professor who looked totally out of place in the hustle and bustle of Yokohama. Even the shop didn't give me the kind of vibes I was expecting. And young Tony here didn't strike me as the type to have an evil villain's lab in the basement.

Something else was going on here.

It was time to improvise. I tucked the vial back into my pocket. Tony's expression faded a bit when the vial went away. The anger in my chest was a low hum, growing steadily in volume, but I kept my tone light.

"Final Breath. What do you know about it?"

Tony didn't move but Mèimei's sharp intake of breath gave them away. I looked to Tony's younger sister and back to him.

His Adam's apple bobbed up and down. "Well, it's a very potent poison that is only effective on Jiārén. The ingredients include fugu neurotoxin and it can actually be readily modified for specific targets if you know what class of talent you are aiming for. Additionally . . ."

Once Tony got going, the words just spilled out of him like he was giving a lecture on crafting the world's deadliest poison. He even turned to the back shelf and brought down a book to show me a reference. The boiling sensation in my belly overflowed and liquid heat flowed into my limbs. I decided to stop him when he opened another book to show me the comparative anatomy between different species of fugu.

I put a hand on the open book, covering the diagram. My fingers clenched, wrinkling the page. Tony's impromptu dissertation on fugu toxin potency stalled in midsentence and his owlish eyes blinked at me. I leaned in close, until I was sure that he could feel the rage baking off my skin.

"Who did you make it for?"

"What? I didn't—"

I shoved the book to the side and it slid across the counter and crashed into the wall. Mèimei cried out as the book shattered a stack of teacups. I grabbed Tony by the shirt before he could pull away and I yanked him forward. His gut hit the corner of the counter and his breath exploded out of him. I slammed his face into the top of the counter and cracked the glass.

Mèimei screamed. Good thing she'd locked the door. I leaned down until I was the only thing Tony could see, with his face pressed to the counter. A trickle of blood seeped into the cracked glass.

This pretty young man somehow had the expertise to make Final Breath, and the gall to talk about it like an academic exercise. Part of me wanted to rage through the shop, but I needed the information more than I needed to vent my anger. An image of Franklin's body swam across my vision, and the memory of the miasma of blood and ginger nearly made me gag. I spoke slowly, and quietly, to keep the anger from consuming me.

"It's already killed one of mine. Tell me who you made it for."

"What? No! It wasn't—"

Colin's scream of pain echoed through my ears.

I banged Tony's head against the counter again. "Someone came after me and my family with your Final Breath. Who did you make it for?"

Before Tony could answer, his sister spoke up. "I told you this would happen!" She stared daggers at her brother as tears ran down her cheeks.

Tony swatted at my arm, trying to pull himself off the counter. "He said it was just a test! To see if I was good enough!"

I leaned down until the glass cracked. Mèimei was in hysterics now and Tony was weeping as well. "Who was he?"

"I don't know! He didn't tell me his name! He . . ."

"What?!"

"They . . . they called him the General! That's all I know!"

I pushed Tony off the counter and he collapsed in a heap behind the counter. Mèimei rushed to her brother and they clutched at each other, both crying openly.

Skies. I'd only heard of the General in passing, from Jimmy Louie when he'd tried to recruit me to his cause. Whoever this shadowy figure was, Jimmy seemed to think he had a grand plan for Jiārén, only I had no idea what it was. I also had no idea who the General was. This entire endeavor had been a dead end.

Frustration gnawed at me but also took the edge off my anger. Tony and his sister were telling the truth. They did not mastermind this.

I reined in my emotions and Tony wilted further under my glare. "You're a fool. How could you think the poison wouldn't be used?"

Mèimei's tears turned to anger as well and she began to beat him with her small fists. Tony curled into a ball under the assault.

"I'm sorry, I'm sorry! I couldn't help it, he made it sound so reasonable!"

As Mèimei continued to pound him, something about what Tony had said finally percolated to the top. I leaned over the counter, which got a yelp from Mèimei, but at least she stopped hitting her brother. Tony's glasses were snapped in half and hanging by one arm. Blood streaked down his face from a cut over one eye. He shied away from me, but stuck on the floor, he didn't have far to go.

"You said the Final Breath was a test. To see if you were good enough. For what?"

Tony swallowed hard. "He needed an amplifier. One he could spread through the air to increase his talent range."

"Did you make it for him?"

"I . . ."

Mèimei punched him in the shoulder. "Tell her!"

Tony had the decency to look ashamed. "I'm almost done."

When Mèimei punched him again, he cried out. "I'm sorry! It hasn't been done before! You know I can't resist a challenge like that."

Something that could increase his range? "What talent type?"

Tony scowled. "He wouldn't tell me, so I'm not even sure how well it will work. He only told me it was for a Black Tortoise talent."

A thrill of fear ran through me like a spear of ice. If a Black Tortoise talent like Uncle Jimmy could increase his range, his charm speak would be incredibly powerful. And Tony here was worried about the efficacy.

"When's he coming to pick it up?"

Tony shuffled his feet, clearly uncomfortable.

"Don't make me ask again," I snarled.

Mèimei pointed to the calendar sitting next to the cash register. It was a small red one embossed with festive gold print and all the significant lunar holidays in red ink. One date was circled with black marker. *9 PM* was written in the square. Two days from now.

There was nothing else I needed from these two. And in two days there would be nothing the General needed from them, either. In my days as the Blade, the emotionless ruthlessness of my office would have closed off this loose end. My father's command to me still rang in my ears, but it no longer held sway over my will. I had found the poison maker, but these people were not the ones trying to kill my brother.

Maybe I was learning something from Fiona.

And, maybe my father's jade chips could still be put to good use.

"Okay, Tony, you and your sister have less than two days to get out of Tokyo. You know who I am, you know who I represent. Let me make this very clear. You will no longer be doing business here."

Mèimei's eyes went huge. "No, please! This place is all we have! We can't—"

"You can and you will."

I reached inside my jacket for the vial of my father's jade chips and set them on the counter. With a little boost of energy the chips floated around the interior of the vial. Tony's expression went all soft again. He knew what this was.

"The Soong Clan does not . . . I do not intend to ruin you. Take this and use it as a seed to set up business somewhere else. Anywhere else. Do not let me find out you are still in Tokyo."

Tony licked his lips but I could see the gears turning. Given what I already knew about him, Tony had the knowledge to utilize them and be very successful.

"We will need some time. All of my books are here, many of them are irreplaceable."

I leaned over the counter again. "Two days. Destroy your work and get out of Tokyo. Trust me, you do not want to be here when the General returns."

My eyes drifted into a scanning state as I watched the crowds here in Yokohama. The visit with the poisoner had yielded intel. Now I just needed more information about this mysterious General.

Jimmy Louie's voice played in my mind, a baffling statement at the time, but now more pressing. "The General is rising . . ."

There was no way Jimmy was just going to shake loose that information. How could I find out more?

In the middle of brainstorming, my phone rang. It was Adam. I definitely did not want to talk to him now. I hit the ignore button.

A moment later, my phone rang again. Tessa.

I moved out of the crowds to find a quieter spot to answer my phone.

"Hey, how is stuff going with the family?"

"Lots of drama as usual. What's up?"

"It's Adam. He's in Tokyo with the sword. He mentioned seeing Professor Ōtsuka today."

My voice rose an octave. "Today?"

"Yes. Could you join him? It would mean a lot to me."

I exhaled slowly, counting to three. "Let me try to wrap up here. I'll call him."

"Great, thanks! Hope everything's okay with your brother. Text me later." Tessa signed off.

I prayed briefly to the heavens to grant me patience so that I wouldn't murder one particular individual who was making my life extra hard. The clock had run out on this Crimson Cloud Splitter issue and I had to deal with it. I return-dialed Adam.

Adam's voice boomed over a rush of urban street noise. "Hey. I think we need to talk. You free?"

The last time we'd been together, I'd broken into his home and threatened him. We did need to talk. "Agreed. Where are you?"

"I'm in Akasaka. Thought I would grab a bite here."

I wanted to reach through the phone line and strangle his thick neck. The egotistical fool couldn't leave well enough alone. No, he had to charter a plane and bop over the Pacific Ocean with a priceless artifact and stroll around with it in Akasaka. There were too many Hoard families in town for Lóng Yá. Word of a missing artifact showing up would spread like dragon fire. He might as well have hung a sign around his neck that read KILL ME AND ROB MY CORPSE.

I had to get him out of here. Tessa's job and life depended on it. "Where are you?"

SEEING A MAN ABOUT A SWORD

Annoyance and desperation made my face hot. Juggling two competing missions was not my forte. I missed my life before the shinigami had entered it, when all I had to do was find artifacts and learn how to blend in with Jiārén.

Now I had to prevent Adam from losing his head, and save Fiona and my brother from a killer. It was a lot.

I exhaled through my nose, frustration making me stab at the screen to double-check his location. He was at Cosmoto, a gastropub in Akasaka. Walkable from the metro. I wove through the crowds to get to the Chiyoda line. It was a quick hop and I exited at Akasaka station.

Akasaka had plenty of bars but it was a quieter neighborhood. In fairness, Adam could have picked a worse neighborhood, like Roppongi with its noisy disco clubs and endless crowds. After my encounter with Kaida, I was amped up and hypervigilant, but the crowds were upscale types who seemed more interested in going to a whiskey club than robbing a hapless tourist.

I stepped onto the glossy checkered floor of the trendy gastropub. The smell of yakitori welcomed me. Suddenly I was ravenous.

It wasn't hard to spot Adam. He was the biggest guy in the bar. He stood up when he saw me, unfolding his huge frame from the booth. Today he was decked out in formal wear, a black blazer carelessly strewn in the booth. The crisp white shirt stretched taut across his powerful physique.

I stopped a few feet short of the booth, trying to gauge his mood.

Our last two interactions hadn't been the friendliest. I wasn't counting on this one being much better.

"Emiko. Thanks for coming on such short notice."

I gave him a tight smile. "You're right, we needed to talk."

His eyes were cool, with none of the playfulness he usually exhibited. The man who had puttered about in Tessa and Andie's kitchen with me was gone. I had gotten used to his open smiles and the warm way he used to greet me, and I felt a strange pang to know that I had been moved into the class of people that he treated as business acquaintances.

Or opponents.

Adam gestured to the booth and I sat down, removing my haori. Sitting close to him in the privacy of the tall leather booths heightened the tension between us.

Adam was nursing a scotch. "Would you care for something to drink?"

I didn't drink but even if I did, having alcohol in this setting would've been a terrible idea. "I'd like some tea."

While Adam spoke with the waitstaff I studied the oblong carrying case on the bench where Adam's jacket draped over it. Clearly my demonstration in San Francisco had done nothing to diminish his enthusiasm for showing this piece.

I could feel its Hoard magic even through the container. Just thinking about how to safely extricate it from Adam and make sure it didn't end up starting a Jiārén war made my head hurt.

"Why are we in Akasaka?" This was a nice neighborhood, but wasn't particularly close to the university, nor were there the plethora of ultra-high-end hotels that I imagined Adam would stay in.

He looked up from his scotch and gave me a half smile. "I keep a flat at the Prudential and I like the food here."

Of course he would have a place at the Prudential Tower. The Prudential Tower was thirty-eight stories tall, with the posh residential apartments starting above the twenty-fourth floor. The units boasted sweeping views of Tokyo and across to Mount Fuji. The Tower rose from the ashes of the Hotel New Japan, which had burned down decades ago. Apparently Adam was not concerned about the rumors of ghosts inhabiting the grounds.

I set Hachi carefully down on the bench beside me.

With a casual tug, he loosened his tie. The tie dangled around the open collar, giving him a relaxed rakish air. He took another sip of scotch and my eyes couldn't help but follow the golden skin of his neck as he swallowed. I drained my tea and signaled for a refill.

"I've been thinking about our last couple of conversations."

"Really? Because you're walking around this town carrying something that makes you a big fat target. So it doesn't look like you've thought about what I've said at all."

He leaned forward in the booth, so close that I could see the amber flecks in his blue eyes. "You confirmed the existence of things I've chased for years. Rumors. Cryptic annotations in old journals. But you said we saw the Lost Heart of Yázì."

I didn't like where this was going. His voice had taken on a fervent intensity that I saw amongst other collectors. Treasure hunters. People like me.

"We did."

His eyebrows drew together and he looked frustrated. He still didn't remember the events of that day, but he desperately wanted to.

"Let's say I believe you."

"I told you the truth."

It still stung that he'd called me a liar. And that he'd been right.

"I can agree not to show the sword in the exhibit . . ." His voice trailed off.

This posturing I knew well. I'd seen Father do this countless times. Adam wanted to make a deal. I suppressed the urge to reach across the table and strangle him with his own tie.

"Let me guess. You'd like some more information," I finished grimly.

Two waitstaff walked toward us and loaded up the small table with platters of beautifully sliced and roasted meats. Golden crisp pork belly arranged in a delicate circle, seared wagyu sliced and plated with ponzu drizzle, crisp bashed cucumbers marinated in rice vinegar and spiced with chili.

We waited in silence as they set down the food.

I was starving. I picked up the tongs and began to serve both of us. He thanked me quietly and we ate in silence like mutual combatants who recognized the importance of sustenance. I could see why Adam liked the place—the food was excellent. The music was good, too, soulful jazz at just the right volume. I cleaned my plate and sipped my green tea.

I couldn't find my earlier annoyance that had fueled my mad dash over here. Instead the tension in my body had eased, softened by the good food.

"Thank you, the food was perfect."

"I'm glad you enjoyed it. Would you care for anything else?"

Somehow it sounded like a loaded question. I shook my head. "No, thank you."

We were so polite, it was painful.

"Shall we resume then?" he asked.

"Please."

Adam signaled the waiter, who popped over and cleared our plates.

"Professor Ōtsuka's lab is actually quite close, in an office park past Garden City."

As an opening gambit, it was a good one because I did not want Professor Ōtsuka to examine the sword at her lab and he knew it. I wanted to grab the sword and shove Adam into a Realm Fragment. But I wouldn't.

So I called his bluff.

"And forever miss out on your chance to know more from an insider about whether those rumors you've been chasing about a secret cabal are true?"

He tilted his head in acknowledgment, his eyes crinkling in amusement. Point to me.

"I do want to know more."

"Today's your lucky day. You relinquish custody of the sword to my clan, my father will swear you in officially, and you will know the secrets that you are sworn to abide by."

He picked up his whiskey glass and took a sip. The air between us had grown taut, and every sound rang louder in my heightened senses. It was the battle readiness that coursed through me before a good fight, familiar, and laced with hot anticipation. I realized I liked this feeling. And that I liked sparring with Adam whether it was on the mat, or verbally.

"This sword was entrusted to me. This is not negotiable."

I leaned back in the booth, Hachi within easy reach. "It appears we are at an impasse."

"How about a walk? We can talk some more."

I agreed.

We were quiet during the walk through hilly Akasaka. He was no doubt turning over various counteroffers in his head. Meanwhile, I found myself scrutinizing every shadow. Even though I didn't expect Kaida to turn up, I didn't like the territory. Too many places for unwelcome elements to hide.

I stopped as we rounded the corner onto a narrow side street. The sky darkened, casting shadows over a lone figure standing in a pool of light under a streetlamp. I tensed.

Too tall, too stocky. Not Kaida.

But there probably weren't many Wàirén wearing bloodred silk hooded robes. And likely none of them had taken the time to etch six-foot-high kanji on the walls. The robed figure clapped their hands together and barked a word. The stifling smell of sulfur closed my throat as the kanji flashed with light and glowed a deep red. A thunderous boom sounded, like the world's biggest taiko drum.

A cloud of oily smoke appeared next to the robed figure. A short, squat figure stepped out of the smoke, glowing with its own internal light. The oni's skin was bright crimson. Bulging ropes of muscle covered every inch of its small frame and its bare chest glistened wetly in the light. Black lines drawn in intricate patterns covered its shoulders and arms, the lines moving as the muscles flexed. It shook itself and thick black smoke poured off the figure. It raised its head to the night sky, exposing the silhouette of curving horns protruding from a wide forehead. It snarled like a wild beast, exposing massive hooked canines protruding from its jaw. It reached one meaty arm behind its back and pulled out a cruel-looking cudgel topped with wicked spikes.

The taiko drum beat sounded again and another cloud appeared, this one in the middle of the street, and another club-wielding oni stepped out of the smoke. The drum beats quickened, and too late I realized the oni were appearing behind us as well, penning us in to the narrow alley.

Word of the sword had spread faster than I'd imagined. A demon master. In plain sight, calling oni into the middle of Tokyo. Adam's chances to return home safely had just dropped precipitously.

Adam tilted his head, clearly confused. "Is this cosplay or have the yakuza changed their uniform?"

As the oni approached, my options dwindled to bad and worse. At least the street was deserted. I pulled Hachi from her sheath.

Adam's eyes narrowed as I drew the sword.

"Should I be worried?"

I turned to face the nearest oni, the heat from its body warming my face. "You should draw your sword, too."

"What do they want?"

"They want to take the sword."

His eyes went flat and hard. "They can try."

Blood and ash, this man was going to get himself killed. "Get ready."

Adam's gaze went to the approaching oni, their horns gleaming wetly in the streetlights. He slung the sword case over his back and nodded, seeming to come to a decision. One of the small apartment buildings on the narrow street was in the process of renovating their entryway. Plastic tarps covered small piles of gravel and sand for new concrete. Adam pulled a length of rebar from under the tarps and returned to my side, his improvised staff held confidently in both hands.

Not bad.

I pushed Adam behind me and got him facing the end of the street we'd come through. I didn't need him watching me deal with the demon master. He took direction well enough and lined up so we were back-to-back. The rebar whistled through the air as he tested the heft of it.

Nearly a dozen oni surrounded us by the time the kanji on the wall stopped glowing. While small in stature, the creatures would more than make up for their size with ferocity and ruthlessness. I had to take out the demon master, and quickly. Once he was incapacitated, the contract to summon the demons would fail and the demons would return to the underworld.

I whipped Hachi in a quick figure eight, loosening my wrist, and nudged Adam with my elbow. "You know what you're doing with that? This isn't a roll on the mat."

"If they think they're stealing from me, they are mistaken."

He sounded serious. Maybe I'd underestimated him. "Follow my lead and keep them off my back."

"On it."

Our backs parted and then the oni were upon us, animal roars echoing off the buildings, the crackling heat of their skins baking off the sweat on my arms. I pivoted between the oni, avoiding their clubs. Hachi flashed like lightning, her bright blade biting shoulders and elbows, severing muscles and tendons. Nothing fancy, that wasn't my style. I just needed to cut these demons down as quickly as possible.

I caught brief glimpses of Adam, taking full advantage of his longer reach and the added length of his improvised staff. He swung the rebar in quick, short arcs, keeping the bulk of the oni at bay, and then jabbed when he could, aiming for knees and shoulders. Just like on the BJJ mat, he was fast for his size, and clearly practiced with a weapon in his hands.

My chest expanded, bringing in more air to my lungs as the fight wore on. My qì cycled through my limbs, filling them with energy like I'd never felt before. Truth had always felt like an extension of my arm, but with the changes Tokyo's Sentinel had made to my meridians, fighting with Hachi was as natural as breathing.

The summoner roared, "Give me the sword!"

His voice was so low it didn't seem human at that register. He'd spoken in Japanese and I responded in kind. "Come and take it."

I swept Hachi low and took out an oni at its knees, hamstrings parting with a sound like a gunshot. The demon went down snarling, spittle flying from its gaping mouth. My left arm was in motion before conscious thought registered, rotating in a wide circle, palm open and pushing. My qì flowed down my arm in a rush and an invisible wall of force slammed into the oni. The demon flew across the street like a cannon shot and slammed into another oni lunging at Adam. The two demons smashed into a vending machine and bent the machine in half on impact.

Well, that was new. I looked at my palm in wonder.

Adam's eyes found mine, wide with exhilaration. "Nice work."

His cheeks were flushed with color, and his eyes held a certain light. He was enjoying this. I shook my head, then turned and ran for the demon master, cutting down the last oni between us with another blast of qì that smashed into the side demon's head. Whoa. That was way more focused than I usually managed. I might not be in my own territory, but with my Hoard Gift awakened, I was stronger now.

The demon master reached into his robes and pulled out a small vial of dark liquid. He threw the vial against the wall and it stained the wall jet black. The sting of ginger flooded my senses.

The demon master stepped into the wall, falling into the dark space of the stain. The power of a dark walker. I put on a burst of speed, throwing stars, which slammed into the unyielding concrete and fell to the ground. Too late. I yelled in frustration and kicked the wall.

Around us the bodies of the oni collapsed into oily smoke that drifted away on the night breeze. I caught the sound of approaching sirens as Adam ran up to me.

I sheathed Hachi. “We need to go, we can’t be here when the police arrive. Your place is close by?”

Adam threw his rebar back onto the construction site and grinned. “Keep up!”

He grabbed my hand and we started running. This guy.

THE PRUDENTIAL

We dashed through Garden City in a crazy run to the Prudential Tower. Between the hills and the concrete, and while carrying an ancient sword, it was perhaps the worst cardio workout ever.

Adrenaline from the battle with the oni and the summoner still coursed through my body, heating me up like a lightning rod. Adam laughed like a loon and raced me, his long legs eating up the pavement despite his inappropriate dress shoes.

Sakura blossoms fell in the wind and stuck to the sweat on my face, and for a moment it felt like I was back in my city where its magic blessed me.

Adam tagged one of the front columns of the Prudential Towers. "I won."

I scowled at him and hunched over to try to catch my breath. "Congratulations."

He laughed again and lifted the sword case high in the air in a circle like he was showing off a trophy.

"Stop that, you idiot."

"I'm celebrating."

I rolled my eyes. Yes, it was good we would live to fight another day. However, we still had a problem. Technically, I had the bigger problem—Jiārén had eyes everywhere, and now they knew I was involved.

Adam lowered the case and held out his hand to me. I stood up and slapped it away. "Consider my offer. I'll take you back to my clanhome, to my father, now."

He set the case down on the ground and scooped a long arm around my waist, pressing me close. "Emiko, I remember now."

His memory had returned.

No wonder he was so happy. I was glad for him, too. My own memories had remained stubbornly hidden and even seeing them through Ogata-sensei's eyes hadn't unlocked everything for me. Pressed against that broad chest, I felt the heat of his body sear through my clothes. I stared at the golden skin of his neck. Adam grinned down at me, a flash of strong white teeth, and then we were spinning. Instincts kicked in and I held on to his shoulder to avoid falling.

"Calm down!"

"I can't."

"Can you at least celebrate somewhere less public?"

He shook his head. Adam lowered his arm and dipped me low after our impromptu waltz and I looked up into his eyes, a bottomless blue. Those eyes invited me to join in his delight. It was hard to resist him in this mood. I was amped up, too, and fighting always heightened my every sense. The moonlight bathed us in a gentle glow and his rumpled blazer only enhanced his appeal.

He lifted me up and twirled out with an extended arm like Fred Astaire. But I wasn't Ginger Rogers. No twirling for me. I stepped out of his arms.

"Adam, we have to hide the sword. Now."

"We did just fine back there."

"What if they had caught you alone?"

"Good thing I had a secret weapon."

He was overconfident and smug. He made me crazy. I couldn't take it anymore. I yanked his lapel and pulled his face close. "Listen to me. You're in danger. You need to turn over the sword."

He tilted my chin with a gentle caress. "I can't do that. It's my responsibility."

His vow to a dead man. His absolute conviction that shone in every line of his strong profile. It was maddening. Talking to him wasn't working. He wouldn't listen to reason. I gave up and gave in, pressing my lips against his in a fierce kiss. My arms slid around his neck and his big hands flexed on my hips, pulling me in tight. Our kiss seared my senses, warmth pooling low in my belly. He groaned and licked at the seam of our lips, nipping and tasting. Adam tasted like whiskey and salt.

Every time we had rolled on the mats or verbally sparred, the spark between us had been unmistakable. I'd been resisting and part of me had known that it would be like this, that once I gave in, I'd want to sink deep into this feeling.

I tugged at his hair, running my fingers against the smooth texture of his skin at the nape of his neck. The feel of his skin tempted me to yank away all the clothing between us.

His hands slid up my waist, squeezing gently. Flames of desire licked up from where his fingers pressed against me. I was awash in heat now. "Adam . . ."

Behind us the double doors of the Prudential Tower slid open. A voice called out, "Konbanwa!"

I broke off the kiss with a jerk, dropping my arms from Adam's neck. Apparently I had lost my mind. I pressed a hand against my hot cheek and drew in a long breath. Adam gazed down at me, his blue eyes unfocused and his lips wet. I took a step backward before I made another mistake and leaned back into him.

This was a disaster. Now he knew how much I wanted him and there was no putting this back in the bottle. I wanted to say it was a mistake, and that it would never happen again. But I couldn't make myself lie about this.

"Adam, we need to get inside."

His eyes searched mine and for once he didn't give me any push-back. He grabbed the sword and then slid his free hand into mine. He'd held my hand briefly on our mad dash here but that had been different. Now it felt possessive, our palms pressed together as we walked—like he was staking a claim. It gave me a weird wash of pleasure and fear. I'd endangered his life and we had no business holding hands.

I stared straight ahead, not meeting the bellman's eyes as we walked into the cavernous lobby. No doubt the bellhop thought poorly of us. It didn't matter what he thought as long as he wasn't a Jiārén spy who could report on my whereabouts.

I hadn't managed to cut the summoner down before he bailed and now he would be reporting back to his handler that the Butcher was with the Wàirén who had Crimson Cloud Splitter. Even worse, word might get back to my father, given his vast information network. I needed to do damage control and fast.

Adam let go of my hand to press the elevator button and my skin cooled as we stood there waiting for the elevator. His exuberant mood of earlier evaporated, and his face was unsmiling. It was like he had remembered that I was the woman who had broken into his place, threatened him multiple times, and also just bashed in a horde of demons. His caution was respect, and I tried to take it that way, ignoring the pang of regret that things couldn't be different between us.

We rode in silence, to Adam's penthouse on the thirty-eighth floor, and it took an eon. Already, the kiss seemed like a faint memory, and the two of us stared fixedly at the elevator doors, anywhere but at each other.

I reminded myself that my goal remained Crimson Cloud Splitter. I needed him to relinquish it before he was killed for it.

"Welcome to my home away from home."

"It's beautiful."

It was. He had virtually no furniture so the views were unobstructed. I wondered how often he used this place. It made no sense to own a place like this and then keep it empty. I thought about the heavy emotion in his voice when he spoke of the deceased Mr. Yamamoto.

Maybe Adam kept this place to stay close to his Japanese host family. It made me fret even more about what I'd have to do and how soon I'd have to do it. That sword endangered Adam and all the Yamamotos, Professor Ōtsuka, her assistants, and anyone who knew of it.

"Would you care for something to drink?"

"Some water, please."

We were back to the painful politeness of earlier.

The silver lining from today's oni attack was that Adam had recovered his memories. Not exactly ideal but at least he knew I wasn't lying.

He shrugged off his blazer and hung it up. My eyes traced the broad span of his shoulders, the muscles of his back as they rippled under his fine woven shirt. I made myself look away.

"Adam, there are dangerous people after this sword."

"Sword collectors are all crazy." He opened the fridge and pulled out some sparkling water.

"You're being naive." I watched him slice a lime and garnish two glasses before splashing in the drink. He had a nice set of knives here.

He passed me a glass, then took a long sip of his fizzy water. "I said I wouldn't display it. That will have to be enough."

I wanted to slam my head against the quartz countertop in frustration. What did I need to say to get through to him? And why did I feel the need to persuade him? The easiest way to resolve this issue was to simply divest him of the sword now. This was how compromised I'd become. The Butcher would have slit his throat and walked out with Crimson Cloud Splitter already.

I wouldn't do that now. Which made this so much harder.

I wrapped my haori closer and tied it snugly. "My offer still stands."

Adam set down his glass. "I accept. But I will discuss this matter of the sword with your father."

Perfect. Then he wouldn't be my problem anymore. And a small part of me would miss sparring with him. But now there were no more secrets between us.

OPENING NIGHT

Surviving a battle came down mostly to preparation. She who is most prepared lives to fight again. She who prepares appropriately also stands a better chance of victory, rather than simple survival.

I surveyed my accoutrements and despaired. I did not feel appropriately prepared for tonight's battle. Fujita-san had laid out a selection of dresses across my futon. I had a clear favorite, a vintage, custom-tailored Yohji Yamamoto.

The dress was a dream of silk pleats, dyed in a gradient from dazzling silver to midnight black. I pulled on the sleeveless gown and marveled at how the fabric skimmed over my skin like light on water. It was beautiful, but not the kind of armor I was accustomed to wearing.

And it was armor, but for the type of battles my father fought in ballrooms with marble floors, where the combatants struck and parried with careful gestures and innuendo. Not exactly my forte. But tonight was the opening gala for Lóng Yá, and everyone would be there. Not going would harm our standing. Luckily, the dress also offered enough freedom of movement for me to prepare for my own kind of battle, just in case.

I pulled out my hairbrush and studied my reflection in the mirror. Simple was best. I braided my hair and coiled it low and tight against my nape. Not giving anyone something to grab. I put the brush back and young Kaida's face stared up at me. I hadn't wanted to admit it before, but I couldn't deny the resemblance. She looked like my mother. I looked like my mother. Ergo, Kaida and I looked alike. That bothered me more than it should have.

Kaida was coming, I was sure of it. It would be too hard to resist, both targets in one place and a lot of people to hide among. I needed to be there to protect my brother.

As if on cue a light tap sounded on my door and when it opened, my brother poked his head in. "Busy?"

I shrugged and pointed at all the clothing and jewelry laid out across my room. He grinned and came all the way in. "Perfect, I need your opinion."

He wore a dress shirt of pale pink silk, open at the neck, and untucked over a pair of joggers. He carried an array of suits on hangers over his shoulder.

I eyed his ensemble. "Even I know that shirt doesn't go with those pants."

Tacchan made a face. "I don't want my slacks to get wrinkled!"

"So, you're just going to stand up all night?"

This amount of worry over clothing was outside of my wheelhouse. Tatsuya huffed. "Of course not, but there's no reason to wrinkle them so soon, is there?"

He whittled his options down to two and held them up in front of his chest. Both were formal silk tangzhuang, but one was a deep rose color with white and silver embroidered cranes on the cuffs and the other was pearly gray with black and white motifs at the neck and collar. The workmanship was exquisite, with the frog buttons arrayed like soldiers down each jacket. "Which one?" he asked.

For once I missed Fiona's presence. As I considered the two jackets, his eyes went from me to the dresses left on the futon, and back to me. "That's the dress you picked?"

I looked down. "What's wrong with this one?"

His eyes drifted back to the futon where the more colorful, outlandish, and impractical dresses lay neglected. "It's fine, I guess."

The tailoring had put this one at the top for me. I stuck my hands into the custom-reinforced pockets and waved them around. "Pockets!"

My brother laughed. "Sure, but that black qipao makes more of a statement, yeah? You walk in wearing that one and I guarantee every head will turn your way."

"I don't want everyone looking at me."

He shrugged and wiggled the jackets. "In that case, which one wouldn't you wear?"

I pointed at the rose silk jacket and my brother smiled, holding it up. "Perfect!"

As my brother carefully laid out his suit, I wound fighting straps around my wrists and tucked in my shuriken. A tanto settled on my thigh, where a slit in the gown offered easy access. The compact blade usually went in my ankle sheath but tonight I compromised to soft leather slippers instead of my usual boots.

Tatsuya eyed me warily as I secured the tanto. "Emi, you know tonight is a party, right?"

We were Jiārén. Just because it was a party didn't mean we couldn't also make time for a fight. "Kaida is still out there."

"We're going with a full squad of Iron Fists, Emi. I think you can relax for one night. Plus, I can't imagine she would try something in the middle of so many Hoard families."

Only the smallest canned magic pieces could come with me tonight. Efficiency was the name of the game. I tucked a few ceramic tiles in one pocket, etched with the character for light. "Tacchan, my job was literally to imagine the things other people wouldn't do."

My brother switched tactics and his voice went soft. "It's my Lóng Yá, nee-san. I just want you to have a good time."

I looked up from my bag of canned magic and smiled. "I'll have a good time if I know you're safe."

He rolled his eyes. "Boring."

I laughed a little in spite of myself. My brother was young, and for him, Lóng Yá was the pinnacle of his life. I went back to sorting through my assets and considered my words before I spoke again.

"I wish tonight could just be about your Lóng Yá, because you've earned it. But there's more going on, and we can't ignore that. What

I can do, is make sure you get to enjoy the night as much as possible, and that will make me happy."

Tatsuya didn't seem exactly happy with my answer, but he didn't argue. He started getting dressed. While he finished up, I slid some of Sally's sparkling gems into my straps near my wrists. Stone limbs. Fire. I considered Nami's crackling blue electricity and added one of the brilliant blue ones as well.

A triple-strand pearl choker made sure I would match the rest of my household. A little thrill of power shivered down my back when the pearls touched my skin. The dark hunger in my belly stirred for a moment, then went back to sleep.

Last of all, I tied Hachi at my hip and pulled on a long black silk kimono jacket embroidered with the clan emblem on the cuffs. I stuffed my other pocket with strawberry cheesecake Kit Kats and called it good.

My brother buttoned up just as I finished. When he turned to look at me I was astonished with the transformation. He looked like a miniature version of my father, but without the hard edges. The clothes made him look older, but his face still had the roundness of youth, even if his brow was creased in thought.

He said, "I get it, but I still want you to have a good time, so there's no way we're leaving without putting some makeup on you."

I winced but stood still as my brother doused my skin with serums and dusted it with powder. The swipe of lipstick was the last straw. "Enough!"

"Almost finished, blot your lips."

Finally the tyrant said we were presentable.

Father's entourage was already lined up loosely in the courtyard when we arrived. Uncle Lau and Kubota-san. Fujita-san. And ten members of the Iron Fists in matching black silk jackets with the silver chrysanthemum embroidered across their backs and the Soong Clan phoenix on their cuffs. Everyone wore pearls tonight, defensive plumage to establish our space amongst our peers. Necklaces, bracelets, pendants, cuff links. The Iron Fist jackets all had matching pearl buttons.

As one, the guards straightened when Tatsuya appeared. If the extra attention made him uncomfortable, he didn't let it show. He simply moved up to the head of the group, and stood on Father's right. Sugi sat on her haunches at his feet.

With the barest nod of his head, Father indicated the empty space to his left. My place for the night. My place always.

The crush at the entrance to the hotel gave me time to evaluate all possible approaches to Tatsuya. Our group stood in a loose circle outside the Royal Lotus Hotel. The streets were empty for two blocks in every direction. Careful management of Wàirén authorities was the hallmark of a strong Jiārén presence.

It was not lost on me that the absence of Wàirén simply meant that the attending Jiārén were more likely to cause trouble.

I grabbed Tacchan's arm and pulled him a little to the left, giving him a little more visual cover from a cherry blossom tree, and out of sight of my pick for an ideal sniper location. The faster we were inside the hotel, the better.

Tacchan grabbed my arm right back. "Look at that. She settled in quickly, eh?"

I followed his line of sight to the group ahead of us. Their contingent of guards wore deep blue shirts with tight collars over fitted slacks. They all wore sampins wrapped around their waists made of shimmering cobalt silk and embroidered with stylized patterns that evoked a sense of water. Sparkles of blue gems winked from fingers and wrists.

The Kohs had decided to show up in force, with a group that was easily four or five times our size. Given the late Old Li's habits, they probably had enough family still at home to double the size of their retinue.

In the center of the group, Sabine Koh cut an impressive figure in a flowing sari of vibrant blue silks. A gauzy scarf covered one shoulder and draped lazily off her arm. The light fabric flowed as she moved, giving the impression that she was floating through water. She sported the necklace of rough-cut sapphires she'd worn at the restaurant.

A parade of Koh elders, also dressed in blue silks, followed her at a respectful distance. Behind the elders, another section of the younger generation, arranged by age with the youngest at the rear. The youngest ones looked to be of age to enter Lóng Kǒu in a year or two. At the rear of the procession I spotted Awang and the rest of the Ice Tsunami Trio. The three of them looked like they would rather be anywhere but here.

Sabine had consolidated her power quickly after our dinner, and clearly with no love lost between her and her brother.

Tatsuya shook his head in disbelief. "Man, that is one screwed-up family."

I barked a humorless laugh. "Like we can talk."

"Hey, we're not plotting to kill each other. There are lines you don't cross."

"Turn it around. What made her decide to cross the line in the first place?"

Sabine's head came up and she turned to look directly at me. I held her gaze as our eyes met across the noise of the crowds and cars. I didn't care what she did to gain control of her family, but I didn't like being her cat's paw. Sooner or later, we were going to have a reckoning. Sabine dropped her eyes first, turning to speak with one of her uncles. The crowds pressed forward and she moved beyond my sight.

All of the Hoard Custodian families would make an appearance today. It was a rare event indeed. We were here, the Kohs were here. The Trans would be along once Fiona finished her doubtlessly extravagant preparations for her hair and makeup. I hoped I wouldn't have to keep her separated from Uncle Jimmy.

With Father's maneuverings, the Soongs were now aligned with the Kohs. My recent dealings with the Trans had brought them into our orbit. Years ago I had satisfied the Talon call to the Tanaka Clan, but I wasn't sure where things stood between our two families. The Tanaka scion was not my favorite guy.

Interactions between Hoard Custodian families were a complex web of relationships. Clearly we were on the outs with the Moks. But the Moks had recently cemented an alliance with the Trans. Tatsuya seemed friendly with Minjae, heir apparent to the Byun Clan, but who knew how my father dealt with the Byun matriarch. That left the Borjigin tribe. The family head wasn't seen in public much. My dossiers were old but said his heir was very ill.

The crowd surged again but this time away from the doors. The hairs on the back of my neck stood up when my father looked in the direction of movement and barked an order to our guards. In practiced motions, the Iron Fists formed a tight circle around us and in unison the guards closed their eyes and began cycling their qì.

I leaned toward my father an infinitesimal amount and whispered, "What's happening?"

He continued to look over the top of the crowd. "Watch."

A few sweet notes rang out, reminiscent of birdsong but from the throat of a man. The music lulled me, at once both gentle and rousing, and I found myself swaying and stepping backward. The crowd began to move and flow like a single entity, a mass of people moving toward a bubble that had formed in the middle. My heart rose with the notes of the song and the bubble grew, filling with a soft golden light. Within the bubble I saw the figure of a tall man and another figure in a wheelchair.

The firm grip of my father's hand on my arm broke me loose. My father had his other hand on Tatsuya, who had already taken a few steps away from us. Tatsuya shook his head and I tried to blink away the cobwebs. I felt like I'd just woken up from a nap. Father pulled us both close and his blue-green aura expanded until it covered the three of us. Whatever siren song had overtaken me dropped away until it was only a dull murmur.

I was about to ask my father again when he shook his head. It was a small motion, but spoke to how much he was concentrating on cycling his qì. I followed his gaze to the open space that had formed in the crowd, and the spectacular figures at the center.

The Borjigin father and son dominated the open space. A loose ring of their attendants held back the gentle push of the crowd. Batuhan, the father, stood in the center with his arms outstretched, as if holding court. He was tall, with wide shoulders and a broad chest. He looked a bit younger than my father. His dark hair flowed down his back, with two small braids at his temples. He wore a cream silk jacket trimmed with deep green and gold, and dark green trousers tucked into tall traditional boots.

His battle cry talent was more associated with war, but he had learned to use it in more subtle applications. With broad, lazy pulses of energy, the crowd mellowed and became docile. Truly this was a talent like no other. The very Gift to alter moods and lift spirits. Batuhan claimed to be descended from Genghis Khan himself, and although that alone was no great feat, I wondered if part of the legendary Khan's success was the ability to rally his tribes with a talent like this.

Batuhan walked with a wide gait, his legs bowlegged. It was easy to imagine him in another era, a grizzled warlord astride a massive horse, thundering over the steppes. He pushed his son's wheelchair as he made his way through the now adoring crowd.

I had never met his son, Ariq, but I did have something in common with him—Ariq had failed out of Lóng Kǒu, too. His reason was essentially the opposite of mine. His talent blazed like a never-ending fire and the constant drain was debilitating. I wondered if Headmaster Chen had been kinder to Ariq when kicking him out of Lóng Kǒu. Ariq and I were like the alpha and omega of Jiārén talent. Too little and you were worthless. Too much and you were equally inappropriate for the only institution available.

Ariq looked younger than Tatsuya. He wore the same cream silk jacket as his father, but it hung loose on his thin frame. I couldn't tell from here but if he stood up, he'd likely be tall like his father. Unlike his father, his hair was chin length, a tangled wave that looked like he'd let it air-dry wet.

As splashy as Batuhan's entrance was, what caught my attention was the sheer amount of blood jade the two of them wore. Gauntlets studded with rough-cut blood jade wrapped their forearms, each stone the size of a walnut. Round blood jade beads were woven into Batuhan's braids. Ariq wore a woven choker on his neck that rippled with flat jade tubes. More blood jade buttons dotted their clothes, closing jackets and cuffs. Rings adorned both fingers and ears. It was a stunning display of Hoard wealth and would overwhelm any other Jiārén to wear so much at once.

My father's aura waned as the Borjigin entourage forded upstream through the crowd and passed us. The doors of the hotel opened only for the Borjigin and then immediately closed behind them. Father's grip on my arm relaxed and when his aura dropped away the battle cry effect was gone. Around us, the Iron Fists resumed their normal formation.

Whatever Tatsuya might have felt as the Borjigin passed, he seemed to shake off the sensation as easily as a dog shaking off water. He popped up on his toes to peer over the crowd. "Do you think we'll be getting in soon?"

I turned to my father. "What was all that?"

The only response I got from him was a raised eyebrow.

Of course, there were no easy answers from him. He didn't want a servant who had to be told everything. He wanted an asset who could filter information and make rational decisions. If I wanted answers, I had to get them myself, preferably before I needed them. I'd have to pay more attention to the Borjigin.

When we got moving again, I grabbed Tacchan to keep him within the relative safety of the center of our group. A bass drum boomed and colorful light flared at the entrance to the hotel. A massive blue-green dragon burst from the doors, snow-white whiskers trailing from the beast's face. The creature let loose a bone-shaking roar and leapt into the sky, circling overhead, its long, sinuous body tracing an undulating circle. A ragged cheer went up from the crowd as we began to file into the hotel through the open doors.

I kept my brother close as we moved forward. "Stay on your guard. This is the most boring, dangerous high school prom ever."

LIGHT AND DARK

Tatsuya hadn't let me leave the house without further smearing pink lip gloss on me. Now it was mostly on my water goblet. I scowled. I had no appetite for standing around, holding a beverage, and making small talk.

A vast collection of the most powerful Jiārén clan heads and their entourages still fit comfortably within the main ballroom of the Royal Lotus Hotel in the center of Tokyo. The hotel was a closely held enterprise involving six clans, all at Bā Tóu or Bā Shǒu level. It was the closest thing we had to neutral territory without entering a Library.

The space sat thirty stories up and commanded breathtaking views of Tokyo's skyline through two walls of fourteen-foot, floor-to-ceiling windows. The ballroom was decorated with minimalist geometry. Huge, square support columns sheathed in gold-veined marble broke up the space, set apart with eye-pleasing asymmetry. Square glass panels set into the floors covered backlit ponds stocked with golden koi. A tasteful display of centuries-old bonsai had been arranged in the center of the room, floating over our heads as if adrift on an invisible breeze. The arrangement of the trees themselves reflected the natural, branching structure of the gnarled limbs. Patterns within patterns, repeating endlessly.

In the center of the room a lone woman stood on a raised platform and made haunting, ethereal music. A circular brazier surrounded her with dancing firelight. The young woman wore a fitted vest and belt covered with small pockets. As she moved within the circle she dipped her fingers into the pockets and sprinkled some sort of powder or tinctures onto the flames, causing them to jump and flare in bursts of vibrant color. Her other hand danced along the edges of the colored flames and her talent transformed the light into beautiful music.

Father glad-handed the Bā Tóu families we encountered and I opted for the fewest syllables possible when called upon to respond. *Yes, I enjoyed San Francisco. No, I did not have a boyfriend yet.* Fujita-san helped me play my part, standing just behind me, close enough to whisper to me without drawing attention. As each family approached, he gave me a quick briefing on each clan head. My own dossiers were slightly out of date, so the update was appreciated.

I knew what Father expected and I made sure to stand at his side, in clear view. I was the Butcher, the prodigal Blade, returned home from her exile to San Francisco. It was the kind of gossip these people loved. It was also a neon sign to Kaida. COME AND GET ME.

Anything to break the monotony would have been welcome.

A new group wandered into our space. They orbited around a tall, older woman dressed in a razor-sharp pantsuit of pale lavender. A necklace of amethyst stones the size of robin's eggs hung from her neck and amethyst rings adorned each thumb.

The progress of the group was slow, given that they matched her pace and she was maneuvering with two forearm crutches to support herself. She set each foot down deliberately and precisely, alternating each step with the opposite crutch. Tap, step, tap, step. Her graying hair was swept back from an ageless face with unnaturally smooth skin. She turned her face to us and one eye was milky white, the other bright and sharp. Despite the crutches and blinded eye, she looked more observant and capable than all of her entourage.

Fujita-san whispered, "Byun A-Yeong. Young Minjae is her best chance in a generation at gathering more power."

Our groups merged with the grace of dancers, bringing A-Yeong and my father together. Sugi's wooden feet clicked against the marble as she stalked amongst the retainers and shadowed my father.

Minjae stood a few rows behind his matriarch, presumably behind his parents. He made eye contact with me and winked. Gods save me from teenagers.

My father bowed respectfully to the older woman. "Byun Halmeoni, how nice to see you in such good health."

Even with all the competing energy flowing throughout the room, the sharp citrus sting of A-Yeong's talent made my eyes water. Minjae's grandmother wasn't quite a truth seeker, but she had developed her empathy talent into a powerful tool. Coming from a family with few combat talents, she had honed her paranoia to a keen edge that rivaled my father's.

A-Yeong's lips curled into the slightest hint of a smile at my father's words. "Zhènmíng, it's always refreshing to speak with such a good liar."

"Oh, come now, you know I can't hide anything from you."

"Do you have something worth hiding?"

"You once taught me that everyone has something to hide."

The older woman turned her gaze to me, her dark eye glinting like a half-hidden blade, ready to strike. The shining white of her sightless eye was a ruse. While she couldn't see from it, she saw plenty. "Not this one, though, hmm? I'd heard of the new Sentinel but I hadn't expected her to be quite so . . . precocious."

A flush of heat started at the base of my spine and ran up to my neck. I stilled my hands and kept them from balling into fists. A-Yeong's eyes crinkled at the corners as if laughing at me as she sensed my reaction. "Don't take after your father, do you? Much more of your mother's side."

I'd been bored before but I was fully engaged now. I knew I shouldn't let this woman get under my skin, but I despised all of this. This elaborate dance where sharks clothed like pretty koi circled each other waiting for blood in the water. I smiled and bared my teeth at her. Let her empathy talent chew on my rage.

If my thoughts were daggers, I hoped they stabbed the Byun matriarch until they gave her a brain bleed.

A-Yeong's smug smile dipped. Her brows drew together as her eyes traveled from me to Tatsuya, and back to my father. "Zhènmíng, the heavens were too generous to you."

My father bowed slightly. "It would be unseemly for a father to be too proud."

The Byun matriarch snorted and took her entourage past us, the quiet tap of her crutches against the marble floor marking her steps. Minjae gave me a small bob as he followed his grandmother and the rest of his family.

Was my father proud of me? A familiar hope rose in me, quickly quashed by pragmatism. He was posturing for the Byuns—no more, no less. I remained a useful tool—no more, no less. My lips flattened in displeasure. This evening would be an endless torment of these Bā Tóu maneuverings.

I turned my attention back to Tatsuya and sipped my water. Minjae bent and had a quiet word with his grandmother. She turned to look in Tacchan's direction and gave her grandson a generous smile. Minjae peeled off from the Byun crew and bumped knuckles with my younger brother. In moments they had assembled a gaggle of teens a short distance away from us.

At the front entrance, the emcee continued to drone on, announcing each family. "Fiona Tran and guests."

Fiona wore a white tulle ball gown that looked wider than my entire kitchen. Silver stars sparkled in the gathers of the fabric. The bodice of the dress was an artfully draped strapless sweetheart neckline. Her long dark hair with fat silver-tipped curls was wrapped into a tall beehive hairdo where more silver stars glimmered. Was that a . . . tiara?

She was tiny so she usually compensated by wearing platform heels. Tonight was no exception, but instead of patent leather, her shoes looked like glass.

Instinctively I looked for Kamon, but saw only the Tran members. To Fiona's left, Linh wore a considerably less festive white silk ao dai over gray trousers, the slits giving her room to move. Willy stood to Fiona's right with a bottle of hand sanitizer at the ready. Looking over who Fiona had brought to the party, I realized I missed Freddy's presence. He certainly would have helped lighten my mood.

Fiona surveyed the room before mincing down the steps in her glass heels.

"Mimi!"

Fiona spotted me and made a beeline for me. I set the water glass down on an empty tray stand and braced myself. Now that she was out in the open, she was vulnerable to Kaida's attacks. And like my brother, Fiona wasn't trying to keep a low profile.

She grasped my arms and leaned in for the European cheek kiss greeting. If there was anything I hated more than a fake air kiss, it was two fake air kisses.

My eyes watered from the cloud of Fiona's French perfume. This close, I confirmed that she was indeed wearing a tiara. Only Fiona could dress like Cinderella and not look like a cosplayer. Instead, she looked utterly exquisite, like a walking confection that could slice you in half with a flick of her talented fingers. Leanna would be in ecstasies at the photos on Yíchǎn after tonight.

I patted Fiona's back awkwardly, uncomfortable with all the eyes on us. I needed to get her somewhere less visible so that I could update her about Kaida and the Jōkōryūkai connection.

To complicate matters, my father chose that moment to step back to my side. Fiona gave him a dazzling smile while I made the introductions.

"It's so nice that Mimi is in San Francisco now. We're very lucky to have her."

"I'm pleased she has found a friend in you."

"Mimi and I have become so close!"

We had? I didn't even need to be here for this conversation. The two of them carried on with an entirely fictional discussion of my life. My eyes drifted over to Tacchan.

My brother stood near the center of a ring of teens, swamped in a colorful sea of silk jackets and sparkling gowns. They were all children of Hoard families and Bā Shǒu families. As expected, they had donned their plumage for the night. I spotted rubies, sapphires, jade, and diamonds. What better use for your children than to proclaim your strength for the coming generations?

As Tatsuya talked in animated fashion with his friends, I took note of several young women either stealing glances or outright staring at my brother. Of course, as the only son in line to lead a Hoard Custodian family, Tatsuya would be considered a prized match. I wondered how the small size of our family figured into the calculus of Jiārén matchmaking.

Even though I'd only been introduced to them the night before, Tacchan's little group looked off-balance without Colin's presence. Something about Colin had completed the trio of friends. Without him, Tacchan seemed a bit vacant, and Minjae simply looked bored. His smiles to the girls around them had a cool edge that said he was trying for aloof but told me he was not having fun. I could relate.

Fiona pulled on my arm, trying to get my attention. She and my father were doing that thing, where they talked about nothing, yet somehow talked about everything. Fiona's crew had intermingled with my father's Pearl Guard, a pleasing pattern of black silk tangzhuangs and silvery gray suit coats. She was talking about business in San Francisco but something drew my attention back across the room.

Tacchan and Minjae had stopped talking. Minjae straightened up, preening for an impressive posse of young women headed directly for them. I counted at least six of them, all lithe curves and dramatic eye makeup. They slink-walked across the room, fording through the crowd. Apparently they'd gotten tired of waiting for the boys, so they were making the first move. Enterprising.

Something twigged in my subconscious and I was moving before I even realized it. I'd long ago learned to obey my instincts and I pulled myself free from Fiona. I ducked through the crowd, weaving my way past little clutches of conversation and roving waitstaff. I circled the room, dropping tiles as I went, and coming around to the group of girls from behind and sliding the tanto from my thigh holster at the last second.

The last girl in the group approaching Tatsuya was just in front of me, hips sashaying in time with the rest of the group. Her long dark hair was styled much like mine—a low bun. Her black dress, though fitted, had long slits up the sides for movement. Her forearms sported a sleeve of elaborate tattoos. She moved swiftly, her stride smooth and sure.

I waited until Minjae and the lead girl started talking to slide my arm around Kaida's waist. She was a few inches taller than me, but that just meant a bigger target as far as I was concerned. I snapped the last tile in my hand and infused a good bit of qì into it.

The Light of Heaven tiles I'd scattered around the room all burst into tiny noontime suns. Crisp white light shone from all the walls, bleaching out the illusions of the entertainers and bringing the musicians' soft melody to a screeching halt. Coming from nearly every direction, the brilliant light also blotted out all the shadows in the room. Voices erupted in confusion and I grabbed Kaida's wrist and wrenched it toward her shoulder blades. She grunted and I dragged her away from the gaggle of girls. I pressed the edge of my blade into the small of her back and marched her across the ballroom and into a quiet corner.

Kaida twisted in my grip and her shoulder came perilously close to popping out. She gave me a lazy smile that had no indication of pain. "Hello, cousin."

The light from my tiles filled the ballroom. Against the night sky, it turned the windows into mirrors. I pressed Kaida into the glass and her reflection smirked back at me. Now that I saw her up close, the family resemblance was obvious. She was no longer the soft girl in the family photo. Jōkōryūkai had burned the fat off her bones, leaving a slender killer corded with lean muscle.

But her eyes. I kicked myself for not seeing it earlier. She had Hiroto eyes. Tatsuya's eyes. My eyes.

I leaned on her, increasing the pressure on her arm. "Stay away from Tatsuya."

"An arrow must fly to its target."

"He's family!"

"He's your family. Jōkōryūkai have no family. To me he's just the job."

Her gaze sharpened. "Oh right, that's the part you failed."

I could end her now. Lacerate her liver, dose her with the Final Breath she was likely carrying and the problem would go away. That was the Blade's way, and Jōkōryūkai's way. I'd already taken Old Li's life. What was one more?

What did my father expect of me? What did I want? I only had a few more moments of the Light of Heaven.

Despite the frigid air being blasted into the ballroom, a slight sheen of sweat glistened along Kaida's hairline. Blood jade adorned her ear, a neat row of studs that ended in a dangling earring in the shape of a bird in flight. At the edge of the neckline of her dress, traces of reddened skin crept toward her neck. Kaida was deep in the throes of blood jade addiction. Madness and death were the next stages.

What did I want? My hesitation was my answer. Kaida knew that I could kill her in an instant and hadn't. Now we were even. She was everything I had been, my past and my possible future, if not for my decision to break my Blade. If I thought my life was worth redeeming, I had to believe the same for Kaida.

I played my hunch.

"You don't want to do this. You let me go last time."

"Think what you want."

"I can help you."

She struggled against me, feral now. "Why would I want help? From you, or anyone in your cursed family?"

With a sickening wet pop, Kaida's shoulder pulled out of joint. Her wrist suddenly hung loose in my hand and she used the slack to twist free of my hold. She backed away, her arm hanging obscenely. Through it all, Kaida hadn't made a sound. We faced each other and her eyes rolled wildly, the whites visible in her mania.

I holstered my tanto. "Stop this. The blood jade is killing you."

"You're jealous. It makes me stronger than you ever were. I'm a soldier for the General."

I had to keep her here in the bright lights. If she made it out to the balcony, she'd walk into the shadows and get away.

"Mimi! There you are." Fiona's pert voice came out of nowhere. Kaida stomped on my foot and bolted out the balcony doors. I turned but Fiona had reached us. I had to keep Fiona away from Kaida. Even with one useless arm, who knew what the blood jade would drive her to?

I pushed toward Fiona, practically carrying her in my effusive response to move her. "Hey, hi. Let's move this way."

When I looked back over my shoulder, Kaida was gone.

Fiona arched a delicate eyebrow at my heavy-handed relocation.

"What was that about?"

"That was Franklin's killer."

"She looks enough like you to be your sister."

"She's my cousin."

Fiona's eyes widened. I quickly filled her in on what happened in Golden Gai. The wheels in Fiona's head started turning when I told her both our families were targets of the same assassin. Her eyes turned calculating.

"Does this change anything for you?"

Trust Fiona to cut right to the heart of the problem. Colin had taken a poisoned blade for my brother. Could I do any less? Of course

I wouldn't hesitate to protect Tatsuya. But protecting my brother didn't require me to kill my cousin, did it?

My voice went flat. "No. I'll take care of her."

Something in my tone must have convinced Fiona. She pursed her lips. "Don't be too hasty. I want my pound of flesh for Franklin, but I need to know who's pulling her strings."

As much as it annoyed me to agree with Fiona, I knew she was right. Now that Tatsuya was also a target, I wanted to know who and why. Once again I had the sinking sensation that my father already knew, and he was simply waiting for me to catch up.

I pitched my voice low for Fiona's ears only. "Do you know who the General is?"

Fiona looked at me blankly, her fox-fur falsies fluttering in confusion before she shook her head.

I had nothing else to go on. Jimmy Louie, Ah Tong, and now Kaida had all invoked the General. Even Jōkōryūkai backed the General. Whoever he was he was, it seemed like his plans were accelerating. And what would make Kaida so fanatically devoted to the General? Who could command that kind of awe and fear but remain unknown to someone as savvy as Fiona?

"He's pulling the strings, Fiona. I'm not sure why, but he wants you and my brother dead. There's something bigger going on here."

Her mouth flattened. "There's always something bigger going on. But that doesn't mean we lose focus from the problems in front of us."

I liked this side of Fiona. "Does this mean you'll stay out of Kaida's sights?"

She frowned at me. Well, it was worth a shot.

Fiona's eyes tracked over my shoulder and went stone cold. I froze and stretched out my senses, trying to get a read on who might be behind me that would cause Fiona to have such a reaction. When the aroma of sesame hit me I put a hand on Fiona's shoulder.

"Go. Keep Linh close. I'll catch up with you later."

She dragged her eyes back to mine and forced some cheer into a smile that didn't go any further than her lips. Fiona leaned in for another set of breezy air kisses.

"Watch your back," she whispered, and then she walked away.

I put on my own smile and turned. "Hello, Uncle Jimmy."

OLD ENEMIES

Jimmy Louie was the nominal head of the Louie Clan in San Francisco, rivals to the Trans for power and business in my city. He was nominally the head because he had the bad luck to be born after Raymond, his older brother. But as long as his brother, Dai Lou, remained alive, Uncle Jimmy ruled from behind the throne, out of respect.

Uncle Jimmy was a fixture in San Francisco for both Jiārén and Wàirén, although Wàirén had no idea just how long the Louies had been a force in the city. As the de facto head of his family, Jimmy had every right to speak with the Sentinel of San Francisco. I just didn't expect him to do so at the Lóng Yá Opening Gala.

For a formal occasion such as tonight, Jimmy had foregone his typical attire. Like everyone else here, he represented his family with his clothing. Instead of his usual warm, grandfather cardigan, he wore a long, black, fitted jacket with a mandarin collar. The cut of the jacket accented his slender frame, and the bold embroidery on the right sleeve and chest evoked the gold his family had an affinity for, as well as the dragons we called our ancestors. The cane with the solid-gold handle completed his look.

Jimmy stopped a few feet from me and gave me a formal, but shallow, bow. Enough for those around us to see that I was being acknowledged, but not that Jimmy was deferring to me in any way.

"Sentinel, if I might have a word with you?"

I didn't like Uncle Jimmy, not after he had rolled me and especially after what his nephew had done to my city in his attempt to steal the Ebony Gate. But he was Leanna's great-uncle, as well as a resident of my city. Even if he wasn't on my side, I had to be on his side. At least a little. I didn't need to make it easy for him, though. I motioned for him to follow me and started a slow circuit of the ballroom. There was no guarantee that Kaida had fled the scene, and I needed to check the shadows for traces of her talent.

After a moment's hesitation, Jimmy caught up and walked beside me, his cane tapping out a steady cadence. As he spoke, I tensed, readying myself for the gentle threads of his power that were sure to reach out for me, to infiltrate my mind and bend my will. The faint smell of sesame paste, Jimmy's talent, remained just that. Faint. No wisps of power threatened me, no attempt to hijack my mind.

Jimmy noticed my hesitation and gave me a gentle smile. "You already proved yourself capable of repelling my power. Why would I try it again, only to risk your anger?"

The admission knocked me back more than an attempt to charm speak me would have, and I changed tactics to cover my reaction. "What do you want?"

"I want what every Hoard Custodian family wants. I want my family to thrive, and for our power to extend into untold generations."

I scowled. "What do you want right now?"

Now his smile became grim. "There's still time to join the General's cause, Emiko. His power is growing faster than I anticipated, but he would still welcome you to his army."

"Who is the General?"

"You'll find out when you pledge yourself to him."

I'd spent too many years in blind servitude. No way was I submitting myself to a new master. "No deal."

Jimmy's voice took on a cajoling tone. "You've just come into your Sentinel power, but that won't be enough to stand up to the General. Don't be a fool and stand on the losing side just to prove a point."

This conversation was going in an odd direction. "I gave you my answer in the tea garden. The answer hasn't changed."

Jimmy's eyes flitted around us, as he checked who might be watching or listening, then he moved closer to me and lowered his voice. "San Francisco is my city, too. I would not want the city to lose its Sentinel. And . . ."

For the first time since I'd started dealing with him, the unflappable Uncle Jimmy looked distressed. I rolled my hand to keep him going. "And?"

It looked like it pained him to speak. "Leanna looks up to you. She . . . You are a good influence on her, Sentinel. She needs that."

I would have been less surprised if Jimmy had hauled off and swung his cane at me. We shared a strange moment, my shock at his admission, and what I presumed was his embarrassment. But Jimmy Louie wasn't the kind of man to lay his cards on the table like this. Especially not to me.

"Nice try but using Leanna to try to win me over is a new low, even for you."

Jimmy put his hand on my arm and stopped us. "I'm serious."

His fingers gripped my arm with the strength of conviction. His eyes bored into mine, willing me to receive his message. His expression was earnest, like someone opening up to a friend. For a split second, I believed him.

Leanna was a good kid who'd inherited the same kind of messed-up childhood as me. Uncle Jimmy was clearly invested in providing for her. He doted on her as if she were his own daughter. Maybe a small part of me hoped that there was a chance for Leanna to have a normal life. At least something different from my own.

But that wasn't who we were. We were Jiārén, and our lives were hard. And I had chosen my path.

I pulled Jimmy's hand off my arm. "Suksuk, it was nice speaking with you. Please enjoy the rest of the gala."

Jimmy's eyes fell as I turned away from him. I hadn't taken two steps when a plume of icy mist wove around the ceiling in the form of a sinuous dragon. The dragon left sparkling icicles dangling from the light fixtures in its wake. Either the illusionists had expanded their repertoire dramatically or my least favorite Hoard Custodian family was somewhere in this ballroom.

A flash of yellow chiffon swirled past the corner of my eye. My stomach sank as I saw the group of people approaching us. Yellow topaz gems accented blue silk jackets and the acrid scent of burnt tea reached my senses.

A loud voice boomed from behind the group. "Oh look, the oath-breaker."

Broken Claw. I turned to face them and plastered on a cool expression.

The party was resplendent in navy suits with yellow ties. They sported various brooches and rings heavy with imperial topaz, the golden stones glowing with a heart of inner fire. As if on cue, the enforcers spread apart, forming a wide aisle through the middle of their group. They bowed as one as Tanaka Kenichi, self-proclaimed weather god, appeared at the far end of the aisle and lumbered toward me.

Unlike his goons, he wore a formal hakama, a long navy affair over a striped kimono. The hakama was trimmed with bright yellow silk and embroidery. Topaz gems had been worked into the embroidery and made the garment sparkle like a night sky full of stars. Given that he weighed in at probably over a hundred and fifty kilograms, the kimono and hakama were probably a good deal more comfortable than a suit.

The years had not been kind to him. His hair had thinned, leaving behind a shiny expansive forehead. His lids drooped low over narrowed eyes but didn't mask the hate that radiated from them. A younger willowy woman in a frothy yellow chiffon ball gown simpered next to him. Her gown was draped artfully over one pale shoulder. This had to be the most recent Lady Tanaka. A fancy fan hung on a delicate gold chain on her slim wrist. She wore an elaborate feathery blue-and-yellow carnivale mask encrusted with topaz trim. Her mint-green aura looked weak next to Tanaka-san's bright orange, but I didn't discount Lady Tanaka. Even píng-level speed talents were formidable.

The Tanakas liked to boast they were descendants of bā xià, the eighth son of the Dragon Father. Their affinity for water and weather was legendary, as was their treachery.

Tanaka-san's jowls quivered as his big throat worked. "You were a fool to cross me, and an even greater fool to return to Japan."

I tipped my head. Not quite a bow. I wouldn't bow for this blowhard. I had beaten him on his home territory. He knew it, I knew it, and his servants had witnessed it. "Tanaka-san. How is your son?"

His son had killed my cousin Tai, nearly killed me, and started a war with the yakuza. Not a very smart lad, and only slightly higher on my gift list than Ray Ray Louie.

"Ask me yourself," a raspy voice called out.

Claws and fangs, why were the gods testing me like this? My vow on Golden Gai was going to be my undoing.

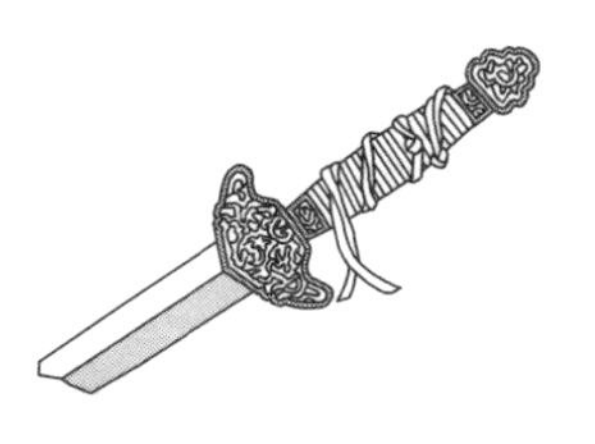

SHE DID THINGS THE HARD WAY

Junior Tanaka appeared from behind their guards and stood beside his father. He wore his shirt unbuttoned at the top and the skin on his neck was an angry shade of red. The scars of old blisters marked a precise arc across the top of his chest. His collar was gone now, for at least a year if my math was right, and he looked scarecrow thin next to his father's massive frame. Honestly, anyone looked like a scarecrow next to Tanaka-san.

When we'd first met, Junior had been stocky, verging on fat, following in his father's weighty footsteps. But his time in the Arctic confines of Mohe had whittled him down to a feral animal of sinew and bone.

Mohe was our solution for Jiārén who couldn't be troubled with playing by the rules. It was about as far north as you could get in China without tripping into Russia. Just north of the little town of Mohe, set in a mountain of permafrost, was our prison for Jiārén. The entire structure was a feng shui nightmare. Mirrors in the wrong places, hallways that led nowhere, hollow walls filled with salt. Everything was proportioned to upset one's harmony with the world and to block the movement of energy. Every prisoner was also fitted with a heavy silver collar, etched with mercury, that suppressed their Hoard Gift. Only one clan had the skill to both apply and remove the collars, so even if a prisoner escaped Mohe, at best they would be lost in the subarctic permafrost, completely bereft of their talent.

This part of the ballroom had been crowded only seconds before, and was now miraculously empty, save for me, the Tanakas, and their entourage. Even Uncle Jimmy had disappeared, which confirmed everything I'd assumed about him. On the fringes of the space, the gala continued, but many eyes were turned our way. Jiārén couldn't resist a fight, either watching or participating. Tonight, it looked like everyone was content to merely spectate. I had to handle the Tanakas on my own.

From behind Junior Tanaka, another figure stepped into the open, a man I instantly recognized because he'd intruded on the peace in my city recently, and caused Adam's electrocution amnesia. Haruto Watanabe, dressed in a haori with Tanaka colors and wearing his katana, stared at me with death in his eyes.

I guessed he hadn't forgotten his trip to my city, either. Coming home empty-handed was a less than optimal outcome for him. Perhaps Tanaka-san had made his displeasure clear? Either way, Watanabe looked more than ready for a rematch. I made a show of looking past Haruto and Junior, and speaking to Tanaka-san.

"Are you sure Junior is up for this?"

Tanaka-san glowered at me but it was Junior who spoke. "We're going to show you your place!"

I tugged at the collar of my gown. "You've got quite a tan line there, Junior, but sure, I've got time to teach you a lesson."

He sneered at me. "When a wild dog appears at your door, you send a dog to deal with it!"

If Watanabe had any thoughts about his master referring to him as a dog, it didn't show on his face. In fact, nothing showed on his face, other than a need to strike out at me. Junior Tanaka stepped up behind Watanabe and laid a hand on his shoulder. After a few whispered words, Watanabe nodded and stepped forward. As one, the Tanaka entourage moved back and gave us space.

In this, the Tanakas were finally doing something smart. They'd already tangled with us once and lost. This time, by sending a Watanabe out to do their dirty work, they could keep the conflict at enough distance to avoid bringing my father into the mix. At least, that was my conclusion about their logic. I didn't see any reason why my father would bother to insert himself here, unless it profited him or our family.

The problem was, this wasn't my kind of fight. It wasn't Watanabe, but the remaining Tanakas. Would they be content to walk away when I defeated their errand boy? The mass of sharp icicles dangling from the ceiling seemed to give me that answer.

Frost bloomed across the floor, spreading out from Watanabe's feet. An icy wind whipped up and blasted stinging chips of ice at my face. The wind kicked up the tails of his jacket, exposing the imperial topaz gems sewn into the lining.

Junior had charged up the gems when he'd put his hand on Watanabe's shoulder, giving his man short-term access to his ice talent.

I hated ice talents.

But at least here, in the confines of the ballroom, Tanaka Senior hadn't charged Watanabe up with his weather and lightning talents.

I'd had enough practice. I could work with an ice talent.

Watanabe methodically drew his sword. I took the opportunity to put mental tabs on all the people lined up behind him, and note which ones might enter the fray at the wrong moment. Watanabe took his stance and a thick crust of ice armor formed over his shoulders and arms. My knuckles ached at the sight of all that ice. I decided to needle him first, and left Hachi in her scabbard for now.

"Aren't you getting tired of being the Tanaka's whipping boy? I already told you, we don't feud with underlings."

Watanabe bared his teeth. "You got lucky last time, Soong. It will not happen again."

Outside of the open space afforded us by the crowd, guests continued to laugh and mingle, unbothered by our impromptu duel.

Someone called out, "Silence!"

The Tanaka group settled down, but the crowd around us carried on as if nothing had happened. Odd.

With a shout, Watanabe launched a volley of ice at my head. Fire and ash, if I never had to face another ice talent in my life it would be too soon. I brought my right hand up in a circular pattern, the motion pure muscle memory. Qì flowed through my arm as easily as water flowing downhill and I shunted it through the Dragon Breath crystal. A spout of orange and yellow flame burst from my palm, creating a halo of fire before me. The ice shards sizzled and evaporated as they flew into the flames.

The murmuring voices around us died to nothing after our first exchange. The gathered guests might play aloof, but everyone here hungered for blood. This was just the appetizer. The tension in the room was thick enough to carve with a blade; we were about to move on to the main course.

Watanabe pushed another surge of freezing wind at my face as he bolted toward me, his sword held low as he ran. At the edge of my vision, Lady Tanaka disappeared in a smear of yellow.

The trick to dealing with speed talents was to not look at where they were, but to predict where they would end up. I'd pegged Lady Tanaka as the most likely to enter the fight, as she was also not a blood Tanaka. When she disappeared, I guessed she would come at my back while Watanabe struck at me from the front.

I backed away from Watanabe to throw off the timing they had worked out, set myself in Lady Tanaka's path, and planted my feet. I'd barely ignited the stone limbs crystal when the young woman plowed into me, ramming her gut into the hardened point of my elbow. With my legs suddenly as heavy as granite obelisks, it was like she'd run into the side of a building. Before she collapsed, I grabbed her forearm with my off hand, pushing enough qì through the other crystal to send blue arcs of electricity crawling up her arm. Her spine bowed as her whole body spasmed and she dropped her steel-tipped fan. I kicked it and it spun wildly across the marble floor.

Watanabe was on me a split second later. I dropped Lady Tanaka, spun to face him, and drew Hachi in the same motion, bringing my wakizashi across my body to block his strike. As we passed each other I pushed enough energy through the Dragon Breath crystal to use it all up in one go. With my repaired meridians, the improved effect engulfed Watanabe's head and torso in crackling orange flames.

The man fell to the floor, rolling and screaming, as fire and superheated steam roasted him from all directions. I kicked Watanabe's sword out of reach as well and turned to face Tanaka-san and his son.

Junior's face was nearly purple from rage. An icicle as thick as my thigh cracked off the chandelier. The icicle fell, aimed right at my head. I tensed to roll away. Midway down the massive chunk of ice wobbled and slowed, then flew across the room and planted itself upright in front of my brother and his friends. The girls around them clapped at my brother's display and Minjae began chipping bits of ice into their drinks. Tacchan gave me a wink and turned back to his friends.

Enraged, Junior screamed and slammed his good hand down on the floor, shattering all the icicles above us. Oh, dear.

A loud clap rang out from my left and I was awash in the smell of pepper and sawdust. The falling ice froze in midair, then drifted slowly to the ballroom floor. The icicles twirled around themselves like birds in an intricate mating dance. In moments they found a new arrangement and rose again in the shape of a phoenix in flight. A small chorus of oohs and ahs went through the crowd and polite applause rippled around the room. My father smiled and gave a slight bow. Sugi flicked her tail, a staccato of wooden clicks. And with that, the partygoers went back to their drinks and merriment, our conflict resolved to their satisfaction.

Tanaka-san and Junior watched my father, their eyes wary. So they weren't as stupid as they seemed. In fact, only the two of them seemed to be capable of conscious thought. The rest of their entourage stood still with blank, happy expressions on their faces, despite what had just happened to Haruto.

I caught a whiff of black sesame under the scent of my father's talent and turned slowly. There, behind the Tanakas, Uncle Jimmy gave me a grim look and a nod of his head. Unable to rouse their men, Tanaka-san and Junior turned and left, abandoning their escorts, and even Watanabe and Lady Tanaka.

Uncle Jimmy picked his way through the crowd of vacantly staring guards, leaning lightly on his ornate cane. He reached into his coat pocket, pulled out Lady Tanaka's fan, and handed it to me. "I think you dropped this. The spoils of war."

Assistance from my family was strange, but I could accept. Help from Uncle Jimmy was an alien concept I could not understand.

I repeated my question from earlier. "What do you want?"

He took a moment before answering, then pressed the fan into my hands. "I want the Sentinel of my beloved city to thrive, so that my city may thrive. I also want Leanna's lessons to continue. For both of those things, you must remain alive and healthy. Please reconsider your answer."

I kind of wanted him to take a whack at me with his cane now, just to get things back to something like normal. At my stunned silence, Jimmy simply gave me another bow.

"Enjoy the rest of the gala, Sentinel." He turned and walked away,

I stared at Lady Tanaka's fan and tried to make sense of things. When I looked up I found my father across the ballroom. His expression said that I should be beside him, so I stowed the fan and walked over. If the events of tonight had seemed odd to him, he gave no sign. The look he gave me showed no disappointment, which was a win in most circumstances.

My father said, "Has the matter been concluded to our satisfaction?"

Again, he made my actions sound like plans he'd put in motion.

Had he?

"Yes."

He nodded once, a precise, sharp movement. The best version of his approval I could hope for. "Excellent. Retrieve your brother."

It was time for business.

PLANS

It took another fifteen minutes for Jimmy's charm speak to wear off the Tanaka guards. Until it did, the party simply flowed gracefully around them as well as the unconscious forms of Watanabe and Lady Tanaka. Jiārén were nothing if not adaptable.

The Tanaka guards woke up in the same moment, and there were a few panicked seconds where they tried to regain their bearings. Unable to find their masters, they finally settled on bundling up Watanabe and their mistress and exiting the gala as quickly as possible. I didn't envy the reception Watanabe would get once he regained his senses.

We spent the next few hours making the rounds of the ballroom. I noticed that my father seemed to have a specific order in which he wanted to speak with everyone, because he skipped over some who we then came back to later. After the second hour I stopped trying to determine what his methods were. I'd never been fast enough to keep up with his schemes.

I spent most of the night thinking about my encounter with the Tanakas. Specifically, playing and replaying my conversation with Uncle Jimmy. Was Jimmy really concerned for me? If so, how did that rate against his pledge to the General? Part of me wanted to ask my father about it, but a bigger part of me felt I needed to figure this out on my own, without my father's opinion coloring my perceptions.

At two in the morning Father decided that we had stayed long enough, and it was an appropriate time for us to leave. Which only meant that we stayed another hour so that we could find all the appropriate people to say goodbye to.

Fiona was one of the first to find us as we made our rounds. She leaned in close for another pair of air kisses and whispered in my ear. "I'll see you at Lóng Yá."

"Does that mean you're lying low until then?"

She made a face at me. "You're no fun anymore. But since you must know, Kamon has asked me to keep him company while he's sequestered with the other judges. So I'll be behind the school wards until the Tourney." She shook her head. "He doesn't seem to understand I have responsibilities to the clan."

I nodded and made a noncommittal sound.

It was good news that stung a little, but I appreciated Kamon's attempt to keep Fiona safe. It also made my life a little easier. Fiona safe behind the wards meant Kaida's targets would narrow down to Tacchan. I could keep my brother safe. I also refused to think about Kamon and Fiona curled up together in some cozy ryokan.

I bade Fiona good night.

During a lull in the goodbyes, I worked up the nerve to lean a little closer to my father and whisper low enough that only he would hear. "Thank you, for earlier."

He was scanning the crowds, looking for someone, and he didn't move so much as a muscle to indicate that he had heard me. After a long enough moment that I thought he actually hadn't heard me, he responded. He did not look at me as he spoke. "You always stand to my left, do you not?"

"Yes."

My father turned to me now, his eyes lit with quiet intensity. "Then I am always standing to your right."

When I got back to the estate, it was quiet. I placed my clothes in the bin outside of my room. Maybe Fujita-san could work his magic. I really did love this dress. I just hadn't been expecting to fight Kaida and the Tanakas in it this evening.

I could have killed Kaida tonight but didn't. We were even, sort of. I mean, we would be if she weren't still committed to killing Tatsuya and Fiona. But they were safe for the time being.

In the end, Father and Tatsuya had my back. It was the first time that I'd ever experienced that. It felt good. Right.

But also fragile.

I cleaned Hachi, wiping the blade down with the camellia-scented oil and then rubbing it softly with the oil cloth, letting the rice paper nuguigami absorb the excess oil. This was my habit—clean my blades, then clean my body.

I gathered my thoughts as I sank into the deep wooden tub. My cousin was the General's henchman, and she was also Jōkōryūkai. Which meant the two were aligned. But why? Why would the Association support this shadowy General?

Again, the urge to ask my father was there, but tempered with the desire to puzzle this out on my own. I also doubted he would give me a direct answer. Unfortunately, soaking in the tub for thirty minutes was a refreshing experience that yielded no insights into Kaida's motivations.

When I was clean I walked over to the vanity and pulled out her photo. Young Kaida looked up at me. Had she already been a disciple of Jōkōryūkai in this photo? My mother had to have known. As always, my mother managed to avoid being around when her talents could have been helpful. Like saving her son from being killed by another dark walker.

Frustration gave way to a familiar acidic anger that had been slowly eating away at me ever since the shinigami had made the Talon call. I knew that I had never lived up to her expectations, but Tatsuya was her golden boy, the shining one who would be Head of the Clan someday. And yet, she'd bartered a Talon that had endangered our immortal souls.

What kind of mother did this?

My mother.

I laughed bitterly. My mother was the type of person who did this. What did that make me? The Byun matriarch's words from the gala echoed in my mind. "Don't take after your father, do you? Much more of your mother's side."

I didn't like that. I hated it that it might even be true.

I looked in the mirror, brushing out my long hair. Mother had brushed it for me when I was little, then braided it just like she did her own hair. I did the same now, running the bristles against my scalp and then winding the long slick strands into some semblance of order. The braid lessened the shock of seeing that bright white streak that the city had marked me with. The resulting braid was long, falling to my rib cage. I stood and walked to where I had set down Hachi.

I didn't have to be like her. I didn't have to do things like her.

I couldn't change my face but I could do this.

With one smooth motion I sliced off my braid, my hair falling free and fanning out around my jaw. I tossed the braid on top of Kaida's photo.

My body felt pounds lighter, and I rolled my shoulders and stretched my neck. I pulled on a robe and walked to the Bǎowù hé to meditate in the sound circle. I wouldn't be getting much sleep tonight so I might as well charge up my qì.

Tomorrow, I would bring Adam to swear to the Hoard and I would need every bit of fortitude I possessed to manage Father and Adam in one room.

The elevator ride down the thirty-eight floors of the Prudential Tower felt like an eternity, the silence between us heavy with unspoken tension. It was a total one-eighty from the playful banter I was used to, the way he'd danced with me in front of the building. His enthusiasm had been infectious. Now he was all furrowed brows and flattened lips and it put a hot stone of guilt in my gut. Especially since it was my fault.

But he'd agreed to swear to the Hoard, and discuss possession of the sword. My primary objective was to keep him and Tessa safe, and this was the best I was going to get for now.

At least I had Bāo with me today.

Adam looked at Bāo, who flicked his long tufted tail with disdain.

We walked through the lobby with only the sound of our shoes on the marble floor to accompany us. I still hadn't figured out who had attacked us earlier. It could have been anyone, though the Tanakas were my first guess due to the proximity and timing. But a dozen Jiārén families could have well-placed informants in the university's antiquities department, my own father included.

We exited the building into sunny weather, the kind of spring morning in Tokyo that made you almost forget you were deep inside the city. The air was crisp, and the street was quiet. It was a short walk to the train station and then we would be on our way to clan-home. Easy.

As if the tension between us wasn't enough, the relative ease of this morning set the rest of my nerves on edge. I sorted through the collection of tiles in my pocket by feel. One of them was etched on both sides, an extra contingency.

We walked in uncomfortable silence, Adam's long legs making both Bāo and me trot to keep up. As usual, bystanders avoided Bāo, seeing only a very large dog. We walked past the area where Adam had spun me around in his impromptu waltz yesterday evening. Now in the bright light of day, the wonder of the evening sparked by the mad dash after fighting the oni seemed even more remote.

The Tower was surrounded by beautiful landscaping, a burbling brook and sandy shores blending seamlessly into glossy black pebbles. Despite the high traffic of the neighborhood, the tall plantings and running water created an illusion of privacy for the residents of the Tower.

A loud rumble broke the quiet.

One hand reached for Hachi and with the other, I pulled on Adam's sleeve to tug him close as I looked for the source of the noise. The sound rose to thunderous levels and the previously calm brook now churned with white water.

Daylight dimmed as if a blanket had been thrown over us. The scent of sulfur made me gag, acrid and overpowering. A summoner. Maybe even the same summoner as last night. Oh good. I could extract my pound of flesh.

The summoning bubble closed overhead, creating a suffocating darkness that separated us from the Tower and the busy streets nearby. The light that was able to filter in was deep red, and turned all the features inside the bubble into dark shadows.

Bāo snarled, and his crimson ruff stood on end. His snout lifted high as he scented the new intruder.

The frothing brook kept rising until it formed a standing wall of churning water. The wall of water flexed and bulged, and then a tusk pierced it, followed by another one.

Oh no. Please no.

A massive shaggy crown rose above the wall, then two deep-set blazing red eyes came through. An ushi-oni, a demon bull, loomed over us, water streaming from its gargantuan height. Instead of four legs, it had six, and they hinged like spider joints, emerging from a bulbous, segmented body. Black, spiny hair covered its legs and each one ended in a talon as long as my arm.

This was a massive summoning. Even a gāo-level summoner would have to be nearby to do this. I prayed to the heavens that he was tapped out.

The demon opened its maw, giving us a nightmare view of fangs and a sinuous black tongue. I'd never fought one of these before but I remembered one more piece of lore about the ushi-oni.

"Adam, this oni spits venom. Get behind me."

Adam's eyes were wide with horror. A demonic bull with spider legs was not cosplay, nor some cool animatronic robot. While he'd accepted that Jiārén lived within his city, his brain was having a hard time catching up with the reality of what that meant.

"Adam!"

He shook himself and stepped back. I slid in front of him and readied Hachi. She was sharp but the question was: was she sharp enough to sever an ushi-oni's chitinous limbs? This seemed as good a time as any for my contingency. As I watched the demon for its next move I pulled the tile from my pocket. The Chinese symbol for Mountain was carved on one side. Last night I'd carved Oda's six-pointed Tokyo star on the back side.

The tile heated as I poured my qì into it as fast as I could. The ushi-oni took a step toward us, one taloned foot cracking through concrete like an eggshell. It reared up and roared, yellow-flecked spittle spraying from its mouth.

I threw the hot tile into the water under the demon's abdomen and backed us up. I sent up a prayer to the Dragon gods and snapped the other Might of the Mountain tile in my pocket. In an instant, gravity increased two- to threefold in a tight radius around the tile, directly beneath the demon's low-hanging belly.

Like the gods themselves had come down, the ushi-oni was crushed into the water, splintering the surrounding pavement and sending up a billowing cloud of dust and water. The concrete fractured out and away from the demon along six lines. The demon screamed in pain, the sound like shearing metal.

"Give me the sword!" a guttural voice bellowed.

I looked over my shoulder. A flutter of scarlet robes told me our old friend the summoner was back.

Before I could answer, Adam threw back his head and let out a loud howl. He ripped open the case to Crimson Cloud Splitter and tore out the katana, holding the scabbard in two hands overhead. "You mean this sword?"

Adam spread his legs apart into a wide stance and unsheathed the katana, wielding the katana in his right hand in a classic overhead pose and holding the scabbard in his left hand. "Come and take it!"

I admit, I was not expecting that response. On the other hand, Adam was as tall as a tree and had the wingspan to match, so he would be a tough opponent. Maybe I should've had Adam face the ushi-oni.

We had ended up back-to-back again, just like last night. For this moment, I savored being allied with Adam again. The suspicion, the doubt, all of it fell away as we faced this threat together.

The ushi-oni struggled out of the water, each step an ominous scrape as its talons carved away the pavement. Chunks of concrete flew up around us, dust and rubble churning with the water, splattering muddy debris on my face and arms. My heart pounded, but my mind cleared as I mapped out my kill zone. I would try the eyes.

"Bāo, protect Adam."

My foo lion roared, a deep rumble of rage, and stalked over to Adam's scabbard side.

Now or never. I couldn't wait around to see if the contingency came through. I activated my stone limbs crystal to shield me while I ran in close. I narrowly dodged the oni's snapping jaws and got under its head. Grabbing the nearest leg, I vaulted up to land on its wide head. I wrapped my hands around Hachi's pommel and brought the tip of my blade down into the demon's eye.

"Hai!" Hachi sank deep and putrid fluid spilled out. The demon reared again with an unearthly screech, but the Mountain tile kept it pinned in place.

I hung on for dear life and pushed, forcing the blade in to the hilt. It had to have a brain, right? Either the demon's head was too big or Hachi was too short or maybe it didn't have a brain because the cursed beast kept roaring and writhing, trying to throw me off.

The throbbing beat of a taiko drum pulled my attention back to the summoner. Oily clouds of black smoke surrounded him and the three husky oni shielding him. Their curved horns gleamed in the darkness, and I watched in growing alarm as Adam dodged their clubs. He and Bāo were acquitting themselves well against the oni, but they weren't making any progress.

I yanked out Hachi, my hands slippery with goo, and stabbed the remaining eye. It had to be less dangerous if it was blind, right?

The ushi-oni screamed again and its jaws opened wide, its sinuous black tongue whipping out. Blind and crazed now, it spewed yellow venom in a long arc. The venom splashed over Adam's head and neck. No, no, no!

Adam cried out and went down on one knee. One hand pawed at his neck while the other kept his sword up as he tried to fend off the club-wielding oni. Bāo bit the oni in the leg and shook his head, shaking the oni like a rag doll. The club sailed away. Adam fell to his knees, his face contorted in pain.

Frantic, I smashed my Dragon Breath crystals into the gaping holes I'd made in the ushi-oni's eyes. The demon's face ignited with a whoomp.

I jumped off the demon and landed hard, my momentum carrying me into a forward roll as I rushed to Adam. He collapsed and Crimson Cloud Splitter landed on the ground with a clatter. I threw my bubble of Steel Wind. The charm shattered next to him and the hardened air shield snapped into place around him. I spun to take on the remaining two oni.

With an overhead strike, I hacked off an arm. Screaming, I thrust in and up, a Y-cut to finish the demon. Hot, ethereal blood sprayed then dissipated as the demon dissolved into oily smoke. Spotting the summoner through the haze, I threw two shurikens, aiming for the empty spot in the hood.

The summoner dodged the blades, but Bāo lunged and bit him on the arm, dislodging the hood. The red silk fell back to reveal a bald man with a face covered in tattooed hanzi. A glowing topaz gem the shape and size of a beetle was embedded in his forehead. My stomach rolled in revulsion.

The summoner wrenched himself away from Bāo, tearing his

robes. He threw down a black vial, and another black portal appeared at his feet. He fell forward and disappeared into the darkness.

Adam groaned as the Steel Wind faded. "Emiko . . . the sword . . ." His voice trailed off.

A bolt of white light pierced the summoning wall. Hope rose in my chest as the tip of a blade followed, cutting through the dark veil. The rest of the naginata followed through the hole.

"Ki-ya!" Oda Tanaka jumped through, his manic eyes swinging wildly from Bāo, Adam, me, and the katana to the screaming demon behind us. As before, the Sentinel was an imposing figure in his armor, towering over me. His eyes darted left and right like a panicked animal, but he'd heard my signal and come to help. I hoped I could help him as well.

"Tanaka-san, look at me." I pushed qì into the Pearl in my chest and willed that power to reach out to him.

Maybe it was something about the tone of my voice, or maybe my power resonated with his, but his eyes turned down to me and lost a little of their manic brightness.

"Emiko." He seemed to take in the situation again. "It's dangerous here. There's an ushi-oni."

I kept my voice pitched low. "I know. And your city needs your help."

Bāo snuggled up next to Oda's leg, bumping his head under the big man's free hand. Oda absently began scratching my lion behind his ears. "I want to help but . . ."

He took a step back and his foot brushed against the fallen sword. Oda looked down and his eyes locked onto Crimson Cloud Splitter.

"Tanaka-san, we need to . . ."

He wasn't paying attention to me anymore. Oda knelt, the movement almost reverent, and he traced a finger over the polished wood of the scabbard. His motions were hesitant, almost afraid, as if he thought the sword might break. I knelt next to him and tried to catch his eye.

"Oda, do you know this sword?"

His voice was a whisper. "This was my father's katana."

With a grunt, Tokyo knelt, set down his naginata, and picked up Crimson Cloud Splitter. He turned it this way and that.

Adam lifted his hand, but was too weak to protest further. I squeezed his shoulder.

Brandishing the katana, Oda charged the ushi-oni with a full-throated bellow. Crimson Cloud Splitter glowed silvery blue, as if filled with lightning. In a blur of motion and searing white light, Tokyo cleaved the limbs off the ushi-oni. With a gravity-defying leap, he landed on its back and took off the demon's head, the lightning blade sizzling through the flesh. With a quaking thud, the massive head splattered into the mud and ash.

No wonder everyone wanted this sword.

"What . . ." Adam looked stunned, his lips slack with disbelief. Bāo placed a big paw on Adam's thigh and headbutted him gently. Adam blinked, distracted by a giant foo lion who now wanted petting.

The corpse of the ushi-oni started smoking and crumpling into itself. As Oda walked back over to us, the body collapsed into a mound of ash. The tension on the Sentinel's face had smoothed out and his eyes had a still quality like looking into deep water. This serenity was new. Granted, I'd spent limited time with Oda thus far but the calm man walking toward us now bore little resemblance to the Sentinel who could barely contain the chaos that had roiled through him.

Adam coughed and curled forward to cradle his ribs.

"Please, we have to purge the venom," I implored Oda.

The Sentinel tilted his head, a quizzical expression on his face. He tossed Crimson Cloud Splitter back and forth between his meaty hands while he stared at Adam.

Clouds and rain, I wished Popo were here. The ushi-oni venom did not seem as deadly as the demonic serpents that had nearly killed me, but with every heartbeat, more of the venom cycled through Adam's body.

Finally Oda set down the katana. He bent and cradled Adam's face between his rough palms. He picked up Adam's wrist and listened to his pulse. He tsked. "It's good we fixed you earlier, Emiko. I would not be able to do this alone."

Fighting the urge to bristle at his characterization that I was broken, I nevertheless couldn't fathom how I would be able to assist. "What do you need me to do?"

Oda tapped two fingers on Adam's sternum, right where his heart chakra was. "Here."

I followed his lead, placing my forefinger and middle finger, curved at the knuckles, as the Sentinel directed. He took my left hand, extending my arm straight out, and pointed the two longest fingers in the classic jian pose. It was like a very awkward tai chi stance.

Oda braced Adam's back and placed both palms flat, and began to palpate against Adam's lungs from behind. Adam coughed and wheezed. Oda began to hum and as the notes ascended I realized he was warming up for Dragonsong. With an unearthly keen, the Sentinel mimicked the dragons of the Realm and slammed both hands against Adam's back. White light so bright it was almost blue blazed from his hands and out of Tokyo's eyes. It jolted Adam's torso and he began to spasm.

Where my fingers touched his heart chakra, white light sparked. Lightning shot up my fingers and along my forearm, prickling my skin. My Gift woke, a hungry thing that gobbled up the lightning and demanded more. Reflexively, my fingers dug into Adam's chest as if trying to scoop up everything inside. My head fell back as the power spiraled up my arm and cycled with my qì. I took everything, an empty well filling to the brim as Tokyo continued to sing, the ululating sounds vibrating through all of our bodies. I didn't know what was happening and I couldn't control it.

"Ka!" Oda gave one last push and moved away from Adam.

I couldn't move, locked in place by the cold energy coursing throughout my body. My vision blurred and all I could feel was the rush of my Gift, alive and seeking. Always seeking. My nose burned from the scent of ozone and smoke. I swayed but Tokyo grabbed my outstretched arm and his voice lowered an octave, descending notes. My vision began to clear as I felt the lightning stretch across my extended arm.

"Tui!" He stomped a giant sandaled foot and now the swirl of power pooling in my belly speared out of my two fingers, a blade of light breaking through the dark sky.

I toppled over, my fingers leaving Adam's chest. My fingers buzzed from the remnants of power.

Adam shook like a dog flinging water, then turned away and retched on the sidewalk. Thick green phlegm poured out of him into the rubble.

Oda took out a small bottle from his jacket and poured it over Adam's face. I hoped it was water.

The Sentinel nodded, satisfaction wreathing his face. "Yes. It is gone."

I took that to mean that we had purged the poison. I nodded weakly. I felt hollowed out, already missing that feeling of fullness. My talent lay quiescent for now, but could I contain it?

Tokyo's Sentinel picked up Crimson Cloud Splitter, and his voice was reverent. "She calls me. Her voice is so clear."

He ran a broad thumb over the tsuka and he began to hum. The sword seemed to vibrate in his grasp and a white glow ran up the blood groove, a cold fire within. Tokyo continued to hum and then he flicked two fingers against the blade, as if striking a tuning fork. The resonant sound made my teeth rattle. Tokyo rested his palm against the flat of the blade, silencing her. He graced us with a beatific smile.

"The city is quiet."

Oda slid Crimson Cloud Splitter back in her scabbard and looped it in his belt. "I will keep her safe."

He picked up his naginata and bowed low to us before turning to push through the dissipating smoke. With a flash of purple light Oda vanished and Crimson Cloud Splitter ceased to be my problem.

I sagged with relief. Adam would be safe now and, by extension, Tessa.

Adam wiped his face with his shirt. He closed his eyes and resignation bowed his shoulders now. It hurt to see him shrink into himself as he watched Oda take the katana. But what choice did we have? My chest ached and I pressed my forehead into my knees.

Bāo licked my cheek, his tongue rough and scouring.

As my eyes readjusted, a line of blacked-out sedans pulled up to the curb outside the Prudential. When the lead car stopped, the doors opened and Nami and Fujita-san stepped out. Fujita-san's eyes tracked unerringly to Adam as Nami made a beeline for the wreckage of the Prudential's landscaping. More of my father's soldiers poured out of the remaining cars and spread out across the street, cordoning off the area. Before the hour was up, the whole block would be cleaned.

Fujita-san moved toward Adam but I waved him off with a shake of my head. It was too much. I couldn't ask him to swear to the Hoard today. Adam swept his gaze over Nami's crew as they went to work. Yet another hole torn into the fabric of his reality. He'd taken a beating today, but the hurt in his eyes had nothing to do with that.

His slumped posture and darkened eyes were a stab of pain through my chest. Just a day ago he'd been so full of life. I'd brought him to this. I'd done this to him. Before I could say anything to him, Adam heaved himself upright and limped back into the building.

He didn't look at me once.

Crimson Cloud Splitter was off the table now, and he and Tessa were safe.

I told myself that I had done my best, but it was cold comfort.

TRAINING DAY

I watched as Tatsuya animated the rocks and twigs in the courtyard, steadily building up a topo map of the Tourney course. Around us, the household came to life in the morning light. A small group of Iron Fists jogged the perimeter, singing a bawdy marching cadence in low voices. Another group on the far side of the courtyard went through their Dragon Steps in pairs with the occasional flash of qì stirring the surrounding trees.

Next to the main house, Lulu Āyí and her youngest granddaughter walked the trees, coaxing the fruit along with their talent. They pulled down fat pears and my mouth watered at the thought of the crisp, tart fruit slices that would await us later in the kitchen. Maybe I would stroll through the fruit orchard after practice and eat a snow peach right off the tree.

The clatter of pots and the sweet scent of steamed dough wafted from the open windows of the kitchen and set my stomach growling. These were the scents and sounds of the Soong estate and I had missed them when I had been in my self-imposed exile in San Francisco.

Despite the chaos we had wrought to the courtyard the night of my homecoming, Fujita-san had set everything back to rights. Fresh lanterns hung along the railings. The ash from the fires had been swept away. Hardly any char marks showed on the stone.

The two píxiū maintained their stony vigil on the perimeter of the yard.

We had work to do, first. Tatsuya expressed utter confidence in his ability to navigate the maze and place in the fastest eight finishers. For once I shared his confidence. The maze was a final exam for each graduating class of Lóng Kǒu, a chance for every student to know once and for all where they stood amongst their peers. Tatsuya's year had very few strong families, allowing him and his friends to cluster at the top of the rankings. For them, the maze was almost a formality.

But after the maze was a whole different story. Tatsuya had spent his years at Lóng Kǒu playing with his friends. After the maze, some of his friends would be playing for blood. For many of the mid-tier families, a top eight finish was good, but not enough. Strategies would change, and friendships would die on the sword of family. In order to maintain our family's position of strength, Tatsuya had to acquit himself well.

That's where I came into play. After the maze was basically a variation of capture the flag. Funny thing about the strategy for that. One way to win was to get to the flag the fastest. The other way was to cripple your opponent to prevent them from reaching the flag before you.

With Jiārén, you had an equal split about which approach they would take.

I was the weakling with no talent. Any strategy I would implement for myself would be to take out my opponent early. I sensed Tacchan didn't think like that.

"Who do you expect to face in round two?"

"Now with Colin out of the picture, probably Minjae, Thùy, Balen, or Chariya."

He gridded them out for me, just like the day I'd come home. Now that I'd seen what my brother could—or more accurately, couldn't—do, I had more concerns.

I studied where Tatsuya had classed his opponents. As a child, every Jiārén learned where they stood on this diagram. More than almost anything else, your position on the Sì Xiàng determined where you stood in the hierarchy of Jiārén. Somewhere on this diagram was my Gift. I had never heard of a Gift like mine. Something so repugnant would have stood out in any text on Hoard Gifts. Even

Tacchan's puppetry, if it were ever revealed, would only be considered frightening. Not an abomination.

I shook myself and returned to the task at hand. When I had time, I would need to speak with my father about my talent and why they had hidden it from me. For now, my priority was to prepare my brother for the most difficult fight of his life.

"Who do you consider your most difficult opponent?"

"Thùy."

"Why?"

"She's a harmonic. She's gotten a lot stronger this year. She can put out a twenty-meter field that can dismantle all of my constructs. That would take me out of the running for the final round."

We couldn't let that happen. Tatsuya didn't seem to care about winning so much as not losing. This meant he needed to finish every round. When the reins for Soong Clan passed from my father to Tatsuya, he couldn't afford to be seen as weak. A weak clan head invited trouble in the same way that a rotting corpse invited vultures.

In a painfully tedious bracketing exercise, Tatsuya and I walked through the various permutations of his possible opponents. None of them were good. My brother was strong, and he had only tapped into a fraction of what he would later be capable of. But he was oblivious and I couldn't teach situational awareness in a day.

That left only one option. We had to fight dirty. That was how I'd survived all these years—by going low before a powerful talent could chew me up.

"Tell me about Thùy's clan and affiliations."

"The Hoàngs are from New York. I'm not sure if they're aligned with any Custodian families . . ."

When my brother's voice trailed off, I lifted a brow.

"Well, she does have this silver necklace she wears." Tatsuya shrugged. "Could be nothing."

Or it could be a gift from Fiona's clan.

"So we know her range is twenty meters. She's really strong. How long can she hold it?"

"I don't know."

"Does she need to face the field or is she the center of the harmonic field?"

"I don't know."

"So you don't know if she is a radius talent or line-of-sight talent?"

Tatsuya shook his head in frustration.

"Where is round two going to be held?"

"Gotenshita Park, after sunset."

I could work with that. Tatsuya mounded up the pebbles and leaves to mimic the terrain of Gotenshita park. I charted out where I would normally wait. Unsurprisingly, Tatsuya hated every bit of my approach and he made sure I knew it.

"It's my last year at Lóng Kǒu. This is supposed to be my last hurrah. I shouldn't be planning to win by stabbing all my friends in their backs."

"What do you think you're doing this for?"

As usual, he was clueless. "What?"

I grabbed him by the shoulders and turned him around. On the other side of the courtyard Lulu Āyí stood under the persimmon trees, carefully tending the new buds on the low-hanging branches.

Tacchan looked back at me with a painfully confused look on his face. "Āyí?"

I swatted him across the back of his head. "Yes, you idiot. Her, and everyone else who works for this clan, who depends on our strength to keep them safe. You're going to take over the clan someday. It won't always be just about you, so you need to start thinking bigger than yourself."

He at least had the decency to look humbled. "You sound like Father."

Ouch. "Well, if you sounded more like him, I wouldn't have to be the one doing it."

"It was supposed to be you. You're the eldest."

The words echoed between us, thick with resentment. The worst part was that he was right. I was supposed to lead the clan. If not for my blocked meridians, who knew how I would have done at Lóng Kǒu? That was just another wound to probe when I had the time. For now, Tatsuya needed to accept his role.

In an eyeblink I was in my little brother's face, staring him down. Even though he was half a head taller than me, I managed to look down my nose at him. I squeezed down on my roiling emotions and waited for him to continue.

Tatsuya dropped his head for a moment and then met my gaze, his eyes bright with emotion. "I. Don't. Want this."

"You are the future of the clan."

"I never wanted this. I was supposed to help you lead. Not the other way around."

"If you're unhappy with your fate, go speak with the Dragon Father." Skies. I was really starting to sound like my father.

My brother's voice cracked as it rose to a shout. "Father let you get away with everything! He let you walk away from us! From me!"

Heat radiated from my brother like an open flame, and several rocks around us floated off the ground, caught up in the intensity of his anger. And beneath that anger, I smelled the distinct tang of real fear. With that, the tight knot of stress in my core unfurled and faded. I held my little brother's shoulders and waited until the rocks drifted to the ground.

"Tatsuya. I'm sorry I left you. But I came back. I will always show up for my family. Now you have to as well. I . . . I can't lead."

I hadn't told him about my Gift. It didn't matter, in any case. No one would ally with a clan whose Gift could steal your own. With luck, I wouldn't tell anyone about it. Because if word got out about the horrific Gift I'd been cursed with, keeping our clan intact would be the least of our worries.

Tatsuya's anger ebbed. "But . . ."

"No buts. You will lead the clan someday and I will cut down anyone who stands in our way."

My brother's gaze roved around the courtyard before settling back on me. His shoulders shifted slightly, his presence seeming to solidify under my grip. He took a deep breath and the pepper and horseradish smell of his talent surrounded me. A handful of rocks rolled across the courtyard and tumbled together into a crude doglike figure as high as my ankle. A rattling sound like a rock slide grew louder and in moments the two of us were ringed by a small collection of rock-dogs.

Tatsuya's eyes shone. The hurt wasn't gone, but the fear had been pushed aside. He nodded once. "All right. Who's first?"

My brother picked himself off the gravel and wiped the blood from his nose. He said something, probably a curse of some kind, but I couldn't hear it over the ringing in my ears. At the top of a little rise, Xiǎo Huā stood looking down at the both of us. She was by far the tallest member of my father's Pearl Guard, as well as the most senior beneath Kubota-san's command. Her hand-to-hand combat skills were legendary, comparable only to her notorious temper. I had sparred against her several times and each affair had left me drained for an entire day.

At present, she was bored.

Tatsuya lifted a dozen rocks off the ground and they swirled around him in a complex pattern. He stretched his hands out and the rocks took off along a dozen different paths, looping around the courtyard, narrowly avoiding the other members of our household to take circuitous paths back to Xiǎo Huā.

She pivoted in place, watching for the incoming missiles. When one approached, she opened her mouth and sang a high, ringing note that scraped at my ears like tinfoil. The incoming rock shattered in midair. She turned and blew the next one out of the sky as well.

I picked up my own rock and threw it at my brother's head. Without turning to me, Tatsuya redirected one of his orbiting missiles and deflected my rock.

I palmed a Dragon Breath crystal. "Good! But it won't just be rocks coming at you."

My qì ignited the crystal and a fountain of orange flame leapt from my hand, aimed at Tacchan's feet. As he danced away his missiles drooped and wobbled in midflight.

"Concentrate! Your qì moves where you will it!" Strange, to hear the lessons I could not learn coming from my own mouth.

Xiǎo Huā pulverized three more missiles, but each one got a little closer, narrowing her margin for error. Tatsuya pounced, sending the rest of his missiles in. I noted with approval that he'd varied the speed of some of them, trying to throw off Xiǎo Huā's aim. Kubota-san's lieutenant spun in place, picking the missiles off one and two at a time while my brother watched, his hands rigid before him.

I launched myself at him, aiming a kick at his head. He dodged and backpedaled, making room between us. I pointed to Xiǎo Huā.

"Go! Put one hand on her!"

"What? You said—" Tatsuya huffed.

"Go!"

Tacchan's aura blazed and he bolted off to the right as a trio of rock-dogs assembled themselves and ran off to the left.

My brother's missiles fell from the sky, the last one barely a foot from Xiǎo Huā when it became a cloud of rock dust. She whirled to find three granite hounds charging at her with a sound like an avalanche. Tatsuya ran in as well, coming at the soldier's unprotected back. The nearest dog pounded in and opened a mouth full of jagged teeth made from chipped rocks. Xiǎo Huā opened her mouth and stomped her foot into the ground. This strike was a massive bass drum beat. Rocks and dirt jumped into the air in a ten-foot circle around her. My brother's constructs fell to pieces under the sonic assault. I clapped my hands over my ears as the sound wave took my brother in the chest and tossed him back ten feet to land on his butt. A trickle of blood ran from one of his ears. I opened my mouth and cracked my jaw, trying to relieve the ringing in my own ears.

I waved to Xiǎo Huā. "Okay, okay. He's had enough."

She gave me a small shrug and walked off the small hill and back toward the guard barracks. "I'm off duty for a while. Let me know if he wants another go."

Tatsuya groaned and picked himself up off the ground. "I almost had her that time."

"You were doing okay from afar. But you won't always be able to do that. Sometimes you'll need to get in close."

"Look, I think—"

A shadow passed over us and I instinctively ducked away, my hands flashing to my waist to grab Hachi. Tatsuya screamed as a dark form crashed into his chest with a roar and bore him to the grass, the two of them tumbling over each other and down the small hill. I ran after them, panicked fears racing across my mind, imagining Kaida slicing her blade across Tatsuya's belly before I could reach them.

I found my brother pinned under a massive píxiū, the winged lion's head as high as my chest, its massive paws nearly covering Tatsuya's torso. A pair of forked antlers swept back from the creature's head and curving fangs protruded from its wide mouth. It roared again and shook itself, long white whiskers whipping back and forth. Only now did I detect the smell of white pepper.

The píxiū turned its massive head to me, dark eyes sparkling bright. Its skin flexed and flowed, still the mottled gray of the granite the statue had been carved from. My father walked out from the guard barracks.

Broken Claw. He'd been watching the whole time. He stopped beside me and we both looked down at my little brother, pinned under my father's animated píxiū. Where Tacchan's píxiū had been an animated statue, my father's creation breathed. In fact the beast's broad chest did rise and fall as it brought its nose down to brush against my brother's head.

My father crossed his arms and the píxiū clambered off my brother and sat obediently at my father's feet. "I have another strategy for you. It will be difficult."

I resisted the urge to roll my eyes. "If 'more difficult' means he wins, I vote for more difficult."

Tatsuya sat up, rubbing at his chest. "What is it?"

Our father's gaze slid over my hair, lingering on the blunt edges that now framed my chin before moving to my brother. "Something that I need to pass on to you. To both of you. Now that your sister is . . . better, I think the time has come."

Tatsuya looked at me, confusion creasing his brow. I shook my head, putting him off for now. My brother's chances in Lóng Yá were the main concern here. I didn't need my drama wasting his time.

If my father noticed our little exchange, he gave no hint. "Our family has many treasures that will become your responsibility. This is the only one you have yet to see."

My brother perked up at this, his eyes wide and eager.

Our father closed his eyes and a low, thrumming hum started in his chest. My eyes widened and found my brother. I'd heard Tokyo's Sentinel warm up with notes like this. Father could only be doing one thing—Dragonsong.

While our Hoard Gifts were bestowed upon us by the power of dragons, this literally was the power of dragons. With enough qì, enough focus, enough practice, and enough talent to not be destroyed in the process, Jiārén could emulate the words of the ancient tongue of the dragons and perform tremendous acts of power.

In the Realm, the Nine Sons of the Dragon created beautiful, intricate creations with Dragonsong. They built soaring structures that dwarfed the clouds and terrible weapons that cracked the world. Dragonsong was a language that defied human comprehension, sung in unearthly notes of beauty and brutality.

To claim that Jiārén knew Dragonsong was like claiming to have read all of Confucius's writings, when all you knew was one word, from one scroll, that you happened to see. Dragonsong was a fundamental force of creation and destruction, and Jiārén weren't even screaming babes mimicking their parents. Even so, the infinitesimal fragments of Dragonsong that we had kept were carefully preserved, passed down in oral tradition, and protected more zealously than any Hoard artifact.

Oda had sung to purge the venom from Adam. To witness Dragonsong once in a decade was stunning, to experience it twice in one day was beyond my imagining.

The humming in my father's chest built in volume and my very bones vibrated in response. The courtyard was empty, except for the three of us. Father had sent everyone away, just to show us this. I cycled my qì, feeling the texture of my father's energy as he drew toward release. I had never considered the possibility that our father knew a fragment of Dragonsong. With my blocked meridians, it had never even occurred to me that I might be able to harness Dragonsong.

The moment my qì harmonized with my father's nearly brought me to my knees. The countless hours he'd spent, teaching me despite my failings, the easy patience he'd shown me with every lesson. I had always wondered why he bothered to teach his broken daughter. It was like he'd known how things would turn out in the end.

The hum was a crackling buzz in the air now, louder than any human throat could make, the sound crushing down on my ears. My father's eyes flashed open and he whirled, arms swinging wide into a downward strike. He opened his mouth and the hum crescendoed and morphed as he yelled, "Tui!"

A tidal wave of energy crashed out of his arms. The píxiū at his feet was pulverized and blew apart like a bomb. The flagstones beneath us crumbled to pieces and were blown away, the blast wave digging a triangular trench that stretched from my father to the far side of the courtyard. One of the persimmon trees tipped and fell into the trench. My father made a face at the fallen tree.

Tatsuya was beside himself, mouth hanging open in wonder. "Woah."

My father straightened up and flicked an imaginary mote of dirt from his sleeve. "That is the Dragonsong my father taught to me. The closest human word we have to translate it is 'push.' The result is simple, yet effective."

Father looked from my brother to me. "Who wants to try first?"

I tipped my head at Tatsuya. He was the one headed into Lóng Yá, not me. He needed to increase his arsenal and this would be an exponential leap. Also I did not want Tatsuya to witness me attempting it. If whatever was within me awoke, I didn't want Tatsuya to see it.

My brother closed his eyes and began to hum. Father guided him gently, keeping Tatsuya on key. They did this several times, even as Tatsuya faltered. For all the difficulty I had with my father, he had always been and remained a patient instructor. He continued in this fashion, having Tatsuya cycle his qì and harmonize to the Dragonsong.

Tatsuya worked, his diligence clear, but his throat struggled to produce the correct notes. Father nodded as if unsurprised. He reached into his jacket and drew a slender stick from an inner pocket. I squinted. That wasn't a stick. It looked like a hollow bone from a bird. Given the color, it was *old*. Then I realized what it was. It was a dragon wing bone. Skies and clouds, I couldn't believe it.

Father rolled it in his hands and I noticed it had carvings and predrilled holes on it. He held it up to Tatsuya. "Watch."

He blew softly and a piercing note rang out across the courtyard. He tapped his fingers as he blew into the dízi and the notes rose in a familiar unearthly crescendo. Father handed the instrument to Tatsuya.

Tatsuya turned the dízi around in his hands, his fingertips tracing the carvings. His eyes held a mixture of fear and wonder. When he brought the instrument to his lips, he replicated Father's tune perfectly.

Father nodded. "Faster."

Tatsuya played the notes again and this time the hum built up in my chest. My brother felt it, too, and his aura flared wild and bright as the power of the Dragonsong saturated us.

"Now push."

Tatsuya stomped his foot and pushed with both hands, the flats of his palms directed at the fruit orchard. Like a bowling ball tearing through pins, six trees toppled and splintered across the courtyard.

Uh-oh. Lulu Āyí was not going to like that at all.

Tatsuya's mouth gaped open and he held the instrument gingerly now, as if it were a neutron bomb. I guess it kind of was. Of every single item in our Hoard, this had to be the most precious. I'd never heard of such a thing and I researched Hoard items for fun and profit.

Father gestured to the wing bone. "You cannot bring a weapon to Lóng Yá, but a musical instrument is permitted."

Maybe that was a loophole that someone like Thùy would also exploit. My lips turned down. "Tatsuya, you might need to use it."

He frowned. "I hope not."

Father stepped close to Tatsuya and forced him to wrap his loose fingers firmly around the instrument. "Take it inside. Study it."

I felt a stab of disappointment. It's not like I needed to know Dragonsong, but I had wanted to try it.

But Tatsuya needed it, so maybe I could try it someday in the future, after Lóng Yá. I watched my brother hold the precious item close to his chest as he turned to walk back to the house. Maybe I could pick a pear and then head to the kitchen to see if the Pearl Guard had left any buns or if they'd just moved through the breakfast buffet like a swarm of locusts. I turned away but my father's voice stopped me.

"Now it's your turn."

"But Tatsuya has the dízi."

"You don't need it."

He always did that to me. Somehow he managed to set his expectations of me so high that I both feared failing and simultaneously strived harder to meet them. Underlying it all, though, was always his utmost confidence in me. He had never given up on me.

Because he knew.

I threw caution to the wind. "You've always known, haven't you?"

My father's poker face was the stuff of legend. "Known what?"

"About my talent. And my meridians."

"That is not a question."

I fought the urge to stomp my feet and rage at him. How did he always manage to do this to me?

He said, "Perhaps you should consider what you are hoping to learn, before you ask your question. But for now, do you, or do you not, want to learn the technique?"

Again with the choices. And if he was bargaining for giving me the confirmation that I was almost sure of against teaching me the Dragonsong technique, it was no contest. I calmed myself and nodded for him to continue.

Father gestured with his hand, motioning me closer. He hummed three notes. I did the same.

"Good, now cycle your qì."

I did as he instructed and hummed the notes again.

"Faster."

As I did so, the vibrations from my throat rippled out across my chest, an ever-expanding ocean of sound. The puny sounds of my throat morphed and I felt my throat chakra release as if a latch had opened. My father slammed two fingers into the spot in my spine that aligned with my heart chakra. Once dormant, my talent awoke and quested outward. It took and took, finding my father's Gift familiar and necessary. My qì cycled incredibly fast, the momentum and power near bursting within me as I sang. I stomped my foot and flung out my arm in an arc toward the remaining píxiū. A pulse blurred the air and the stone guardian crumbled to dust.

It was strangely quiet after. No more Dragonsong. My chest heaved and I felt as if I'd sprinted while being chased. I stared at the pile of dust that once been a majestic píxiū. My Gift deflated, no longer fed by an outside source.

I looked at my father. He wore a pleased expression. He'd been right. I hadn't needed the dragonbone because he'd shared his Gift with me. I'd gobbled it up and been able to direct it at the píxiū.

And I was right. He'd known all along about what I could do. He'd just chosen to hide it from me my entire life. All the shame I'd experienced after being expelled from Lóng Kǒu, the years he'd sent me away to Jōkōryūkai stretched out in a montage of pain. To know I'd had a Gift, even a horrifying Gift, would have given me some small comfort. Now my talent had awoken and I could choose never to use it. Never to make it another weapon my father could direct.

I made the question as direct as possible. "You've always known I had this talent, haven't you?"

Again he showed no surprise at my knowledge. "I have known for many years."

Years of frustration boiled out of me in an instant. "Why didn't you tell me?! All through Lóng Kǒu—"

"Mimi, I am your father, and the head of our clan. It is my responsibility to mold you into the kind of Jiārén who will ensure our clan legacy endures for generations."

He raised his hand to me. "In this, I have succeeded. And you should ask yourself, given the nature of your talent, how would Lóng Kǒu have been different for you, had you known?"

"But—"

"Your path was always going to be difficult, Mimi. I only ever tried to give you the tools to prevail in your endeavors."

He was right, again, but my anger wanted to keep lashing out. It would get me nowhere, though. I would never win, not against him. He'd probably planned for this exact conversation. I turned away from him and stalked to the house. I didn't need pears or buns—I'd lost my appetite.

ENTERING THE DRAGON'S MAW

Today was Tatsuya's big day.

Lóng Yá was the crucible from which Tatsuya had to emerge as the victor. He'd spent the night with the menagerie in the Hoard treasure room. I spent it walking through countless scenarios on how I would neutralize Kaida before she could kill my brother.

None of us got much sleep. Well, maybe except for Uncle Lau. I'd heard him snoring while I'd checked and rechecked my provisions for today. It would be a long day, with all three events of Lóng Yá being stacked within less than twenty-four hours. From sunrise to past midnight.

There hadn't been much point in trying to sleep since we had to be ready to go by two hours before dawn.

We all dressed carefully for the occasion. As usual, I simply wore what Fujita-san had laid out for me before augmenting it with my special touch. Today was a charcoal-gray boatneck tank of fine wool over lined wool trousers. The fabric moved easily and had lots of pockets, some of which were hidden in the waistband.

I slid two crystals into those secret pockets. I was definitely taking this outfit back to San Francisco with me. In my opinion blades were the perfect accessory for every occasion, but I also wore a short single strand of perfectly matched creamy pink pearls. Fujita-san had given me a beautiful lightweight trench coat, the fabric a blush pink with a sheen like the inside of an abalone shell. I paired it with low-top black Onitsuka Tiger sneakers. This outfit was so somber and restrained that if it weren't for my tattooed arm, I'd look like a banker walking from the metro.

I patted my pockets one last time, mentally walking through the locations of my provisions. Finally, I strapped on Hachi and made my way downstairs.

Down in the kitchen, Uncle Jake and Lulu Āyí had been busy. The steamer trays filled with buns were stacked high, and vats of boiling soybeans steamed up the kitchen.

Lulu sliced up her giant pears, arranging them into artful displays. Uncle Jake winked at me, then with a lazy gesture started juggling the pears in the air with his talent.

"Oh, Jake. Stop that." Lulu tsked, waving her knife around.

"I'm just checking which ones are ripe." Jake grinned.

Lulu rolled her eyes. Jake knew very well that his wife only picked the ripe ones. They were all perfect, of course. But I appreciated Jake's efforts to lighten the mood in the kitchen. It was a serious day and we were all here hours earlier than usual.

Uncle Lau marched in, his brisk steps like that of a soldier. It did feel a bit like we were an army regiment headed out to engage the enemy. Only they were our own people and yet we couldn't trust anyone. He poured his tea, then slurped his Dragonwell tea noisily before piling more bāo onto his plate. He set his teacup down and looked over at Jake. "Send over some of the nai wong bāo, Jake."

"You got it." Jake snapped his fingers and two steamer trays hovered in the air to drop down before Uncle Lau.

Clearly the momentous occasion had not interfered with Uncle Lau's appetite. I sat down and Uncle Jake floated over a pot of tea for me. Nami looked up from her bowl of rice and grilled mackerel briefly to assess my weapon choices for the day. She grunted approvingly when she saw my straps and Hachi. The students couldn't bring weapons, and while we weren't supposed to go in loaded for bear, we could still remind people that the Soong Clan was a combat house.

After breaking into some pork buns and slurping down a bowl of savory soy milk, I felt a little more awake.

I nabbed a nai wong bāo from Uncle Lau's bin and he smiled at me. In this room, these were the people I trusted. In San Francisco, I'd been lucky enough to grow close to the Sun family and Tessa. Maybe Freddy. When I'd broken Truth and renounced the Blade mantle, I thought I would be alone forever. That my family would never forgive me. I was glad I'd been wrong.

Tatsuya poked his head in. "Uncle Jake, any xiǎo lóng bāo?"

"For you, of course."

Wow. Uncle Jake had really pulled out all the stops. Xiǎo lóng bāo was a two-day process, making the gelatin cubes, freezing them, preparing the delicate wrapping, and then freezing it all again before steaming them to yield the delicious soupy goodness. Unless it was a special occasion, Jake didn't make XLB dumplings.

Tatsuya was graduating today after six years at Lóng Kǒu. I guess it didn't get more special than that.

I assessed my brother's eyes and skin tone. He looked refreshed from his time in the Hoard treasure room. His skin gleamed with health, the normally pale tone flushed with a slight pink as if he'd gone out for a run. The whites of his eyes were so clear they held a blue tinge and his eyes and thick straight brows looked inky dark in contrast.

He wore a pale pink blazer over a gray T-shirt and gray jeans. Pearls studded his belt buckle and he sported two pearl studs all the way up the shell of his left ear. He took off his blazer and hung it on the chair next to me and sat down. Uncle Jake slid two bamboo trays of XLB in front of Tatsuya, who promptly slid the black vinegar trays over to dunk his dumplings into.

I pouted. "Uncle Jake never makes me XLB."

"Yeah. I'm his favorite." Tatsuya slurped noisily.

I hoped he burned his tongue.

Tatsuya devoured sixteen XLB and asked for more. I shook my head. I knew I should eat more but the combination of the early hour and nerves had diminished my normally hearty appetite.

The distinctive click of wooden rings sliding together sounded and Sugi strode into the kitchen followed by my father. His eyes lasered in on Tatsuya and he gave a small nod of greeting. Father had eschewed the silk jackets today and sported a charcoal wool Tang suit, trimmed with silver threads and seed pearls. With the arrival of my father, we were the perfect family portrait.

Except for my mother. I shoved down a spurt of anger. It was Tatsuya's big day—a day I'd never attained for myself. Surely my mother could get dispensation from Bā Shǒu to attend her son's Tourney run.

Father put his hand on Tatsuya's shoulder and gave a firm squeeze. "You will do your clan proud today."

Tatsuya swallowed a mouthful of dumpling. "Yes, Father."

I set my teacup down. "Mother should be here for Tatsuya today."

Almost in unison, Father and Tatsuya turned to stare at me.

"Of course your mother would be here if she could. But what she is doing is beyond anything you could imagine. It is for the good of all of us," Father responded calmly.

Tatsuya nodded his head. "It's okay, Neesan. She talked to me before she left on assignment. I understand."

Father's response, I expected. His eyes shone with admiration when he spoke of his wife—a quality that would have been endearing if it didn't always end with a rebuke for me. Tatsuya calmly shoved another dumpling into his gullet, unfazed by our mother missing out on the culmination of six years of his training at Lóng Kǒu.

If it didn't bother him, why should it bother me? But it did bother me.

My fingers squeezed into tight fists and then relaxed. My expectations were unrealistic. It didn't matter to her that this was Tatsuya's big day. She wasn't showing up for him. But I was.

I punched Tatsuya lightly on his arm. "Take it easy on those XLB or you'll be too slow to run the maze."

Lulu walked over to us and slid a plate of sliced pears onto the table. "Have some fruit."

Tacchan smiled and snatched up a slice with his chopsticks. "Thanks, Āyí."

She patted him on the back. "You'll need your energy today. Would you like some persimmons, too?"

Tacchan nodded.

Lulu pointed at me. "Mimi, go to the front to pick some for your brother. Somebody smashed all the persimmons in the backyard."

I sputtered. "That wasn't me!"

Lulu crossed her arms and stared me down.

I scowled at Tacchan. "Fine. I'll go get you your persimmons." I tossed down my napkins while he snickered, then stalked out of the kitchen with a basket.

It was still early, not even dawn. As I stepped off the front landing, my steps faltered, unprepared for what I saw.

Under the glow of the red lanterns, Adam towered over Fujita-san, and they spoke in hushed tones. Yoko-obaachan stood next to Adam as well, the gray of her tightly permed hair glinting red under the lanterns as she bent over his hand.

Bright red blood dripped from his palm, and Yoko chanted softly over it.

Sugi sat next to his knee, and the wolf's ears swiveled at my approach, a soft snick of wood.

While Father was inside, his ever-faithful companion kept watch over the newest member of the Soong Clan. This must have happened while I was in the kitchen stuffing my face with steamed buns—Adam had sworn to the Hoard.

After the disaster yesterday, my father had taken matters into his own hands. I should have been relieved, but I felt strangely left out.

I strode over to them, interrupting the odd tableau. Adam saw me first and tipped his head. "Emiko."

The expression in his eyes was unreadable. "Adam."

He straightened and all at once I was struck by the incongruity of him here, in the heart of my clanhome. Despite the ridiculous hour, he wore a suit and tie, the fine gray fabric looking almost purple under the lanterns. His tie was pink with a white sakura print. My gaze lingered on the tie because his tie pin was silver, with a single glossy pearl. A Soong pearl.

Adam looked more relaxed than I would have expected for a guy who had just stepped through a Realm pocket, bled for a vow to a Dragon's Hoard, and was being tended to by a healer and shepherded by an animated wooden wolf.

Fujita-san's eyes darted between us and he tapped Yoko on the shoulder. She nodded. "Hai."

With another gesture, Adam's wound sealed, the skin of his palm healing with a neat curved scar. It was exactly the size of Sugi's jaw. Adam's eyes widened in wonder and he turned his hand this way and that.

He bowed deeply to Yoko and thanked her profusely in Japanese.

Fujita-san smiled at me. "Emi-chan, I hope you ate."

I nodded. He wrapped an arm around Yoko and they walked back into the house.

That left me to walk Adam out. I stared down at Sugi, willing her to leave. She sat on her haunches, the deliberate click and slide of polished wood telling me she wasn't going anywhere.

With a sigh, I set down the basket. Tacchan was going to have to do without his persimmons today. I gestured to the pathway for Adam to follow me into the bamboo forest. I should have been pleased. The sword was safely in Oda's hands, and Adam had sworn to the Hoard, so my duties were concluded. But it seemed like a hollow victory, with no winners.

We didn't speak, and the only sound between us was the crunch of gravel and Sugi's clicks as we walked under the tall archway of green bamboo. We exited the path and to my relief, Sugi stayed back while Adam and I crossed into the front house.

Adam pushed aside the noren panels and gave the ceiling crane ornaments a wide berth, which told me my father had given him quite a show of his power to ensure Adam's acquiescence.

I stopped, uncertain of what to say. Finally I settled on, "I'm sorry."

Adam gave me a mirthless smile, the planes of his face shadowed in the darkness of the front house. "Are you?"

Irritation made my tone sharp. "I did everything in my power to handle this peacefully."

He gave a hard laugh. "Peacefully."

"Why are you mad? You should be happy now. Every rumor you've chased for years is true. You can lay the mystery of the Yamamotos' ancestors to rest. They were Jiārén. Kenji is descended from Jiārén. Now you know all of it."

Adam spread his arms wide, but his voice was soft. "All of it? Emiko, you told me nothing about yourself. Your family is the Soong family of Soong Pearls. You weren't breaking Jiārén secrets to tell me that."

I sputtered. "I have nothing to do with that business."

He shook his head. "Imagine my surprise when your father mentioned he owned the penthouse units above mine. And that you lived there for a time. You never bothered to mention it. You treated me like a fool."

I had. I lowered my eyes in regret.

Adam's voice lowered. "Anything you asked me, I answered. I was an open book for you. I thought we were getting to know one another but it wasn't just Jiārén secrets, Emiko."

He took a step back from me. "You lied about everything you are."

The unfairness of it seared me and my face flushed hot with shame. I said nothing in response, could think of nothing to respond with as he pivoted and stalked away.

Traffic around Todai University's Hongo campus had been redirected until the area was a virtual ghost town. Our entourage entered the grounds through the historic Red Gate, and in the pale light before dawn we arrived at Sanshiro Pond. The picturesque body of water sat in the center of the campus, and the small island in the middle of the pond hid the Gate to Lóng Kǒu.

Just for tonight, a Dragon Wing bridge had been constructed to provide entry. Two stanchions had been set up on the edge of the pond, slender pillars of polished wood, each topped with a sphere of milky jade the size of a softball. A matching set of jade spheres waited on the island.

When it was my turn, I stepped up to the jade stones with my brother.

Tacchan stopped beside me. “So, do we just—”

It was like a giant cushion of air picked us up from below. In a split second the cool morning air was rushing past our faces as the glassy surface of the pond whipped by below. My brother whooped and his voice echoed across the water.

I pointed ahead of us. “Get ready!”

The island loomed and the jade stones on the other end of the bridge flared to life. Another cushion of air caught us. The cross-winds whipped at us and snapped the tails of my trench coat out behind me. Tacchan let out an excited yelp as the ground jumped up to meet us.

I landed neatly on bent knees with my coat flaring out around me, my boots leaving a deep indentation into the earth.

Uncle Lau crowed. “Ha! Perfect landing!”

Once we were all across, my father got us organized again and as a group, we crossed through the Door that led to the massive Realm Fragment housing Lóng Kǒu.

Stepping back onto the grounds of Lóng Kǒu was more surreal than I had anticipated. Coming at dawn meant the campus was still shrouded in the mist, much the way it felt in my memories.

The school was set behind a circular rampart of ten-foot-high whitewashed stone walls atop a gently sloping ridge of earth. Grass covered the earthen rise in a carpet of verdant green, stark against the white of the wall. Thirty-foot magnolia trees with their clusters of delicate white blossoms stood sentinel outside the wall, far enough away to discourage anyone from trying to use the trees to breach the walls. The top of the wall was notched every fifty feet with a narrow opening that gave the guards a clear view of the exterior grounds.

The only access through the outer wall was through four massive moon doors that marked the cardinal directions. Our family and retainers approached the East Gate. The rosewood timbers that curved around the heavy door were painted a brilliant blue, and a sinuous dragon with a serpentine body decorated the door, carved into the old wood.

I had walked through this very door, the last time I had left. I tried not to read too much into this coincidence. During the school year, students only used the gates associated with their houses. For large events like Lóng Yá, everyone simply used the East Gate.

My father walked at the head of our party, with Tatsuya and me just behind him. Uncle Lau and Fujita-san trailed behind us, and a small contingent of the Pearl Guard fanned out behind them, guarding our flanks. We all wore our family colors, but the more overt Hoard pieces had been left in the vault today. Lóng Yá was about the students, and there was an unspoken rule to allow the student competition to play out without family interference.

Of course, this simply meant that everyone tried their best to cheat anyway.

As we crested the small rise and entered the East Gate, the interior of the grounds opened up before us. The closest building to us was Dragon House, a two-story wooden building topped with bright blue tiles. Stonework dragons with glittering cobalt scales twisted along the rooflines and guarded the doors. The early fingers of sunlight speared through the horizon, bouncing gold-white sparks off the blue scales. My breath caught in my throat at the sight. It hadn't been the best year of my life, but some parts of Lóng Kǒu had been good. Especially in Dragon House.

Beyond Dragon House was the main school, an ancient, multilevel building, all weathered timber built in intricate lattices and interlocking supports. Today flags from the Hoard Custodian families hung from the roofline, flapping in the light breeze. The school was a round structure, five stories tall, and flanked by dozens of smaller buildings that radiated out from the central hub.

As the building went up, delicate arched pathways stretched out, connecting to smaller classrooms that floated like moons in orbit. Some of the classrooms sat on white clouds, some on shifting masses of rock and earth. One of the bridges was made up entirely of twisting vines full of flowers that bloomed and died as you watched. The vines reached out into space and spread into a massive platform, supporting a small cottage built out of rough-cut bamboo.

I had never liked walking those pathways. It was too exposed, too vulnerable. The roof of the central building was a massive cone of lacquered wood shingles in deepest red. There was only one way to access the roof, and I had needed to evade guards and traps to get there.

I could just make out the other three houses, Bird, Tortoise, and Tiger in the distance, directly opposite from Dragon. Between the houses were vast sparring fields and training grounds, set up to accommodate students with a dizzying array of Hoard Gifts. All that space had been taken to construct the maze, a rambling structure of stone and raw lumber that sprawled across the school grounds, winding its way from house to house, and fully encircling the main building.

As we neared Dragon House, our party stopped behind another group waiting to enter the dormitory. I groaned inwardly at the sight of all the lavender. Tatsuya perked up and went up on his toes, looking for his friend.

His eyes lit up. "Minjae!"

The taller boy turned and waved, smiling. The boys began moving toward each other when my father's hand shot out and grabbed Tatsuya by the wrist. At the same moment Byun A-Yeong leaned over and stuck out one of her canes. The cane tip hit the path with a crack, blocking Minjae's path.

Minjae took one look at his grandmother and the boy deflated, turning away. The Byun matriarch's eyes traveled from my father to me. She smiled, the expression coming nowhere close to her diamond-hard eyes, and turned away to lead her party up the stairs and into Dragon House.

Tap, step.

Tap, step.

My father turned to Tatsuya. "Family first."

Tatsuya nodded slowly and the Soong party moved as one to enter Dragon House.

Dragon House was smaller than I remembered. And today it was also emptier. Many years had passed since I'd been there, but it still smelled the same—a mélange of spices and dry wood. My earliest and clearest memory of Lóng Kǒu was arriving at the dormitory and nearly panicking at the sensory overload. Our home had always been crowded, the grounds populated by guards, house staff, and other retainers loyal to my family. Other children my age had been an infrequent occurrence. As the eldest child of a Hoard Custodian family, I had all the advantages of private tutoring from the best teachers. Lessons in the arts, sciences, and physical fitness to prepare me for my future.

None of them prepared me for Lóng Kǒu.

Hundreds of teenagers living in one building, packed in and stewing in a rich broth of hormones, bravado, and pride. Although not every student came from a Hoard Custodian family, every student had some claim to power and glory. Everyone had at least one exceptional aunt, or cousin, or grandfather who had defeated some fell demon, or ghost, or noxious creature of the night. Our families filled us with the legends of our ancestors and sent us off to Lóng Kǒu to make our own mark.

It was a miracle we didn't eat each other alive before even getting to the Tourney.

The qì dampeners in the dorms helped. I finally felt them as we walked into the dorm, a low-level numbness that set into my bones. Everyone else in our group felt it. I saw it in the tense shoulders and twitching fingers all around me. Tatsuya shook it off the fastest since he had still been living here a few weeks ago. My father didn't show any effects at all. But then again, my father was very good at hiding things.

My blocked meridians had made the dampening ward a moot point for me during my disastrous tenure over a decade ago. But the wards gave the school some assurance that the students would be somewhat limited in their ability to cause mischief when out of direct supervision. The wards could not stop anyone from accessing their qì, they just made it much more difficult. It was not a coincidence that the school only designated viewing areas within the dorms for the visiting families. If putting all our most talented children in one building was dangerous, putting all their parents together was ludicrous.

The west side of the building, facing the main school, had been converted into one large room that held nearly every powerful family amongst the Jiārén. The entire west-facing wall had been transmuted to glass, allowing us an unobstructed view of the beginning of the maze. As a Hoard Custodian family, our family had a place of honor, roped off and separate from the rest of the crowd. The Pearl Guard broke ground through the crowd and eased our path to our seating area.

"Mimi!"

Guess I didn't have to look for Fiona. She'd found me first.

Given what she was wearing, it was a testament to how distracted I was by re-entering Lóng Kǒu grounds. Fiona was never one to hide her light under a bushel, and today was no exception. She dazzled the eyes with a halter-top pantsuit of silver sequins. The band around her neck showcased her sleek bare shoulders and elaborate silver cuffs circled her biceps. Her long dark hair hung in fat curls, the edges tipped with white. Fiona had managed to nail the look that Xena warrior princess would have if she were a Barbie doll going to a disco club. She looked perfect, at ease with herself and at home in these surroundings.

In a swirl of warm air, Fiona rushed over to me, arms outstretched in a hug.

As always, I found myself taken aback by her effusive greetings. I hated the bowing and the "Sentinel" formality but this open warmth also left me feeling awkward.

I patted her on her back and waited for her to release me. "Hi, Fiona."

Linh stepped up and gave me a short bow. I nodded back. Linh, I understood. No air kisses and loud greetings from her. She was all business, her sleek gray suit custom-tailored to house an array of weapons. Her high-necked white blouse was adorned with a slim silver bar pin where the highest button would be. Understated and lethal. Linh was my kind of girl. Which raised Fiona even more in my estimation because she employed such a capable team.

Fiona slung a friendly arm over my shoulders, which she could only reach because she had four-inch-platform-heeled white boots on.

"You know, I can refer you to a good hairstylist in San Francisco."

"Forget my hair. You have bigger problems."

"Any word on the General?" Her voice was low and soft.

I shook my head.

It had taken me a while but now I had come around to Fiona's point of view. Kaida was a killer. But we were all killers. The General was the decision maker.

Fiona flipped her hair. "Everyone who is anyone is here. The General must be, too."

She had a point. Although I wouldn't have been here if I could have avoided it. Guess that would have made me a nobody, which was the way I preferred it.

"The Louies are allied with the General. Keep an eye on who Jimmy and Raymond talk to."

Fiona's eyes narrowed. "Jimmy made the wrong play here."

I agreed. "Who else do you think is part of the General's faction?"

Fiona gestured broadly across the grounds. "There are eight families. If you tell me that the Soongs are not part of this then that leaves six I need to worry about."

"Even the Kohs?" I didn't think my father would have done a deal with Sabine if he thought she was part of the General's sinister plans.

Fiona tilted her head, clearly weighing what she knew. "Maybe Old Li, but he's gone now."

A familiar resentment rose up in me and I looked away before Fiona saw something in my face that was better hidden.

Linh started, a sudden tenseness in her shoulders before she relaxed again. I turned to find Kamon prowling toward us, his navy trench swaying gently with his long strides. The sober color only served to enhance the fiery orange corona of his aura.

I drank in the strong lines of his face, searching his eyes before I caught myself, and schooled my expression into a neutral mask.

He looked a little frazzled, and his face relaxed with relief when he saw Fiona. "Fi, I'm sorry the meeting took so long."

She waved a careless hand. "You don't have to worry about me, I know you have all those judge duties." She turned to me. "Besides, Linh and Emiko are here."

Kamon nodded, and he smiled warmly at both of us. "For which I'm grateful."

Fiona curled a hand into the crook of his elbow and slid close. "For the last time, I am fine. I can handle myself."

He tilted her chin up. "Can you stay in the salt zones?"

"Don't be ridiculous. I'm going to every house."

I watched this interplay with some sympathy. Some of the pavilions had salt zones that neutralized most talents. If she stayed in the salt zones, then Kaida wouldn't be able to get to her and I wouldn't have to worry about Fiona as a target. The houses were warded, too, but going to and from every house continually exposed Fiona to Kaida's dark-walking.

I looked up at the rising morning sun. It would be many, many hours until sunset, and the maze run was over. Surely Fiona could stay safe until then.

I tried to give Fiona an assist. "I'm sure it will be fine if Fiona just stays out of the shadows."

Fiona gave a tinkling laugh. "Oh, Mimi. I never pay attention to that unless I forget my sunscreen."

I rolled my eyes. "If you die before the students finish the maze, I'll be really annoyed."

She let go of Kamon and tapped my bicep lightly. "Mimi! I knew you cared."

I looked to the clouds and heavens for patience. "Just imagine Freddy running your empire in San Francisco."

Kamon let out a bark of laughter and even Linh's lips quirked.

Fiona huffed. "You don't have to be mean, Mimi."

"Don't call me Mimi."

AZURE DRAGON OF THE EAST

A reedy voice called over the murmuring voices in the viewing room and my spirits sank even further. The families quieted and everyone turned to the front of the room where a thin man in voluminous robes waited for everyone's attention. Dark, narrow-set eyes scanned the room. His pale complexion contrasted harshly with the brilliant red of his ornate robes, which included peaked shoulders that increased the width of his body by another foot on each side. Bright gold embroidery decorated the robe, showing the animals of the four cardinal directions bowing in obeisance to the wearer.

Subtle.

Chen Li Wei, oily headmaster and chief administrator of Lóng Kǒu, brought his bony hands together and smiled beatifically over the crowd. When the voices quieted to his liking he began speaking.

"Welcome, honored guests and family, to this year's Lóng Yá competition. Lóng Kǒu is honored to host this, our most revered tradition, once again . . ."

I couldn't help it. I zoned out. As the headmaster droned on about family and tradition, I made my way closer to the massive window to get a look at the maze. Li Wei's eyelid twitched when he noted me moving as he spoke, but he turned away and continued. Perhaps his voice rose a note or two. Fine. He and I had never quite seen eye to eye, even on the first day I'd shown up. I'd been terrified of him back then, but now looking at him, I couldn't help but notice just how small he was. I got close enough to the west wall to put my hand on the glass.

Up close, the massive construction for the maze was even more impressive. Each year the structure was built anew, and each year the design was changed to prevent anyone from cribbing notes from the previous year's students. Here, at the start of the maze, rough-cut bamboo staked out a huge swath of lawn like an animal pen.

The maze structure started at the far end of the pen, the wooden edifice as wide as a rugby pitch and two stories high. A recurring motif of the four cardinal animals had been painted onto the dark wood and hewn stone. Beyond the first wall, the roof of the structure was clouded, as if the maze was filled with fog. When the students entered, the fog would be cleared, allowing the spectators to watch the students attempt the tests.

Li Wei's voice rose to a fevered pitch, extolling the strength of the 104 students who had survived to the end of their term. "The maze tests the student's control of qì. Hoard Gifts, while flashy and exciting, do not compare to ultimate control of qì! The maze is the true test of Jiārén!"

I'd heard that he gave the same speech every year. Based on the glazed eyes around the room, my information was right. Judging by his clothing and his impassioned speech, this poor man was overcompensating for his own bottom-rung Gift. I pitied the young girl I'd been, for ever fearing this sad little man.

Eight matching doors stood at ground level, evenly spaced across the building. Each led to the first room of the maze, and the first challenge for the students. Each door had only one complete path to the exit. You could pass all the tests, and still lose yourself in the maze and finish dead last.

Students would be let into the maze eight at a time, based on their class rankings at the end of the school year. Tacchan would be in the first group to enter. Once the first group had progressed past the first test, the second group would enter. It was the height of ignominy to be surpassed by a student who started after you. The maze was each student's last, best chance to improve their rankings before the year ended.

The growing murmur of voices told me that the headmaster had finished his exhortations. My skin crawled and I knew someone was standing behind me. I turned to find the headmaster next to me, his hands steepled at chest level, a dour look on his face.

I dipped my head in a marginally respectful manner. "Headmaster."

He didn't bother trying to minimize his sneer. "I had hoped the circumstances of your departure would have assured you would never return."

"I believe it was your assessment, Headmaster, that I could not be taught."

Li Wei's eyes widened. "Impertinent. I see your time away from us has not improved your disposition."

All around us, families moved to find their seats. So many powerful Jiārén in one room, and Li Wei felt his time was best spent harassing me? As much as I wanted to take the headmaster down a notch, I couldn't screw this day up for Tacchan.

My old headmaster leaned into me, smelling like liniment oil. "You were a disaster from day one. The best thing I ever did for this school was to throw you out."

Father appeared out of the crowd behind Li Wei, saving the skinny man from my wrath. He gripped Li Wei by the arm, a seemingly casual gesture but I caught the subtle press of his fingers into the headmaster's meridians.

My father smiled, all teeth. Sugi appeared at my father's side, paws clicking on the hard floor, her marble black eyes like bottomless pits. "Chen Lau Shi! So nice to see you! Stirring speech, as usual."

The headmaster wobbled a bit then recovered. "Soong Xian Sheng. I warned you that your daughter was not permitted to—"

"My daughter is my chief of security. Surely you would not intrude upon the security of any families attending Lóng Yá?"

The headmaster's neck convulsed as he swallowed and finally nodded. My father nodded as well. "Excellent. She'll be on her way, then."

I took my cue and left the headmaster in my father's capable hands. Tatsuya found me as I crossed the observation room. He had a half-eaten pork bun in one hand, and a pineapple bun in the other.

"Really? You're eating again?"

"What? I'm still hungry."

I looked around us. Minjae was nowhere to be found. I pulled my brother to a quiet corner and took the pineapple bun from his hand. "Tacchan, I need you to stay focused. Even if the maze is a cakewalk, you need to do well."

Tatsuya scarfed down the rest of the pork bun and grinned. "And I keep telling you, this is the easy part."

His eyes narrowed and he checked around us before lowering his voice. "What did Father mean earlier? When he said you were . . . better?"

"No. We are not talking about me right now."

"Why not? What else can I do now to prepare for the maze? Nothing! Tell me what Father was talking about."

"He wasn't . . . it isn't . . ."

Broken Claw, why was this so hard? I cycled my qì and held my hand out, palm up. Tacchan's eyes widened and he put his hand above mine, palm down. His qì cycled up and our energy swirled together between our palms. It was basic stuff and didn't do anything but tickle your palms. It was the kind of thing you taught your kids when they were little. And I'd never been able to do it with my brother.

I pulled my hand away before Tatsuya could get too excited. "That's it. That's what Father was talking about."

I could see the gears spinning behind my brother's eyes. "What about—?"

"No. No Gift that you need to be worried about. This isn't important right now. You need to get through the maze."

Tacchan's eyes sparkled and he struggled to keep his voice down. "This is great! We are going to kick butt!"

His face split into a wide grin and he lifted his fists to me. I rolled my eyes and bumped knuckles with him. At least he was happy. A massive gong rang at the far end of the observation room and all talking ceased.

Li Wei stood on the dais at the end of the room. "This year's Lóng Yá will now commence!"

Tatsuya blew out a long breath. He seemed to shrink almost, as if trying to compress his qì.

I hoped our preparation had been enough.

The headmaster signaled and we all bowed to each of the four directions.

"Dōng júe gōng."

"Nán júe gōng."

"Xī júe gōng."

"Běi júe gōng."

Li Wei clapped his hands together after the fourth bow and a thunderclap of sound broke open the eight doors, pulverizing them into dust. Flames shot out of the tops of the entrances, so hot they were blue in color. The sky above turned into a hot hazy blur. The maze was open.

Tatsuya gave me a nod and moved off. He found Minjae and the two of them made their way down to the maze entrance. In moments students began entering the starting area and sorting themselves into little clusters. I found an open spot and scanned the crowd, spotting several of Tacchan's friends.

Tatsuya had pointed out Thùy to me earlier. Hoàng Thùy Lê went by Thùy to her friends. Straight bangs framed a delicate face and round cheeks. The slender young woman had grown up in New York but the Hoàng Clan held significant standing in Southeast Asia.

Despite the pomp and circumstance of Lóng Yá, Thùy had shown up in a champagne velour tracksuit and spotless white Puma sneakers. She looked up to the observation window and lifted both arms, hands balled into fists. A cheer went up behind me. Thùy winked and waved to the crowd. She exuded an effortless cool, one that my brother clearly lacked. I could see why he had concerns about her.

Thùy moved to the front of the pack and approached the eight doors that led to the maze. The remaining seven top students of this year's class gathered there as well. A wave of nervous energy passed over the students like a storm cloud. Necks were cracked and arms shaken loose.

I studied the other five students standing next to my brother. Tatsuya had grouped Balen and Chariya as top eight candidates for his class. There was only one other girl. That had to be Chariya Seng. The Seng Clan were aligned with the Moks, a mid-tier but strong family. The Seng Clan had started out in Cambodia but now had a base in Vancouver. Perhaps the Moks had sponsored Chariya. That would be in line with their recent overtures with Fiona. Locking down some West Coast alliances would give them access to friendly ports in San Francisco and Vancouver.

Unlike Thùy, Chariya had dressed for the occasion, elegant in a pink pantsuit and cream low-top boots. She'd pulled her wavy black hair back into a low ponytail. She and Thùy traded a look with each other. Chariya bounced on the balls of her feet. She seemed eager to get started.

I couldn't figure out which of the remaining boys was Balen. Ultimately, it didn't matter. Only their maze results mattered from this point forward.

A low gasp echoed throughout the crowd and everyone looked up. A floating structure appeared over the maze, casting a shadow over our faces. The citadel floated on a bank of pristine cotton-candy clouds. Golden banners with roaring dragons, soaring fenghuang, and rearing qílín adorned the walls of the citadel and snapped in the wind. From this floating fortress, the judges for this year's Lóng Yá would be able to observe everything without being bothered by pesky Jiārén.

Chen Li Wei clapped his hands again. The flames over the doors died down, dissolving into thick streamers of smoke. The smoke twisted into itself and swirled into the sky, shaping itself into a whirling ring. With another clap from the headmaster, the smoke broke apart into four segments, each chasing the others around the circle.

Brilliant color bled into the smoke, turning the four segments blue, red, black, and white. Faster and faster the smoke raced in a circle and the bleeds of color morphed into the four cardinal animals. The students hooted and applauded from the grounds, some of them punching their fists into the air.

A pounding drum rhythm began as the four animals flew faster, smoke breaking apart now and mixing the colors together. The drumbeat reached a hammering crescendo and the colors split into eight separate coils of multicolored smoke. The coils descended to the students and shaped themselves into various animals from the zodiac. A ram made of smoke appeared above Tatsuya. It brushed against his outstretched hand and the ram's color shifted to blue-green. A rabbit leapt in front of Thùy, thin puffs of smoke above its tail. Its color changed as well as she waved her hand through the smoke. Minjae had been given the dog as his smoke guide. The remaining five students all found themselves standing behind a different animal from the zodiac, each colored according to their specific auras. The top eight students of Lóng Kǒu bent their knees and set their eyes on the door in front of them, ready to run for their lives.

I let out a long slow exhale. Tacchan could do this.

With a bang the smoke guides flew into the maze and the students chased after them.

The maze run was on.

VERMILLION BIRD OF THE SOUTH

Li Wei left the dais as the crowds began to disperse and families moved to find a better view of the students.

Li Wei's enormous hanfu robe was so wide that he took up the space of three men. He bowed low to the Byun matriarch and he gestured expansively. The headmaster tapped his wrist, as if there were a wristwatch hidden in the massive sleeves of his hanfu. Minjae's grandma remained impassive but dipped her head in response to the headmaster's words.

The Vermillion Bird House was situated in the southern portion of the maze. With no small amount of relief I found the outer stairwell and flew down the three flights of stairs along the outer wall of Dragon House. Fujita-san and Uncle Lau would stay behind to see the later batches of students run the maze. However, I only cared about my brother and who he would face.

I wanted to watch these first eight finish.

The iron gates to Bird House were thrown open. Scarlet silk tapestries hung on each face of the double doors, heavy gold thread embroidery depicting two sharp-beaked Zhūquè facing each other, their lush tail feathers fanned out high.

I stepped through the gates and up the landing into the great hall of Bird House. Ornately carved rosewood chairs and sofas with stiff high backs were pushed to the edges of the room, clearly set up to accommodate the large number of spectators that would be here today. Long scrolls with brushed lettering decorated the walls, their words echoing with history.

A mere week ago, students had lounged around in these uncomfortable chairs and goofed off. Today they would be running the maze as if their very lives depended on it. Poor Colin wouldn't be participating today and his future livelihood literally depended on that. All because he'd stepped in front of an assassin's blade to save his friend.

Other Jiārén kids wouldn't have done it. Minjae had been there, too, and he hadn't done it. And now we couldn't even give Colin a place in our clan.

I hated it.

My father's words notwithstanding, I still believed our clan owed Colin and needed to repay our debt.

As if on cue, two canes thumped behind me. Great. Maybe Byun A-Yeong really could read my mind, and had arrived as if I had mentally summoned her. I was almost directly in the middle of the great hall, too far from any of any of the exits to leave without running, and I wasn't about to run from the Byun matriarch. I stepped to the side to allow her entourage to pass.

A-Yeong's raspy voice echoed in the large lobby, punctuated by the tapping of her canes against the bamboo floor as she crossed the great hall. "Young Sentinel. Enjoying your return to Lóng Kǒu?"

"I'm just here for my brother."

Hateful woman. She knew very well that I had been kicked out.

She continued her slow progress across the marble floors, her dupioni silk trousers whispering with her steps. The matriarch's several attendees fluttered about her, adorned with lavender cashmere scarves. Some wore long purple cloaks, shrouding their features as they moved through the hallway. They passed me, but Minjae's grandmother stopped right next to me.

A-Yeong turned and gave me a cool smile, none of it reaching those sharp eyes. Even the milky one seemed to stare into me, seeing every chaotic emotion within me.

"It must be satisfying to come back with such a storied career. The Blade of Soong House, and now the Sentinel of San Francisco."

"You mean instead of coming back as just someone who got kicked out?"

"Just so. Your time after Lóng Kǒu was clearly so much more fruitful."

I gave her a bland smile. "I was fortunate in that I could continue to serve my clan."

The matron clearly knew I hadn't been at some Swiss boarding school. Now she was fishing. I wasn't about to confirm her suspicions.

"The clan is secondary to the Association." A-Yeong tsked dismissively.

Okay, we were just going to come right out in the open, then. I'd made my opinions on family clear when I fled from Jōkōryūkai. I arched a brow. "On the contrary. Family first."

She straightened up and looked down at me. "We all know what the Association asks of its members. You owe everything you are to them."

"I owe my existence to my family." To my father, mostly.

"Family is fleeting, a blink of an eye to a dragon. You are a strong woman, Sentinel. You would do well to think like a dragon. Should your house fall, you would have nothing. Nothing but the Association."

"Then I'm grateful my house is strong."

She tapped her cane on the floor, emphasizing her words. "No, young Sentinel. You are strong."

"Thank you for your kind words."

A-Yeong lifted her cane and waved it in the direction of the maze. "This, window dressing, today. It means nothing, understand, girl? Your brother may be powerful, but he is not strong. He may become strong, but he is not strong now, when it is needed. Your father knows this and does nothing."

She pointed a finger at me. "Without you, your house has no future."

She leaned into me and for a sickening moment, her milky, blind eye peered all the way to the core of my being. The citrus scent of her talent flared and A-Yeong could see all the secret shame of my childhood and the awful desire to be better than I was. She had the grace not to gloat.

"You didn't spend years in America without thinking about the possibility of a life without your family. You don't need to disappear when the door closes on the time of the Soongs. Take a page from your father's book, girl, and make plans for the future. I, for one, can think of great things for you to accomplish, Sentinel."

With that parting shot she pivoted, the taps of her canes marking her progress through Bird House's sprawling lobby. I seethed as she walked away but bit my tongue. Her insinuation that my brother was weak worried me, but to paint my father with that same brush was laughable.

Instead of following after the Byuns, I left and walked along the perimeter of Bird House seeking the outer spiral of stairs. I raced up the steps, eager to make up the time I'd wasted fencing words with A-Yeong and to burn off some of my anger.

From the roof of Bird House, I had a clear view of the southern portion of the maze. I kept my eyes peeled for the blue-green ram that Tatsuya was chasing.

I spotted a section of the maze where several routes funneled into one large room. The walls were rough-cut stones the size of melons, mortared together with mud and dirt. Eight doors lined the far wall. One of the doors burst open and Minjae flew through, his long legs carrying him at top speed. A second after him another door shattered out of its frame and my brother jumped through a cloud of sawdust and splinters, his arms held up to protect his face.

The walls of the room flashed and the mortar between the stones glowed a deep red. The boys bolted for the far side of the room where eight closed doors awaited. Their guide animals flew across the open space.

When Minjae reached the center of the room the walls came alive, undulating as the stones shifted in place. With a rumbling crack, stones flew from the walls and careened into the boys.

Minjae lifted his hands as he ran and brought them both down in a chopping motion. Qì flashed through the air and shattered two stones in half. He leapt over them and raced to the exits.

Three stones zigzagged through the air, bearing down on my brother. Tatsuya raised a hand and clenched it into a fist. The stones burst into dust, pulverized by the force of his qì. He waved his arms as he ran through the cloud of grit and punched his fist forward, shattering the door ahead of him. He hit the door just a step behind Minjae.

As the two boys exited the room, the remaining entrance doors blasted open, banging against the rock walls. The rest of the top eight ran through the doors, led by Thùy, following close on the heels of her guide rabbit. The stones that had been chasing my brother broke off and attacked the new students.

I didn't care to watch the other students. Tatsuya had been right, he was finishing the maze with ease. The only question was whether he would finish first. How much did he want it, compared to Minjae?

The next viewing station was Tiger House, a relatively short walk from here. Tatsuya and Minjae had to take the long way around the school grounds, and find their way through the maze as well.

I ran.

WHITE TIGER OF THE WEST

Tatsuya was more than halfway done with the maze. Watching the smoke guides for the first eight had been unexpectedly tense. The morning sun rose higher, casting golden light around the beautiful Lóng Kǒu campus. Tiger House loomed to the west, still cast in shadow.

Lóng Kǒu had a deceptively simple layout but the pathways and wards leading to Tiger House were decidedly more complicated. Those who lived in Tiger House cultivated Dragon senses. The obvious paths that led to Tiger House were guarded by any number of deadly or near-deadly traps. Those with superior sight or reflexes could evade the traps. A few lucky ones simply flew past them all. The residents of Tiger House reworked the traps on a weekly basis, even keeping the changes secret from their own housemates, holding to fanatical beliefs about the survival of the fittest. For the rest of us mere mortals, we had to navigate a safer route.

Wide rock formations marked the entrance to Tiger House. The entrance was almost hidden beneath towering piles of stones, as if daring one to enter the darkness within.

During my time here, brief as it was, I had visited Tiger House once. Even now, its massive size and layout looked harsh and imposing.

"Look who left San Francisco."

I whirled around. In a jaunty red skirt and frilly edged blazer, Stella Mok stood atop a low rise behind me. When we'd last met, I'd literally pulled the earth out from under her, leaving her ranting and raving. She didn't look much happier today. Like all Jiārén, Stella had a knack for nursing a grudge, feeding it bitterness and pride to keep it hot and fresh.

Beyond the borders of my city, I wouldn't be able to pull the same stunt as last time. No doubt Stella had been biding her time, waiting for an opportunity to meet me again on neutral ground. Although technically as an earth talent, there was no neutral ground around Stella.

Stella flicked her fingers and her talent washed out beneath my feet in a wave, claiming the ground beneath us in a wide radius. Message received. I had done it to her in my city and now she was repaying the favor. With a gentle tilt of one wrist a scree of gravel slid off the columns next to me and forced me to step back. She smiled with smug satisfaction.

If I could make it to the Tiger House, the qì dampening inside would make it difficult for Stella to use her talent. Unfortunately, there was plenty of ground for me to cover between here and the threshold of the house and she was powerful enough to open the earth and swallow me whole. No one would find my body after.

The ground beneath me buckled and tilted, forcing me to scramble to keep my footing. There were probably a handful of traps between me and Tiger House if I ran in a straight line. Most would only take off an arm or a leg if I was lucky. Stella's qì pulsed under my feet, thick with the threat of destruction. If I stayed here, Stella would throw rocks at me until I tired out and then grind me into paste.

To hell with it. I crushed a Dragon Wind crystal beneath my boot and let the gust of air propel me into Stella. I landed hard, scrabbled for purchase, and made a grab for her right ankle. She cried out and slid her Ferragamo pumps into a cross-stance, making the earth extend in a pillar to bring her up above my reach.

Typical. No one liked it when I got up close and personal.

I scrambled up the rising pillar, dust coating my face and clogging my throat. Like a goat, I slapped two hands down and kicked with my back legs, using a boost of qì to reach Stella. I rammed my shoulder into her knees and felt a satisfying pop. She screeched and toppled backward.

I pinned one forearm against her hip and crawled my way up her body, twisting my hands into the expensive fabric of her clothes. I took the opportunity to wipe my face on her blazer, drawing a look of horror from her. My mouth stretched into a grin that bared my teeth.

"Don't mud wrestle a pig, Stella."

She shrieked and smacked a hand down on the rock, sending a spray of dirt over us both. Stupid. If I'm going to smack anything, I smack my opponent. I pulled my fist back, readying for an uppercut to knock her out.

"Ladies!"

It wasn't just the voice, although it was certainly beautiful, the tone rich and resonant. The kind of voice that could make a grocery list sound compelling. Something shifted in my chest as the sound hit my ears, my anger and belligerence fading away.

I lifted my head and turned to face the owner of that gifted voice. In doing so, I saw that Stella had a razor spike of rock poised to lance through my side. That would have hurt. Her rock spray had been a feint and I'd fallen for it.

Stella's face had gone slack, her eyes taking on a soft admiration for Batuhan's compelling voice. As the creases around her eyes smoothed out, she released her hold on the earth and the pillar of earth and rock slowly lowered us back down. We tumbled onto the grass and I rolled as far from Stella as possible. The Borjigin met us at ground level, father and son. They were dressed identically in cream tunics lined with fur trim and trousers tucked into soft cream boots. Batuhan stood behind Ariq's wheelchair, his legs spread and his hands on his hips. The breeze kicked and rattled the beads in his hair, revealing blood jade ear piercings. Again I was struck by the enormous amount of blood jade they both wore. They had chokers of it around their necks, gauntlets around their forearms, and I suspected they had it on their belts, too. Ariq wore multiple rings on both hands, all blood jade.

It was lunacy. They wore enough blood jade between them to

enrich two families, more than enough power to go to war or drive a dozen men to madness. Anyone sensitive to blood jade would feel the two of them coming from a mile away. In fact, my teeth were already buzzing.

I stumbled as I stood up, hands on my head, trying to block out the crackling qì that emanated from the Borjigin like heat from a smelter. Stella's face went from placid to nauseated and she fell to her hands, her knee bent at an awkward angle. She cried out as she went down.

Batuhan tsked and bent to give her a hand up. "There, there. Can't have that, can we?"

His aura flared, thick as spring fog in the city, and that bubble I had seen before at the gala spread out from his body. Stella's eyes glazed over and a soft moan escaped her lips as it enveloped her. With an audible crack her knee popped back into place. Stella didn't even flinch and never once took her eyes away from Batuhan's.

I didn't know what he was doing, but I knew I needed more of it, the way I needed air to breathe. I took a stumbling step toward the shining beacon in my mind that was Batuhan, knowing that if I got close enough I would be content to stay by his side for the rest of my days.

He turned to me and grimaced. The golden bubble vanished and I gasped at the release. "Sorry about that. I meant to dial it down."

Batuhan returned his attention to Stella. "On your way then, dear."

Still dazed, Stella smiled like a smitten schoolgirl and walked away on unsteady feet. She'd completely forgotten about me. I wasn't sure if I should be relieved or insulted.

Batuhan returned to Ariq's wheelchair and gestured for me to proceed before him. "Come. This path to Tiger House is already clear. We still have plenty of time to get to the viewing area before the top eight arrive."

I hesitated, just long enough to be impolite. Putting myself in the path of this man's talent was not a good idea. If I thought Uncle Jimmy had been bad, Batuhan was exponentially more powerful. I was coming up with some kind of excuse to beg off when Ariq spoke up, his voice deeper and richer than his thin frame suggested. Even if he hadn't inherited his father's talent, he'd certainly gotten the voice.

"Please join us, Ms. Soong."

I studied Ariq's aura. It was almost crumpled onto itself as if trying to unfurl, but being sucked back in. It practically vibrated from some internal push-pull. I'd never seen the like before.

Batuhan's request I could refuse. But this young man? Not within me.

I nodded and moved onto the pathway.

Walking into Tiger House seemed truly like walking into the dragon's maw.

The observation room in Tiger House was set up similarly to Dragon's. Batuhan positioned his son's wheelchair for an optimal view of the maze. His retainers had already set up what looked like a coatrack next to the spot for the wheelchair, in front of a silk dividing screen painted in lush watercolors, depicting the Sons of the Dragon. Nine dragons in subtle shades of blue and green twisted through pristine white clouds. With practiced efficiency Batuhan removed his gauntlets, belt, and choker, and hung them up on the coatrack in close proximity to his son. He patted his son on the shoulder and they shared a quiet word before he walked back to me.

I followed him to a spot by the viewing window just out of earshot from his son. He rubbed at his arms where they'd been covered by the blood jade. "It gets a little tiring, after a while, carrying the blood jade. But you do what you must for your family, right?"

"Of course."

He had been wearing enough blood jade for five or six people and his only complaint was that it was a little tiring. I was getting a contact high just being this close. It reminded me of Koh senior and how he must have felt at the Shanghai Lotus while we crowded him with our blood jade finery. That memory left a bitter taste in my mouth. I tried to refocus on the stately gentleman in front of me.

"Why do you wear it?"

If he was surprised at the directness of my question he didn't show it. "My son. It keeps his talent at bay and allows him to function. If I may say so, your bluntness is refreshing."

"I find it easier than the alternative."

"Yes, you would, wouldn't you? Ogata-sensei didn't tell me about you."

I kept my face impassive. I'd sworn an oath of secrecy when I was with the Jōkōryūkai. I didn't speak of my time there and I didn't talk about Ogata-sensei. It seemed highly unlikely he would be speaking about me with anyone outside of the Association. Between the Byun matron's talk of the Association and Batuhan's mention of Ogata-sensei, I felt disoriented. How did they know about my affiliation with Jōkōryūkai? Were they fishing?

"I'm not sure I know what you are referring to."

"So cautious. Admirable. You are a credit to your clan."

I bowed my head a slight inclination. "Thank you for your kind words."

I didn't know how many times I was going to have to say that phrase today but it was already grating.

Batuhan gestured in his son's direction. "Truth is the best policy. I wanted to talk to you because I see that you carved out a life for yourself outside of Lóng Kǒu. My Ariq will need to do the same."

Ariq looked up from his study of the dome, chatting with another clansman. Where his father had a fierce intensity, Ariq had the open gaze of an innocent. Had I ever looked like that? Felt like that? Maybe before I'd attended Lóng Kǒu, but I couldn't recall it. Maybe that's why I wanted to train Leanna as long as I could. Before she had to give up that openness.

Ariq's talent was likely off the charts, a variant of his father's Gift that chewed through all the ambient power of the blood jade and still looked hungry.

I'd never had power like that. Couldn't imagine it. And yet, seeing how frail the young man looked and how worried his father was, I didn't envy him one bit. Ariq seemed sheltered from the cutthroat nature of Jiārén life. It was a testament to my parents' pragmatism that they never shielded me from the realities of our brutal society.

My road hadn't been the conventional one but my eyes were wide open. It wasn't comfortable, but it was the way I preferred it.

"Change is coming, Emiko. I've tried to speak to your father about this but he remains stuck in the past."

I did not have a good response for that. I wasn't privy to my father's machinations but he was still the head of my clan. Also, I wasn't happy with someone else criticizing my father. While I didn't always see eye to eye with my parents, that was our private family drama.

I settled on a noncommittal statement. "Ours is an old clan."

Batuhan waved a hand dismissively. "Look at what we've become. Shadows of what we are supposed to be. In a few more generations, we will be gone, victims of our own infighting. Jiārén need to change."

"Change is difficult." Soon I was going to run out of aphorisms.

"Those with vision must rise to the occasion. You can be part of it, or you can be crushed by it."

Wait, was this a job offer? A threat? I was too strung out by all this dancing around between Minjae's grandmother and Ariq's father. This was my own fault for leaving my father's side to get here early. These people and their double talk were exhausting and above my paygrade.

"I leave those decisions to the Head of the Clan."

Batuhan laughed, a booming sound that carried throughout the rooftop area. A half-dozen men in cream tunics scooted closer. His clansmen surrounded me. I didn't reach for my blade but I shifted my body weight slightly.

"Enjoy the rest of Lóng Yá, Emiko. We will speak again, soon."

His power bloomed, filling the air, thick and hot, and his men's eyes took on the fever-bright shine of bloody fanaticism. It would be problematic to get my back to a wall so I willed myself to keep my hands loose and simply bow and turn away. I took measured steps but the sensation of presenting my back to such a powerful person made the space between my shoulder blades itch.

I found an empty spot along the glass. I caught the maze in the corner of my eye. Several guide animals bounded along the roof of the maze, none of them my brother's. I'd missed him. Cursing the chatty Borjigin, I backed out of the room, bolted from Tiger House, and ran to Tortoise.

BLACK TORTOISE OF THE NORTH

If Bird House was flashy and bright, Tortoise House was restrained elegance. No gates barred the entrance to Tortoise House. Two once-mighty stone pillars stood in front, crumbling into ruin but wreathed in small white blossoms that climbed through every crack and crevice. Birds flew here and there, the quick darting movements giving the space vibrancy despite the aging structure.

Gray pebbles lined the walkway, which narrowed into a curved wooden bridge over a small lake. Lotus blossoms floated on the dark surface and the rippling water made a soothing soundscape for the entrance to Tortoise House. I wouldn't be able to scope out the perimeter here because a broad waterway surrounded the house, giving the structure the appearance of floating on a large rock.

The moon-shaped wooden doors swung open and I stepped into the waiting area within. As I walked by the double doors, I noticed they weren't simply a round shape but actually carved as the tortoise, the aged surface smooth and dark. No stiff furniture awaited guests within Tortoise House. Instead meditation cushions were strewn about, round and colorful.

I looked for the stairs but unlike the multifloor structures of Dragon House and Bird House, this place had a slight slope and the hallways made switchbacks that led ever gradually higher to a mezzanine and then above. It was ingenious and meditative, the sheer number of steps it took to wind ever higher up to the rooftop.

Unfortunately the long walk gave me too much time to consider just how many blades were aimed at my family. In rapid succession, both Byun A-Yeong and Batuhan had bluntly suggested that my family was falling from power, and soon. It was small comfort that both of them were interested in retaining my services afterward.

I had to make sure my father knew. There seemed to be a larger game at play here, possibly more than he anticipated. It was not uncommon for families to take swings at each other, to try to carve away some enterprise or territory. But plotting to eliminate an entire family? A Hoard Custodian family?

My mind refused to extrapolate forward. There were too many possibilities, and guessing at them without more information was useless. Enough to say that the absence of our family would completely upend Jiārén politics and the existing power structure.

And in that eventual chaos, someone would step into that vacuum to seize power.

The General.

The people who had invoked the General all spoke of him in reverent tones. Even the unflappable Uncle Jimmy. After meeting Batuhan up close, he was the most obvious suspect. And his pitch to me had been all about upending the status quo. He would be ready to take advantage of the chaos if my family lost power. He probably already had three other members of Bā Tóu in his pocket. If my father was removed, he would have the majority. He could shape Jiārén life as he saw fit.

I was nearly to the roof and stopped in my tracks, stunned at my insight. This was why we were targeted with the Trans. If either one of our families were removed from Bā Tóu, Batuhan won.

Did my father know all this already? Did he know that by agreeing to protect Fiona I was single-handedly thwarting Batuhan's plan to seize power?

No. I couldn't think like that. Big plans were not my forte. I knew what I could do, and that was enough. I could protect Tatsuya. I could try to protect Fiona.

I got moving again and when I reached the roof, two people were already there—Chen Li Wei and another proctor. Just like the headmaster's extravagantly wide scarlet hanfu, the proctor's hanfu was also majestically oversized, as wide as she was tall, but dyed in the rich blue of the tapestry that hung in Dragon House. Their ceremonial outfits were so wide that if they stretched out their arms, their robes would still keep them a foot apart.

I did not want to speak to the imperious headmaster again. After my little tussle with Stella and my verbal sparring with the Byun matriarch and Batuhan, I was on my last nerve. If that pompous jackass even looked askance at me, I would toss him off the roof.

It's not like he could expel me twice.

I pivoted and stepped behind a wide column that would give me some cover from the headmaster and the proctor, while allowing me to look for Tatsuya's smoke animal guide. The ram horns were distinctive and I spotted Tatsuya closing in on the final challenge. Where was Minjae? I looked for the smoke dog, craning my neck.

"Emiko!"

A voice I hadn't heard in over a decade. I turned to greet her, and was stunned to realize that it was the proctor. I blinked and tried to merge my memories of my friend from Dragon House with this elegant woman in the azure silk robes that were as wide as my Jeep. When we were twelve, Hana had the plump cheeks that spoke of a soft childhood with lots of sweets. Her disposition had been the same, sweet to her awkward roommate—me. Age had honed the planes of her face, revealing delicate bones and showcasing her fine dark eyes against milk-pale skin.

Hana was one of the few good memories from Lóng Kǒu I had, one of the few students who had not written me off once the extent of my failure was common knowledge. Much like my father, Hana had taken me under her wing and found time to tutor me after classes, trying to push me past my blocked meridians. I was never sure what she had seen in me to commit so much of herself to me, but when I'd left, she was the only one I'd known I would miss.

As a resident of Dragon House, Hana had a combat-grade Gift.

She had her aura pulled in tight but enough of the crimson radiated outward, with almost invisible silvery stripes. Kinetics were plentiful among Jiārén but Hana was a gāo-level the likes of which was rare. She wielded her kinetic skill with a surgical level of precision. I'd also never encountered anyone with a range like hers, which was probably lucky for me. Also like my Uncle Jake, Hana hadn't expressed any interest in joining an elite guard squadron. She'd found the perfect place for her talent and her good nature—teaching snotty-nosed Jiārén hotshots.

Maybe her time tutoring me had stirred something inside her.

Hana took my shell-shocked expression as smoothly as ever and stepped in to give me a hug. I wrapped my arms around her and did my best to ignore Chen Li Wei's pointed stare. Hana squealed and crushed me.

I patted Hana on the back. "Hana! Ribs!"

Hana released me and held me at arm's length, her eyes taking me all in. "You cut your hair!"

Her eyes refocused, staying just above my head. "Oh my goodness!"

Hana's eyes turned serious in a heartbeat and she raised her hands, passing them over me, hovering just over my shoulders. Her qì brushed against mine, a soft touch of subtle energy. She drew in a sharp breath. "Wow."

Li Wei cleared his throat and looked pointedly at Hana. Hana grabbed my arm and dragged me away, waving merrily. "Be right back, Headmaster!"

I allowed Hana to pull me away, getting me out of dealing with Chen Li Wei again. Hana led me down a level to another room with a wide balcony that still gave an excellent view of the maze. She pulled a couple of chairs over to the edge of the balcony and we sat.

Hana grinned, a wicked little smile. "Don't worry about the maze. I designed the last quarter. No one's getting through it in under an hour. Your aura looks so different! Spill. I want all the details."

For a short time, it was like we were back in school, huddling together in one of the study halls, commiserating about classes. Well,

Hana commiserated with me, since she aced all our classes. I stumbled my way through a heavily edited version of recent events, giving Hana the impression that becoming the Sentinel had unblocked my meridians. Which wasn't entirely untrue, but keeping my contact with the Tokyo Sentinel private seemed to be the correct thing to do, so I followed my gut.

Hana's eyes narrowed at parts of my story but she seemed to take most of it at face value. In return, she caught me up on her life since Lóng Kǒu and how she ended up becoming one of the youngest faculty in the school's long history.

Her eyes glowed when I told her about taking the Sentinel mantle for San Francisco, a smug smile gracing her lips. "See? I knew you would make something of yourself. Tang Lǎoshī always said so, too."

Now it was my turn to look astonished. Tang Lǎoshī's name only evoked a feeling of utter dread that sucked at my insides and memories of being excoriated in class for my poor coursework. "Are you sure you've got the right teacher? All I remember is Tang Lǎoshī browbeating me for taking shortcuts."

Hana nodded, her eyes sparkling. "You may not have done the homework the way it was intended, but you got the right answers. Tang Lǎoshī admired your innovation, even if he couldn't say so during class. After you left, he would always talk about how you were his most refreshing student in a decade."

She hunched over, squinted her eyes down to bare slits, and affected a rattling, raspy voice. "'That girl was something! Li Wei was a fool to expel her!'"

Hana's eyes went wide again and she clapped her hands over her mouth. She looked around us and when she saw we were still alone she burst into laughter. I laughed with her, and it felt good, really good to laugh again. I wondered what Freddy was up to right now. I would have to tell him this story later. If I got back home again.

A horn sounded from below and Hana shot to her feet. "Here they come!"

In the time we had been talking the rooftop had become crammed with spectators. I picked out A-Yeong along the packed guardrail. The old woman stood in a small semicircle of open space, the crowd held back by her guards, allowing her to stand with her crutches spread to either side of her. Her gaze found me and she lifted one delicate eyebrow to me, the one over her blind eye, before returning her attention to the maze.

Not creepy at all.

A roar went up and I turned back to the maze. The covered structure ended in a solid wall of mortared stone that bordered a grass-covered field. No doors provided any exit from the maze. The last fifty meters of the course were a straight shot across open ground. The end of the maze was a massive golden moon gate, sculpted to look like the roaring, open mouth of a dragon. The morning sun winked off sharp fangs of gold that hooked in from the top of the gate. A collection of eight red silk sashes hung from the fangs, golden numbers embroidered on the ends. The first students to pass through the final gate and grab a sash would go on to the next round.

A section of the maze wall flowed open, the stones rolling away from each other to make a small hole. Minjae's lanky form shot through the hole in a dive. He hit the grass and tumbled, coming up and spinning back to the maze.

He was haggard, his cheeks sunken and sallow, the fatigue plain in the slump of his shoulders. The whole course had taken him just over two hours to run, but he looked like he'd just crossed the Gobi with a single canteen of water. Somewhere in the maze he'd lost the top buttons to his shirt, his chest was covered in a sheet of sweat, and his wavy hair was plastered across his broad forehead. Minjae hauled his arms up and clenched his hands into loose fists. The stones moved back into place, sealing the hole he'd come through. He seemed to relax, his arms dropping to his sides, and he turned and jogged for the finish line. A roar went up from the crowd above us.

Hana gave a quiet laugh. "Does he really think it's that simple?"

Halfway across the field Minjae simply vanished from view as if the earth had swallowed him whole. Cries of dismay erupted from the crowd.

In that instant the walls of the maze blew open at two points. Tatsuya crawled through one hole and Thùy pulled herself from the rubble of the other. Both were filthy, covered in dirt and dust, wobbling on their feet, eyes glazed over. Thùy had lost one of her sneakers and the one she'd kept was drenched in mud. Shallow cuts and crusted blood covered Tacchan's arms. They stared at each other for a bare second before they turned and lurched for the finish line.

Minjae pulled himself out of the hole that had been hidden under illusion, his head coming up through the grass. When he saw Tacchan and Thùy bearing down on him, he scrambled over the lip. My brother and Thùy both put on a burst of speed when they saw Minjae ahead of them. Thùy bounced into the air on a sputtering burst of qì, avoiding one of the hidden traps.

Tacchan did the same but he stumbled on his landing, going down hard on the grass. Even from up here I heard the air explode from his lungs. He popped up and I recognized the hard light in his eyes as he ran after his friend. My brother had found the fire inside himself, the desire to conquer, to win. But anyone could see he'd found it too late. Minjae passed through the moon gate, pulling the sash with the golden number one, tangling the sash around his chest as he fell, gasping.

A raucous cheer went up as Thùy took the second sash. My brother took the third sash just behind her. Thùy limped away from the boys and collapsed to her knees, her shoulders heaving. Tatsuya staggered over to Minjae, both of them breathing like blown horses. Tacchan offered Minjae a hand and pulled his friend to his feet. They embraced briefly but now the action was laden with stiff formality. My heart ached for my brother. Even from this distance I could see the wall that had sprung up between them.

BANQUET

The next round would begin at sunset. That gave us the late afternoon to do something that our clans all loved to do. Eat a big banquet feast.

Though my time here at Lóng Kǒu had not been a walk in the park, I'd never had any complaints about the food. Also, my visit with Hana had reminded me that maybe I'd had a friend here, too. She'd been warm and welcoming, not holding it against me that never once in the last thirteen years had I contacted her. I was embarrassed that I hadn't maintained contact but it wasn't like I could have a pen pal while entrenched with the Jōkōryūkai.

Though my memories of Lóng Kǒu were dominated by the shame I'd felt at being expelled, I did remember the lavish meals. Mealtimes were serious affairs here and I fully expected the world-class chefs to pull out all the stops for the esteemed guests.

My mouth watered as I thought about the fried namazu skewers I'd had upon returning to Tokyo. That seemed so long ago though it had been less than a week.

I wandered down to the school's main pavilion, a vast field of manicured grass situated just south of the central building, the Temple of the Yellow Dragon. Dozens of round banquet tables covered the main pavilion with acres of ivory linens. Students and their guests milled about the perimeter and trickled their way to the tables, weaving complex patterns as they found their seats. Around the edges, formally attired waitstaff as well as semiautonomous clouds of smoke mingled through the crowd offering drinks and trays of appetizers.

The qílín citadel passed overhead. I stopped and watched the majestic structure land in a flurry of mist and clouds.

Lóng Kǒu took pains to appear neutral and that meant being careful about not having Hoard Custodian families overrepresented in the citadel. That left retired faculty members, notable families such as the Zhao Clan, and the Jiārén entities who were not in fealty to Custodian families. Popo had even been a judge once.

The mist settled down, mere wisps now. In a rush of movement, the judges descended from the cloud citadel. A hush fell over the pavilion and even with all the jaded Jiārén present, jaws dropped open throughout the crowd. The first judge to come down towered above the gathered spectators, his broad shoulders a foot above anyone's head and his midnight-black wings arced another six feet over that. The tengu's ruddy skin nearly glowed in the early evening light, contrasting against the sleeveless black leather tunic covering his chest.

The tengu was talking animatedly with another judge, a barrel-chested man dressed in shining green scales. The tengu's large nose bobbed up and down as he spoke. The man dressed in green nodded along and as he moved the scales along his neck caught the sunlight. I blinked in amazement. I didn't know wani could wander so far from the ocean.

Another half a dozen judges descended the stairs, each one dressed more fabulously than the last, all of them oozing the power of Old Ones. I glossed over all of them, though, because one of the judges was apparently flying. I blinked. It wasn't the banners come to life, it was an actual qílín, a flying unicorn, with a body like a massive plow horse, eagle wings, and a head like a dragon, and covered in a glossy coat of shimmering gold. The golden coat morphed into scales of gold down the creature's legs, ending in silvery-white hair that covered the qílín's fetlocks. A magnificent mane and beard of silver flowed about the qílín's head as if it were underwater.

I never thought to witness such a sight in my lifetime. Though qílín had come from the Realm with our ancestors, they'd parted ways with Jiārén and hidden in shrouded valleys and remote peaks in Asia. When they deigned to shape-shift and walk among us, they didn't stay long, finding our ways to be violent and crass.

This was a Lóng Yá Tourney for the books, where an already rarefied atmosphere would become legend. Not only were two Custodian families meeting in the final eight, but it would also be the year the qílín came. Chen Li Wei was already insufferable as it was. He would be henceforth intolerable.

The sight of a shimmering flying qílín dazzled me so much I almost missed the rest of the judges. They moved down the golden staircase and one man in particular moved in a way that caught my breath.

Kamon.

Halfway down from the citadel, Kamon's head jerked up like a predator scenting prey. His eyes narrowed and found me across the pavilion. My heart thudded in my chest.

A high-pitched voice cried out. "Kamon!"

Kamon's head turned just in time to catch a flowing form of silvery chiffon that launched into him at top speed. Fiona fell into Kamon's arms and beamed up at him, her million-dollar smile at full wattage. Kamon, ever the gentleman, set Fiona to rights and offered her his arm. He turned to the wani and appeared to make introductions between Fiona and the wani. The wani's aura was a band of solid green around his head, marking him as a magical entity like Kamon. It had been a long time since I'd seen any of the wani. In fact, the last time had been with Kamon by my side. The wani bowed low over Fiona's hand, his long, curling hair falling off his shoulders. His dark eyes glinted as his lips curled into a wicked smile. Fiona tittered.

They made a picture-perfect tableau. With Kamon turned away from me I ducked down and lost myself amongst the incoming partygoers.

My eyes nearly bugged out of my head as the last two judges descended the stairs, a petite woman in voluminous white and gold robes, and a floating, sinuous white serpent with glittering scales. When they reached the grass Iron Serpent transformed into her human form, a full head taller than her companion, and dressed in the flowing white silks I remembered from our encounter on the Golden Gate.

She had said we would meet again.

The two women spoke for a moment and then as one, they both turned and looked directly at me. They were clear across the pavilion, and dozens if not hundreds of people stood between us. And yet I was certain they were both looking me directly in the eyes.

Iron Serpent gave a dainty wave, her waterfall sleeves falling back to expose one pale hand. She gave a little laugh and bid her friend goodbye.

The shorter woman continued to stare at me. Her long russet hair was tied back in a simple tail, exposing peaked, tufted ears that swiveled of their own accord and dark, luminous eyes like pools of ink. But the truly notable thing about her were the glossy, luxurious tails that peeked out from under her robes. I had seen a húlí jīng before, but never one like this, with tails so numerous that they fanned out beneath her gown in a mesmerizing ripple.

The fox spirit finally looked away and slowly took in the pavilion, full to bursting with the most powerful families from the Jiārén community. She looked bored. After a moment she turned and walked off, leaving her fellow judges and heading for the ginkgo trees that surrounded the pavilion. She sat at the base of one of the trees and leaned against the trunk, closing her eyes as if to take a nap.

I found our table where most of our clan was already seated. My brother had his head down on the table, whether from fatigue or shame, I wasn't sure. I sat next to him and shook out my napkin. Whatever was going through my little brother's head, there was nothing we could do about it right now, and the best cure for an aching heart was an endless parade of excellent food.

In San Francisco my diet consisted of Kit Kats, takeout, coffee, and tea. Tessa had long given up on finding anything of substance to eat in my house. In two years I still had yet to put more in my refrigerator than leftovers and sriracha packets. While coming back home to Uncle Jake's homemade cuisine was a treat, a full-blown Lóng Yá banquet was something I'd probably never get again and I intended to take full advantage.

Somewhere, a bell was struck and the din of the crowd died to a murmur. Li Wei stood at the end of the pavilion and began speaking, his thin voice extolling the efforts of all the students in this year's Lóng Yá. Our table was just a bit too far away to hear him so I elbowed Tacchan. He lifted his head from the tablecloth just in time as our first course landed on a pillow of air.

The round dish contained a bright orange mound of uni. The raw sea urchin smelled of the briny tang of the sea and hovered off the plate, supported by a tiny vortex of smoke. If I was guessing correctly, Lóng Kǒu was really pulling out all the stops, and we were getting kaiseki for dinner, a multi-course tasting menu focused on local and seasonal foods. Kaiseki in Wàirén restaurants was already a pricey affair. Kaiseki for hundreds of ridiculously discerning and worldly Jiārén? This meal budget had to be equivalent to the GDP of some nations.

After another second the smoke whirlwind wobbled and collapsed, dropping the uni onto a carved bamboo spoon. Tacchan and I bumped knuckles and ate. The appetizer hit my tongue and for a split second, my troubles vanished in a haze of salty deliciousness. As the smoky, briny, tangy uni went down my gullet the next course arrived, the covered ceramic plate balanced on small clouds. In addition to an army of chefs they had to be employing a platoon of air and wind talents just to serve the diners.

I uncovered my plate and took a deep whiff, decorum be damned. This meal was going to be amazing and I intended to get the full effect. A delicate slice of fish sat on a mint leaf, surrounded by assorted pickled spring vegetables.

Tatsuya raised an eyebrow when he opened his plate. "Are they all going to be this small?"

I picked up the fish by the mint leaf and popped it in my mouth. "Quality, not quantity, little brother."

The flavors exploded in my mouth, a familiar blend of tangy and umami, the namazu I'd had from the hawker stand in the Glorious Emerald Pagoda. A once-in-a-lifetime fish, and I'd just had it twice in a week.

The dishes blurred after that. A traditional kaiseki might have a little over a dozen dishes, but I lost count on about the twentieth plate as the cuisine began to branch out to showcase food from the broad spectrum of Asian countries. Father was a more judicious eater than Tacchan and I were.

Tatsuya begged a few plates off Father. "You going to eat that?"

Sugi sat absolutely still between Tatsuya and Father, her dark eyes glinting under the night lanterns as my brother ate his portions and Father's plates, too. It was weird, but I sensed that Sugi liked Tatsuya better than me. Like if I tried to pilfer one of Father's portions, Sugi would take off my arm. An image of the curved scar on Adam's palm rose up in my mind and I shook it off, unwilling to let it mar this evening.

After the last course, Tatsuya leaned back in his chair and drummed his fingers on the table, his gaze roaming the pavilion. At the front of the pavilion, the speeches had started, with the headmaster introducing guests of honor and praising students of distinction from the graduating class. In other words, the boring part. My brother kept up the rubbernecking until he found Minjae in the crowd. His eyes brightened and then his shoulders slumped when he saw his friend, probably reliving the end of the maze. He stood abruptly, pushing his chair back from the table.

"I'm still hungry. I'm going to go find some more food."

My father gave a small nod. After Tatsuya left the table my father tilted his head in the direction my brother had walked off and three of our Pearl Guard left the table, following Tatsuya at a respectful distance. We were in the true competition of Lóng Yá now and my father would leave nothing to chance.

I checked the time. The sunset challenge would start as soon as the speechifying was over, but I needed to get back to Yokohama tonight. I needed to confirm the General's identity. Whatever else happened tonight, I was going to have to beg off soon.

I scooted around the table until I was closer to my father. He took no notice, and seemed to be intently watching the activities at the main table. I opened my mouth and hesitated. Goddess, why was this always so hard? Why did this always feel like I was unprepared for a test?

Before I found the words to ask my father, a gentle breeze washed over the entire pavilion like a sigh, carrying the subtle scent of jasmine. I turned to the head table, zeroing in on an expanding circle of soft golden light.

Batuhan stood in the center of the dome, his arms outstretched, a benevolent smile on his face. There was something about him that made me want to get closer. I leaned forward and focused on him, curious to hear what the man had to say.

Someone picked up Tatsuya's chair and sat down next to me, blocking my view of the head table. Irritated, I shifted my chair to get a better view.

Whoever had sat next to me huffed. "You looked so bored until now."

Without warning, a finger swiped across my upper lip, leaving something wet and sticky under my nose. The sharp, iron scent of blood flooded my nostrils and I jerked back like I'd been slapped. I swiped at my face and my hand came away bloody.

The húlí jīng sat in Tatsuya's chair, sucking on her finger. "Better?"

Batuhan's power washed over me again, tugging at my mind, drawing me toward him like a whirlpool. The man was speaking, but his words were garbled, like I was listening through water. All around the pavilion, heads nodded and glassy eyes stared with adoration. My father was one of the few attendees who didn't nod along, his arms crossed over his chest, brow drawn down and furrowed. His chest lifted and fell in a steady rhythm.

I realized he wasn't intently paying attention.

Father was cycling his qì.

It was rarely a bad idea to follow his example. I drew my focus inward and began cycling. A small hand covered mine and I looked up to find the húlí jīng had drawn close to me, right inside my personal space. My eyes fell to the multitude of tails splayed out around her chair. No one else seemed to notice that one of closest things we had to an immortal was sitting next to me. I fought the urge to pull away and took a deep breath.

The húlí jīng smiled. Her teeth were small, very white, and very sharp. "No. Not like that. Like this."

Your qì was deeply personal, your very life force, which we learned to move in order to power our talent, sending it out into the world with our Hoard Gift. Whatever extraordinary feats Jiārén were capable of, controlling another's qì was not possible.

Except, it seemed, for the húlí jīng. Somehow, her power, gentle as spring sunshine, nudged my qì as I cycled. I had the distinct vision of standing in the shadow of a massive giant, her power towering over me like a mountain. My qì moved through my mended meridians, patiently guided along a new path, a path unavailable to me before the Tokyo Sentinel's work. After a moment my qì flow smoothed out, almost cycling on its own. As it did, my vision and hearing cleared and my focus sharpened.

The húlí jīng took her hand off mine. "There you go. Practice the new cycling pattern so you do not forget it. Visualize your qì moving through you like electricity through a wire. It creates a field as it moves, similar to an electromagnetic field, and can protect you from certain talents."

My father flicked his eyes to me and nodded slightly before returning his attention to Batuhan. Batuhan seemed to be talking about the students, praising their efforts through the maze. Pretty boring stuff, but the Moks looked like they were hanging on his every word.

"Jiārén should be striving to increase our strengths, rather than fighting amongst ourselves. With Chen Lǎoshī's gracious permission, I will demonstrate."

The crowd quieted as Batuhan closed his eyes and placed his hands out in front of him, palms facing out. He sang a high, clear note that echoed across the pavilion, carrying the Borjigin's Hoard Gift with it. Several people fell out of their chairs as the wave of power passed over them. A few people broke down and cried. The wave passed over me with a shiver and when it passed, I felt clean, like I'd just stepped from a scalding hot shower. The scrapes and bruises I'd amassed from my scuffle with Stella Mok had already faded due to my improved healing but now even the lingering mild aches from rolling around on the rocky grounds faded in a soothing wash. The note faded into the night and several students shot to their feet, exclaiming with delight.

A few tables over, Minjae sat up a little straighter. The hollows under his eyes had been erased, and the gleam of lazy confidence had returned to his eyes. A-Yeong reached over and patted his head, clearly pleased. I scanned the crowd and saw the same results at every table. Batuhan had used his Gift to restore the students.

A wave of applause rippled across the crowd. Impressive. In one swoop he'd saved each of the competing families a fortune in herbs and elixirs their kids would have needed to start the sunset challenge. A man with a Gift like that could command armies to march to the ends of the earth.

Batuhan continued, "These students represent the next step in Jiārén advancement. It is up to us, the elders, to mold the new generation to continue the strength of dragons. Every year Wàirén grow more numerous, and their world encroaches on ours. Soon we will be—"

The húlí jīng moved until she filled my field of view. "This is boring. You are interesting."

Even my father did not seem to notice the fox spirit at the table. An immortal was asking for my attention. The best course was to give it to her.

"Uh . . . thank you?"

Her ears flicked back. "You are Emiko Soong and you are the most interesting person here."

She gave the pavilion a cursory glance. "I have seen all this before. The schemes and plots, the rise and fall of clans."

The fox turned her dark eyes to Batuhan. "He thinks he is being clever. Original. Ha!"

Despite the húlí jīng's dismissiveness, the rest of the audience was still largely held at rapt attention. Byun A-Yeong even nodded along to Batuhan's words, and I doubted that woman agreed with anyone more than once a month, just on principle.

Batuhan raised his voice now, carrying across the pavilion. "Are we not the descendants of dragons? Since when do dragons cower and skulk in shadows? What lessons are we teaching our progeny about their birthright? What . . ."

The húlí jīng's small hand grabbed my chin and turned me to look at her. Abashed, I resumed cycling my qì and the Borjigin's Gift released its hold on me. "Sorry. His talent is quite strong."

The fox sniffed. "Not really. Not at this distance. For the full effect you need to be right next to him. I studied another like him ages ago. Would you believe the strength of his talent drops off as the inverse of the square of the distance, just like gravity?"

I blinked. Had the húlí jīng just cited a physics equation to me? "You're not what I would have expected from a húlí jīng."

The fox spirit laughed, a loud, yipping sound, and wiped a tear from her eye. "See? I knew you would be interesting. Do you know how many people here would speak to me like that?"

At the look of horror on my face the húlí jīng laughed again and patted my hand. "It is fine, really. Refreshing, even. All the fawning and bowing when people meet me becomes tiresome."

Strangely enough, that was something I could relate to.

She put her hands together in a wai and inclined her head to me. "You may call me Most Exalted Heavenly Madam Yao."

I put my hands together as well and bowed, trying to find a depth of bow that was greater than Madam Yao's but also not so deep as to appear fawning. She laughed, another high-pitched yip, as I stuttered through the motions.

Madam Yao slouched into her chair, getting comfortable. "This is nice. I have not had someone so interesting to converse with in an age. I usually do not come to these, you know. I send one of the kits. It is always so boring, the same thing every year. Do you know why the húlí jīng remain neutral in the affairs of Jiārén? Why there is always a fox at Lóng Yá?"

I shook my head. I had never considered what place the húlí jīng held in our society. I had heard all the stories, of course, but despite their great power, they kept to themselves. And the idea of being gal pals with a nine-tailed húlí jīng was both enticing and terrifying.

"Because when you live to be a thousand years old, the lives of Jiārén are barely ripples in the river of life. We watch you, but only to confirm that you are not diverting the course of fate. Your petty squabbles are nothing to us."

"That's . . . depressing."

The húlí jīng smiled, baring her sharp teeth again. "Yes! And that's why you're so interesting. Or might be. Possibly."

"I'm sorry, but I don't understand."

Madam Yao's eyes narrowed and landed on my father's back. "I would not be surprised if your father has kept you in the dark about this. It is enough to say that events have been foretold that will turn ordinary ripples into forces that can reshape the river of fate."

She leaned back in her chair and looked up to the night sky. "The first ripples in the water are occurring here. At Lóng Yá. This year."

She waved a hand in the direction of the judges' table. Kamon was deep in conversation with the man dressed in the green scales. "Everyone came. The wani, the tigers, tengu, even the qílín deigned to come down from their mountain. Something will happen to tip the scales and we all wanted to be here to witness it."

Cold dread landed in my gut and spread out to my limbs. Madam Yao was right. As usual, I wasn't seeing the whole picture. What was happening this year that had attracted the attention of so many powerful figures? Did my father know? How did this relate to the General?

"And you. You are one in a millennium." One of her tails flicked and confusion kept me silent. I didn't know why Madam Yao had taken such an interest in me.

At the front of the pavilion, Batuhan was still speaking. ". . . is our duty to our children to ensure their future. To train them to face the challenges that will test them. To prepare them to defend our way of life. They will be soldiers and we—"

Screams and shouts exploded from the crowd as the qílín materialized out of the night sky and landed on one of the tables, smashing it and sending dishes and drinks flying. It was massive, at least ten feet at the shoulders, and it tossed its head, razor-sharp horns flashing in the torchlight. Its flowing silvery whiskers and mane whipped back and forth as hooves the size of dinner plates stamped down, crushing the table to splinters. The qílín reared up, front hooves slicing through the air. It blew a high, piercing whistle and hundreds of hands flew up to cover ears. Some people ducked beneath their tables.

In seconds the entire pavilion had gone silent.

Iridescent eyes glared over the crowd and the qílín spoke, its strangely harmonic voice echoing directly into my head. From the looks I saw around me, everyone was getting the same transmission. "This bores us. Commence the next round."

The qílín reared again and launched itself into the sky without another word.

Chen Li Wei stood on shaky legs and tried to take control of the crowd as Batuhan graciously took his seat, waving all the while to his adoring fans.

Across the pavilion, several people stood, including my father. They converged on the main table and eight heads of powerful clans left a Hoard piece in front of Chen Li Wei. It was only eight small pieces of Hoard gold, but it was enough to give a mid-tier clan a huge boost in power. Whoever won Lóng Yá would significantly increase their clan's standing.

I looked from Batuhan, to my father, and then to the húlí jīng, snippets of Batuhan's speech coming back to me.

I turned to Madam Yao. "Is Batuhan the General? Is he going to create the ripple?"

Now she just looked disappointed with me. Her dark eyes bored into me and it was like staring into infinity, making me feel very, very small. "Oh, no, little phoenix. It is you."

SUNSET CHALLENGE

The banquet had left me full from the delicious food, and befuddled from the cryptic words of the húlí jīng. Madam Yao had flounced off to join her immortal colleagues and I had been left to finish off the remaining bowls of green mung bean soup with sago pearls. Three bowls later, my mouth was happier but I had no further insight into what Madam Yao had been saying about me.

But apprehension weighed me down as I walked to the sunset challenge. I had left this place under a cloud of shame—I did not want to do anything that could jeopardize Tatsuya's standing here.

I told myself that we had prepped as much as possible. It was now up to Tatsuya to step up to the challenge remaining.

The maze running served two purposes. First, it force-ranked every single student that year by their completion time. Second, it bracketed the top eight finishers and allowed a couple of bonus rounds where those eight students could face off in one-on-one challenges.

The proctors knew in advance who the top eight would be going in. The reason was straightforward—only members from combat-grade houses would advance. If you were a student from Bird House or Tortoise House and had one of the top eight maze run times, it didn't matter, you would not be facing another student in the last two rounds. If a student's talent was growing wondrous crops, it wasn't a good idea to pair them off against a student who could smash them with Dragon Limbs.

The headmaster began reading off the pairings. Two large scrolls unfurled at the gates, the next matches set forth. Tatsuya inhaled sharply, stress blazing off of him like heat from a furnace. This wasn't going to be the cakewalk the maze had been. He'd be in there on his own. I couldn't help him anymore. Against the darkening sky, my brother's silhouette made him look slender. I knew he was physically strong and his Gift was powerful, but I lamented the thing I loved about him—his gentleness. He shied away from hurting anyone.

I couldn't say I had that problem. That fundamental difference between us was what made Tatsuya my loveable brother and what had made me the Butcher.

The two scrolls held four names each. Four students who would compete amongst themselves for two spots in the final battle. Depending on their placements, this was where friendships died in Lóng Yá. Each pod of four students would be transported to a Realm Fragment, ensuring that no student had any advantages of prior knowledge. The students had to not only compete with each other in the Fragment, but also manage basic survival tactics. Two golden sashes were available in each Fragment, for the four students who would advance.

At last, the headmaster called out Tatsuya's match. He would be facing off against Chariya, Balen, and a young man I hadn't seen finish the maze. I squinted at his red belt. Maybe a kin to the Moks. Tatsuya exhaled, a long, slow expulsion of air. His shoulders relaxed and the relief on his face was obvious. Chariya was the strongest candidate in his bracket, and a powerful kinetic. She had strength and accuracy but we were unclear about her range. I'd watched her in the maze and she had confidence that radiated from her sure movements. She wasn't going to be a pushover, but Tatsuya had trained against the many kinetics of the Pearl Guard. He wasn't worried.

Balen was from Dragon House and might have been a problem in one-on-one combat, but in the second round, where Tatsuya would have room to work around him, he could neutralize Balen.

In any case, the relief on Tatsuya's face was clear. Anything other than competing with Minjae or Thùy in this round was acceptable. Based on our training, it was also his most straightforward strategy. And with all the students ensconced in the Fragment, Kaida would have no access to my brother. Perfect.

I clapped a hand on his shoulder. "You've got this."

My father nodded once to Tacchan, a quick, decisive motion, and then walked off into the crowd. He didn't look back. The majority of our retinue followed him, except for the three guards who had shadowed Tacchan after dinner. My brother watched our father walk away, the expression on his face unreadable. Tacchan was too old to have been expecting words of encouragement from our father. He had done his part, raised Tatsuya to be strong, and given him the tools he felt Tatsuya needed to succeed. Now it was all up to my brother.

The crowd parted, making space for the students. Chariya, Balen, and the young man with the red belt stood next to Tatsuya. Minjae, Thùy, and two other Tiger House students formed another group a few feet away. Eight kids who were all probably decent friends, suddenly reduced to awkward teenagers again, sizing each other up with stolen glances.

Ragged cheers burst from the crowd of onlookers. Of all the students, Minjae and Thùy seemed to be the most at ease. Thùy's clan stood out in the crowd like a pack of tourists, cheering and hooting encouragement. It was a little disconcerting how rowdy the Hoàng Clan was. They had brought champagne rally towels that matched Thùy's tracksuit, and the whole contingent whipped the towels in the air as they cheered. A few of the kids, clearly taught to keep a low profile, shied away from the loud display. Thùy reveled in it, pumping her arms in the air and prancing back and forth like a prizefighter before a bout. With each pass in front of the crowd, her family's cheers grew.

An air horn blared, followed by an obnoxious buzzing sound.

A rotund man in Thùy's entourage, dressed in a too-tight matching tracksuit, was spraying gold confetti over the crowd from what looked like a modified water gun. Skies above. I wasn't a stickler for decorum but Thùy's family acting like they were at a Mets game did cause me to raise my eyebrows in surprise. I cheered up when I saw Chen Li Wei's expression. He looked positively revolted, which had me feeling a bit more warmly toward the portly man waving the spray confetti gun around.

The irritated headmaster blew a piercing whistle, calling for silence. The Hoàng Clan cheers died down slowly despite his withering glare. "Silence! The top eight will be transported to their respective Fragments soon. One judge and one healer will transport with the students to ensure adherence to the rules. Once in the Fragment the students will . . ."

Tatsuya wandered away from his cohort and sidled up alongside Minjae. The Byun matron stood on the far side of the clearing, her crutches planted wide around her. When Tatsuya punched Minjae lightly on the shoulder, her one dark eye zeroed in on my brother. I tensed, ready to throw myself at the hateful woman.

Minjae turned and the two boys studied each other for a moment. Whatever tension held them back passed like an errant wind and they began throwing playful punches at each other, laughing as they went. Minjae's grandmother frowned before turning away. The boys hugged each other fiercely and traded grips, the tension from the maze forgotten for now.

Whatever happened the rest of this night, I hoped their friendship could withstand it. My phone alarm chimed. Time to go. I caught Tatsuya's eye and tilted my head to him. He had everything he needed. I melted into the crowd and bolted for the East Gate. I had a date at the Herbalist's.

Yokohama at night was a very different experience, one I found familiar and comforting. It was always a bustling area but at night the shadows grew long and dark, providing even more anonymity. My business and my prey both preferred the dark.

There were plenty of tourists and locals alike on the street, but Yook Bo's small side street was already deserted. Broken streetlamps let the shadows creep in deeper, the darkness thick with dread.

I slowed as I stepped into the darkness. The lights were off at Yook Bo.

Good. I hoped that meant they'd left town already. My original plan had been to stake out the place and watch for visitors. I crept up to the door and peeked in, and my heart dropped.

There was just enough light from the street to show the broken crockery strewn across the floor, mixed with shattered glass, tea leaves, and books. I was too late.

Cold sweat broke out on the back of my neck as I pushed the door open. I stepped inside and let the door swing shut, staying out of the dim light. The smell hit me first, the stinging stench of sulfur like a freshly lit match. Adrenaline surged and I tightened my fingers on Hachi's grip.

I stayed motionless for a count of five, listening for any hint of an ambush. Sometimes the best way to find a trap was to step on it. I dropped a Dragon Limb crystal into my left hand and drew Hachi to high guard. I moved into the shop, keeping my back to the wall. The interior of the shop was nearly pitch black. Once inside I stayed still for a moment, letting my eyes adjust and stretching my senses out into the room.

The smell hit me again, harder and stinging the back of my throat. The demon summoner had been here. So the Tanakas were working with the General, along with the Byuns. Who else? The Moks?

My shoulders tensed at the thought of Tacchan competing against A-Yeong's grandson. Was Minjae in on it, too? If so, I had just left Tatsuya surrounded by vipers. I had to get back to Lóng Kǒu.

As I stepped forward, my senses told me what I had been dreading. Broken Tooth, there was a body. I couldn't see it yet, but I'd been around enough death to know the feel of it. The utter finality of a once-living person reduced to a lump of rapidly cooling meat. If anyone else was in here, they were better than me at hiding in the dark. I crouched slowly, holding the trench coat away from my body to reduce the noise. As my eyes opened to the dark, the shape of the body revealed itself in the middle of the floor.

Tony lay on his stomach, but his sightless eyes stared up at the ceiling. Skies. Something had clawed at his face, leaving parallel tracks across his cheek. I sheathed Hachi but kept the crystal in my left hand and crept to Tony's body. I turned his body and jerked open his silk vest, popping the buttons and riffling through the inside pockets. Nothing. No bottles, no vials, no paper packets of powder. Not even a wallet or money.

The door burst open behind me and I spun. The shelves were too tight to draw Hachi so I pulsed my qì down my left arm and shattered the Dragon Limb crystal. Bloodred energy engulfed my hand like a torch and raced up to my shoulder. Gleaming red and purple scales erupted over my arm as my muscles thickened. Fire and ash, I could get used to this.

I met my attacker with the palm of my hand. Something crashed and shattered over my enhanced arm. My attacker let out a strangled cry and lunged at me again. My arm shot out, clipping my assailant in the shoulder and spinning them around. I followed in close and wrapped my elongated dragon fingers, talons and all, around my attacker's neck. I squeezed gently, enough for the talons to press into the soft flesh. I needed answers, not another dead body.

My attacker pounded both hands on my Dragon Limb, but they might as well have been trying to knock down a tree. I dragged them across the shop toward the dim light filtering in from the open door.

Skies.

I dropped Mèimei to the floor where she curled into a ball, clutching at her neck, her eyes red and puffy from crying. I closed and locked the door and turned on the lights, which just pushed Mèimei into a fresh crying jag as it lit up her brother's mutilated body. Another time, I might have been more gentle, but I needed fast answers tonight.

I crouched, using my body to block the view of her brother, and staying well out of her reach. "Mèimei. I need you to focus. I need to know who did this."

The girl trembled, her shoulders shaking with the strength of her sobs. "He . . . he . . . he said he was almost done. He told me to get my bags . . ."

Broken Claw. He hadn't destroyed his work. "Did he finish it?"

She shook her head. "I don't know. He sent me away."

He'd known what might happen. The girl collapsed into tears again, her hands clutched around a parcel wrapped in brown paper. Probably whatever Tony had sent her for. An errand to save her life.

I stood and moved behind the counter, leaving Mèimei to her grief while I looked for clues. I couldn't console her anyway, I didn't have the words to help her. Behind the counter with the cash register an open doorway led to a tidy office where Tony kept a computer and a file cabinet alongside his workbench. The workbench was in shambles. But there was a rather thick bundle of cables exiting the back of the computer that disappeared into the ceiling. Jackpot.

I went back outside and hauled Mèimei up to her feet. She flinched away from my Dragon Limb and I had to clamp down on her arm to keep her from bolting. She thrashed in my grip. The smell of her brother's blood was thick in the close confines of the little shop, clashing with the herbal scents of tea and ginseng. I had to get this done quickly, before the poor girl lost her mind.

"Mèimei, I know this is hard, but I need to know who did this. I need you to show me the security footage."

The girl wailed, boneless in my arms, her hands reaching for her brother's broken form. My back strained to keep her upright. I pushed her up against the wall to keep her from moving and spoke through gritted teeth. "He's dead! Your brother is dead. Find the thing inside you that wants to find his killer. Find the thing that wants revenge. Someone killed your brother tonight. That doesn't make you weak. It makes you mad!"

As I spoke, Mèimei's eyes cleared, the shine from her tears crystalizing into anger. She seemed to finally recognize me. When she spoke her voice was a bare whisper. "You're the Butcher."

"Yes." There was no denying it. Not at a time like this.

"You'll get them."

I gave her a quick nod. I wasn't normally in the revenge business, but this time, our priorities aligned. I could use it and not feel like a total heel for manipulating Mèimei's emotions.

The young woman relaxed and I let her down. She marched into the back office and sat at the computer, quickly pulling up their security software. The video wound backward until it showed her brother alone in the shop, and two people coming in the door.

The taller figure sported a familiar long cloak and two long ends of a lavender scarf fluttered as he strode in. The woman beside him prowled with an easy stride, her smooth gait like that of a dancer.

Beetlehead, the oni summoner. And Kaida.

I had to get back to Lóng Kǒu. Something big was happening tonight. Kaida. The demon summoner who had waltzed right past me at Bird House covered up by that voluminous purple cloak. The General, whoever he or she was. All of it bouncing around in my head and swirled up with the húlí jīng's words. Somehow it all made sense, but I didn't have the vision to see it.

My father might, though. That triggered another idea. "Mèimei, what did Tony do with the jade from my father?"

She'd pulled herself together, and was cleaning up the shards of broken ceramics. She paused with the dustpan in hand. "Nothing, yet. He was planning to do some tests tomorrow."

"Where did he keep it? Do you have a safe?"

Mèimei laughed bitterly. "We get broken into at least once a month. We gave up on a safe long ago. He kept the jade in his pocket, where he keeps—kept anything that valuable."

I hadn't found anything on his body. It was possible that the demon summoner or Kaida had taken it. Kaida for sure would have recognized the jade for what it was. My father would be able to confirm. Maybe he could help in more ways than one tonight.

I turned to go and found Mèimei on the floor again, sniffling quietly as she picked up broken bits of teapot, studiously avoiding the area around her brother's body. My mind flashed to another market stall in another time, again with the jarring odor of blood clashing with the ordinary scents of the business. I had stood over another broken girl in that shop as well. Only that time, the damage and grief had all been due to my actions.

"You can't stay here. The people who killed him. They'll be back."

Mèimei stopped sweeping and looked up to me from the floor, her face a mask of despair. She didn't make a sound. Jiārén life chewed people up every day of the week. Small-time operators like Tony lived only at the whim of powerful Custodian families. Tony and his sister were just more collateral damage from the schemes of the powerful.

I grabbed one of the last Kit Kats from the counter and turned it over. Japanese Kit Kats had a blank space on the wrapper for short messages. I grabbed a marker from the cash register and started writing.

"Go to Shinjuku Station." I pulled a narrow bar of gold from my pocket. "This will get you into the Emerald Pagoda and buy you passage to San Francisco."

I handed her the gold and the Kit Kat. "Find Vitality Health Services in the Inner Sunset district. Ask for Grandma Chen and show her this note. She'll know it's from me. She can hide you until I get there."

She took the items from me, her motions robotic, and shuffled to the office and closed the door softly. I could only hope she took my advice. I didn't have time to do anything else. I made for the door and ran, praying I wasn't too late to stop Kaida.

MIDNIGHT MATCH

When the portal spit me out at the edge of Lóng Kǒu campus, the anxiety, guilt, and distress had tied my gut in knots. The familiar and unwelcome side effect of portal travel meant that I hunched over the manicured shrubs and vomited in front of the towering golden moon gates.

I breathed deep and cycled my qì the way the Old One had showed me. The pain in my stomach immediately loosened and in that moment I realized that I should have done this while crossing the portal. For so long I had accepted that I had been lacking and taken my portal sickness as a penance. No longer.

My steps quickened as I sped across the vast campus. Despite my inner turmoil the darkness held a velvety quiet that wrapped around me in familiar comfort.

A high whistle pierced the night followed by a shower of rockets exploding in glitters of fiery white sparks. A smoke animal plumed in the wake of the rockets, the distinctive shape of a purple dog overhead. The Byun heir had completed the sunset challenge first. Whoever finished next would face him for final placement to determine first and second place in Lóng Yá.

I had to assume that Beetlehead had beat me back here and delivered the amplifier that Ah Tong had created for the General. I'd been gone nearly two hours. Tatsuya should be close to completing the sunset challenge as well and then gearing up for the midnight match. He knew to stay in the warded areas while he waited.

The arena for the final midnight round had no wards. Kaida would be able to wander freely through the crowds, her talent boosted by blood jade.

Another shrill whistle followed by rockets exploded overhead. I looked up, breathless, and saw the smoky outline of Tatsuya's ram. He was done. He'd be facing off against Minjae. I ran toward the lights, anxious to see him.

I found him behind a protective circle of our Pearl Guards, their shoulders set close to completely enclose an area of the pavilion for our family members. The formation melted open briefly to let me inside. My father and Tatsuya sat at a repurposed banquet table. Colorful lanterns rose high above us and cast golden light over a sparkling variety of colorful vials scattered across my brother's side of the table, along with a growing collection of empty vials.

My brother's jacket was shredded open across his back, the fabric scorched and tinged with blood. One of the sleeves had been torn off at the elbow and the skin on his forearm was an unhealthy shade of pink.

I sat down next to my father. "On to the next round, then?"

Tatsuya set down an empty glass stained with traces of some red liquid. Even from where I sat, the smell was so strongly medicinal that I winced in sympathy for Tacchan. He belched into his fist and then squeezed at his nose. "Blood and ash, that's worse coming up than it was going down! Yes, on to the finals in the main stadium. Thủy and Balen. Me and Minjae for the Winner's Pot."

Father pushed a vial into my brother's hands, the liquid inside jet black with hints of blue. "Now this one."

Tatsuya grimaced, popped the top off the vial, and tossed back the contents before scrunching up his face as he swallowed. The bitter smell of herbal remedies wafted across the table and the skin on his forearm lightened and smoothed out.

Outside of our protective detail, several families, including the Byuns, clustered around Batuhan's camp. The soft gold glow of his talent formed a warm bubble of light around them. Tatsuya yelped as he downed another vial of medicine. Everything on the table probably cost my brother's weight in gold. Not only were we not partaking of Batuhan's charity, we were doing it very obviously in front of everyone.

"I take it we are not friends with the Borjigin, then?"

My father opened a small pillbox, the top inlaid with mother-of-pearl, and handed two small green tablets to my brother. "These two with the next one. No, we are not his friends. What have I taught you about the price of gifts?"

The answer was a reflex. "Nothing is free."

My father grunted, his version of pleased agreement. "We can take care of Tatsuya on our own, with no need to incur any debt, implied or otherwise. True gifts are rare enough, especially amongst Jiārén. Look to one's actions, and not their words, to determine their intentions."

I glanced over the collection of families waiting to enter Batuhan's sphere of influence to heal their kids for the next round. My father knew a lot more about what was happening tonight than he was letting on. As always, I was still catching up. But tonight, for once, I didn't feel so far behind him.

"Baba, I think Kaida is here."

His hands stilled for only a moment, and then he resumed arranging the remaining vials for Tatsuya. He waved Fujita-san over to the table. "Please make sure Tatsuya finishes these in this order. Emiko and I will be discussing business."

Business. With that word Fujita-san wouldn't interrupt us unless the world was cracking apart around us, and even then he might hesitate. Fujita-san nodded and then with two sharp claps called his companions, the scent of his talent gentle and sweet. Two large Ural owls landed in the lantern stands above us. Their dark gray feathers fluffed out and then settled as they turned their heads this way and that. They would give warning if they sensed a portal opening near Tatsuya.

Uncle Lau moved closer to Tatsuya and signaled Nami. She moved into position where she could keep an eye on our owl guards. When they hooted, Tatsuya could animate his own shields and Nami would call down her Raijin lightning strikes. It wasn't perfect but there was no such thing as perfect safety in Jiārén life.

My father walked away from the table and I followed him. Out of earshot of my brother, I told Father everything I'd seen in Yokohama, my encounters with Byun A-Yeong and Batuhan, and my suspicions about the General and his plans. If anything I said surprised him, he didn't show it.

My father reached into his jacket and pulled out a small glass tube, a twin to the one I'd given Ah Tong. One small chip of jade floated inside the glass. "I gave you all but one of the chips I imbued with my power. This one will lead you to the others. Give me your hand."

Had he always known he was going to have to track them down? Or had he made plans just in case? My father's mind was like a spider's web, making connections no one else could see, far before they were even hinted at.

I put my hand in his.

My father cycled his qì, the flow of his energy a cool tingle where our palms met. He looked me in the eye. "You know what you need to do."

Fire and ash. The last thing I wanted was to use my accursed talent. As usual my father left me with only terrible choices. Use my talent, or leave Kaida free to attack my brother. Be my father's pawn, or not. In the ineffable calculus of my father's schemes, my talent was just another lever to be pulled. One more variable to track.

Ever since I'd broken Truth, my life had been a string of awful choices. But they'd been mine. Even if my father had been pulling the strings, I had still charted my own fate. I wasn't going to let my brother down, whatever my father thought. I cycled my qì and my talent awoke, a hunger stirring in my belly at the convergence of my meridians.

My talent reached out and found my father's, cooing over it like a predator sniffing at a fresh kill. I dug into the hunger, like wrapping my hand around the nape of a jungle cat, pushing the animal down, asserting my control. I had to be careful. If I let it off its leash, it would run loose, and I had no idea what that meant. The hunger bucked under my control and steadied, then licked out at my father's power. The scent of white pepper flooded my nose and suddenly the jade in the vial called out to me as clearly as a bell.

I opened the tube and popped the jade into my mouth, sticking it between my cheek and gum. It pressed against my cheek, turning me to the left, and slowly moved toward the front of my mouth as I turned.

My father grunted as he watched me. Again, all the praise I was ever going to get. Did he ever consider what his schemes would cost his children?

Of course he did. But the cost was never enough to tip the scales.

"Baba, the amplifier that Ah Tong made. If Batuhan is the General—"

My father held up his hand and closed his eyes, his breath even, cycling his qì. Under his lids, his eyes darted back and forth as if in dream sleep. His eyes snapped open. "Do not concern yourself with Batuhan. Protect your brother. Find Kaida. Do what you must to stop her."

I would follow my father's orders and protect our family, but Kaida was our family as well. I had set her on this path. I swore I would not be the one to end her life.

Tatsuya yelled and jumped up from the table, hopping around waving his hand at his open mouth. "Hot! Hot! Hot!"

My father's lips drew up in a small smile. "That was the last one. I forgot to warn him about it."

His smile faded. "Find your cousin."

My father walked away, leaving me to it. It had always been like this. When he gave me an assignment it was almost as if he forgot about me until it was finished. My brother's life was on the line today.

I would not fail.

I pushed through our Pearl Guards, the jade in my cheek leading me to the thickest part of the crowd.

A buzz of energy raced through the crowd as anticipation built for the final matches. The crowd began moving as one, making its way toward the main stadium. The final matches would take place there, an ultimate test of the students' skills. The playing field was tailored to allow each student to use their Hoard Gift to their maximum ability. These matches were legendary for how students were pushed to their limits. Some students were pushed beyond those limits.

In order to allow competition at this level, the main stadium had no wards, no qì dampening, no proctors to contain the students. It also meant that Kaida would be able to emerge anywhere in the stadium. My brother had enough trouble paying attention to one opponent. Dealing with Kaida as he was fighting his best friend . . . the thought chilled my blood. I had to find her.

When I'd fought her at the train station, she'd easily eluded me. Her Gift was powerful and she was better trained than I was. But I had a couple surprises in store for her.

Tonight Kaida would be facing a different opponent. Someone who had grown up around another dark walker.

I didn't want to kill her. Just killing her would have made my task easier. I'd made myself a vow on Golden Gai. I wasn't my father's weapon anymore. Kaida was our blood. In some twist of fate, she had fulfilled my obligations at Jōkōryūkai. Shame washed over me. She didn't deserve to die.

I wouldn't let her kill my brother, but I would do everything in my power to spare her life.

As I slipped through the crowd, the jade chip slid along my jaw until it was directly under the center of my lip. The tugging sensation increased as I drew closer to the Byun Clan, until the jade felt like it was about to fly out of my mouth. A gentle waft of rotten ginger and the jade chip in my mouth fell quiet.

Broken Claw. She'd jumped. She'd been right here. But now I had confirmation. She had my father's jade on her. I could track her.

I followed the crowds into the stadium. My brother was here. So was Fiona, but she would be well guarded. I'd done all I could for her so I could focus on protecting my brother. Unless I was mistaken, Kaida would be here. I just had to be ready for her.

Bells rang out and the crowd roared its approval. The final four students entered the stadium. The last two matches would play out simultaneously. This was the main event for Jiārén every year, our Lunar Year monthlong festivities packed into a single day. I picked my way through the stadium, dodging people rushing to find their seats before the event began.

Tatsuya entered through a small door at the far side of the stadium. He looked so small down there by himself. Minjae appeared at a door opposite my brother's. My brother's side of the stadium had been set up with plenty of raw materials for him to work with. Piles of stone and brick had been scattered about his half of the field. On Minjae's side bright metal objects like massive gongs had been set into the earth and hung from wooden scaffolds. No, not gongs. Parabolic dishes. Amplifiers for a harmonic talent. If Minjae could find the right spot on the field, the amplifiers could turn the whole field into mush.

Gods. They could kill each other several times over with all that. I shook my head. How was this, any of this, useful other than as blood sport?

The bells rang again and the matches started. I stared, unable to look away as my brother raised his hands and animated several piles of stones. He built his defenses first, a rapidly twisting network of stone and brick surrounding him like a miniature hurricane. His troops came next, rock dogs and rams, loping away from him at top speed to chase down his friend.

Minjae ran across the field, his talent lashing out, harmonics screaming like nails on a chalkboard and shattering my brother's constructs. When one of Tatsuya's constructs got too close, Minjae lashed out with pure qì and broke it apart. Tatsuya was right. Minjae was very good. If Minjae had the stamina to maintain this pace, he could outlast my brother. Tatsuya would have to keep the pressure on him, keep Minjae on his back foot and force a mistake if he hoped to win.

The jade tugged on my cheek, drawing me to my right, away from Tatsuya's match. I tore my eyes away from my brother and headed after my cousin. We'd given Tatsuya all the help we could. The fate of his match was solely in his hands now. My job was to make sure no one interfered.

I cut across the stands and was nearly deafened by a chorus of raucous singing from the crowd at my back. Thùy emerged from the door beneath us and her contingent of family and clan members broke out into an upbeat hip-hop song with lots of yelling and screaming. Thùy danced her way across the field, bopping along to her custom walk-on music. On the far side of the stadium, Balen emerged more sedately and settled himself into a nook between two large trees. Balen's aura flared a deep green and the trees on either side of him cracked and swelled, lifting him up as their roots chewed through the turf, snaking out like bark-covered serpents. The families on Balen's side roared in approval as Thùy's clan faltered at the sight of a gāo-level plant master.

The bell for the third-place match rang out and Thùy ran forward.

I elbowed my way through the mass of people. If I found Kaida in this mess, we were going to have a hell of an encounter with so many people around us.

There. I caught the scent of rotten ginger as the jade in my mouth jumped again, pulling me forward. A swish of black hair bounced away, just ahead of me. I plunged forward, keeping my eyes on her. Someone yelled as I pushed them down to the ground. My hand shot out, weaving through bodies until it landed on an arm in a dark sleeve with gold accents.

I curled my fingers into the fabric and yanked back.

Kaida's face swam out of the crowd and her hand came up. Instinct took over. I couldn't draw my blade in these conditions. My free hand shot up and caught her by the wrist. Metal gleamed and my cousin's blade stopped just short of my neck. I locked my elbow against my body and fought her to a standstill, Kaida's little knife quivering in the air just above my sternum.

Around us, the crowd continued to cheer for Thùy, oblivious to the drama happening in their midst.

My cousin's eyes were shot through with twisting veins of red and black and a sheen of sweat coated her forehead. Stray bangs of her dark hair were plastered across her face. Gods, the heat radiating off her body was like a furnace.

She smiled, showing all her teeth. "Hello, cousin. Enjoying the show?"

Her other arm whipped up and I let go of her sleeve to catch that hand as well. I yanked that hand down, trapping it against her body. The motion dragged down the neck of her shirt, exposing the ugly red lines crawling up from her heart.

"You're killing yourself, Kaida. This isn't worth it."

"How would you know what something is worth? You're such a disappointment. Always quitting when the road got hard."

"Tatsuya is your cousin! Your family!"

Kaida's eyes glinted, hard as river rocks. "I have no family. You saw to that! You and your mother!"

She jerked her arm down and back up again, breaking my hold on her wrist. The blade flashed again. I ducked and jabbed my fingers into her shoulder for a strike at her meridians. Maybe I could cripple her powers. Kaida cried out as my strike landed and the blade dropped from her nerveless fingers.

I reached for Kaida as she fell. Metal glinted and I pulled my head back, arching my neck. A hot line of pain flared across my cheek. Kaida rolled away, knocking down two more revelers, and came up on her feet, another short blade held lightly between her fingers.

She licked her lips, her grin growing to manic width. The red tracks had crept up to her neck, extending beyond her collar.

I had to save her. "Kaida, the blood jade is killing you."

"You're wrong. The blood jade makes me strong. Stronger than you. The General has made me strong, he's made me his weapon."

On the far side of the stadium a scream pierced the night, the sound reaching into my belly and turning my body cold.

Tatsuya.

He screamed again and the crowd roared in response. In my moment of hesitation, Kaida's talent blossomed, drenching the humid night air with rotting ginger. She fell into the shadows beneath her and disappeared. The jade in my mouth fell quiet.

I turned and ran to the other side of the stadium.

My brother was in trouble.

Tatsuya and Minjae stood within arm's reach of each other in the center of the field. My brother still had his defenses up, a swirling cloud of fist-sized rocks, but Minjae was inside his defenses. Both boys were covered in cuts and scratches. Minjae's shirt had been nearly shredded from him. A bright red smear of blood ran from my brother's ear.

The playing field was a ruin. Tatsuya's constructs had torn up fresh furrows of earth, massive arcing swathes of churned-up dirt large enough to swallow a truck. The amplifiers that had been behind Minjae had been pummeled by Tatsuya's missiles until they were unrecognizable scrap metal and Minjae's harmonic talent had reduced much of Tatsuya's initial stockpile of rock and brick to piles of dust and sand. The grit caught in the whirlwind around the two boys, whipping into a miniature sandstorm. All around the stadium people raised their hands, guarding their eyes against the flying sand.

Minjae opened his mouth and screamed, the sound a high-pitched whine that scraped at my nerves. Several people around me cried out, clutching their hands to their ears. Tacchan's defenses wobbled, a few of his rocks shattering. Minjae had figured out that the best way to attack my brother was from inside his defenses.

My brother went to one knee but held on, his defense steadying itself, the shattered rocks rejoining the flow. Tatsuya stood, sending rocks flying at his friend, even as he backed away, trying to make space between them. Minjae lashed out with his qì, catching the rocks and flinging them away from him.

I sucked in a sharp breath, watching Tatsuya continue to backpedal. Was he really so unused to fighting someone inside his defenses? Or had he lost his nerve? Would he use the wing bone and send Minjae flying into oblivion?

Minjae was laser focused on Tatsuya, his talent flaring around him like a bonfire. Which one of them would slip first? Who would tire out and make the first mistake?

A loud tapping noise started from the far side of the stadium. The sound grew and swelled, until it sounded like a chorus of drums.

At the front of the stands, surrounded by a sea of lavender scarves, Byun A-Yeong stood behind the guardrail, slamming one of her crutches onto the metal railing. Her retinue around her stomped their feet in time to the beat. Even the boys paused at the sound, Tatsuya's gaze traveling up to the stands. Minjae turned and locked eyes with his grandmother.

She stared down at him like a dragon contemplating a mouse and continued to pound out the beat.

In the corner of my eye, fireworks shot into the sky, tracing the outline of a bounding rabbit in brilliant red sparks. Thùy had won her match.

No one cared.

Minjae turned back to Tatsuya, his eyes now flat and dead.

No, no, blood and ash, no! I lunged through the crowd, a useless action. I was too far away and I had no idea what was going to happen.

Minjae set his legs wide and brought up his arms. My brother yelled, bringing his defenses raining down in one last attempt to win the match. Minjae didn't even flinch, didn't dodge. Rocks peppered him where he stood, drawing blood from his arms, face, neck. He stayed where he was and opened his mouth.

Pain exploded in my head, a hot spike of agony that drove itself up my neck and into the base of my head. I grabbed the guardrail to keep myself from falling. All around me people screamed and fell to their knees.

One scream rose above them all. My brother on the field, crumpled to the ground, bearing the brunt of Minjae's attack. Minjae made no noise at all, although his mouth was open. The scene wavered before me, my eyes refusing to focus. Minjae had modified his harmonics. His talent had blended somehow with his grandmother's, turning his shrieking into something that affected the mind directly.

I swayed again, nearly tipping over the guardrail. I cried out my brother's name. I don't know if he heard. I don't even know if I actually said anything. The lights around the stadium strobed as I tried to find my footing.

In the next instant, the pain was gone. I shot to my feet, scrambling down the steps, shoving people aside. Tatsuya lay huddled on the ruined earth, bleeding from both ears and his nose now. Minjae stood above him, his chest heaving, his eyes strangely bright.

Tatsuya uncurled as the pain left him. The two boys made eye contact. My brother's hand moved to his shirt pocket where he'd stowed the flute. I held my breath. If he could get it out, just get a single note, he could turn the whole match. Minjae's attack had been devastating, but it was still nothing compared to a fragment of Dragonsong.

My brother's arm moved past his pocket until his arm came to rest over his eyes. His shoulders began to shake and he rolled onto his side. "I yield."

Minjae's shoulders slumped and tears fell from his eyes. He stood there for two heartbeats staring down at Tatsuya's prone form. Minjae turned away and returned to his side of the stadium. A cheer went up from the opposite side, where no one had been touched by Minjae's attack. Fireworks launched into the night sky and traced out a brilliant purple dog in midleap.

I scanned the crowd until I found my father. He stood perfectly still in the midst of our clan, who were still getting themselves sorted after Minjae's attack. My father looked no worse for wear. He might have only weathered a slight breeze. His face showed neither pleasure nor disappointment. His eyes found me and he tilted his head slightly toward my brother.

Cleanup duty again.

I leapt over the guardrail and landed lightly on the turf. Up close, the damage the two boys had done was remarkable. They were prime examples of the apex of our power. I crouched next to Tatsuya and gave him a moment to pull himself together.

He swiped his arm across his nose and blinked when he saw me. His eyes were red and swollen, his voice thick with emotion. "I couldn't do it."

As someone who had also failed to take the final, irrevocable step of an arduous process, I was in no position to criticize. "I know."

I gripped his arm and gave him a squeeze. "Come on, we can't stay out in the open like this. Let's get you out of here."

He let me pull him to his feet. Minjae's attack had been much worse for my brother. I was almost back to normal, but Tatsuya was still shaky, barely keeping his legs steady as we limped to the exit. I shifted my shoulder, getting more of his weight on me. Gods, when had my brother gotten so big? I still remembered carrying him on my shoulders.

Tacchan groaned and I felt one of his ribs shift. "Neesan, did I screw up?"

"Well, you didn't win. But don't worry about it. It's over now."

"I tried. I did. I just . . ."

He couldn't stand the idea of destroying his friend. "I know you did."

In the stands, my father hadn't moved, and he watched me take my brother off the field, still with that blank expression on his face.

"I let the family down."

"No, Tacchan. You knew the true enemy here was never Minjae."

The true enemy was losing one's compassion. Giving up one's soul. My brother was younger than me, but he was wiser by far. I hugged him close.

I'd been up for nearly twenty-four hours. We were all tapped out. Laboring under Tatsuya's weight and angry at my father for driving my brother like this, I almost missed it. My senses twigged and my reflexes, normally paranoia-quick, were suddenly as slow as tar drying.

By the time I was pushing us to the side, the thick scent of rotten ginger had surrounded me in a cloud. Shadows boiled up from the earth and several people in the stands screamed. An arc of silver flashed out of the darkness and drew a thin line of heat across my left side. Pain buckled me to one side and Tacchan and I tumbled to the ground in a tangled heap of limbs. The jade chip dug into my lip, scraping against my teeth.

Kaida stepped from the writhing shadows, a short blade in her left hand, her katana at her hip. Her eyes were bloodshot and her skin radiated with feverish heat.

"Hello, cousins. Time to finish this."

BALANCING THE SCALES

An icy calm settled over me. I stood and pushed my brother behind me. Up in the stands people pointed and shouted but no one ran down to the field. No one rushed to help. It was the Jiārén way. The only common reaction among the crowd was a widening of the eyes, and eagerness to witness this.

Lóng Yá was our yearly proxy for all-out clan warfare. A polite fiction we indulged in to keep with the old ways, while not driving ourselves to extinction. But Jiārén were descendants of the dragons, and we were bloodthirsty. The crowds looked down on Kaida and me and they yearned for the battle taking shape.

My father hadn't moved an inch since Kaida had appeared. His eyes found mine and he gave the barest nod of his head. He trusted me to finish this. I settled my breathing, unsheathed Hachi, and dropped a tile.

I had to keep her focused on me and away from Tatsuya. If I could buy enough time, Father would be able to get Tatsuya out. My whole rotten childhood, growing up the pitied, stunted member of our family. It had all led me to this moment to use everything in my power to protect my brother.

Had my father planned all of this? I would never know. Anticipation burned through me, the searing knowledge that finally, here was a problem I could solve.

Someone in front of me with a sword, who wanted to kill me.

Her katana was longer, her reach was already a tad longer, and she looked like she hadn't been up since dawn. She had energy and strength to spare while I was already running on half a tank.

Trying to get inside her reach and countering with compound attacks would only work if I could stop her from dark-walking. Her blood jade was also pumping so much energy into her that she was venting qì like a leaky bucket. And there weren't many ways to stop a dark walker.

If I could taunt her to stay engaged with me, I'd have a shot.

I ground the tile beneath my boot. As it snapped I felt the hot rush of Dragon Limbs coursing up my legs. It wouldn't last long but it would give me the little power boost I needed.

My only chance was to keep this fight quick and dirty. My specialty.

I sneered at my cousin. "Are you sure you want to finish? Because you always run away."

"I don't need to run away. You're weak and slow."

I pointed my sword at her and laughed. "Prove it. You want Hachi? Come and get her."

She drew her katana and charged me like an enraged bull. Perfect. I angled my body and sidestepped to parry. The broad side of my sword angled upward, sliding against her blade. Kaida was strong but I got her wrist into an awkward angle. I forced her arms up and met her charge on my hip. Our bodies crashed together but my enhanced legs stayed anchored to the ground like boulders. Kaida bounced off me like a basketball. As she reeled back I lunged forward and stomped down on her foot, the Dragon Limb giving me extra weight. Bones cracked. Kaida shrieked in pain and I slammed a straight left into her neck.

She dropped like a rag doll and I followed her to the ground. When we landed, I pounded her arm into the dirt until she let go of her katana.

Kaida screamed and swung her left arm, the movement wild. I barely got Hachi to block her tanto. The impact rang through my arms, numbing my hands and knocking me back. Hachi dropped from my senseless hands. Kaida bucked off the ground and barreled into me.

Gravity dropped away as Kaida carried the two of us over the lip and into the massive trench in the earth. Sky and ground switched places in nauseating succession. I thudded onto my back, the air exploding from my lungs, and the jade chip flew out of my mouth. Kaida landed on top of me. Her knife sliced through the top of my shoulder and buried itself in the dirt just inches from my head.

I shut out the pain and kicked, planting my foot in Kaida's stomach. With the dregs of my Dragon Limbs I shot my leg out and launched my cousin into the air. Her scream cut off with a sound like a massive tree limb snapping in half.

I stood, my feet squelching into the mud, my limbs heavy with pain and fatigue. My left arm was growing cold, and what felt like a river of blood coursed from my shoulder, dripping off my fingertips. The burst of Dragon Limbs was already gone. I needed to end this now.

Kaida lay sprawled in the mud ten feet away, her right arm pinned under her body at a grotesque angle. Her chest rose and fell in a staccato rhythm, her breath coming in shallow pants. She groaned, the sound morphing into a scream as she wrenched her body upright, her right arm dangling dead from the shoulder socket.

"Kaida—"

Rot, decay, and ginger flooded the trench as Kaida drew on her blood jade. Red veins crawled up her neck and scarlet tears dripped from her eyes. Kaida smiled, her teeth broken and bloody, and she fell into the shadows.

Fire and ash! I spun, realizing too late that the bottom of the trench was swamped in shadow. I turned and ran. My only chance was to run to the end of the trench and get out of the shadows.

Ginger and rot bloomed to my right and Kaida's fist connected with my jaw. Light exploded across my vision and I went down in a heap. I rolled and came up woozy, to find nothing near me. A spinning kick melted out of the shadows directly in front of my nose. My head snapped back and I blacked out.

My eyes popped open. How long had I been out? Maybe seconds. I was lying in the mud, staring up at the night sky. The judges' citadel floated serenely above the field on thick clouds, fine streamers of mist trailing away in a light breeze. The citadel glowed with warm golden light, lit from within the clouds. Were the judges staying to watch me die?

As I struggled to get up, the scent of Kaida's talent swamped me again. This time when she emerged I grabbed onto her and hauled back, pulling her out of the darkness. Kaida screamed, her fingers raking at me.

I let her do it, leaving myself open as she leaned in to strike. My right hand came up and brushed the side of her cheek. If she hadn't been so focused on pounding my face she might have noticed. Kaida landed one punch on my jaw, lighting up my vision with stars again, just as I grabbed the blood jade crane dangling from her left ear and ripped it out.

Now I had her anchor.

A dark walker was lost without their anchor.

Kaida screamed incoherently, clutching at her head. For all the qì she had, without her anchor, a twin to the anchor my mother used, she wouldn't be able to use her talent.

She settled for raining blows down on my head. Dazed from the hit to my jaw, I went down and Kaida rode me into the mud. I got my arms up as best I could, trying to curl into as small a target as possible.

I knew now I couldn't stop her unless I killed her. As Kaida raged above me I cursed myself, my mother, my father, my Hoard Gift, and the cursed path of my life. I'd had few choices. But I could make this choice—I wasn't going to kill my cousin.

The scent of pepper and horseradish filled my nose.

The hunger inside me rose up, as if stretching after a long nap. It went into seeking mode and this was a target-rich environment, filled with a surfeit of gāo-level talent.

I sensed my brother, creeping along the edge of the trench, possibly trying to find a way down.

No! Kaida would kill him!

I opened my eyes and forced my arms up, grabbing Kaida's wrists. She jerked back but I hung on with the force of desperation. I dug my fingertips into the soft flesh of her wrists, drawing blood as I searched for her meridians. I wouldn't kill her, but this would be so much worse for both of us.

The hundreds of eyes surrounding me were a sudden weight on me. But they didn't matter. Only Tacchan mattered.

Kaida screamed, the sound hoarse and primal, blood jade madness driving her mind over the edge. My talent strained like a rabid dog on the end of a chain.

I let it loose.

My qì cycled through my meridians, lighting up my body like a neon sign. Every wound sang with pain, sharp as broken glass. My aura burst free like a spotlight and my talent leapt forward, my back arching off the dirt. An inhuman scream tore from my throat. In a small corner of my mind, I saw a pair of fox ears peek over the edge of the judges' citadel, followed by an ornate, golden horn next to them.

And then my talent, the endless hunger, burrowed into Kaida, sharp teeth sinking into soft underbelly. I kept my eyes open. I would not shy away from this. My cousin screamed again, but my talent gorged, devouring it all—her talent, her qì, and the blood jade energy.

All around me, more talents flared to life. No surprise, really, to see people baring their weapons when confronted with a monster like me. My talent wavered, distracted by the presence of so many rich talents.

No!

I pushed through until I found my talent inside me and forced my will over it. It was like wrestling an alligator, a wild animal unleashed after years of imprisonment. Slowly, I pulled my talent away from the stadium and refocused on Kaida. It sank back into my cousin and fed, stealing my cousin's talent and feeding it back to me.

Like Iron Serpent, I was a thief beyond imagination.

Kaida's energy flowed through my hands, her skin hot enough to burn my palms, and filled me to bursting. My skin felt as if it would split and light would explode from my body. My hair stood on end and tingled with electricity. Sparks crackled along my arms and a tiny stain of darkness formed between my hands.

Kaida's scream faded and her eyes fluttered shut. She slumped, only my arms holding her up now. The hunger kept going, it wanted more—everything it could take.

At the top of the trench, Tatsuya's face appeared. He held the wing bone clutched in one hand, his eyes wide and staring.

I struggled to contain the energy and hold down the hunger. I mentally willed Tatsuya to get back, to get away. I had to do something with the energy my talent had consumed, but it was going to be messy.

I dragged my talent back, reeling it in inch by inch, pulling it away from my cousin. It raged inside me, trying to free itself, shredding at my control. The stolen qì helped. I wrestled it down and squeezed it back into its cage. I grabbed Kaida's limp body and pulled her close to me. I would do my best to protect her.

I cycled my qì, the way Madam Yao had taught me. My chest swelled like the world was about to erupt from within me. I sang three clear notes, my fragment of Dragonsong. Again. Faster. My qì spun through me like a whirlwind. Sudden clarity flashed across my mind. The melody, the notes, my qì, cycling through me, the rhythm of the Dragonsong. Understanding of something glorious tickled at the edges of my comprehension.

My chakras unlocked and the clarity vanished. I lifted my arms and pushed.

I aimed straight up. Any other direction meant blasting into unknown crowds of people. I hoped the judges' citadel had moved away.

The Dragonsong burst forth from me like a bomb, laced with Kaida's dark walker talent. Twisting tendrils of shadow ripped from my arms and converged on a point directly above me. It was like the birth of a dark star. The shadows exploded and howling winds pushed me into the mud.

When the winds cleared I opened my eyes. A dark blot hung motionless in the sky, like an errant smear of paint on a canvas. The edges of the darkness sparkled. The sky beyond was a vibrant purple accented with clusters of bright yellow stars. The floating citadel drifted closer, the Old Ones all gathered at the edge, eyes wide but somehow free from surprise. They looked . . . expectant.

I felt it in my bones before my ears heard it. A vibration of the universe at a level so fundamental that my very atoms responded in kind. The sound built slowly, layers upon layers of delicate creation. When I heard it, tears welled and ran down my cheeks, equal parts joy and terror. The sound was terrifying beauty, the concrete reality of our gods.

For the first time in centuries, true Dragonsong called out to us, the notes ringing high and clear.

A dark shape filled the hole in the sky and then the shape was falling, growing, heading straight for me. The shape twisted, morphed, and resolved into a person that landed heavily in the mud next to me.

My vision narrowed and the rest of the world ceased moving, my stomach clenching into a tiny ball of ice. The woman who'd just appeared out of nowhere wore a neat kimono with impeccable pleats, the creamy fabric spotless and decorated with chrysanthemums painted in delicate watercolors along the hem. A majestic crane in flight soared across her back. Her dark hair was piled neatly into a braided bun at the base of her neck. In classic fashion, despite the fact that she landed so firmly as to leave small craters in the mud, all of the mud splashed on me, as if none of it dared touch her kimono.

She wielded a naginata with a dark blade of chipped stone. Three wooden rings of pale wood rattled at the base of the blade. She held the naginata at high guard, as if expecting an attack from the hole I'd ripped in the sky. Without dropping her blade, she turned to me and dark mirrors of my own eyes stared down at me from beneath dark slashing brows.

"Emi-chan."

My throat closed up, dry and tight. My voice was a whisper. "Mother?"

She nodded, the motion brisk, like my father. Her eyes traveled to the space above my head, to Kaida, and then to our surroundings. "I meant to return sooner. Let me handle the rest."

I blinked. That almost sounded like an apology from my mother. Unheard of.

The qílín landed hard into the mud next to us, its massive hooves splashing mud and dirt everywhere and yet somehow none of it landing on the magnificent beast. Madam Yao sat astride the qílín's back, a pleased expression as she wrinkled her snout. Skies, this was turning into the strangest day of my life.

Madam Yao jumped nimbly off the qílín's back and danced over to us on light feet that barely touched the ground. She stopped next to me and stared straight up at the purple patch of sky, childlike delight on her face.

"I thought I would never see it again."

The qílín blew a dissonant chord and pranced in a happy circle. Madam Yao shot the qílín an exasperated look.

"Yes, yes. It's nice to see home again. Even if it's just for a moment."

I felt very small, huddled in the dirt and mud, beneath these two majestic Old Ones. Was the húlí jīng hinting that she had come over during the Cataclysm?

And my mother. My mother! I was still reeling from the fact that she was even here. Where had she even come from?

Kaida was a dead weight on my chest. I set her gently to the ground and stood on shaky legs. I could just see the stadium over the lip of the trench. Every set of eyes was glued to the open portal. Expressions across the crowd ranged from shock and horror, to wonder and excitement. In the sea of faces, I found A-Yeong and Batuhan, the only two who weren't looking up into the night sky. They both stared at me, A-Yeong's pale white eye spearing me to the mud. Her knuckles blanched white as she crushed her crutch grips.

The Dragonsong grew to a clarion call that pulled at my heart, the sound filling the night sky, blanketing the entire school grounds with thick, ancient power. A sigh floated from the crowd, part relief, part fear. We were descendants of the dragons. Why was there fear?

Madam Yao jumped onto the qílín's back and looked down at my mother. "There's no more time. Come along, Sara."

My mother reached up and the húlí jīng grabbed her hand and vaulted her up to the qílín's broad back, fearless and tall. The two of them stood atop the qílín between the Old One's towering eagle's wings. Madam Yao turned in a circle, her arms out toward the crowd.

"There should be enough, but we will need to work quickly."

My mother stowed her naginata, strapping it across her back. "No choice then. Let's do it."

The qílín took off, sending off a gust of cool night air against my face. I watched in awe as they rose up to the dark gash in the sky. As they pulled away, Madam Yao raised her hands and began a complex series of motions. Subtle, deep power emanated from the fox spirit, an overwhelming force like the permanence of mountains.

Cries and shouts peppered the stadium. Kaida grunted and I looked down to see her blood jade earring studs pulling themselves out of her ear, one by one, leaving bloody holes in her ear. The gems launched into the night sky, chasing after the qílín. The delicate chain of pearls ripped off my neck following Kaida's blood jade.

More cries of dismay and anger and then the sky above the stadium was a glittering net of floating jewels. Rings, necklaces, rare stones and gems, gold, silver, and otherworldly metals, Hoard artifacts stripped from their owners by the gentle magic of an immortal fox.

The scent of several talents flared as Jiārén throughout the crowds strove to regain their treasures.

The húlí jīng smiled gently and waved her hand.

It was like the gods themselves had stamped their feet down and crushed a bug. Every talent in the stadium winked out in an instant, crushed under a will so powerful that it dispersed the qì of a dozen different talents at once.

Broken Tooth. We thought we were so powerful. And this fox spirit had just humbled an entire stadium of Jiārén with barely a thought.

A swirling constellation of jewelry now orbited the qílín who hovered in the air next to the open portal, the fox and my mother perched on its back. The haunting music of the old Dragon gods grew to overpowering volume, pressing me down to my knees. The Dragonsong called to my heart, singing to me to submit.

The whirlwind of Hoard artifacts spun faster until it was nearly a solid wall of metal and gems. Madam Yao and my mother were only visible in brief flashes. My mother raised her arms and the húlí jīng stepped in close behind her. The fox's magic took on the sharp ginger scent of my mother's talent. My mother curled her fingers and reality shook.

The open portal of purple-tinged sky . . . moved.

My jaw dropped open. This . . . this didn't happen. One dark walker couldn't control a portal opened by another. And yet it was happening. The qílín floated to the ground and my mother dragged the portal down with her. I grabbed my cousin and carried her out the far end of the trench.

My mother and Madam Yao dropped off the qílín's back as the portal settled into the earth. The Dragonsong was a deafening roar now, dense waves of power pouring through the portal. The húlí jīng crooked her fingers and the flying Hoard artifacts settled over the portal, blocking the opening.

The fox spirit laid a small hand on my mother's back. "Now, Sara."

Ginger flooded the thick night air. The qílín blew a complex series of notes, ending on a high, shrill whistle. The Hoard artifacts at my mother's feet trembled, the pieces vibrating as if resonating. Gems cracked and splintered into colorful shards. Gold and silver glowed red, then white hot and melted into slag that hung in the air over the portal. The power of uncountable Hoard pieces burst into the night and coalesced around my mother. It was more power than any one Jiārén should be able to handle and still live.

My mother pulled on her talent and the world . . . flexed. A scream tore out of my mother's throat as her power stitched the world together. A blistering wave of heat blew my hair back and the metal and gems fused together into a massive plate set into the earth. Where I had ripped a gash into our reality, my mother and the Old Ones fashioned a Gate from a fortune in Hoard artifacts and the Winner's Pot. The Gate closed with a thump that I felt in my bones, and then flashed, sun bright again. When the light faded the Gate was gone, the trove of priceless Hoard vanished, and all that was left was an indentation in the mud.

Two Old Ones had just closed a portal to the Realm, our ancestral homeland, something no one had seen in over two millennia. And before the portal had been closed, everyone in the stadium had been graced with the sound of actual Dragonsong, proof positive that our Dragon gods, who we had thought killed in the Cataclysm, were still alive.

But none of that seemed to matter tonight because every pair of eyes in the stadium was now trained on me. Despite the wonders we had been witness to tonight, the only thing a stadium full of Jiārén cared about was that my talent had been revealed. One that could steal other talents.

An abomination.

THE EMPTY ONE

With the makeshift Gate in place, the last notes of Dragonsong hovered in the air and faded into silence. Time seemed to hold still for a few heartbeats. My chest collapsed, as if empty, and the hollow sensation remained as if my very soul had flattened. Maybe it was ancestral memory but the brief notes of Dragonsong had pulled me so intensely. The crowd was strangely quiet, too, as if they were experiencing the same emptiness. Well, most of them anyway.

"Abomination!" screamed Chen Li Wei.

It appeared the headmaster was less affected by the Dragonsong and had regained his voice and the wherewithal to target his outrage. To further accentuate his name-calling, he extended one voluminously robed arm and pointed down at me.

His cry echoed throughout the arena. Heads turned.

Madam Yao huffed, her vividly colored tails swishing under the moonlight. She and my mother leapt off the qílín's back and approached us. My mother made for Tatsuya, checking him over for injuries as she whispered to him. The fox immortal floated over to where I knelt and placed a hand on my shoulder, giving me a gentle squeeze.

The qílín flew up and hovered in front of Chen Li Wei. Once they were face-to-face, the qílín stared down the headmaster. "You fail to understand, as usual."

Chen Li Wei drew back in affront but his eyes were wide with alarm. "Impossible. She's a talent thief. Unnatural."

"She is the child of the stars, the Empty One foretold a millennium ago."

The headmaster's voice lowered but I heard the horror in his voice just fine. "Worldbreaker."

Were they talking about me? I found my father in the stands. His face remained impassive as ever.

It was no coincidence that Father had that poem in his study. He made plans within plans. Surely he had planned for this day when my talent would come to light. In a flash of realization, I knew now what my parents had been talking about with Ogata-sensei. He had understood what my Gift was, and that only my meridian blockages had prevented my Gift from coming to light earlier. My talent was so rare that my father would have easily tracked down this prophecy.

It took some effort but I turned to face my mother who stood near Tatsuya, her slender hand on his shoulder. Despite the frenzied manner in which she and the qílín had worked to craft the makeshift mending, she looked calm and unruffled. Her kimono remained spotless and her long silky hair was wound into a neat coil low at the nape of her neck. Unlike my father, Mother wasn't quite as good at keeping the emotion off her face. Her stricken expression told me everything I wanted to know. She knew exactly what the qílín was talking about.

A collective gasp went up from the crowd. The floating citadel descended and before it landed, a massive tiger leapt out, Kamon's stripes glistening under the light of the lanterns.

My breath caught and for a moment, I just admired him in this form, a powerful beast that tore through the stands and jumped over the railings to run toward me.

Madam Yao let out a chuff of amusement as Kamon prowled toward us. When a six-hundred-pound beast looks at you, even when you know they aren't intending to eat you, there's an atavistic moment of fear. My hindbrain screamed, *Run.* My heart swelled and reminded me that this was Kamon. He nudged my side and the warmth of his body began to soothe the hurt and the chill in my bones.

Kaida let out a low groan and moved restlessly. I hadn't killed her. I might be an abomination but at least I wasn't an oathbreaker.

There was a flurry of movement in the stands. Batuhan and Ariq appeared at the front of their entourage. Golden light emanated from Batuhan, and I wanted so badly to go stand in his presence and have it heal my wounds. Instead I bent over and focused on the sting in my lungs and the myriad sharp pains across my body. This was familiar. This was real. I knew how to handle physical pain.

The turmoil inside, the shame I felt for revealing my talent to all and sundry. Those, I had no idea what to do about. The adrenaline that fueled me earlier was gone and I shivered in the chill of the night.

The weight of Kamon's massive head butted against my waist and I set my hand onto his neck, grateful for his warmth and his support.

Batuhan stood over Kaida now, his talent so vast I could feel it smoothing over my skin and hair like a tidal wave of bliss. My cousin looked up at him, her eyes wide with awe. Tears began streaming down her face, leaving streaks in the dirt on her skin.

He held his palm over her head. "Child. Be at ease."

The black and red streaks on her neck shrunk, and she sobbed harder. Ariq hummed and also held his hand out toward Kaida. The other effects of the blood jade madness began to leave her body and I watched in amazement as father and son worked in tandem to heal her.

I'd never heard of blood jade madness being reversible.

It was an overwhelming display of their talent. The edge of the effect splashed out, reaching me and Tatsuya. My fatigue faded and the gouges and scrapes of my skin sealed fresh and pink as if days old.

My mother's face relaxed and she smoothed a hand over Tatsuya's brow, her relief clear on her expressive face.

Batuhan looked at my mother and in his gaze I saw something that made me deeply uncomfortable. I was used to seeing respect mixed with fear when others looked upon my mother. In his dark eyes I saw admiration and a sort of yearning that signaled a history between them. I didn't want to know what that was about.

I clenched my jaw and looked back down at Kaida.

Her wrenching sobs had ceased. She mopped her eyes with the heels of her palms, flicking away tears in impatient jerks. It was a familiar movement, because I did the same after I cried. She stood up and being side by side with her reminded me anew how similar we must look, and that was only the outside. On the inside we shared family ties and years of grueling tests at Jōkōryūkai. Weapons who broke Second Law when our handlers felt it expedient. We had the same ugly scars on our soul. We were a matched pair and both of us would be exiled after this. My cousin to Mohe, me back to my city. It seemed grossly unfair to her.

The blood jade that had made her crazed was gone now. Without that influence, would her eyes still be filled with hate when she looked at me?

So far she had yet to look at me.

She reached for Batuhan's hand and pressed her forehead to it.

"Thank you, General," she murmured, her voice low and raspy.

I inhaled sharply. This was the confirmation I had been looking for. But what was I supposed to do about it now?

My mother took Kaida's hand and gently took it off Batuhan's. The big man took a step back and my mother moved into the space, standing between him, me, and my cousin. Mother was a full head shorter than Batuhan but stood as tall and proud as he did. The naginata at her back helped.

"They are my responsibility now."

When my mother spoke, people listened. There were few foolish or daring enough to cross the Walker of the Void. Batuhan hesitated for a beat, then bowed his head in acquiescence. He pivoted his son's wheelchair and turned to leave, and his entourage followed him out.

I searched the stands for Fiona. With her sparkling silver tiara, she stood out. She was very pointedly not making eye contact with me—instead her gaze was fixed on the massive tiger leaning against me. She couldn't be happy to see her new beau leap out of a flying citadel and charge toward the side of his ex. My heart kicked a bit, a response that I couldn't help. I knew I had no claim here, but he was the one person in my life who knew about the Talon my mother had traded to the shinigami, and what that had cost me. It soothed some of the ragged wound in my heart that he was here at my side.

I wanted to tell Fiona that it was okay, that I didn't have designs on him, that I was just grateful for his years of friendship. She was my friend and I owed her that. But as it turned out, I didn't get to do any of that because Chen Li Wei decided then that he'd had enough of me.

The headmaster's nostrils flared and his forehead shone with stress sweat. I bet he remembered exactly why he'd expelled me in the first place. He pointed his finger at me again, shaking with fury, his voice high and shrill. "You will never have a place at Lóng Kǒu!"

He brought his arm down in a slicing motion and my world turned black. I stumbled backward, expecting to bump into either Kaida or Kamon, and when I met no resistance, I fell on my butt. The inky darkness faded away. The golden light of dawn broke over the horizon behind me and lit up the exterior of the East Gate with its sinuous Azure Dragon. The Gate was closed. I lay back on the soft grass and studied the early morning skies.

Being banished not once but twice from Lóng Kǒu had to be some sort of record.

I should have moved, but I was exhausted. The soft grass was like a luxurious mattress and sleep pulled at me. My family would be out soon and we could go back home. My brother was safe for now. Father would move heaven and earth to protect his heir. I would let him strategize about what to do about the General. It was what he was best at.

I had done what I was best at so my role was concluded.

Even my mother was home, for once. How would I ask her about Kaida? I imagined that after my ignominious exit someone would shackle Kaida. The silver circlet they'd lock around her neck would prevent her from accessing her talent while the Bā Tóu decided her fate.

While my father decided. Would my father punish the niece who'd tried to kill his son and daughter?

At least she was alive. I hadn't killed her. I'd kept my vow.

And I'd done it by giving the most powerful Jiārén a front-row seat to the debut of my awful Hoard Gift.

Talent thief.

Worldbreaker.

Abomination.

I closed my eyes, fatigue washing over me. I wanted to sink beneath the ground and avoid dealing with all of it. When I'd broken Truth and run away from my clan and Kamon, I'd thought nothing could feel worse. But I'd failed to account for the fact that back then I'd had hope for forging a different life for myself. One that didn't involve being the Butcher.

What did I have now?

I wrapped a hand around Bāo's pendant. The hard, familiar ridges of the jade cut into the flesh of my palm as I squeezed. Why hadn't I summoned Bāo earlier when I'd been in dire combat with Kaida?

Bāo's massive jaws could have made mincemeat of Kaida, giving her two opponents to deal with. Her dark-walking couldn't solve for both of us.

I let go of my pendant, unclenching my fist. It was my talent. The hunger had arisen deep within me, impossible to deny. I hadn't summoned Bāo because my talent had risen to the fore, taking over my thoughts. It wanted me to drink Kaida down and I had.

This was why the headmaster had kicked me out again. I wasn't safe to be around.

Would I be able to control my talent next time?

A breeze rippled across my face and I opened my eyes. A large figure stood over me, silhouetted in the moonlight. A qílín, with a cheerful húlí jīng astride its back.

"Aren't you tired of lying in the dirt?"

I pushed myself up to sitting. "I'm just tired."

Madam Yao tsked. "We'll get you home."

The qílín yawned, its enormous teeth gleaming in the moonlight.

"Yes, yes. We are all tired. Emiko will need her rest, too, for what is to come." Madame Yao gestured for me to join them.

That didn't sound ominous at all. I stood up and scrubbed my hands on my pants. My clothes were stiff and grimy.

Like my mother had done earlier, I vaulted onto the qílín's back. Unlike my mother, I rode astride and hugged Madam Yao, holding on for dear life. I had survived a blood jade–powered dark walker today. Surely I could make it home without falling to my death.

Madam Yao patted my shoulder and handed me a smooth white object the size of my hand. I realized as I gripped it that it was a tooth. More specifically a fang. My night kept getting stranger. "What's this for?"

"When the time comes, you may use the Lóng Yá to call upon us."

"How does it work?"

Madam Yao hummed a string of notes and placed her paw on the fang. It glowed softly blue before dimming. I ran my thumb over the fang and it seemed to vibrate softly in response. Old glyphs I didn't recognize were carved along its length. This was a treasure beyond what Jiārén could imagine. A dragon fang imbued with Dragonsong that could reach a húlí jīng. I had done nothing to earn a gift of such magnitude.

I bent my head low. "Thank you."

I only hoped I would prove worthy of the gift.

RETURN TO SF

Click-clack, click-clack, click-clack. The rhythmic sound of wooden shingles pulled me from a dreamless sleep. I opened my eyes to the vaulted ceiling of our family's Hoard room, the intricate scrollwork of the buttresses lit by smokeless braziers set around the walls. A dozen polished singing bowls sat in a wide circle around me and Tatsuya. My brother lay on his back, one arm up over his face shielding his eyes, his chest still rising and falling in a steady rhythm. Sugi lay atop my brother's chest, its beady black eyes staring at me as I slept.

I stared back for a moment before realizing I wasn't going to win a staring contest with an animated construct that never needed to blink. I sat up slowly and reveled in the fact that while I had taken a beating the day before, I actually felt pretty good. My body ached, but it was the good ache born of hard work. I'd fallen asleep on my own hard floors back in San Francisco enough times that sleeping on the gold-veined marble here was a piece of cake.

The wooden wolf tilted its sleek head, watching me. With the animates, I never knew, were they watching me or was it Father? Straightening my back, I breathed deep and tried to ignore the wooden wolf still staring at me as I cycled my qì. The new pattern was already becoming habit, feeling more natural with practice. I considered what Madam Yao had said, about the flow of qì being like electricity, and as I cycled, I reached out to the Hoard pieces in the room. One by one, the pieces lit up in response to my qì, like magnets attracted to each other.

Tatsuya was still asleep, his long lashes dark against his pale skin. He had crashed hard after we'd gotten home. No doubt Uncle Jake would attempt to force-feed the kid significant volumes of jook and bone broth. Uncle Lau would take the other approach and insist on lots of activity.

I wouldn't be here to see any of that.

Though this was my family, this wasn't truly my home anymore. San Francisco was waiting for me. I felt the city call me, its lonely echo reverberating throughout my chest. Maybe I was imagining it but whenever I put my hand on the Pearl, the city's call rang with a clarion quality.

It was time to go home.

What would it be like to step back into the boundaries of my city, now that I'd come into my full flush of my talent? Would it war inside me like two endless factions and drive me insane like it had with Tokyo's Sentinel? I'd survived so much, I told myself that I could figure it out. I would have to—my city needed me.

I poked Tatsuya's cheek with one finger. His nose twitched and his hand rose up to swat at his cheek. I pulled away before he touched me and poked him again.

"Mmmgh. Stop it."

I poked him again, this time on the other cheek. I didn't know when I would get to see him again, so I had to get my licks in now.

"Wake up, sleepyhead. You're all charged up and ready to go. Another glorious day."

Tatsuya cracked one eye open and glared at me. "Why are you in such a good mood?"

"I thwarted a plan to kill my brother and outed myself and my talent to all of the most powerful Jiārén we know. Anyone who might have been thinking to take a swipe at us is probably thinking twice now. I call that a win."

I actually hadn't considered it that way until the words came out of my mouth, but I remembered the fear I'd commanded as Blade. A little fear wasn't a bad thing.

Tatsuya stretched and tucked his arms under his head. He looked thoughtful, and much older than he had only a few days ago.

"Are you upset about not winning?"

"Hm? Oh, no. At least, I don't think so. I'm just . . ." His voice trailed off.

"Minjae?"

His eyes turned sad. "Yeah. Minjae. I know what Father wanted me to do, why he gave me the dízi and the Dragonsong, but . . . I couldn't bring myself to do it."

Freddy had warned me about this, about Lóng Yá tearing friends apart.

I put my hand on my brother's shoulder and squeezed. "You might have lost your friend for a little while. But you didn't lose yourself, and that's more important."

He turned to me, disbelief on his face. "When did you become so philosophical?"

"A Sentinel is wise beyond her years, young dragon."

We held it together for a few seconds before bursting into laughter.

Tatsuya's stomach growled. "Hey, is it time for breakfast yet?"

True to form, Tatsuya was digging into thirds when I gave up. Apparently even near-death was not enough to increase my capacity to put away Uncle Jake's famous jook with preserved fish and thousand-year-old eggs.

Nami led a small group of Iron Fists into the kitchen as I dropped my spoon into my bowl. All of them sported either bandages or newly pink scars, remnants of the chaos in the aftermath of the final round of the Tourney. Apparently things had gotten quite heated after the Old Ones had divested so many Jiārén of their Hoard gems.

The Iron Fists filtered in quietly and my hackles went up as I noticed a lot of jumpy eyes and twitching hands. Nami only had eyes for my brother, though, and I recognized the moment when she released the tension she'd been holding. The relief of seeing someone safe and sound, the one you've been tasked to protect. My estimation of her went up a notch.

Nami came to a stop several steps away from me. The Iron Fists arranged themselves in tight formation behind their leader. Nami brought her hands together at chest level and gave me a stiff bow. Her eyes did not leave me. "Sumimasen, Soong-san, the Iron Fists are in your debt. You kept Tatsuya safe."

Behind her the Iron Fists bowed. To a man they all kept their eyes on me.

This was a marked improvement from before, but the stiff formality and borderline hostile looks were not lost on me. "He's my brother."

Nami rose from her bow and her subordinates followed. "Of course. I did not mean—"

"Just say what you want to say, Nami." The tension was a palpable itch on my skin now, and even Uncle Jake and Lulu Āyí had gone silent. If Nami kept dancing around it like this I was more than likely to punch her.

A crease formed between Nami's eyebrows and she took half a second before finding her words. "We hope you have enjoyed your visit to Japan, Soong-san."

Nami spun on her heel and marched out of the kitchen, the Iron Fists trailing behind her. Tatsuya's eyes were wide with surprise, but there was only sadness in Jake's and Lulu's eyes. The same sadness cut through my heart more surely than any blade. I was Soong, but this was no longer my home. It had started when I had broken Truth, and was complete now that my talent had been exposed.

No one wanted a thief in their home.

The kitchen, once warm, homey, and inviting, was suddenly hot, cramped, and suffocating. I made apologies to Uncle Jake and Lulu Āyí and left.

As I made my way across the house to Father's office I nearly ran into my mother as she closed the polished redwood door that led to her suite of rooms. Two bags of weathered leather sat on the floor at her feet and the stone-bladed naginata leaned against the wall. She closed and locked the door behind her, tucking an ornate copper key into her robes. With a whisper of power she sealed the door with her talent as well. Even if there was a copy of the key, no one was getting into those rooms now.

The sight of her packed bags raised my hackles. "Leaving already?"

I tried for cool and disinterested, but it came out as bitter and angry.

My mother smoothed her hands down the front of her kimono. Today her garment was made for traveling, ivory leather lined with thick fleece. The fabric nearly hummed with power as well and I caught a glimpse of gold cranes stitched onto the lapels. I knew from experience that the thick belt around her waist held several hidden pockets, sure to be stocked with useful herbs and elixirs.

And knives. Always knives.

She reached for me and I nearly flinched. Her fingers touched the shorn edges of my hair, her eyes sad. She traced the white stripe in my hair and a small smile tugged at her lips. Her hand was cool on my cheek as she brushed a stray lock of hair behind my ear. I set my jaw and stared at her, holding her dark eyes—my eyes—refusing to drop my gaze. I hadn't seen her for two years but she didn't look like she'd aged a day. And now she was leaving again, with no explanation, not even any concern for my brother.

She said nothing about my golden aura. Was she proud of me that I was the Sentinel of San Francisco? Had I finally met her high standards?

The blockages that stunted my talent were gone now. Would she comment on that?

"You may find it easier to walk alone now."

My lips tightened. This was bitter comedy. "Did I ever have a choice?"

Her eyes searched mine. "I would have spared you this. I tried. But your steps have brought you back to being the Empty One."

I swallowed hard. That cursed poem.

"When did you know?"

"When your talent truly awoke and you nearly drained your father to death." She looked away, her eyes blinking rapidly. "I was willing to pay anything to save you both."

And she had. Trading a Talon to a death god that nearly cost my immortal soul to redeem.

"The shinigami brought you both back to me, and blocked your meridians."

Her eyes shone with unshed tears. "Between the two, I felt it was the lesser curse for you to bear."

"All these years. You and Father never told me." My voice trembled.

"No. That fault is mine alone."

"Father—"

She shook her head. "Your father almost died as well. When you both awoke, I had already used my Talon. He didn't know, but he pieced it together, years later when you were expelled from Lóng Kǒu."

Mother took my hands in hers. "He has only ever worked to make you strong."

Her voice went soft. "He was so much better with you. Always teaching." She looked away, eyes too bright. "Sometimes I couldn't bear it. I didn't know what to do for you."

And she'd dropped me at Jōkōryūkai's doorstep. "How could you give Kaida to the Association?"

As if giving me to them was somehow more palatable.

Mother's eyes hardened and her voice shook with emotion. "Ogata-sensei had to order your death if he was to save face. I was not going to lose you, not after all the sacrifices I'd made to save you. Kaida was an . . . inelegant solution. But I had to decide quickly, and I don't share your father's gift for foresight."

She shook her head. "I thought it would buy us some time to extricate her, but Kaida was a natural. Ogata-sensei forbade me to interrupt her training."

Bitterness rose within me until it was a sour taste in the back of my mouth. "Why bother? You were nearly rid of me."

She grabbed my arm, her grip strong as steel. "You are my daughter, Emi-chan. Your father has your brother to continue his line, but you will always be mine."

I gaped at my mother's sudden outburst of emotion.

Mother strokes her hand over my long, dark hair, and brushes it carefully with the sandalwood comb. I lean back and take comfort in the sleepy warmth of her body.

Tears fell from my eyes and I could only nod, mutely. I bowed my head and slowed my breathing. Mother leaned forward until our foreheads touched.

"Your path was fated to be difficult. I did what I did to prepare you, if I could not be there for you."

She leaned back until we were eye to eye again and her voice was fierce. "But never doubt, Emi-chan, that I would tear down the heavens for you."

And she had, in a way, just last night. Between this and Father's approval at the gala, my childhood memories and feelings were being recast. I knuckled away the tears. "What's going to happen to Kaida?"

"Returning her to the Association would be her death. Mohe at least will not kill her."

No, only make her wish she were dead. Sadness weighed on me. I hadn't really saved her. Just condemned her to more pain.

My mother bent to her bags and unzipped the larger one. "I want you to have this."

She pulled out a long, narrow package wrapped in soft leather. As she stood she unwrapped it and my heart stopped.

A lacquered black scabbard emerged, the wood polished to a high shine, a crane in flight etched along its length. The tsuba was inlaid with blood jade, carved into another phoenix, matching the shorter sword at my hip. I had last seen it in the dirt after I'd beat it out of Kaida's hand.

My mother presented the katana to me with both hands.

"Her name is Shokaku and she has been apart from Hachi for too long."

She must have seen the question on my face. "You already had Truth, but I still wanted to give you something to protect you. Both of you."

Her face turned sad again. "I do not know where Kaida's path will take her but I think Shokaku is better served in your hands now." Her eyes flicked to my shoulder. "You do need a new sword, do you not?"

My hand came up, almost an involuntary reflex, before I stilled it, my palm inches from the smooth wood.

Mother nudged the sword toward me. "Take it, Emi-chan. Your path grows darker every day. I will feel better knowing you have both swords protecting you."

She was right. I'd had a sense of how things had changed, but hearing my mother say it out loud crystalized it into reality.

"I can't stay here."

Heartbreak etched across her face. "No. Our talents are too dangerous. Spending too much time here makes the rest of the clan uneasy. I decided long ago that it was better for me to stay away."

I'd just come back home, specifically to support my brother. "I would rather stand by my family."

Her face grew sad. "For us, that's too much to ask."

Of course, she knew what she spoke of. If I was going to take advice from anyone, it should be from her, a woman with a talent that was both powerful and reviled.

It felt like breaking Truth all over again, as I wrapped my hand around Shokaku's scabbard. A roaring sound filled my ears when my mother let go of the sword as if I'd crossed a rushing river, with no way of returning.

The hug surprised me. One moment the sword was between us, like a wall, and the next it was pushed aside as Mother pulled me into a tight embrace. I froze, unsure of what to do. Her arms squeezed me, desperately tight. My arms slowly folded around her and I plunged into a sudden sense memory of myself as a young girl, buried in Mother's arms and the warm folds of her kimono. I tightened my grip, to draw out the moment and embed this feeling into my body, to stamp it indelibly into my memory.

She whispered in my ear. "Take care of yourself."

"I will."

She released me and took a step back, taking hold of her naginata and her bags. Her eyes shone with unnatural brightness. Then darkness spilled out of the bottom of her kimono like ink. In the next moment the darkness swarmed over her and she vanished. I wrapped my arms around myself and cradled Mother's warmth to my chest until it was gone.

Before I left, I needed to learn whatever I could about my talent. Jiārén spent their childhood years learning in a controlled environment. I wouldn't have that luxury.

Finding my father proved to be difficult. His office was empty, the animates quiet and dark. I found Kubota-san taking the Pearl Guard through their morning routine, but he didn't know where my father was, either. After a little longer I just gave up and headed back to my room. I needed to pack. I was sure to find him before I left.

Of course, he was in my room.

My bags were laid out on the floor, and my laundry had been neatly folded and organized into piles on the bed. My father sat in the chair by the window, watching the Pearl Guard, his hand absently patting the jade monkey in his lap. Sugi lay over his feet, apparently asleep. Did a wooden wolf even need sleep?

Between his silence and the hug from my mother, my emotions

boiled inside me. I began throwing my clothes into my bag. The sooner I was back in my city, the better.

"You knew." It wasn't a question anymore.

He seemed to take some offense at my statement. "I am your father, Mimi. It is my responsibility to know."

A knot of frustration welled in my throat and threatened to either choke me or make me scream. "Why?"

"Why were you gifted as such? Or why did I not tell you?"

"All those years, teaching me. You never once thought to tell me!"

"Why would I?"

My voice was ragged. "I don't know! Maybe it would have given me some hope."

Father stood and put his hand on my arm. He didn't speak until I raised my eyes to his.

"Hope is deceptive. It will lead to despair, and I would not let you go down that road. Hope is for the weak. I do not hope, I plan. I could not know if or when your talent would grow. I could only give you the training and the skills you would need, regardless of the outcome."

It was always like this with him. He was always right, and he always won.

My anger deflated. "Mother said I can't stay. So I can't even protect Tacchan, when we know Batuhan is still coming for him."

His mouth quirked up at the corner. "I think Batuhan will find his priorities rapidly reorganizing themselves in the near future."

He raised his hand and the jade monkey jumped out of the chair and climbed up his body. In a pouch over its stomach was a silver scroll case. The same one he'd had the day I arrived. My father opened it and presented it to me.

"Your star chart. Written at your birth."

I took it from him, confused. "I don't know how to read it."

My father's lips twitched. "Then learn."

He stood and the monkey clambered up his chest to sit on his shoulders. Sugi roused and click-clacked over to the door before turning back to stare at us.

"We knew your path would not be easy, but a life of purpose seldom is. You have always risen to the task at hand and exceeded my expectations. I expect no less from you now."

With that my father walked to the door. He opened the door and turned back. "It was . . . good to have you home again."

He left and closed the door behind him. And that was all the explanation I was ever going to get from him.

I decided to fly home on a private charter and avoid further interaction with Jiārén at this point. I couldn't handle the way they'd all looked at me in the arena. If I had thought it was bad before when I was the Butcher, I had lacked imagination.

Cleaning my room and packing to return to San Francisco should have given me some sense of pleasure and anticipation. San Francisco was my home now and I loved it. But as I swept the remaining piddly amounts of Kit Kats into my tote, I felt only exhaustion. And dread.

I didn't know what kind of welcome I would receive back on Lotus Lane.

With a heavy heart, I said goodbye to Uncle Jake and Lulu Āyí. There were hugs and tears and bags of dried fruit stuffed into my tote. Uncle Jake handed me a lunch sack for the plane. It made me feel about five years old and headed off to a picnic. I went out to the courtyard where workers were installing new píxiū statues. Uncle Lau bounded high in the air, issuing drills to his troops.

I waved goodbye. With Uncle Lau, there were no tears and hugs, just one tip of the head from him. He was a soldier—he understood when an assignment was over.

And then it was just Fujita-san driving me to the airport. We passed the ride in silence, as was our way. Much of my life, he had been there, offering his quiet support. He wasn't my parent but he'd always done his best to make me feel at home. I owed him so much. But he was privy to most of our clan secrets so I finally had to ask.

"Did you know about my talent?"

He kept his eyes on the road, his fingers loosely gripped on the steering wheel.

After a long pause, he nodded. "When you were very young, we thought you were an animator like your father. You were always with him, and you would animate the carvings and name them. You played with them and they were so vibrant and alive. We thought you would surpass even your father in your animation skill."

I didn't remember any of that. I must have been very young indeed.

His voice grew softer. "Later we realized the reason your talent behaved like animation talent was because you spent so much time with your father. After the incident that brought Bāo to you, we finally understood."

This meant everyone in clanhome had to know. Uncle Jake, Lulu Āyí, and Uncle Lau. Yet they'd never leaked a word of it. A secret of such enormity hidden by a conspiracy of silence. And perhaps love.

My throat tightened, overwhelmed with emotion.

"Thank you."

He parked the car and we were silent, neither of us anxious for me to fly back to San Francisco. Finally I reached for the door handle and pushed the door open. Fujita-san beat me to the trunk and pulled out my duffel. Then he handed me the beautiful pink trench he'd set out for me the day of Tatsuya's Lóng Yá events. It was pristine. I put it on, enjoying the fit and running my hands over the many pockets.

He pulled out a square package wrapped in furoshiki cloth. "For you. Open it when you arrive in San Francisco."

Tears stung the backs of my eyes. I blinked hard and pulled him in tight for a hug. "Thank you for everything."

THE ARCHIVE

My house was still standing when my rideshare dropped me off after midnight. A quick inspection of the perimeter told me my security system was not only intact, but also had been undisturbed during my absence. Perhaps the carpet of jet-black crows blanketing my front lawn had something to do with that as well. The birds turned as one to greet me as I stepped out of the car, hundreds of black eyes glittering with silvery moonlight. I turned to thank the driver and was nearly knocked back as he drove away even before the door had shut.

Now that I was back in my city, my senses had reawakened. With my repaired meridians, the well of power that rested below me felt like an overcharged battery ready to burst. Popo would have a fit the next time she saw me. I waved a hand and the crows took wing, buffeting me with air as they left in droves. In moments they were gone, wheeling into the night sky. One remained perched on the roof of the front house, keeping watch. Well, there was nothing wrong with more security. And maybe they missed me.

On my desk in the front house, I found a tidy pile of mail. Tessa had the code to the front door and she had brought in my mail. Knowing her, she probably had attended to our business bills, too. I spread the mail out, fanning it across my desk. Mostly junk. But one very impressive square envelope stood out from the rest, its deckled edges classy yet rustic. My name and address were carefully penned in a calligrapher's hand. A wedding? It was postmarked before I'd left for Tokyo.

I grabbed a knife from inside the desk drawer and, with a flick, sliced open the heavy paper.

You are cordially invited to the Tien Pacific Museum event . . .

I ran my finger over the embossed wording of the invitation. Tessa's museum. Adam's exhibit.

I didn't know how I would face him. I didn't see any way of backing out of Tessa's big night. What a mess. I turned the beautiful paper over. Bold slashing script sprawled across the back. *Emiko, we should talk. Yours, Adam.*

Skies. I wasn't ready for this. I dropped the invitation back on the table like it was a burning hot coal. I had no idea how I would handle seeing Adam. And it was inevitable I would see him, whether at the gym or at the museum. Even if I gave up the museum gig, I couldn't get away from him. I had responsibilities to him both as a clan member and as the Sentinel. I didn't regret what happened to Crimson Cloud Splitter, but I couldn't see a way forward with Adam, not right now.

I locked up the front house and made my way through the garden to my cottage. The night air cooled my hot cheeks. The sound of the running water and the clean scents of my wards soothed me. Once in my refuge, I crashed on my bed in the back house and stared at the ceiling. I'd only been gone for five days and yet it felt like months had passed.

My body was tired and achy from the ten-hour flight, but my mind was wide awake and racing, still on Tokyo time. I got up and began unpacking, not out of any urgent need, but to give my restless limbs something to do.

Halfway into one of my bags, I remembered Fujita-san's gift. The cloth wrapping was beautiful, the pattern of gnarled black branches and pale pink chrysanthemums spread across the cotton furoshiki. I let a small kunai blade fall into my palm from my sleeve and used the sharp edge to slice through the one piece of clear tape I found on the back of the box.

With the tape split, the package opened like a flower, revealing several pink and green bags inside. Sakura and green apple Kit Kats. A handwritten note with Fujita-san's careful kanji lay atop the little mountain of chocolates.

Emi-chan,

Although you make your home elsewhere now, it was wonderful having you back, even for a short time. I know these are your favorite and I hope they remind you of everyone who misses you. Your father may not say it, but he is very proud of you. We are all very proud of you.

I dug the heels of my palms into my eye sockets, trying to press back more tears. The house was suddenly too close, too stuffy, the walls looming over me. I quickly changed and tied Shokaku and Hachi to my waist. The extra weight was a comfort. I needed something to do. I knew where I needed to go.

It was too late at night to find a reasonable rideshare so I just ran the two and a half miles to the central library. As I ran through Dogpatch and into SoMa, the city's nightlife seemed to follow my progress. Shining eyes watched me from dark alleys. Dark wings flapped above me. I even caught the yips of a scrawny coyote who padded along with me for a few blocks before shying away from the bright streetlights of SoMa.

I cycled my qì as I ran, thinking about what I was about to do. Or rather, trying not to think about it. The closer I got, the more right it felt. I'd been trying too hard last time. It was more about the feeling, and less about the doing.

The library was, of course, closed. I ran across the front of the building and its concrete facade and into the plaza between the library and the Asian Art Museum. The energy of San Francisco hummed all around me like a rushing river. The spot I was looking for was a shining stone in the river that called out to me like a song.

I found it at the base of the Pioneer Monument between the two buildings. On the east side of the base of the statue, a small bas-relief carving in the pale stone. I traced my fingers over the figure, a majestic bird in flight, flowing wings outstretched and a glorious tail of many feathers. A phoenix.

I pressed my hand against the phoenix and cycled my qì in the pattern the húlí jīng had shown me, feeding my energy into the city. The carving glowed with soft golden light and the base of the statue shimmered. I stepped forward and descended into the darkness.

As I walked in the darkness a small light appeared before me, a dull orange glow that brightened and dimmed. I smelled the tobacco before I saw her.

Gu Ma sat in a battered lawn chair, a crooked cigarette between her lips and a dog-eared book of sudoku puzzles in her lap. She had a pencil in her hand and one more behind her ear. Another pencil pinned her gray hair up in a bun at the base of her neck.

She looked up as I approached, her eyes squinting into the dark. "Not nice to just walk in unannounced through the back door."

I stopped in my tracks. My little stunt in Tokyo had really peeved her.

Gu Ma blew out a long trail of smoke and looked me up and down. She pointed a stubby finger at me. "Had a bit of adventure, didn't you? What did you cut your hair for?"

I ran my hand through my hair, suddenly self-conscious. "Uhh—"

Gu Ma laughed, an abrupt, hacking sound, and waved me off. "Ha! It's okay. I don't care what you do with your hair."

She quieted and became serious. "You have to open it, girl. Or I will end you."

The way she said it wasn't a threat. It was a simple statement of fact. She looked a little sad as she said it.

Light burst forth from the rough-hewn walls of the tunnel, illuminating the circular mosaic door and the labyrinth carving on the floor. Behind that door was untold forgotten knowledge. Answers to questions I hadn't even known existed a few days ago. Why were the Dragon gods still alive? How had I opened a portal to the Realm? Where had the Gate gone, after Mother had closed it? What was the prophecy the húlí jīng had spoken of?

I had to open the door. I needed to open that door.

The thing I had realized, was that this was *my* door. I was the Sentinel of San Francisco. The door wasn't *closed* to me. It would only open *for* me.

I spun my qì through my meridians and drank in the power of my city. My veins filled with fog off the ocean, tinged with sea salt and drenching my city in its mist. Crystal cool power filled my body as I drew on the wellspring of power at my feet. I pulled it toward me, bending it to my will. The city's power merged with my repaired meridians and settled over my shoulders like a favorite coat.

The mosaic on the wall shifted, the pieces flowing through the rock. With each passing second I saw a new pattern in the gray and blue stones. Faces, trees, the rushing ocean, a crow's wing, the setting sun.

I pushed the pieces into place, finding the pattern that felt the most natural, the most right. Wings outstretched, head high and triumphant, flowing tail feathers snapping in the wind. The phoenix.

The door flashed brilliant blue and white and cracked open. I released the power inside me and stepped forward to open the door.

Behind me, Gu Ma chuckled. "Not bad for someone so young."

She folded up her chair, tucked it under her arm, and walked away, into the darkness. "He's waiting for you. Don't dally."

Oda sat at a small reading table a few rows in from the outer wall. A desk lamp cast a warm pool of light around the table. His gigantic naginata leaned against one of the bookshelves, and Crimson Cloud Splitter was strapped across his back. He wore a pair of reading glasses perched on the end of his nose.

A leather-bound book with yellowed pages lay open on the table, the pages densely packed with kanji.

Tokyo's Sentinel looked up as I approached, and he smiled. His eyes were clear and bright, the hollows gone from beneath them. In fact, he looked like he'd had a restful vacation since the last time I'd seen him. I released the tension I'd been holding. Crimson Cloud Splitter was with the right Custodian. I didn't like the way I'd had to get it to him, but I couldn't fault the outcome. Maybe I was more like my father than people thought.

I settled into the chair across from him. "You're looking better."

"Feeling better, thank you."

His hand strayed up and he brushed a finger over Crimson Cloud Splitter's handle. "This has helped."

"Gu Ma said you were waiting for me?"

"You had a busy trip to my city. Made some trouble."

I opened my mouth to protest but he held up a hand to stop me. "Did some good, too. But things are happening. Things that some people have been waiting a long time for."

Oda thumped one beefy finger on the open book. He closed the book and spun it around to me so I could read the cover.

Poems of the Soong Dynasty

"Emiko, how much do you know about prophecies?"

ACKNOWLEDGMENTS

Last time I thanked my family for humoring me as I squeezed out writing time between work and kids. This time, my wife deserves an extra tip of the hat for making it possible for me to set aside my day job so I could take a running leap at this writing thing. I'm positive that joining me on extended travel to cons and other countries for research was just an unforeseeable cherry on top for her.

Thank you, Julia, for being the best writing partner ever, and for being born with the other half of my writing brain.

Also, thank you to the readers who found Emiko during her first year on bookshelves, whether in stores, in libraries, or on your e-readers. Anyone willing to give a debut author a chance is a winner in my book. Thanks.

~Ken

I could not have imagined writing this book with anyone else. We were young and fearless once, and then we got old and cranky. These stories were always waiting for Ken and me to come back to them. I'm lucky in my friends and I'm grateful that we get to put our stories out into the world with the support of our loving family and friends and our top-notch publishing team.

Writing is a solitary endeavor but making a book is a huge team effort. Thank you to my cheerleading team at home—my husband and sons. Thank you to my law partner, Katie, and my colleagues at the firm, who held things together so that I could launch *Ebony Gate* into the world. Thank you to my first reader, Karna, for always believing in me, for Kevin who remembers my earliest writing voice, and for Will, my stalwart fantasy tastemaker.

We are forever thankful for our agent, Laurie McLean, who helps us navigate the realm of publishing and is always our advocate.

We couldn't have asked for a more amazing team at Tor to work with, from our editors Claire Eddy, Sanaa Ali-Virani, and Eli Goldman, to the incredible publicists and marketing gurus Ashley Spruill, Saraciea Fennell, Laura Etzkorn, Julia Bergen, and Emily Mlynek. Ken and I are immensely thankful for the eagle eye of Hannah Smoot (who apparently is better at counting days than we are) who ensured the continuity of the story and a million other details.

A thousand thanks to our amazing audio team. It was a dream to work with a talent such as Natalie Naudus. We appreciate the tremendous efforts of Natalie, Katy Robitzski, and Chrissy Farrell to bring this vibrant production to life (especially me because it ensured my husband actually listened to the books)!

A big thank-you to Ken's parents for all the Chinese language help, and Nicholas and Kat for reading the books and recording the pronunciations. (It had to be you, because Ken and I flunked out of Chinese school together.)

One of the most beautiful things about this step in the author journey for me has been finding friends who have helped me navigate the vagaries of publishing, explained things to this baby author, and lent a sympathetic ear when I needed it. Thank you to Brittany Greenway, for teaching me so much about bookselling, and being a friend.

Thank you to Andrea Stewart, Sunyi Dean, and Ronnie Virdi for answering all my questions and taking me under your wing. Thank you J.R. Dawson and Emma Mieko Candon for your friendship and overall awesomeness this debut year. I'm sorry Twitter imploded but I'll always be grateful that we found each other there.

Big thank-you to Jennifer Estep for being a straight-up legend. You've inspired me so much.

A special shout-out to our Writers of the Wulin chat group for answering all our various questions about language, swords, Asian myth, Asian foods, and overall camaraderie: Tao Wong, JC Kang, Jo Wu, Rinoa Koh, JF Lee, Mina Ikemoto Ghosh, and Ai Jiang. Thank you Professor Yasmin Yoppen for the incredible font of knowledge on East Asian religion and myth that powers our group discussions. Thank you Ben for your friendship and support, and Ariya for your Thai language help!

To Kendrai Meeks and R. L. King, I'm so lucky I met you two at the beginning. I appreciate your wisdom and friendship and look forward to many years of indie brainstorming together.

Shannon Fox and N. V. Haskell, I'm so happy that Superstars brought us together. I'm rooting for you!

I'm fortunate to live in the Bay Area so that I can see writer friends in person, and their support and friendship has meant so much to me. They turned up for me, they ate dumplings with me, they ate cupcakes with me, they met me at bookshops. It's an embarrassment of riches. I'm talking about you, EJ DeBrun, T. A. Chan, Victoria Shi, Essa Hansen, Amy Z. Chan, Hana Lee, and Kemi Ashing-Giwa. Please never move away.

Middle school me could have never imagined a future where readers could find me through social media, sharing posts and videos appreciating our books. This is truly an amazing era to be a creative and to form these direct connections with readers. Thank you Penny, Katie, Sammie, Lorraine, Zana, Bean, Luchia, Carole, Ash, Elle, Christina, Joshua, Lili, Bri, and the entire B2Weird crew! Your early enthusiasm helped fuel us through this trilogy.

We so appreciate the booksellers who have championed this book. In an ever-growing marketplace, it means so much to us that booksellers have hand sold these books to readers who wouldn't have otherwise found it. Simeon, Maryelizabeth, KelleyAnn, Donna, Megan, Justin, Stacy, Carmen, Jeff, Kalani, Cari, Rene, Kel, Lillian, Lloyd, and so many more. Thank you from the bottom of our hearts.

~Julia

ABOUT THE AUTHORS

Nicole Gee Photography

JULIA VEE likes stories about monsters, money, and good food. Vee was born in Macao and grew up in Northern California, where she studied at UC Berkeley and majored in Asian Studies. She is a graduate of the Viable Paradise workshop.

Ann Dang

KEN BEBELLE turned his childhood love for reading sci-fi and fantasy into a career in prosthetics. After twenty years he came back to books, writing about plucky underdogs and ancient magical artifacts with deadly secrets. He and his wife live in the Pacific Northwest and he still dreams of growing perfect tomatoes.

Bebelle and Vee have written together since middle school.